Children of the Rat

Books by Eleanor Fitzgerald:

Novels

The Ministry of Supernatural Affairs
Night People

The Black Carnation

Children of the Rat

Other Works

Oxford Junction

The Forest

Anthologies
Hymns for the Gallows, Volume One: The Trial

Hymns for the Gallows, Volume Two: The Last Meal

Hymns for the Gallows, Volume Three: The Hanging

Anima, Volume One: The Signal

This is a work of fiction. Names, characters, places, and incidents either are the product of the author's imagination or are used fictitiously. Any resemblance to actual persons, living or dead, events, or locales is entirely coincidental.

Copyright © Eleanor Fitzgerald, 2023

The moral right of Eleanor Fitzgerald to be identified as the author of this work has been asserted in accordance with the Copyright, Designs, and Patents Act of 1988.

All rights reserved. No part of this book may be reproduced in any form on by an electronic or mechanical means, including information storage and retrieval systems, without permission in writing from the publisher, except by a reviewer who may quote brief passages in a review.

Cover Art Copyright © Eleanor Fitzgerald, 2023

First paperback edition November 2023

ISBN: 9798856414614

Published Independently

Contents

Author's Note and Content Warnings..........................ix

Part One: Echoes in the Mist......................................1

Chapter One – The Wizard's Apprentice.....................3
Chapter Two – Fight of the Century...........................13
Chapter Three – Hickory Dickory Dock....................23
Chapter Four – The Third Eye Opens........................31
Chapter Five – Agent of Chaos..................................41
Chapter Six – Going on the Offensive.......................51
Chapter Seven – Get Out or Die.................................61
Chapter Eight – Black Cats Bring Bad Luck............73
Chapter Nine – Class Nine Event...............................85
Chapter Ten – Together in Electric Dreams..............95
Chapter Eleven – Thou Shalt Not Kill.....................103
Chapter Twelve – Whatever Pain May Come.........113
Chapter Thirteen – Don't Stop Moving....................121
Chapter Fourteen – Know Your Enemy...................129

Interlude One – Tides of Flesh.................................137

Part Two: Danse Macabre..141

Chapter Fifteen – The Reichardt Drop.....................143
Chapter Sixteen – A New Day Dawns.....................153
Chapter Seventeen – Welcome to the Wishbone Collective...163
Chapter Eighteen – Residue and Retina Burn.........171
Chapter Nineteen – Mealtime Chatter.....................179
Chapter Twenty – Arming the Dogs of War...........189
Chapter Twenty One – Together We Fight.............199
Chapter Twenty Two – Rats in the Run...................209

Chapter Twenty Three – There Are No Coincidences 219
Chapter Twenty Four – The Cold Heart of Progress 227
Chapter Twenty Five – Unforced Errors..................239
Chapter Twenty Six – Listen to Your Heart.............249
Chapter Twenty Seven – No Place For Heroes........257
Chapter Twenty Eight – Cracking the Code............265

Interlude Two – The First Generation......................273

Part Three: The Bluesky Protocol............................279

Chapter Twenty Nine – Alone in the Bitterness.......281
Chapter Thirty – Vibe Check, Failed.......................289
Chapter Thirty One – The Wandering Fool.............299
Chapter Thirty Two – Arrows Alongside the Lightning 309
Chapter Thirty Three – Her Dreaded Master...........319
Chapter Thirty Four – Midas Eyed Girl...................329
Chapter Thirty Five – Doom Spirals........................339
Chapter Thirty Six – Down to the Waterline...........347
Chapter Thirty Seven – We, the Living...................357
Chapter Thirty Eight – Ride of a Lifetime...............365
Chapter Thirty Nine – Dog Days Are Over.............373

Epilogue – Scattered to the Winds...........................381

Acknowledgments..391

About the Author..395

Author's Note and Content Warnings

I have drawn from my own experiences and knowledge to create this novel, and have taken some creative license with the geography of Dartford and certain aspects of history and medical science.

I don't think that any of my minor changes are so large or egregious as to be plot- or immersion-breaking.

I hope that you will forgive me my little tweaks in light of the tense and frightening narrative that I have produced.

There are also some content warnings that I would like to point out in advance, although I will not be too specific; I do not wish to spoil the plot, after all! This will be the last mention of these warnings so that the story may unfold uninterrupted.

- **Body Horror**
- **Medical Horror/Surgery**
- **Torture**
- **Graphic Violence/Bloodshed**
- **Institutional Violence**
- **Mind Control**
- **Transphobia**
- **Kidnapping**
- **Suicide/Self Harm**

Thank you for choosing this novel, dear Reader. I hope you enjoy reading it as much as I enjoyed writing it.

THE MINISTRY OF SUPERNATURAL AFFAIRS

Pugnamus In Obumbratio

For Ben, a fellow writer and possibly the kindest man I have ever met.

You're truly one of the best of us.

And for Steve, my late father.

You handed me a copy of The Rats, by James Herbert, one rainy afternoon with a playful little grin on your face.

I hope this is what you had in mind.

Part One: Echoes in the Mist

Chapter One – The Wizard's Apprentice

The Stranger

"Fuck!"

The sprinting figure ducked as another bullet whistled past them, leaving swirling eddies in its wake. A series of muted pops followed and there was a snickering sound as the volley hit the blackened concrete less than a metre from the Stranger's head.

I have to get out of here.

The plan hadn't just gone wrong; it had been doomed from the very start.

The Stranger's reinforced boots slipped as they skittered down a debris pile, contaminated ash and dust kicking up behind them. The lenses of their makeshift gas mask were fogging up as they sweated with exertion. Behind them, more muted gunshots; Carmichael's goons now carried suppressed weapons.

I should never have trusted that fucker in the first place!

The bullets zinged around the masked Stranger, trails through the shimmering fog fading in their wake. The twisted wreckage of the derailed trains had finally been dismantled and moved to a warehouse, but the carriages that remained intact on the rails were left in place for decontamination.

The rectangular cars loomed above the destroyed houses. Through the dizzying fog, they looked like giant fallen tombstones; a darkly ironic memorial to all those that had perished on that awful day.

It was towards these that the Stranger now ran.

The bank was strewn with shattered brickwork and the charred remains of the railway sleepers that had been thrown clear in the initial derailment. Every surface was slippery with ash or slick with the noxious, oily smoke that still lingered over the devastated town.

The Stranger looked behind them and saw four figures in black pursuing through the debris. Their body armour, jumpsuits, and breathing apparatus was all state of the art, allowing them to move virtually unencumbered whilst still being protected from the swirling poison.

They raised their weapons again, Heckler & Koch MP5's with reflex sights and suppressors, and fired at the Stranger.

The bullets clanged and ricocheted off the sleek metal surface of the train. The Stranger threw themselves flat to avoid the deadly storm of lead.

"Cease fire, cease fire!" The leader's voice was muffled by his mask, but it echoed clearly through the fog. "We are not to damage the remaining cars!"

A reprieve at last! The Stranger smiled behind their gas mask, but their glee was short lived as two of the men swapped their firearms for telescopic batons.

"It's gonna be like that, then?" The Stranger's voice was tired, but determined. They reached under their long, chemical resistant coat and pulled out a sturdy entrenching tool with sharpened edges.

They reached into a pocket with their other hand and slipped a small, but deadly push knife between their fingers.

"Just leave me alone," the Stranger yelled as the two goons closed in, "and we can all just walk away from this!"

One of the men twirled his baton with a mean chuckle.

"I don't want to hurt anybody!" The Stranger's voice was strained and they wished that they could wipe the condensation from the inside of the claustrophobic mask. Still, the armed men drew ever closer and the Stranger hefted the sharpened shovel in an attempt to look menacing.

Is this even going to get through all their body armour?

The first of the men leapt forward, bringing the baton whipping through the air as he went. The Stranger stepped to one side, moving entirely on instinct, and brought the shovel swinging through the air over the top of the man's strike.

Their combined momentum send the metal edge into his neck, and he screamed wetly as the modified tool cut through his throat. The Stranger freed their weapon with a panicked kick and the body rolled down the slope.

The other man swung his baton into their ribs, breaking at least one and sending the Stranger sprawling on to the ground.

Through their gas mask, they could see a tangled mess of metal rods and rails at the bottom of the hill behind them. As the man brought his baton down for a second hit, the Stranger roared and kicked their legs upward into his stomach, sending him flying over their head and down the hill.

The blood curdling scream that followed was enough to confirm their impact with the jagged pile of steel.

"Two down, two to go," the Stranger wheezed. They got to their feet, one hand gingerly holding their broken ribs. The two remaining men looked at each other before the leader put one hand to his head and radioed their commander.

"Yes, sir. Of course, sir."

The Stranger strained to hear the man's voice through the thick fog.

"...killed two of our men already." There was a pause, and then the man nodded. "Understood, sir."

The leader tapped his one remaining compatriot on the shoulder and the two of them retreated into the fog.

Some luck at last, the Stranger thought, smiling behind their mask. The brief uplift of their mood did not last long, however, and the distant whine of rotor blades spinning up soon wiped the grin off their face.

"Why can't anything ever be easy?"

"God, I hope this still fucking works," the Stranger muttered as they swiped an electronic key card through the lock and keyed in the code. The rotor blades reached full speed as the words 'Access Denied' flashed up on the little screen by the door.

"Finley, you absolute cunt!" the Stranger roared. The sound of an aircraft taking off reached their ears and they could make out a distant shape moving through the fog towards them. They pulled their hand back and punched the panel in frustration. The little push knife stabbed through the keypad and shorted out the mechanism; with a hiss and a crackle, the locks thudded open.

The Stranger slipped through the door, pulling it closed just as a bright halogen searchlight illuminated the area around the quarantined cars. The car they had just entered was windowless, so they were safe for now.

They'll switch to thermals soon enough, the Stranger thought as they pulled the tight hood of their coat down and removed their gas mask. They took a deep gulp of cool, clean air and sighed contentedly. The hood had held their wild, untameable hair in its messy bun, but now that it had been removed, several stray locks fell out of the bobble to frame the Stranger's shapely face.

She caught sight of her reflection in one of the dormant command consoles; high cheekbones, a pointed chin, sharp nose, and defined jawline all would've been handsome on a man, but were statuesque on a woman.

She would've looked unapproachable and intimidating if it wasn't for the warmth in her grey eyes and her lopsided, slightly goofy smile. Her teeth peeked out from underneath her top lip, giving her a cheerful, almost rodent-like appearance.

I look pretty fucking good, she thought proudly. *I've come a long way.*

Outside there was the distinctive thrum of rotor blades passing close overhead, followed by the purr of an electrically accelerated chain gun. A brief scream followed, but it was soon snuffed out. The Stranger froze in place, terrified to make even the slightest sound.

Her heart thundered in her ears and she hoped that it would not be loud enough for the drone to pick up on. A single tear rolled down her cheek as terror gripped her. When the unmanned aircraft finally moved on, she breathed a ragged sigh of relief.

"I need to get out of here," she said softly, "but not until I get what I came for."

She moved to the sealed metal pod in the centre of the carriage; it was surrounded by a layer of bulletproof polycarbonate glass. She didn't have the codes to unlock the pod or the glass, but she had come prepared.

Both locks were digital and too complex for the Stranger to hack, even with their custom codebreaker machine. *We're gonna have to get analogue with this shit,* she thought with a grin. She pulled a blowtorch, an aerosol can, a small hammer, and a box of ceramic shims out of her little backpack; these would get her into the metal pod.

She selected a portable ultrasound machine, the kind normally used by midwives, albeit one that she'd made a few modifications to, and attached the probe to the glass with sticky contact gel. She switched on the machine and dialled up the frequencies until the bulletproof glass began to ring softly.

She smiled and put on a pair of protective goggles. The glass began to crack as she cranked the amplitude of the ultrasonic waves. Once it was weakened enough, she picked up one of the chairs by the computers in the carriage and smashed the glass to pieces.

An alarm began to blare and red lights flashed in the carriage as well as on the outside of the train car. The Stranger looked around in panic; she'd been certain that the alarm was deactivated in the crash.

I'm going to need to get out of here fucking sharpish, she thought as she hammered the ceramic shims into the spaces in the pod hinges. Once they were in place she began to heat the metal with the blowtorch. When it was glowing, she used the coolant in the aerosol to crash the temperature down.

She repeated this process twice for each of the three hinges. Once they were all suitably heat treated, she tapped the shims deeper into the grooves that they were now firmly stuck in. The brittle metal cracked and shattered under the force and she pulled the door of the pod open.

Inside was a mannequin, that should've been wearing the Stranger's prize. Instead it was completely unadorned, except for a note pinned to its chest.

"Better luck next time, Elsie," she read angrily as her eyes flicked over the familiar looping script. "All the best, Finley."

I'm going to wipe that smug grin off his little face, Elsie thought as she gathered her items back into the bag. Outside, the rotors roared as the drone sped towards the carriage. She pulled a compact firearm from her backpack and screwed a wide barrel into place. She broke open the weapon and loaded a large bullet into it.

She donned her gas mask just as the chain gun spun up once again. The rounds tore through the carriage as she burst out into the swirling fog. She snatched a strange mess of electronics from her belt; it was about the size of a cricket ball and covered with bulbs and small speakers.

She tossed it away from her and it began to strobe and shriek as it hit the ground. The small helicopter drone came down lower, its chain gun focussed on the distracting object. It opened fire as Elsie shot at it with the strange rifle.

The bullets from the drone tore through the distractor, shredding it, as the heavy round from Elsie's gun hit the main body of the aircraft. The armour piercing shell got through the outer layer of the autonomous vehicle before it broke apart. The salty expanding foam contained within forced its way through the inside of the drone, gumming up machinery and shorting out electronics as it did so.

Elsie had formulated the mix to be exothermic in its reaction, and the faltering drone burst into flames as it spun out of the sky. A smile crossed her face behind her gas mask as the damaged aircraft crashed into the ground mere metres away from her. She hurried over to it, pulling one of her many specialised multi-tools from her belt. She ran her gloved hand over the surface of the drone, making reassuring noises as the robot's electronic brain died.

"I'm sorry," she said softly, "I didn't want to hurt you. I never meant for you to be used for something like this."

Once the electronics had all burnt out, she pried open the access panel and removed the fried computer core. She also detached the electronic accelerator from the chain gun and put both devices into her bag.

I'm sure I can find a use for these, or sell them at the very least; not a wasted trip after all.

Before she could move, an eerie sound drifted through the fog. She cocked her head to one side, trying to catch the location of the noise. Every time she thought she had it, however, it slipped out of her mind and seemed to move elsewhere.

What is that?

Before Elsie could get her head around it, the sound faded and all that was left was the muted hubbub of the town and the growl of distant traffic.

She pushed the cover shut, and frowned at the words emblazoned on it; Eigenforce International, the largest and most powerful company on earth. The drone, the train, and the goons were all owned and deployed at the whims of Finley Carmichael, the richest man in the world.

Elsie snarled at the memory of him, and fought the urge to kick the downed drone.

Finley, she thought, *my mentor, my only friend, and my worst enemy.*

She got to her feet just as her name was yelled into the mist.

"Elsie Reichardt!" The voice was a man's; his accent was peculiar, but distinctive. "I think you're a mite late, girl."

"Fucking hell," she muttered as she backed away from the man's voice. "This just keeps getting better and better."

She turned on her heel and ran just as a gunshot rang out through the mist. The high powered round zipped through the air, catching Elsie in the shoulder. Even though the metal plates she'd sown on to her coat took some of the force, she still screamed in pain.

I've got to keep going, she thought fearfully. *I can't let him catch me.*

"You keep on runnin' girl," Mad Dog called after her as he chambered another round, "we ain't never gonna stop chasin' you!"

Chapter Two – Fight of the Century

Chloe

Chloe Turner coughed and spluttered as she dashed to the bathroom. She hit the sink at full speed, bending double over the ceramic basin. She coughed once again before hawking a thick globule of blood streaked phlegm into the sink.

She rubbed her teary eyes as she watched the disgusting blob slip stringily down the plughole. She flicked on the taps to flush it away before giving her face a quick wash.

Fucking bullshit chemicals, she thought angrily as she towelled her face dry. She peered at her reflection in the mirror, still horrified at her own appearance. *At least the blistering faded quickly enough.*

Parts of her face were discoloured and disfigured from the toxic smoke that swept through the town in the wake of the derailment; one of her eyes was almost completely red, aside from her oversized dark pupil.

"I'm never going to look normal again," she muttered sadly. Whilst Chloe had always been considered a plain looking young woman, she now looked downright freakish.

Her phone jingled softly in her bedroom and she trotted down the tight corridor in response. Instead of a call, she realised that it was her ten minute warning alarm; she had to finish getting ready now or she would be late.

"I hope Beef and Candy win this one," she muttered as she pulled a clean t-shirt over her head. She would've favoured ripped jeans, but she wanted to protect herself from the fog; *better late than never, I guess.*

She settled on a pair of tight faux leather trousers and heavy boots. She tied her long hair back instead of leaving it loose. It was a glossy black colour, except for the bright white streak that the toxic smoke had left in it.

At least that looks cool, she thought with a smile. She added a gold necklace and a few bangles to her ensemble and smiled. Her good eye twinkled prettily as she admired her appearance in the mirror. Her gold nose ring was an endless point of contention between her and her parents, but they had relented slightly; the derailment and resulting fire had been hard on all of them.

She pulled one of the respirators that her father had sent her from the internet from its box on her dresser. The flimsy blue surgical masks that the government had provided were next to it. *What a fucking joke,* she thought angrily, *it's as if they don't care if we live or die!*

She also picked up a pair of goggles and a raincoat before she trotted downstairs. She poked her head into the kitchen to see if her brother was there, but the house was empty aside from her. She poked her head around the corner to check that the back door was locked and screamed.

A large rat, with beady black eyes and matted oily fur stood on its hind legs and looked right at her. She screamed again; it was the largest that she'd ever seen. She scrabbled for something to throw and her hand closed around her father's heavy University Challenge quiz book. She hurled it at the rat with all her might, missing it by a whisker.

The rodent didn't even flinch.

"What the fuck?" Chloe yelled. "Fuck off, will you?"

It regarded her with its dark eyes; if she didn't know any better, she would've sworn that it was sizing her up. *Rats aren't that smart,* she thought. Her fear was rapidly replaced by anger and she gestured violently at the pensive rodent, which did not react.

A curious sound echoed from outside, and the rat turned tail and scampered into the downstairs loo. Chloe moved after it and was horrified to see it scrabble up over the toilet seat. It jumped into the bowl with a splash and vanished around the bend.

"That's fucking horrifying," she said as she slammed the lid shut and piled heavy bleach and cleaning chemical bottles atop it. "That should keep you out!"

Her phone jingled again in her pocket; she needed to leave immediately or else she was going to be late. She jiggled the door handle, ensuring that it was locked before heading into the living room. She went to the family whiteboard where her tickets were supposed to be, but instead the little magnet was sitting there all alone.

She traced her fingers over the magnet, and her first guess was confirmed. The image of long pale fingers, complete with painted and manicured nails, taking the tickets filled her mind and she let out a low, exasperated groan.

"Shy," she grumbled as she headed out the door, "I am done with your bullshit!"

The walk from Norman Road to the Fairfield Leisure Centre normally only took Chloe five minutes or so, but since the derailment her lungs ached any time she walked too quickly. Nowadays it took her closer to ten, but she always left in plenty of time.

Her footsteps echoed through the fog. Although it was barely eight o'clock in the evening, it was already dark. She turned her collar up and wished that she'd brought a scarf; the early November air was chilly and the dampness of the persistent fog drained the heat out of her with frightening efficiency.

A gentle pattering sound to her right caught her attention as she passed the access road that ran along the back of her street. She slowed down and squinted through her goggles into the darkness. A blur of motion made her jump, but she soon calmed down when she realised that it was just a fox.

It trotted up the road towards her and a chill ran down her spine. The creature's tongue was lolling out of its mouth and its eyes were rolling madly in its skull. It panted rapidly as it moved, its rail thin ribs visible through its greasy, patchy fur. It slavered and yelped as it approached her.

Is it rabid? Whilst rabies wasn't endemic in the United Kingdom, Chloe vaguely remembered someone telling her something about the disease and bats. She backed away from the fox, moving towards the foggy road. It snapped at the air and charged towards her.

She took a step back and kicked it squarely in the ribs, flinging the deranged animal into the middle of the tarmac. It hit the ground and screeched before scrabbling its way towards her once again.

A car horn blared as a vehicle loomed up out of the mist, but the fox simply stared at the oncoming headlights. The car hit it, dragging its raggedy frame beneath the wheels. The driver didn't even stop, and sped on through the swirling gloom.

"What the fuck is going on?" Chloe muttered as she went on her way. "What was in that train?"

She reached the leisure centre without further incident, and made her way inside. Once she was safely out of the fog, Chloe pulled off the respirator and goggles. She took a deep breath of the filtered air and looked at the other people milling around.

Most of them were in their mid twenties, much like Chloe, although several of the patrons were markedly older. Music played over the speakers as the small crowd waited for the doors to the gym area to open.

What is everyone looking at? Chloe wondered as she noticed that several of the people were staring into the empty space where the vending machines had once been. She slipped between a couple of men in biker jackets and saw what, or more accurately *who*, held everyone's attention.

A white man with dark curly hair and a circle beard was strutting his stuff as Sledgehammer, by Peter Gabriel, played over the speakers. He wore a pink longline fur trim coat, a pale green ruffled shirt with matching trousers, and pink over-the-knee lace up canvas boots. A flash of gold liner framed his dark eyes, which were half closed as he danced. His painted fingernails flashed in the fluorescent light as he moved, oblivious to all those around him.

"Who is that?" Chloe wasn't sure if the man in the biker jacket had asked her directly, but she felt compelled to respond.

"He's my brother," she said, already tired of his antics. She walked forwards and grabbed his hand, startling him. "Shy, stop making a scene!"

"Oh, hi there, Noor!" Shy Turner said warmly. He wrapped his arms around her, squeezing her tight. "It's good to see you!"

"I've told you, I want you to call me Chloe!" Her voice was sharp, although she never could stay mad at her brother for long. "Nobody is going to buy couture designed by someone called Noor!"

"They absolutely will!" He grinned at her. "I would, that's for sure."

"Forgive me, but your current outfit doesn't exactly fill me with confidence."

"Oh, boo!" He tittered slightly as he continued to shuffle in time to the music. "Why is everyone afraid of a little colour? Worried they might actually enjoy themselves?"

Before she could respond, the bubbly young man spoke again.

"Ooh, this is my favourite part!" He practically squealed with excitement and began dancing again.

Try as she might, Chloe could not find fault with his moves. *He's a weird little guy,* she thought fondly, *but he's got heart.*

Shame he's such a fuckup.

"Shy, do you have the tickets?" she asked loudly over the music. He nodded in perfect time to the drum beat. "Where are they?"

He reached into his coat and brandished the tickets at her with a smile. She took them as he began to snap his fingers and rock his hips as the song intensified. *It is a good song,* she agreed with a smile as she began to shuffle along too.

There was a clunk as the doors were opened and his eyes snapped open. He slipped his arm through hers and ambled into the gym area for the evening's entertainment.

"Do you think Jim and Delilah are slated to win the belt?" Shy asked excitedly as they waited for the match to begin.

"Beef and Candy," Chloe corrected. Shy rolled his eyes and shook his head. "What?"

"It's not enough for your friends to have stage names, but you all need cool nicknames now?" He chuckled when she nodded. "Whatever you say, Noor."

"Chloe," she muttered darkly.

"My apologies. I'm guessing that Beef and Candy would like a lift home tonight with all their stuff?" He added a little sarcastic stress to the names, but his overall tone was not unkind. "Unless Beef has brought his little runaround with him."

"Jim is Candy," Chloe corrected, "and Delilah is Beef. I'm sure they would appreciate a ride home, Shy. They're always super tired after a fight."

"Ladies and gentlemen," the announcer said from the centre of the ring, "welcome to the final fight of the season! Here the Dartford Tag Team Belt is up for grabs, but who will walk away with this prize? Let's welcome our contenders into the ring!"

Chloe cheered loudly whilst Shy launched into a joyous grito as Beef and Candy strode into the room.

"Local champions, unbeaten for two straight seasons; Hacksaw and Sledgehammer!" The announcer waved his arms to encourage the crowd to cheer for the masked pair. "Will they defeat their opponents to take home the belt, or will they fall at the final hurdle?

"Let's meet the villains of tonight's show!"

"Wow!" Chloe said when Beef and Candy swaggered out of the changing room in their civilian clothes. "That was a hell of a fucking fight!"

"Damn right it was," Beef said with a huge grin. She had the title belt draped over one shoulder and a swagger in her step. "Drilled like a fucking ballet, too, weren't we, Candy?"

"Legit," Candy said as he flexed his muscles to Shy's delight. Both wrestlers were tall, muscular, and the kindest people Chloe had ever met. Whilst they brought their terrifying personas into the ring, they were absolute sweethearts to the core.

"So, do you folks want a ride?" Shy asked.

"If you're offering, slick," Beef said with a grin as she slapped him on the back. The force nearly sent him sprawling. Candy laughed as Beef winked at him. "Although we should give you a lift every now and then, don't you think?"

"I guess," Shy said before he yelped in surprise as Candy deftly picked him up and put him into an effortless fireman's carry. "Oh, I could get used to this!"

The four of them made sure that their masks were securely in place before stepping out into the swirling fog. Somewhere in the park behind them lurked the fairground that had been abandoned on the night of the fire; it was too contaminated to move, so it had been left behind as a grim monument to the suddenness of the derailment.

Chloe shuddered and wrapped her coat tightly around herself. *How the fuck did it get so cold?*

"Fuck me," Beef said as they walked towards Shy's van, "this fog looks like it's getting worse! We haven't had a single clear day for weeks now."

"Yeah," Candy said quietly as he put Shy down next to the driver's side door. "I'm actually thinking we should get out of town for a while, you know?"

"What makes you say that?" Chloe asked. *I've had exactly the same thought ever since the derailment.*

"Just a feeling; like something is about to happen." Candy's voice was quiet. He tried the door handle, but it was still locked. "Whenever you're ready, Shy."

"Guys, are you seeing this?" Shy asked, almost too quiet to be heard. Chloe and her friends joined him on his side of the van. She gasped when she saw what had stunned him almost to silence.

A dozen rats were staring at them from the edge of the car park, all in a perfect line. Their beady eyes were glinting in the hazy fog-filtered light, and their little noses sniffed the air around them. Then, simultaneously, they all turned towards the darkness of the bushes and scampered away, as if called by some unseen master.

"Maybe you're right, Candy," Chloe said softly. "Perhaps something weird is going on here."

"No shit," Shy said as he unlocked the van. Chloe didn't respond, but climbed into one of the back seats.

I think it's too late to leave, she thought as they drove through the darkness. *We're stuck here now, for better or worse.*

We have to see this through to the end.

<u>Chapter Three</u> – <u>Hickory Dickory Dock</u>

Elsie

Elsie groaned and grimaced as she fished for the bullet that was still in her shoulder. She hadn't dared remove it the night before, not with Mad Dog and his team hot on her heels.

She fought back a scream as she wiggled the surgical tweezers around in her flesh, searching for the round buried in there.

"Fucking hell," she moaned as tears streamed down her face. She continued to move the tweezers around and her eyes widened in relief when the metal pincers closed around the tiny fragment.

With a shuddering gasp, she pulled the bullet out and dropped it into the bowl of water. The blood bloomed and blossomed into little crimson chrysanthemums as she stared at the submerged metal.

I'll patch myself up in a second, she thought. There was a pounding sound on the bathroom door, followed by an angry man's voice.

"Fucking hurry up in there, bitch!"

"I'm nearly done!" Elsie yelled in response. A bus station bathroom was not the best place for impromptu surgery, but it had a variety of exits and the surprising lack of cameras would hide her from her pursuers long enough for her to catch her breath.

She rummaged in her bag and pulled out a small device; it was about the size and shape of a television remote control. She held it against the wound in her shoulder and gritted her teeth before pushing the button to activate it.

There was a stinging sensation as the gadget sprayed hydrogen peroxide into her wound, sterilising it, before it clattered rapidly and shook in her hand.

Elsie screamed as her little machine stitched her wound closed with surgical precision. Once the needlework was done, it sprayed an aerosolised dressing over the injury, sealing it. With a deep exhausted sigh, she placed the machine back in her bag and smiled. *That should do for now,* she thought, *although I should try and get some antibiotics just in case.*

She looked down at the bloodstained bullet and frowned; something about the situation was not right. Mad Dog always preferred to hunt humans with a bow, so why on earth would he use a rifle? She peered closer, her nose almost touching the water, and her stomach lurched at what she saw.

The banging on the door resumed, more insistent this time.

"I'll be out momentarily," she said as she packed her things away. She shouldered her bag with a grunt and tossed the contents of the bowl into the toilet. She hit the flush and watched as the bullet, along with the blinking GPS tracking dot embedded in it, swirl down the drain.

They'll be on top of me any minute, she thought, panicked. *I need to get out of here.*

I need a distraction.

She opened a pouch on her belt and extracted a single marble. This one was made of clear glass with a flash of red in the centre; she'd felt good about this one when she first saw it.

Elsie leant against the door, one hand on the lock, and listened to the music of the universe. *Please find me a way out.*

Her eyes half closed as the bus station filled her mind, frozen in that instant. For the briefest of moments, Elsie could see how it all fit together; the interlocking systems and actions that made up the world she lived in.

It's a clockwork universe, she thought with a smile, *and the melody is all for me.* A thin golden halo appeared around certain people and objects, and she pulled open the door.

The loud man who'd been pounding on the door was directly in front of her and she gave him a calculated shove, dropping the marble as she did so. It skittered across the floor as he staggered back, arms wind-milling.

His hand caught on a stranger's bag, ripping an already worn strap and sending a bottle toppling out on to the floor. The bottle and marble rolled in opposite directions, with the former tripping up a child who was trying desperately to keep up with his mother.

He fell sideways, slipping into the path of an oncoming bus.

The driver panicked and whipped the vehicle to one side, colliding with another bus with a loud crash. Across the room, a young woman who'd stooped down to pick up the marble that had stopped at her feet straightened up suddenly at the sound. She knocked the bus station custodian backwards; his broom handle lurched as he moved, smashing through the safety glass of the fire alarm and setting it off.

People looked around in confused panic as the siren blared and the automated voice told them to quickly exit the station.

Amidst the chaos, the man who'd been outside the bathroom looked left and right to find Elsie Reichardt, but she had vanished into thin air.

"You must be Elsie!" The handsome young man smiled at her as she entered the living room of her small home. He wore a simple white polo shirt and white trousers; strangely enough, he was barefoot.

"What are you doing in my house?" Elsie said angrily. There was no need to ask his name; most people on the planet would recognise the face of Finley Carmichael. He ran a perfectly manicured hand through his artfully styled dark hair and chuckled.

"I'm here to talk to you, Elsie. I've a proposition for you; a business collaboration, if you will." He perched on her sofa and gestured for her to join him. Elsie remained standing and he shrugged. "Suit yourself. Word on the street is that you are quite the inventor, Miss Reichardt. Is that true?"

"Perhaps," Elsie said warily. "What does the *Modern Midas* want with me?"

"Modern Midas!" Finley laughed and shook his head. "The press do love their alliterative titles, don't they?"

"What do you want from me?" Her voice was hard and her fists were clenched.

"Like I said, I have a business proposal for you."

"No. I don't want anything to do with you."

"At least hear me out; no harm in listening, is there?" he said, waving her concerns away with an idle hand.

"I suppose not," Elsie murmured before taking a seat in her favourite armchair. "Well, Mr Carmichael, you have three minutes of my time. Make your proposal and do it quickly."

"How would you like freedom, Elsie?" He smiled at her and his icy blue eyes glinted. "Freedom from poverty, from legal red tape, from the Ministry of Supernatural Affairs?"

"How do you know about that?" Elsie asked, shocked. Whilst she wasn't yet on their radar, she was careful to avoid tangling with anyone else like her just to be on the safe side.

"Unimportant," Finley said, dodging the question. He picked up a penny from the table and began to fiddle with it. "What's relevant here is that I have always been able to spot a good investment; untapped resources, unrealised potential, assets that have yet to reach their full value. I see that potential in you, Elsie.

"I want to give you the freedom to create, and I can. You know that, don't you?" He smiled at her shocked face. "What more could you hope for? Come with me, and together we will make Prometheus feel small; we'll have greater visions than God himself, and the power to make them reality."

"Why me?" Elsie asked, her voice soft and contemplative.

"Because I can see what you are, Elsie, even if you cannot." He handed her the penny as he rose from the sofa. "Just think about it, okay? We'll be in touch in twenty four hours for your decision."

He strolled out of the room and she heard the front door shut behind him. She looked down at the penny in her hand and gasped.

It was made of pure gold.

"Where are you keeping it, Finley?" Elsie muttered as she limped through the smog filled park. She'd extracted her collapsible walking stick from her backpack once she was out of the view of any cameras, along with swapping her gas mask and stowing her coat.

Recognition software could identify someone from their gait and stance, even if their face was obscured; Elsie's awkward hobble with the walking stick was carefully constructed to fool such programs.

Never underestimate your protégé, Finley, she thought with a smile. The stick clacked as she moved and using it made her shoulder ache, but it was far too dangerous to go without it. *If Mad Dog is here, the game has changed,* Elsie realised.

"Maybe he doesn't have it," she said softly. "Perhaps it's in with all the reconstruction materials and debris."

It would be a good place to start, if I can get in.

"What I wouldn't give for a good old fashioned internet cafe," Elsie said wistfully. She managed three more steps before a huge grin broke out on her face. "There's always a computer at the library!"

She turned smartly on her heel and came face to face with the largest rat she'd ever seen. It looked at her with its dark, intelligent eyes and took a careful step towards her. She took three hurried steps back, but the rat followed.

"Shoo!" Elsie said loudly, flapping her arms. "Go away!"

The rat squeaked excitedly and two more slipped out of the undergrowth, just as bold as the first. They scampered towards her and for a moment Elsie was certain that one of the rodents grinned at her.

"Leave me alone," she yelled before lashing out with the walking stick. She caught one of the rats in the mouth, casting it aside where it landed with a whimper. The remaining pair still pursued her, albeit at a safe distance.

This is not normal, Elsie thought fearfully. *Rats do not behave like this!*

She glanced around, looking for a landmark to help orient her, but the swirling fog was thicker now than it had ever been; she was well and truly lost.

"Help!" Her voice was shrill and panicked, and the rats chirruped excitedly in response. "Are you hunting me?"

Her words were uneven; she was on the verge of hysterics. She lashed out at another rat, but it ducked under the blow and scurried past her. She glanced over her shoulder and saw that half a dozen rats had gathered behind her.

"Oh shit, oh fuck, I'm going to get eaten by rats!" She squinted through the lenses in her gas mask and saw someone walking towards her through the fog. It took her a few seconds to realise that the size of the person meant they were most likely a child. "Run! Stay away, the rats are here!"

One of the rats leapt at her, but she brought her heel down on its skull with a crunch. The figure grew closer and closer, stumbling and slouching as it came.

"Get out of here, kid!" She groaned with exertion as she swung the walking stick at the assembled rodents, scattering them for a few seconds. The child was saying something as it approached. "I can't hear you, kid, but you have to run, okay?

"You need to trust me!"

"Mummy," the child moaned, "Mummy, I'm so

cold."

Elsie could finally see the soil that stained the child's hands and the glassy look in its eyes. Her heart began to pound in her chest and a scream erupted from her lips. She glanced at the circling rats, and then back to the shuffling child.

"Mummy, please!" The child reached for her, but she shoved it out of the way with the walking stick. Unfortunately, the child hooked its fingers around her stick and yanked it from her hands with freakish force. Unbalanced, her assailant fell over, and Elsie seized her moment.

I hope they don't follow me.

She hopped over the prone child and sprinted into the swirling mist. The rats did not pursue her and she sobbed with relief. She did not stop running until she reached the wrought iron railings at the edge of the park.

Her gloved fingers clung to the slick cold metal as she wept behind her gas mask.

"It was only a child, Elsie," she reassured herself, "just a strange child and a weird group of rats. Children can't hurt you."

If that's true, said the little voice in her head, *why am I so frightened?*

Chapter Four – The Third Eye Opens

Chloe

"I heard there were more break-ins last night," Candy said between bites of his burger. "People around here have gone crazy if you ask me."

"They've always been crazy," Beef replied as she dipped her chips into her milkshake. "Now they've got an excuse to act that way, though. Don't you agree, Chloe?"

"Yeah," Chloe said absent-mindedly. She rolled the peas around her plate with a fork; her appetite had completely vanished and her wounded eye was beginning to ache. "I'm sorry guys, I think I'm getting a migraine."

"That's the third time this week," Beef said as she put a muscled arm around Chloe's shoulders. "Have you spoken to the doctor about the headaches?"

"I can't get an appointment this side of Christmas," Chloe said sulkily. "Not even a telephone consultation."

"We could take you to the hospital," Candy said, starting on his second burger. "We'll stay with you for as long as you need; ride or die."

"They're not taking in anyone who isn't on death's door," Chloe sighed. "Given all that's happened, I'm not surprised. Everyone in the town is getting sick, and what's to blame?"

"Capitalism," Candy said with his mouth full. The two women nodded. Beef was about to say something when a shriek from the street caught the trio's attention. Shy burst into the Wimpy, a panicked look in his eyes.

He glanced back and forth until he spotted his sister and her friends. He grinned at them and trotted over to join them, grabbing a chair as he went. Beef sighed heavily as he sat down whilst Candy gave him a broad smile that was mostly cheeseburger at that point. Chloe buried her head in her hands as the pain throbbed through her eye.

"Hey gang," he said with a smile, "what's going on?"

"Why were you screaming?" Candy asked, concerned. "Is someone picking on you, Shy?"

"No, I was getting chased by rats, actually." He chuckled nervously and glanced at a menu as the waiter came over to take his order. "Hi, Robbie, can I just get a cheeseburger, some chips, and a sparkling water float, please?"

"A sparkling water float?" Robbie looked at Shy and shook his head disapprovingly. "Are you fucking serious, Shy?"

"If you can have ice cream in a sparkling soft drink, why can't said beverage be water?" Shy held his hands up, as if appealing to the heavens. "It's an arbitrary line, dude."

"You're an abomination," Chloe grumbled without looking up. "Just get him a coke, Robbie; you don't have to put up with his bullshit."

"Don't order for me, Noor," Shy said. "Fine, seeing as I'm at a table with a bunch of narcs who refuse to see beyond their own narrow world view, I will change my sparkling water float to a banana milkshake please, Robbie."

"With whipped cream, fudge pieces, and a flake?" Robbie asked, already knowing what the answer would be.

"Please." Shy's eyes lit up as he remembered something. "Can I get a couple of Bendys on the side please?"

"Sure thing, man, as long as I don't have to know what you're gonna do with them." Robbie said before walking away.

"You're gonna get sacked one day, Shy," Chloe muttered.

"Why? I'm just ordering from the menu, Noor!" Shy's eyes glinted in the way that only a mischievous younger sibling's can. "They can't fire me for that."

"If you keep coming in to order fucked up things, they might make an exception just for you." *Besides,* she thought groggily through her headache, *you have your little side hustle going on.*

"Noor, are you alright?" Shy asked quietly, suddenly aware that his sister had not looked up once since he had appeared, uninvited, at their table.

"It's just a migraine, Shy," she mumbled. "Just leave it, alright?"

"How long have you been having migraines?" Shy asked, suddenly curious.

"It's the sugar," Candy said after chewing slowly.

"What?" Shy replied, thoroughly confused.

"You can't have an ice cream float with sparkling water because it doesn't have any sugar; it throws the balance off." Candy smiled broadly at them all, pleased to have worked out the answer to their float conundrum.

"Thank you, Candy," Chloe said, slurring her words slightly. "I... um... don't feel so hot, guys."

Before anyone could respond, Chloe Turner blacked out and fell from her seat, hitting the cold clean tile floor of the Wimpy with a resounding thud.

"Where am I?" Chloe whispered as she got unsteadily to her feet.

She felt light headed and confused, much like she normally did when she realised she was dreaming. She stood in the Wimpy but it was strange; something about it was off, sterile even. The clock on the wall had stopped, frozen in the instant that she had passed out.

Chloe reached out for it with her right hand and gasped as the clock restarted. The more outstretched her right hand was, the faster the clock sped through its motion. She pulled her hand back, and the clock returned to the original time.

"That's fucking wild," she murmured as a small smile crept on to her face. "I wonder..."

She extended her left hand and, as she expected, time flowed backwards. *Very interesting indeed,* she thought. She moved her left hand through the air and felt her fingertips catch on something.

She couldn't see anything, but in her mind's eye she half saw, half imagined a great latticework of threads and strings that spanned all of creation. The threads touched everything and linked in ways that were impossible to describe, let alone understand. She fumbled to find a name for such a thing, but the words came to her automatically, as if they'd always been there and she was remembering them after a long time asleep.

"The Tangle," Chloe murmured. She brushed her hand through the threads once again and hooked one with the tiniest tip of her fingernail. "What happens if I do this?"

She plucked at the thread and the scene before her trembled and blurred. In a heartbeat it had reformed and she was looking at a scene involving two strangers she had never seen before; one was an impossibly beautiful woman and the other an older man with a walking stick.

Who are you people?

She pulled her hand back, and the scene returned to the frozen Wimpy.

"This is amazing," she muttered. "I could spend my entire life here."

She was about to reach her hand out once again when a sharp pain in her chest snapped her focus away. Chloe rubbed her sternum and frowned. From somewhere far away, she heard Shy's voice; it was distant and muted.

"Come on, Noor!"

He sounds upset.

"Come on! Robbie, hurry!"

There's that pain in my chest again.

"Don't you fucking die on me!"

What!?

There was a quiet whining noise, followed by a flash of lightning that sent her whole world blazing white. She screamed, but the sound was fractured and distorted, as if scrambled on a video tape.

"Again!" Shy's voice was desperate and tearful. "For fuck's sake, Robbie, zap her again!"

There was another flash and the frozen world collapsed. Chloe left the strange world of the Tangle behind and sat bolt upright with a gasp in the Dartford Wimpy. She took a deep, ragged breath and looked around at her friends.

"What happened?" Chloe croaked as Shy removed

the defibrillator contacts from her skin.

"You died, Noor," he said, his eyes full of tears. "You dropped dead."

I don't think it was anything as simple as that, she thought darkly.

Not in the slightest.

"What!?" Beef yelled angrily into her mobile. "Her fucking heart stopped beating in the middle of dinner; how can that not be an urgent case?"

Chloe took a sip of Shy's milkshake as the dispatcher tried to calm Beef down. *Good luck with that,* she thought with a smile. *You're lucky that you're down the phone line and not here in the restaurant with her.*

"An appointment with her GP? Are you kidding me?" Beef rolled her eyes so hard that the person on the other end of the call must've heard it. "Well what do we do if she collapses again? She should at least be looked over by paramedics!"

Chloe looked away as Beef moaned in frustration; whilst her friends believed her case was particularly urgent, she was actually feeling a lot better in herself. Better than she had been in a long time, in fact.

"Just leave it," Chloe said firmly. Beef looked at her and raised a questioning eyebrow. "I mean it! Just let it go.

"I'm fine now."

"You actually look pretty good, all things considered," Shy said warily. She noticed that his eyes were full of curiosity and was even more alarmed when her normally tactile brother moved his hands to avoid contact with her skin. "Are you really feeling better?"

"I am," she replied with a nod. "The headache is gone and I..."

No, that's fucking crazy, she thought. Shy's reply made her question if he could read her mind; not for the first time, in fact.

"I got chased here by bunch of highly intelligent rats," Shy grinned as he spoke, "so nothing you can possibly say will be more outlandish than that."

"I feel different," Chloe said. Her usual grumbles had faded and even the pain in her chest was receding at a startling rate. She could feel the strange presence of the Tangle, like some otherworldly hum. She reached out and felt in the air for a vibrating thread, but her fingers moved through the empty space without resistance.

"Different how?" Candy asked. He had been watching her silently since she had been revived. Whilst they sometimes made quips about him being slow, there was a brightness and insight in the large man's eyes that gave her pause.

"It's like my body is different; tighter and more powerful, if I'm going to describe it." She paused for a moment, unsure of just how honestly she should answer. "I feel like there's suddenly more to everything and I'm super keyed into it, if that makes sense?"

Her friends were silent, so she weighed up her options before deciding to be completely open with them.

In for a penny, she thought.

"I think I can see the future, or at least have the possibility of that. The same with the past too." Chloe looked at Shy who was chuckling and shaking his head. "Don't you believe me?"

"You know I'd stick with you through anything, Noor," he said with a smile, "so of course I believe you."

"Really?"

"Hell yeah," he said. He gestured to Beef and Candy. "There's something strange about the two of you, too. Do you feel any different?"

Both of Chloe's friends nodded, much to her amazement.

"What about you, Shy?" Candy asked pointedly, reaching out for him. Shy nimbly got to his feet with a grin, deftly avoiding the other man's touch.

"Just the same as I ever was." He cocked his head at them. "So, anyone want to come with me to look into these creepy rats?"

The three of them looked at each other for a moment before Beef slowly shook her head. Chloe and Candy followed her lead.

"I'm sorry, Shy," she said, "but I think we've got bigger fish to fry than a few weird rodents."

"Well, I guess I'll see you later then." Shy looked pointedly at Chloe. "Take it easy, Noor, okay?"

"I will do. You be careful out there," she replied with a grin, "Shy Turner, Rat Detective."

Her younger brother chuckled as he strode out of the Wimpy, slipping his mask on before he entered the swirling mist. *He didn't pay for his dinner,* Chloe realised.

Slippery little shit.

"We should talk about this somewhere a bit more private," Beef said in a low voice. "We should find out what we're really capable of too."

"To what end?" Chloe asked, already smiling at the answer she knew her best friend would give.

"We could change the world, Chloe." Beef couldn't control her excitement and she had a grin that was a mirror of Chloe's. "We could do anything!

"Our new lives start tonight!"

Chapter Five – Agent of Chaos

Archer

"This is fucking ridiculous, Roxy," Archer said as his partner threaded her car, a Porsche 911 Carrera 4 GTS, through the late evening traffic. He shuffled awkwardly in his seat as they zipped along, tugging absent-mindedly at his seatbelt. "Why do they need us for this job? Can't the Regulars handle a few weird rats?"

Roxanne did not answer; instead she focussed her attention entirely on the road ahead of her. Archer took this as permission to bitch and gripe about their assignment to his heart's content. The insulating glass muted the sound from outside the vehicle, making his agitated Northern Irish voice seem even louder.

"If I'm being honest, Roxy, this is downright insulting, although I can't say that I'm surprised." Archer glared through the window at the dark English countryside. "Where was the fucking Ministry when that rogue Fomorian was tearing through Glenarm last year?"

Roxanne sighed heavily as she changed gear.

"Don't give me that, Roxy! You know I'm right! The locals had to band together to drive the fucking thing back into the sea with no help from those in Westminster, but they send fucking Ravenblades to deal with rats because they're bothering people in the Home Counties?" He scratched at his seatbelt once again and drummed his feet against the floor.

"Do you want me to pull over?" Roxanne asked softly.

"No, I'll be fine," Archer said through gritted teeth. "Are you sure I can't take this thing off?"

"Positive. If we crash-"

"I can just transfer my momentum, Roxy."

"Your reflexes aren't that fast." She shook her head softly. "You'll transfer your brains through the fucking windscreen if you aren't wearing your belt."

"Hmm." Archer wanted to protest but when he was in her car he followed her rules. *Better that than in some tin can on rails.* He shuddered at the thought of the derailment that had taken place the previous month; *no matter who you are, burning to death is one of the worst ways to go.*

"Besides," Roxanne continued, "there's definitely more to this than just rats, Treen."

"What makes you say that?" He shifted in his seat, frowning.

"Things are never that simple, and definitely not for us."

"How much further?"

"About twenty minutes, although..." Roxanne's voice trailed off as a traffic jam loomed out of the darkness before them. She mellowed her voice into a gentle soothing tone. "It might be a bit longer than that. Why don't you go through the case file again and remind me what we're up against?"

"Sure," Archer said with a stressed sigh. He pulled out his Ministry issue tablet and keyed in his password. "So, this all kicked off with the derailment back in October. Two trains ended up on the same track as they approached the bridge at the centre of Dartford; one was a freighter carrying all kinds of horrible chemicals and the other was a private charter belonging to...

"Oh shit."

"What?" Roxanne drummed gently on the steering wheel as the Porsche crept along the tarmac. "You miss something on the first read?"

"I did," Archer said quietly. "I skimmed over the details of the crash; I didn't think it would be hugely relevant."

"Foul play?"

"Mhmm."

"I can't believe someone deliberately caused that crash," Roxanne said sadly. "How many people died in the end?"

"Total count was over a thousand, I think," he muttered as he skimmed through a series of photographs. "Somebody definitely went out of their way to get both trains on the same track, but that isn't actually what caused the accident."

"Oh?"

"The second train was driverless. Whoever programmed it did a piss poor job; it ploughed right into the chemical freighter, which had stopped." He shook his head in disgust. "An automated train had no fucking place on that line, but the owner isn't exactly the kind of man to take no for an answer."

"Who's the owner?" Roxanne asked, although her tone suggested that she already knew the answer.

"Finley Carmichael." Archer grimaced as he said the name. "Over a thousand fucking people; what a complete and utter prick."

Finley Carmichael, billionaire and Exception, had been a thorn in the Ministry's side for almost a decade. He had been using his wealth and political influence to interfere with their investigations and operations wherever he could; rumour had it that he was planning some kind of coup against Mohinder Desai, the Director of the Ministry of Supernatural Affairs.

Just one more thing for them to privatise, Archer thought bitterly. *He's already got more money than god; what else could he possibly want?*

"Forget about Carmichael for a moment," Roxanne said. "What are we actually up against?"

A thin mist was starting to fill the air as they crept ever closer to their destination. Wisps curled through the darkness like ephemeral serpents, twisting this way and that between the snarled traffic. Roxanne took a moment to ensure that the windows were firmly shut.

"There have been several reports of rats acting strangely," Archer said with an exasperated groan, "along with a few instances of unusual behaviour in the local population."

"Violent?"

"Sometimes, but there are at least..." he paused as he counted, "four instances of spontaneous heart failure in ordinary humans, followed by sudden revival. All of the subjects were exposed to the toxic smoke from the accident and they all reported feeling changed by the experience."

"Near death experiences will do that to you," Roxanne said flatly.

If anyone would know, it's you, Roxy.

"Is that all?" she asked.

"This last part is unsubstantiated," Archer said carefully, "but there have been sightings of ordinary humans exhibiting supernatural gifts."

"We find new Ceps all the time-"

"No, these are people that have been ordinary their whole lives, Roxy." Archer looked at her, his eyes gleaming with excitement. "I think that we might be dealing with an honest-to-god bona fide Induction Event."

"That's impossible."

"I'm not so sure about that."

"We understand how Exceptions evolve, Archer!" Roxanne's voice was sharp, almost angry. "New variants don't just appear out of thin air, especially not in a population with no previous abilities. Induction is a myth, Archer."

"I'm not the only one who thinks it's possible, Roxy, but I am one of the few who will openly talk about it. There are more of us than you think."

"And just look what happened last time someone tried to prove it!" She looked at him, her eyes wild. "Are you really arguing for a repeat of Project Lamplight, all to prove your own personal hunch?"

"Of course not!" He turned away, shamefaced. "I wouldn't wish that on anyone."

"I should hope not," Roxanne said, her clipped tone making it clear to Archer that they were done with that topic.

It doesn't mean I'm wrong, though.

"I've never seen fog this thick before!" Roxanne said unhappily as they cruised through the streets of Dartford. Her satellite navigation system had faltered when they left the main road; the derailment had shut many streets and diversions were everywhere.

Their unfamiliarity with the town was compounded by the thick blanket of noxious smog that covered the entire area, leaving the two Ravenblades well and truly lost.

"Why are all the streets named after trees!?" Archer

cried as he looked through the atlas that Roxanne kept in the glove compartment. "It's almost like this place is designed to be confusing! Where are we trying to get to?"

"Wyvern Close," she said as she peered through the windscreen into the night. "The Ministry has rented us a house for six weeks; hopefully we'll be done a lot sooner than that, though."

"I hope so," Archer said as he looked up from the book. "I think you should take that road over there."

"Where?"

"There, on the left."

"I can't see it; there's too much fucking fog!"

"Just turn left now!" Archer flailed with his hands. "Now, Roxy!"

"Alright, alright-"

There was a thud as the Porsche clipped a man who had suddenly appeared in the swirling mist. He let out a cry as the car knocked him to the ground. Roxanne let out a strangled scream as she stepped on the brake; Archer had already unclipped his belt and was opening his door when they came to a stop.

Fucking hell, he thought as he took an unfiltered breath of the smog. It burned his eyes and stung his nose. He coughed once, hard, and pulled the neck of his t-shirt over his mouth and nose as he looked around for the fallen man.

"Hey," he yelled, "are you hurt?"

There was a groan from the ground nearby and Archer deftly made his way around the front of Roxanne's Porsche towards the sound. He trailed his fingers over the lurid paintwork; Viper Green, if he remembered correctly.

He blinked rapidly as he moved, clearing the tears from his eyes. *I can't imagine what it must be like to live here!* He pushed his free hand into his pocket, fumbling for the goggles that he had brought to mollify Roxanne.

He slipped them on with a sigh of relief. He glanced around, bouncing on the balls of his feet and lightly stepping back and forth as he looked for the fallen man.

It feels good to be moving again.

There was another groan and Archer immediately zoned in on the man's location. He took a step towards him and the prone figure, barely visible in the thick fog, let out a terrified scream.

"Get it off me!"

Archer dashed forward and dealt a swift kick to the largest rat he had ever seen, sending it skittering into the night. As he slowed, he reached down to tug the man to his feet. Archer pushed his momentum into the man, sending him upright with almost no effort.

"Thank you," he said breathlessly, and Archer realised that the man was barely out of his teens.

"Sweet Jesus, you're just a fucking kid!" He took a step back in shock just as something leapt at him out of the darkness, snarling as it did so. It passed between the two men in a blur of fur and fury. "What the fuck was that?"

"Get back in your car!" The young man's voice was firm, if a little frightened. "Get away from here whilst I distract them!"

"What is happening?" Archer yelped in pain as something bit his leg. The strong fabric held, but he was still badly bruised. Another bite followed, and then another. He lashed out around him, letting his momentum flow like a raging river, but the rats were too fast for him.

It's like they can predict my every move!

Again and again the rats attacked, and Archer began to realise that in his exhausted state he was no match for their coordinated onslaught.

"Get out of here!" Archer yelled at the kid. "Get in the car and tell Roxy to go!"

Instead of doing as Archer had instructed, the young man reached out and took the Ravenblade's hand in his. There was a brief flash of rainbow light and the sensation of an electric shock shot up Archer's arm. He felt strange and weak; definitely not his usual self.

"Ooh, pistachio!" The young man quivered slightly before turning smartly on his heel and delivering a savage kick to a rat that leapt out of the mist. He let his body carry on moving, then twisted sharply to transfer his momentum into a downward punch, slaying another rodent.

Archer looked on, his mouth agape under the makeshift mask, as the strange young man fought off the swarm of vermin that had surrounded them.

Oh my god, Archer thought after a particularly dextrous set of blows sent the last of their attackers scurrying off into the gloom, *he's using my gift.*

How is that possible!?

The man turned to face Archer and grabbed his hand a second time. Another flash of light and an electric jolt accompanied the contact, and Archer felt like himself once again.

"Did you just take my power?" His words were muffled but the stranger seemed to hear him.

"I just borrowed it for a moment," he said playfully. "I hope that I wasn't being too forward!"

"How did you do that?" Archer asked, but the young man just giggled before prancing off into the night; his pink coat swished through the mist, leaving eddies in his wake.

What the fuck is going on?

More movement in the mist caught his attention, and he quickly returned to the car. He shut the door and pulled his shirt from over his mouth before letting out a long sigh.

"What was all that about?" Roxanne asked as she started the engine once again. "Did something attack you?"

"Yes it did," he said breathlessly. A small smile crept on to his lips as they got underway once again. "You know, Roxy, you were right; this is definitely a job for us.

"It looks like there's something more happening here, after all." He grinned at her. "We're way beyond the fucking pale this time."

"Should we withdraw?" He shook his head and she smiled at him. "Good; you know I love getting swept up in a crazy case! What's our next move?"

"Throw away the ruby slippers and hold on tight!" Archer said with a laugh. "I've got a feeling this is gonna be one hell of a ride!"

Chapter Six – Going on the Offensive

Elsie

Elsie breathed a sigh of relief when the swirling smog began to glow with golden light. *Sunrise,* she thought, *at long last.* The sound of rats scurrying past the door of the abandoned flat had filled her with dread for the past two nights, but luckily they had remained outside.

"At least there haven't been any more drones," Elsie muttered as she got to her feet. She let out a satisfied groan as she stretched out her cramped muscles. The injury in her shoulder was now little more than a dull ache and she smiled at her body's resilience.

"It's good to be different." She walked from the cosy sitting room into the galley kitchen and started looking through the cupboards. "Empty, empty, empty, and... well, what do you know!? Also empty."

Her stomach growled and she frowned. It would be easy enough to head out for half an hour or so to grab some food, but she ran the risk of Mad Dog picking up her trail once again. She shuddered at the thought and decided to endure the hunger for a little while longer.

I'm going to have to leave here soon, she mused as she leant against the fire damaged worktop, *or else Finley might beat me to reconstruction site.* She traced her fingers through the dust and soot that stained the kitchen, horrified at just how much damage had been done even so far from the accident.

"Why didn't the train stop?" Elsie muttered angrily as visions of fire and destruction flashed in her memory. "I programmed it myself; the collision avoidance was built into the fucking hardware!"

She yelled in frustration and lashed out at one of the cupboards. Her heavy boot crashed through the flimsy chipboard, sending fragments falling into the space behind it. She struggled to get herself free and her stomach rumbled once again, accompanied by a sharp pain.

He's trying to starve me out, Elsie thought tearfully, *and as soon as I go anywhere near a shop or restaurant he'll be right on top of me. I've heard him brag about it enough times.*

"What sort of a sick fuck hunts human beings!?" Her voice echoed around the small space. Mad Dog was not the only fucked up person that Finley had introduced her to, but he was certainly the most dangerous.

"I've hunted men, I've hunted women, and I've hunted children," he'd told her when they first met, his eyes glinting with unhinged malice, "but I ain't never hunted me a transsexual before. Soon as the boss says I can, and he will, I'm a-coming for your hide, girl. I got a spot on my wall picked out, just for you."

It had taken her far too long to see Finley Carmichael for what he was, but realising just what kind of people he surrounded himself with had been the first small stones of an inevitable landslide of realisation.

Now all that's left is to undo everything we built together.

Elsie felt her lip tremble as grief gripped her heart. He had been right in their first meeting; they had created wonders that she would never have dared to attempt without him. Her earlier inventions and gadgets were crude by comparison, almost ugly in their simplicity.

I will never have children, she thought sadly, *but I have brought life into this world.*

The dying whirr of the downed drone filled her mind and she slowly sank to the dusty kitchen floor.

I never wanted to hurt anyone or harm anything.

Elsie blinked back the tears of loss as she finally tugged her boot free. She shook her head, trying to clear the single word that constantly rattled around it, but it continued to echo long after her other thoughts had fallen silent.

Murderer.

She closed her eyes, desperate to shut out the chemical scarred kitchen and the swirling fog beyond the blackened glass; her handiwork, her fault. She drew her knees up to her chest and tearfully voiced a question to the empty house.

"Why does it always end up like this?"

There was no name for what Elsie Reichardt was, but Finley Carmichael had suggested either Mechanic or Archimedes. Elsie had rejected those names; both weren't accurate enough and the latter was far too grandiose.

I'm just Elsie, she'd thought. *Nothing more, nothing less.*

It had been Dylan Weiss, Carmichael's Head of Technology, who had finally stumbled on a term that felt correct.

Composer.

"Everything is connected," her grandmother had told her, time and time again, "and nothing that happens does so alone. This world has a rhythm, if you know how to listen to her; it takes practice, but a quiet mind will hear her music.

"You will know her plan by the notes she plays."

Iris Reichardt had been one of the most divisive avant-garde composers of the twentieth century and Elsie's only guardian for the majority of her childhood. Iris had known that her grandchild was special; that she could also hear the heartbeat of the universe.

Although it had taken over twenty years, Elsie had finally learned to not only hear the hidden music but also to change its tune to suit her needs. With practice she had realised that the correct push applied at the right place and time could alter the events of the world in drastic ways.

She'd likened it to ripples in a pond when explaining it to Finley; one touch would disturb the water but a deliberate pattern of intervention would create waves from even the stillest surface.

With care and precision she could weave a symphony of seeming chaos into the most perfect and targeted order. She was hesitant with her gift at first, however; sometimes, indeed a lot of the time, there would be unexpected consequences or unforeseen ripples in the wake of her music.

Newton's third, she thought with a sad smile. *If you bump the universe, it bumps back.*

But the more she practised and played, the more she realised that there were layers to the tune; every object had a note of its own and she could follow the chords and cadences to create and invent machines and devices beyond anyone's comprehension.

Even her own.

Her gift was not without its drawbacks, however, and they were not limited to the unforeseen outcomes of her meddling. The most powerful compulsion was the one that was common to all great artisans and visionaries; if one had the ability to create something, then it must be created regardless of the consequences.

"And look where that's got me," she muttered to the empty kitchen. "I was too focussed on whether I could that I never even considered if I should've been making all those toys for Finley."

She let out a deep sigh. She was no longer angry with herself, but instead was deeply tired of scrabbling to fix her mistakes. *Pandora was my magnum opus,* she thought sadly, *and she's in the hands of Finley fucking Carmichael.*

Never has there been a person who deserved her less.

"It's no good," she said suddenly as she got to her feet. "I can't hide from Mad Dog forever and I need to get Pandy back before Finley works out how to use her. I need to get into the reconstruction site."

However, she thought as she gathered up her things, *I'm going to need some help.*

The music thumped and blared as Elsie sipped her drink. Lady Natasha's was an Exception only establishment, so she felt reasonably safe from Mad Dog and his capture team. Finley Carmichael could still walk in, of course, but she was confident that he would not dare to show his face anywhere in Dartford; not after his automated train had caused such an awful catastrophe.

Lady Natasha's existed in a twilight space when it came to Ministry oversight; it was both officially sanctioned but also served as a haven for Exceptions who wished to avoid the attention of the government operatives.

Elsie, however, was using the club to rendezvous with someone who could assist her with accessing the reconstruction site. Such services did not come cheap but she still had access to the account that Finley had set up to fund her inventions and research; thankfully he had not thought to freeze her cards.

Unless he's expecting me to use it, she thought as her blood ran cold, *and Mad Dog will zero in on me right away.*

"Are you Elsie?" asked a handsome dark haired man; he was in his late thirties and covered in tattoos. Elsie looked up at him and his eyes flashed with animal shine, confirming her suspicions. She nodded and gestured for him to sit. "I'm Silas Cherry, pleased to meet you."

"A pleasure," Elsie said as she shook his hand. She had to lean in close to be heard over the music. "You come very highly recommended."

"I'm sure, and I have the price to match." He took a moment to look around them, ensuring that they weren't being watched. "So, is this a classic asset retrieval job, or is there going to be some, uh, close contact work?"

"I'm not entirely sure what you're asking," Elsie said carefully. Silas blinked slowly, clearly frustrated. *He's more pretty than handsome,* she thought idly as she waited for his response.

"Are we going to be breaking and entering with the aim of theft or murder?" Silas asked.

"We're taking back something that's mine, so neither."

"If you need to break in, it's still theft, dear."

"Mhmm."

"Where's the place?"

"They've set up a prefab building in Oakfield Park-"

"We're going after the accident reconstruction site!?" Silas raised an eyebrow, suddenly uncomfortable. "You didn't have anything to do with that, did you?"

"Of course not!" Elsie lied. "I'm looking for something that was lost in the mayhem of it all, and I think it might be stored away there. If it is, I'll take it with me, but otherwise everything else will be completely untouched. Does that sound fair?"

"Fine by me. Give me a couple of hours to get split up and meet me at the south end of the park." Elsie nodded as he spoke. "My usual fee is three thousand, upfront, but..."

"What?" There was a pause before Silas Cherry spoke once again.

"You're Elsie Reichardt, aren't you?" His voice was low and conspiratorial, but there was an almost reverential edge to it also.

"Yes."

"Rumour has it you can build anything. Is that true?"

"More or less. What do you need?" She pulled out a notepad and began scribbling.

"A codebreaker; another client needs me to interfere with some automated location or something, but I can't for the life of me work out how to get through the final security systems. Can you make something like that?"

"I already have," she said with a small smile. "It's worth a lot more than three thousand pounds, but you seem like you have a real need for it."

"You'd give it to me?" Silas said, his eyes wide with excitement.

"No, but I'd lend it to you," Elsie said with a smile.

"You go and get set up; I'll see you soon."

"In a while, crocodile," Silas said as he left her sitting by herself in the noisy club. Elsie watched him as he walked away; his skin rippled and pulsated as he moved, seemingly bringing his tattoos to life.

I wonder if that's how he's linked?

Finding an adult Swarm, let alone one for hire, had been quite a surprise. Their ability to fragment their mind and share it with the creatures that made up their particular entourage made them useful spies and strategists, but prolonged separation could cause a wealth of psychological problems.

I can't imagine what it must be like if one of their bound dies, Elsie thought.

Silas Cherry seemed to be stable, but the only way for her to be sure was to see him in the field.

"Please let me pull this off," she muttered before downing her drink. She stretched slightly, left a tip on the table under her glass, and went to leave the club.

Across the dance floor, a bearded young man with gold eyeliner followed her movements with keen eyes. Elsie turned around as she reached the cloakroom, certain that someone was watching her. When her gaze passed over the man's table, she found it empty. She shuddered and took her coat gratefully from the attendant.

I can't wait for this to be over, she thought. *This town gives me the creeps.*

"One last task," she muttered as she stepped into the swirling mist, "and then I can get the hell out of Dodge."

Her mind was full of thoughts of Mad Dog and his nightmarish barbed arrows. Elsie was certain that there could be nothing worse than him lurking in the

glistening fog.
  Little did she know just how wrong she was.

Chapter Seven – Get Out or Die

Chloe

Chloe shivered and pulled her coat even tighter around her chest. The nights were growing colder and darker with each passing day, it seemed, and the horrible fog showed no signs of lifting.

If anything, she thought as she walked, *it's getting worse.*

Chloe kept her wits about her as she made her way through the swirling mass towards Candy's house. There had been too many reports of disappearances since the derailment, especially after dark, not to mention the sharp increase in animal attacks too.

"What the hell is in this?" Chloe murmured through her mask as she swished one hand through the glistening silver droplets that hung on the air before her. "This isn't like any fog I've ever seen before."

She jumped as a black cat darted through the street in front of her. It regarded her with eerily human eyes for a moment before raising its eyebrows and continuing on its way. Chloe leant against a nearby tree, trying to catch her breath and slow her racing heart.

You're getting skittish, she thought with a nervous giggle. Still, laughter aside, she couldn't help the image of the rabid fox from entering her mind, eyes wild and tongue lolling as it charged at her. She shuddered once again and went on her way, her pace swifter than before.

Chloe slowed when a searing pain suddenly tore through her chest. She began to cough and splutter as she staggered along; her mouth was filled with the salty metallic tang of blood. With one scrabbling hand she ripped the mask from her face and spat a globule of stringy blood streaked saliva on to the glistening pavement.

The fog filled her chest as she gasped down lungfuls of tainted air, and she retched as the acrid plasticky stink stung her nose. Her coughing intensified and she lost her footing, falling to her knees. Her throat burned as she inhaled the swirling fumes and her vision darkened a little. She flailed around, looking for her mask; in her discomfort, she had dropped it.

Her goggles had misted up due to her panicked perspiration and now she was disoriented; all turned around and lost in the poisonous gloom. There was a gentle tapping sound to her left. Her eyes were full of tears and her nose streamed bloody mucus as she turned her head in the direction of the noise.

Chloe let out a strangled scream when she found herself face to face with a huge greasy rat, its twitching nose mere inches from her open mouth. It looked at her with glassy dead eyes, not unlike a doll's, chittering and chirruping as it did so. It took a hesitant step in her direction, and then another.

"Fuck off!" Chloe yelled before collapsing into another fit of uncontrollable coughing. She winced as a sharp spike of pain flared up her left side; she had cracked a rib with the force of her cough. The rat darted forwards and nipped at her left hand as it hung loosely at her side.

"Ow!" Chloe reacted instinctively, snatching the creature up by its tail as it turned to flee. She heaved it over her head and brought it crashing down into the pavement, yelling all the while. "No, no, no, no, NO,

NO!"

She brought the rat down again, crushing its skull and severing its spinal cord, but in her frenzy she didn't notice the rodent grow limp in her grip. Instead she continued to bludgeon it against the concrete, splitting its head open and spilling its blood and brains across the floor. Only when it was a pulpy mess dangling from a barely recognisable tail did she regain enough control of her emotions to stop.

She let the mangled carcass drop to the ground with a wet plop. Her lungs seared with pain as she inhaled the toxic fog and a small part of her wanted to just lie down and suffocate. *It would be easier,* she thought. An eerie sound drifted through the air, but she could not pin it down; it was at the very edge of her hearing. Something about it pulled on her soul and she found herself getting shakily to her feet.

Chloe took three unsteady steps in the direction of the curious noise, wheezing and spluttering as she went. Thick bloody saliva hung from her mouth in rancid strings and her bloodied hands swept and clawed and the fog. Her eyes rolled madly in her head and she let out a guttural moan, gently shrieking like a rabid animal.

Suddenly there was a weight on her shoulder and she felt the sharp sting of claws on her exposed cheek. She cried out in pain, clutching at her wounded face. The inky black cat leapt to the ground and stared at her.

"What the fuck?" she managed to say between coughs. Chloe's mind fought to stay in control of her body, but the mist sapped her strength and will. Her right foot took another shuddering step, seemingly of its own accord.

"Get it together!" hissed the cat angrily before it

batted something across the ground. Chloe looked down, her eyes barely focused, and saw her mask. With trembling fingers she fitted it to her face and exhaled, hard.

With the mask now cleared, each breath came a little easier. She turned to look at the cat, but it had vanished. *Did it really talk,* she wondered, *or am I just going crazy?* Chloe looked down at her bloodied hands before hurriedly wiping them on her coat. The blood still oozed from the bite wound, but it wasn't serious.

"Maybe I should take the rat with me," she murmured as she searched for the rodent's carcass. "They might need to know if it was rabid or something..."

Her voice trailed off as her eyes settled on the bloodstained concrete. Her heart thundered in her ears and she took a terrified step backwards when she saw the shattered remains dragging themselves towards her, one gory inch at a time.

How is this possible!?

Adrenaline flooded her body and she let out a terrified scream. Chloe Turner ignored the burning in her lungs as she fled through the foggy night. Behind her, the bloody carcass continued to ooze its slow, gelatinous way along the pavement.

"Are you sure you didn't imagine it?"

"I'm sure, Beef!" Chloe's voice was filled with frustration but she kept perfectly still as Beef brought the clippers close to her head. "It wasn't a trick of the light either; I smashed that rat to pieces but it just kept coming!

"It was horrible."

"It sounds it," Beef said softly as she buzzed the clippers through Chloe's hair. Although she kept her head stationary, Chloe's eyes followed the drifts of black hair that drifted to the bathroom floor. "Ooh, yeah, this undercut is gonna look fucking sick when we're done."

"I hope so," Chloe said excitedly. She'd expressed an interest in getting a snazzier haircut after the incident in the Wimpy a few days earlier, and Beef had been happy to do the honours.

It had been a strange evening, truth be told, but her friends' total honesty about what was happening to the three of them had been refreshing, especially after weeks of bullshit and misinformation about the toxic fog.

Chloe, Beef, and Candy had all been exposed to the initial wave of chemical smoke, but instead of perishing like so many residents, it had changed them instead. All three were faster and stronger than they had been before, and it wasn't just Chloe who had developed some kind of supernatural talent.

Whilst her newfound ability to enter the Tangle was at best unstable and at worst life threatening, Chloe Turner was determined to refine her skills. Whilst the unfettered viewing of the past and future she'd experienced in her near death state was what she strived for, she'd started to get flashes of intuition about what was to come or glimpses of the past when she handled certain objects.

Her power was only just beginning to blossom, but she already showed tremendous potential. Unbeknownst to her, Chloe Turner had developed the gift of a Double Janus Seer without the necessary genetics; an occurrence believed to be impossible by the Ministry of Supernatural Affairs.

Candy's gift had shocked Beef and Chloe, partly due to its simplicity but mostly because he had been using it in plain sight ever since the derailment; if given enough time, he could mentally solve any problem. He'd also explained that he never forgot a single thing he read or was told, and he could reach out to other people and borrow some of their cognitive abilities to speed up his own calculations.

"The only downside," he'd said with a shy smile, "is when I start on a problem I can't stop until I've finished it."

Chloe had been amazed by the journal full of mathematics and other calculations that he'd sheepishly shown them when Beef asked for proof of his talent. What had surprised his wife and wrestling partner the most, however, was their bank account.

"I can't believe he's been gaming the stock market for weeks," Beef said as she looked at Chloe's new hairdo. "I still can't get my head around the fact that we don't have to worry about mon-"

"You okay there?" Chloe asked as her friend's eyes glazed over slightly.

"Locked and loaded, Bowman," the stocky wrestler whispered, before she yelped in pain. "Ouch!"

Beef's blonde plaits jerked sharply as she tossed the clippers to the ground. She gingerly rubbed the small burn on her hand whilst Chloe made sympathetic noises.

"Another shock?" asked the Seer, and Beef nodded. "How many is that today?"

"Eight so far," Beef said sulkily. "I can't believe that you and Candy got such awesome powers whilst all I ended up with is the ability to always have a mobile signal. That's such bullshit!"

"Hey, don't sell yourself short," Chloe said with a wry smile. "You can always find a phone signal *and* you get regular electric shocks from any device you handle."

"Ha ha ha, bitch," Beef said, "if you keep this up I'm gonna shave your whole head! What will mummy and daddy say then?"

"They're in Lahore for three months," Chloe replied. "By the time they get back, I'll have enough hair for a pixie cut."

"I maintain that it's out of line to leave you in charge of your deadbeat brother for three months whilst they go off gallivanting round Pakistan."

"Shy isn't a deadbeat," Chloe said defensively.

"He sells drugs out the back of the Wimpy Burger," Beef said, one eyebrow raised. "That's pretty fucking deadbeat to me."

"He's still my brother, even if he has made a few unfortunate decisions, and he's capable of taking care of himself." Chloe turned to face Beef and caught sight of her reflection in the mirror. "Damn, you did a really good job!"

"Of course I did," Beef said with a self-confident smile.

"Girls, dinner is ready!" called a man's voice from downstairs.

"Be there in a moment, Mr B!" Chloe called in response. "Do you want any help clearing up in here?"

"No, you go ahead. Tell Errol that I'll be down in a few minutes; it'll give him plenty of time to fawn over your new look." Beef winked at Chloe as she left the bathroom and trotted down the stairs.

She nipped softly down the corridor and into the

little kitchen where Errol Baxter, Candy's father, pottered around the cramped dining table. Chloe took a deep breath, enjoying the spices that scented the air. Errol turned to look at her and beamed.

"Oh my, who is this beautiful young lady?" he said, a twinkle in his eye. "If you've come to sweep my sweet boy off his feet, I must tell you that he is already spoken for."

"I've only eyes for you, Mr B," Chloe said with a laugh. "Dinner smells amazing."

"I do the best I can with what I am given." He took one of her hands in his and gently guided her to sit down. "Now, has my boy told you about his little surprise gift to me?"

"He hasn't," Chloe said as she looked at Candy. He gave her a wry smile. "Are you allowed to tell me?"

"Of course!" Errol said excitedly as he set four dishes on the table. "He has, along with my wonderful daughter, paid for me to take a holiday to Falmouth for two months to see my sister. What a generous pair they are!"

"You won't say that when we put you on a train to Cornwall," Beef teased as she walked into the room.

"You wicked girl!" Errol said with a laugh. "It's a shame that the two of you can't come with me; I think a few weeks under the Jamaican sun would be good for you, Dee."

Beef stepped around the table, giving Errol a peck on the cheek as she went. Both her and Candy had moved back in with Errol Baxter after his wife had died three years earlier. Chloe had cautioned them against it; three big personalities in a small house had looked like a recipe for trouble.

She couldn't have been more wrong.

Errol had been delighted to have them move in and had treated Beef like his own daughter. *I'm glad it all worked out,* she thought as she tucked into her delicious dinner; Jamaican Brown Stew with a side dish of Rice and Peas.

She looked at Candy from the corner of her eye. He was a man of few words, but he wore his emotions and intentions on his sleeve. *He wants his father away from all this,* she realised. *Somewhere safe.*

"When do you leave, Mr B?" Chloe asked with affected nonchalance.

"Tomorrow morning," Errol said with a huge grin. "James was quite firm that I go as soon as I could; winter in this country is no good for an old man, after all."

"I'll help you finish packing after dinner, Errol," Beef said around a mouthful of stew. "This is incredible, as always."

"Such kind words, thank you."

The conversation remained light throughout the meal. When they were finished, Beef and Errol went upstairs to resume his holiday preparations whilst Chloe and Candy took care of the washing up.

"I'll be happy when he's safe," Candy said after a few minutes of silence.

"I feel the same way about my parents being in Lahore."

"You and Shy are welcome to stay here, if you like. I don't like the thought of you being so close to the lake."

"What's wrong with the lake?" Chloe asked, her expression puzzled.

"I'm not sure, but it's always felt a bit ominous, you know?" He dried a few plates before continuing. "Mrs

Danforth, you know, from down the road, she disappeared a few days ago; nobody has seen her since Oliver's funeral."

"Do you think she..." Chloe hesitated for a moment. "Do you think she killed herself?"

"That's the theory, but there was no note and her back door was wide open." He shook his head. "Something terrible is happening here, Chloe."

"Why now?"

"Something was set free by that fire..." Candy lowered his voice. "Something evil."

"I'm starting to think we developed these gifts for a reason, Candy," Chloe said. "Maybe we're supposed to stop whatever is happening here?"

"Where would we even start?"

"I have an idea," Chloe said as she looked through the little kitchen window. In the distance, its glowing lights visible through the fog, was the tallest building for miles around; Junction Tower, the beating heart of the Eigenforce International Freight Depot.

"When do we go?" Candy asked as he followed her gaze. Chloe let her eyelids fall, half closing them as she felt for the merest hint of the Tangle. It twanged under her questing fingertips and her eyes snapped open.

"Tomorrow night," she said, suddenly certain of their path. "We need to be entering the western stairwell from the eighteenth floor at exactly eleven o'clock tomorrow."

"What happens if we don't make it?" Beef asked from the doorway. Chloe hadn't heard her approach; for such a muscular woman she was surprisingly light on her feet. "Well?"

Chloe's mind filled with the memory of the

dismembered rat inching its way across the concrete towards her and she shuddered.

"We die," she said softly.

"Who's we?" Beef said, putting an arm around her. "The three of us?"

"No," Chloe said, her voice trembling with fear.

"Then who?"

"Everyone."

Chapter Eight – Black Cats Bring Bad Luck

Elsie

Elsie's heart thundered in her chest as she waited in the swirling fog for Silas Cherry. The sweat-covered rubber of her gas mask clung to her face like a shroud, making her feel trapped and claustrophobic even though she stood under the open sky.

Why hasn't this fucking mist shifted yet? Elsie thought angrily. A block of high pressure had lingered over the town in the wake of the disaster and the still air had not been disturbed by even the slightest breeze. It was unusual, for sure, but not strange enough to draw more than a cursory mention from the meteorologist she had seen on the news a few days earlier.

What are we going to find in there? Her eyes peered at a luminous spot in the fog where the Reconstruction Centre was. From the pictures on the television she had seen that it was surrounded by a razor wire topped chain fence and was patrolled by security day and night.

Elsie's mind kept coming back to the taunting note Carmichael had left for her at the crash site. He knew that she'd come for her greatest invention and he had been one step ahead of her.

I saw the case get loaded on to the train, she thought as she worked her way through the possibilities. *I know you wouldn't transport her any other way, so the research car must've been a deliberate red herring.*

She had seen almost a dozen men flee that particular carriage during the accident; each man was armed to the teeth and ready to fight. Finley Carmichael had clearly wanted her to go after Pandora and he'd laid a trap for when she did.

I was never supposed to see that note, but if I did you would've had ample time to transport her out of there whilst your goons tried to murder me.

Oh my god, she realised, *you must have had Pandy in the main freight storage this whole time! It's the only place you could quickly smuggle her out of in a pinch.*

Elsie's eyes looked at the glow once again.

The main freight car of Finley Carmichael's automated train had been almost totally destroyed in the crash and any objects that survived, along with other scrap and debris, were taken by the investigators before the billionaire's goons could retrieve it.

"You're in there, aren't you?" Elsie said with breathless excitement. As devastating as the crash had been, she built Pandora to withstand such an ordeal.

Her greatest invention was hiding in a crash investigation team's warehouse, unharmed and untouched. Elsie was certain that Finley hadn't got his hands on it yet; if he had, he would be hunting her instead of Mad Dog.

"I never should have created you in the first place..." Her eyes glazed slightly behind the gas mask lenses, but snapped back into focus at the sound of rustling from the undergrowth beside her.

She whirled around, drawing a strange looking pistol from the pocket of her greatcoat. Ever since her encounter with the rats she'd made sure to travel armed.

"Show yourself!" Elsie hissed into the dark. There was another rustle as an inky black cat leapt out from a bush. It looked up at her, its shimmering eyes glinting with mirth.

"Jumpy, aren't we?" The cat's voice was that of a man and Elsie sighed with relief and lowered the gun.

"God damn you, Silas! I might have shot you!" She shook her head in disbelief as the cat stretched out and rolled lazily on to its back. It looked up at Elsie, expecting a tummy rub. "Cut that out, you pervert!"

The cat hissed as she kicked it gently. It growled at her for a moment before leaping on to her shoulder. It pointed at the glow with a paw, and she nodded.

"Is your body nearby?" She asked as they made their way carefully towards the reconstruction site.

"Yes," Silas purred, "and it is well protected; no need to consider fucking me over when we're done."

"I wasn't going to!"

"I would," the cat said with a dark chuckle. It looked up at the loud hooting of an owl.

"One of yours?"

"Mhmm. I've got a few crows on standby too, ready for a distraction, along with a wealth of other night creatures." Silas looked at her with his feline eyes, one brow raised in an uncomfortably human manner. "So, Elsie Reichardt, what is it that we're pilfering tonight?"

"None of your business."

"You made it my business, sweetheart."

He has a point, she thought. She opened her mouth to respond when she felt the cat stiffen; it dug its claws into her shoulder and its fur stood on end.

Elsie responded, ducking down low. There was a soft moan in the mist, muffled by the precipitation and distance. Beneath it was the same eerie sound that she'd heard at the crash site; once again it slipped away whenever she tried to focus on it.

What the fuck is that?

The first rat came into view seconds later, shortly followed by dozens more. They ran silently, bouncing over the damp grass; all moved as one, completely uniform.

Elsie felt the cat on her shoulder twitch as Silas fought to keep his body's natural instincts under control.

Once a cat, always a cat, Elsie thought. Despite her witty observation, she did not smile; instead she realised that she was shaking in terror. Another moan rang out, much louder than before. Elsie's heart almost stopped.

Those are words.

"Hhhhhhheeeeeeeellllllppppp mmmmmmeeeeeeee!" The first shambling figure staggered into her field of vision and she carefully lowered herself into the slightly overgrown grass, desperately hoping that it would conceal her.

The figure was not alone. Eight more, ranging in size from a small child all the way to a towering adult, slouched and shuffled into view as they crossed the park in the wake of the rats.

They cried out as they moved, their words all variations on a theme; loneliness and fear.

Elsie began to sob into her gas mask, silently praying to whatever deity would listen. *Please,* she begged, *don't let them find me.*

After an agonisingly slow five minutes, the unsteady creatures moved on. Elsie let out a shuddering gasp, relieved that she'd escaped their notice.

Please don't let that be the ZX, she begged silently.

"Silas," she whispered as she got to her feet, "what was that?"

"I have no idea," the cat hissed nervously, "but whatever it is has control of all the rats in at least a ten mile radius.

"It's a real shame. I always enjoyed being a rat."

"I'm sure you did," Elsie muttered. She wondered if the awful creatures and the train derailment were linked, but deep in her heart she suspected that was the truth.

Did I set all this in motion? Is this all my fault?

"Let's get this over with," she whispered to the cat as it resumed its place on her shoulder.

"Agreed. I don't want to be out here any longer than absolutely necessary."

The two Exceptions approached the chain link fence at a crawl as Silas's owl swooped ahead, scoping out the area beyond the barrier. Elsie carefully drew her pistol once again and flicked off the safety.

She smiled as she felt the reassuring weight of it in her hand. The grip was moulded to her measurements and the ergonomic design was absolutely perfect. All the weight lay in the heavy battery and the magnetic coils that shrouded the barrel.

It was a prototype weapon, inspired by a commission she'd received earlier in the year to create a handgun for an invisible assassin. It electrically accelerated small tungsten rods to an absurd velocity by the time they left the barrel to silently shred whatever stood in their way.

She'd dubbed the accelerator pistol the "Reichardt Scanline"; the interference caused when the weapon was fired would disrupt any nearby monitors with a distinct pattern of distortion.

The owl signalled the all clear.

With the Scanline in hand and Silas on her shoulder, she got to her feet. The black cat deftly leapt through a gap in the razor wire, its form blurring like an inkblot as it did so.

Elsie marvelled at the sheer usefulness of her accomplice's gift; there was little question as to why he'd taken to moonlighting as a thief.

After stepping through the sharp wire, Silas's cat form nimbly leapt downward at a diagonal angle, hitting the gate latch as he went. There was a sharp buzzing sound and the way through the fence swung open. Elsie grinned as she followed him into the compound.

"Where is everyone?" she hissed as the cat resumed its perch.

"I don't know. I can't see anyone, that's for sure." The owl wheeled overhead once again before taking a swooping path through the chain enclosed space. "It's too fucking quiet for my liking, that's for sure."

Elsie was about to open her mouth to respond when the faint pitter-patter of approaching footsteps caught her attention. She turned in the direction of the noise just as a human shaped hole formed in the fog beside her.

Silas yowled as he leapt from her shoulder as something whipped through the mist with a metallic whisking sound.

She brought her arms up just in time, catching the garotte with her wrists. The wire cut into the thick sleeves of her overcoat, as her assailant groaned and pulled with all his might.

She felt a knee collide with her lower back and she dropped to hers with a grunt. Her attacker took the opportunity to pull the garotte upwards; Elsie shifted her arms to compensate but the deadly strand was still perilously close to her throat. The two of them thrashed and struggled, disturbing the mist enough to obscure the assassin's form and preventing Silas from coming to her rescue.

Elsie closed her eyes and let her thoughts cascade in a torrent of sound and colour. She saw herself taking the commission for the Scanline and reading up on Ghosts; she had been especially interested in the physics of their gift, along with the fact they were practically unkillable with conventional weapons.

I am not conventional, Elsie thought with a flash of inspiration as she flicked the weapon's safety on. Sensing that she had a plan, the Ghost kicked her once again, dealing a savage blow to her kidneys. The Composer roared in pain and anger as she dropped the weapon and the garotte closed around her neck.

The Ghost yelled in triumph, which was all Silas Cherry needed. A pair of monstrous bats swooped in through the mist and hit the invisible attacker in the face, biting and clawing where their eyes should've been.

The assassin let go of the garotte to swipe at the flying mammals, freeing Elsie. She snatched up the Scanline and deftly cross-wired three of the magnets with her nimble fingers before hitting the trigger.

The resulting burst of interference was at the exact frequency to react with the Ghost's invisibility. With a scream he snapped into view as layers of his skin sloughed off, leaving him bloody and defenceless. She continued to pull the trigger, over and over, as Silas brought all of his creatures to bear on the incapacitated Ghost.

After what seemed like a lifetime, their attacker finally shuddered and went still. Not one to leave anything to chance, Elsie pulled out her little push knife and drove it into the base of his skull, severing his brain stem.

Amongst the ruined flesh she saw a familiar, albeit faded tattoo and she realised who their attacker was.

"Mitchell Rawlings," she spat angrily, "one of Finley's goons. I only met him once and he made my skin crawl."

"It looks like you returned the favour and then some," said the cat wryly. "Was he Ministry?"

"No, some American mercenary with a criminal record as long as my arm. Finley has a fondness for dangerous felons and ex-soldiers." She turned to look at the cat. "Thank you for saving me."

"Any time. You and I make a hell of a team, Elsie Reichardt; we could make a lot of money if we worked together, you know."

"I'll take it under advisory," she said as she strode across the ground to the building. "If Rawlings was here, that means that any security is dead. We need to be quick and careful; Carmichael never sends anyone alone."

"You know an awful lot about how he thinks," Silas said, his voice dripping with suspicion. He did not press the issue, however, and followed her into the prefab warehouse.

Elsie instinctively brought her hand up to her mouth in shock, only to have her glove smack into the gas mask. Bodies were strewn about the warehouse; both

Crash Investigation security personnel and Finley's armoured goons.

Silas padded past her and dispassionately examined the corpses. He made the occasional tutting sound, along with an exclamation of surprise here and there.

"Well," he said matter-of-factly as he sauntered back over, "what we have here is a two stage killing."

"What?" Elsie remarked, her head still reeling at the carnage before her. Silas sighed heavily and settled on his hind legs, gesturing with one paw in an uncomfortable pantomime of humanity.

"The security chaps in the orange vests were clearly in the employ of the investigation team. They were already here when our assault force broke in. I'm guessing they had inside help to get through the fence quietly." He glanced back at the door. "The Ghost was shadowing them, possibly even without their knowledge; a part of me thinks that he was there to kill the assault team if they saw too much, but that's just speculation.

"Anyway," the cat continued, "by hook or by crook Carmichael's soldiers gain entry to the compound. They round up all the patrolling security officers and corral them in here. This fellow, the one closest to us, tries to make a break for it or attacks one of the hired guns; either way the outcome is the same and all the investigation personnel are slaughtered."

"How can you possibly know all this?" Elsie asked, both intrigued and frightened at Silas's deductive skills.

"This is not my first rodeo," he said tersely, "and I'd rather keep my past to myself. I did show you the same courtesy, after all."

"Of course," she said quietly. "Sorry, Silas, I didn't mean to intrude."

"No harm, no foul." He smiled at her, which was a truly upsetting sight; no normal cat could possibly wear such an expression. "We're getting to the exciting part now. All of the sensitive wreckage and debris is behind that door over there; the damage around the frame suggests that the soldiers were trying to get in, but they failed. I'm guessing that whatever you're looking for is back there."

"What happened to the soldiers?" Elsie asked. They were strewn about the floor like discarded toys, with their limbs twisted in all manner of unnatural angles.

"They were interrupted whilst trying to break into the room. Their assailant was a single person who fought at close range; a combination of freakishly powerful unarmed strikes combined with some highly skilled blade work." Silas cocked his head to one side, thoughtful for a moment. "Judging by the shape and depth of the stab wounds, I'm going to hazard a guess that this is a Ministry operative.

"Regardless of their origin, our new attacker killed every single one of Carmichael's hired guns before trying to get through the locked door." Silas grinned at her. "He also failed to get in. Given that the Ghost was still around and the bloodstains are still moist, I'd hazard a guess that this all happened no longer than an hour ago.

"We're lucky we weren't caught in the crossfire."

Elsie did not reply. Instead she ran across the room and immediately set to work on the digital security panel set into the door. It was a complex system that had several redundancies and multi-factor protections.

It would've taken an experienced thief over an hour to get it open.

Elsie smiled as the door unlocked only seventy eight seconds after she'd started working on it.

"That was impressive," Silas said as he returned to her shoulder. She reached into the darkness and an automated light flashed into life, illuminating the space inside. Elsie ignored the majority of the twisted burnt wreckage and focused on searching for Pandora.

"Oh my god," Elsie said sadly as she stumbled on a crude pile of ruined machinery, torn to pieces like some bizarre puzzle. "Pandy, what did this to you?"

Pandora, the automated environmental protection suit that Elsie had designed, was completely destroyed. She traced her fingers down the damaged edges as she blinked back tears; she had hoped to recover her intact, but now Pandy would be added to her growing list of dead creations.

The damage was unlike anything else the room contained. There were no scorch or burn marks, and the suit had been ripped apart, systematically. She began to quickly gather Pandy's pieces into a bag.

I can't rebuild you, she thought sadly, *but I won't leave you for the vultures either.*

"What's this?" Silas asked as he jumped from her shoulder to look at a collection of pale broken stone. It was another anomaly, completely untouched by the flames. "Given where it is in the reconstruction, I'd hazard a guess that it was right next to your suit. We should take some of it with us."

"Agreed," Elsie said as she swept some of the stone fragments into her bag. Once everything was gathered, she put the bag on her shoulder and turned to leave.

She was mid stride when she saw something that stopped her in her tracks.

"What do you see?" Silas asked, peering in the direction of her gaze.

"The cargo door," Elsie said, "is smashed outwards; that's the opposite direction to where the chemical train impact would've come from. How can that be?"

"Maybe Finley Carmichael had something alive in here," Silas suggested. "We'd need a cargo manifest to be sure."

"Then we should go find one," Elsie replied with a smile, "if you're up for coming with me?"

"You know what they say about cats and curiosity," Silas said with a chuckle as they exited the room. "Wild horses couldn't drag me away!"

Elsie felt relieved that she would not have to continue on alone, but the sight of the shattered door was burned into her mind.

Something broke out of that train, she thought.
Finley, what the fuck were you keeping in there!?

Chapter Nine – Class Nine Event

Archer

"Are you going to be okay without overwatch, Bowman?" Roxanne Wagstaff asked, her voice filling the earpiece that Archer Treen wore. "None of the scopes can penetrate this fucking fog."

That's a bad sign, he thought, but kept his worry to himself.

"I'll be fine, Wags. Just be ready to go if it all kicks off, yeah?"

"Locked and loaded, Bowman." Roxanne said.

They always used call signs when carrying out an operation, which was unusual for Ministry Agents. In fact, it was so notable that most people simply defaulted to calling Roxanne by hers; whilst he inexplicably remained Archer, she was now known almost exclusively as Wags.

"I sure wish Malarkey had chosen to join us," he said as he made his way across the fog clouded park. "It would be good to have someone in the mix with me on this one."

"I asked about a secondment, Bowman," Roxanne said through the earpiece, "but nobody is available."

"Who did you ask for?" Archer asked, slowing his pace slightly. When there was no response, he tapped the microphone taped to his throat. "Wags?"

"I asked for Hillgreen," Roxanne said softly, stopping Archer dead in his tracks.

"The fuck, Roxy!?"

"Call signs only, Bowman!" Her voice was sharp. "Look, she's the only person who can match you when it comes to close quarters combat, and she's a Ghost; just think about how valuable she would be in a fight."

"I don't fuck with Ghosts, Wags. I won't fight alongside someone I can't see." Archer bounced lightly on the balls of his feet. "Besides, have you heard the rumours coming out of Oxford these days?"

"She isn't a cannibal, Bowman."

"She fucking is! They were dealing with vampires or some other mental shit like that, and she got bitten." He shook his head in disbelief. "The word around the Ministry is that she ate Joseph Evans after she killed him."

"She did not!"

"Then why is the file sealed, huh?"

Silence.

"You've not got a fucking answer to that one, have you, Wags? We're Ravenblades; we have maximum clearance and we aren't allowed to see her formal debrief?" Archer paced back and forth on the grass, fingering the knives that were strapped to his jumpsuit. "Something is fucking wrong in that city, Wags. It does things to people."

"She freaks me out too, Bowman, but she's one of the best out there."

"I heard she murdered Gideon."

"Lola Oriole killed Gideon Frost, Bowman," Roxanne said with considerable exasperation. "Hillgreen didn't lay a finger on him; hell, nobody would be able to kill him, especially not a Ghost."

"Why would Lola do that?"

"She's unstable," Roxanne replied, although she did not sound convinced. "They sent her to Betony Island for a reason."

"Either way," Archer said as he cast his gaze

towards the hazy glow of the reconstruction compound on the other side of the park, "I'm on my own tonight, Wags. Are you sure that the thermal scopes won't-"

He stopped speaking as the muted sound of gunfire reached his ears through the fog. He quickly triangulated its source; the compound. He immediately broke into a sprint towards the distant lights.

"Wags, are those security personnel armed?"

"Only tasers, I think; did you hear something, Bowman?"

"Gunfire," Archer said as he built up speed. "I'm going in hot, Wags."

"Roger that, Bowman. Weapons free." He could hear the envious smile in her voice. "Good hunting."

The chain link fence loomed up out of the fog before him. Archer smiled underneath his mask and dropped forwards, transferring his weight on to his hands. He bent his arms, absorbing the momentum he'd built up with the sprint, and then straightened them. The perfect transference of force catapulted him into the air; he cleared the razor topped fence with ease.

He rolled as he landed on the other side, preserving his momentum and immediately reaching his top speed once again. Archer breathed easily and steadily as he went. An articulated lorry with a shipping container loomed before him; the top edge was aligned with the windows on the prefab warehouse opposite.

Archer made a beeline for the side of the lorry and pushed his momentum against the solid steel of the container, allowing him to run up it with ease. As he reached the top he kicked himself backward, flipping through the air and smashing through the window.

He sailed through the warehouse and tried to grab every detail that he could. *I'm bound to miss something,* he thought as he fell through the air. He envied Roxanne's gift tremendously, but he would not trade his own for anything; being a Tumbler was just too useful.

"I count twelve," he reported just before he hit the ground. He rolled as he did so, moving in the direction of the nearest man. The intruder wore high spec military gear and carried a bullpup assault rifle, which he now aimed at Archer. The Tumbler pushed off against the ground, leaping over the burst of gunfire.

Archer slapped one hand into the soldier's gas mask as he soared over him, putting a portion of his momentum into the blow; the man crumpled as his skull shattered. *Eleven.* Before the corpse hit the floor Archer landed and was already running once again. He grunted with exertion as he accelerated to his top speed of forty four miles per hour.

Archer Treen's gift as a Tumbler wasn't unnatural speed or strength; instead he could perfectly transfer and preserve his momentum. Whilst not inherently as powerful as other Exceptions, he had trained hard since he was a small boy and was now capable of incredible feats of acrobatics, athleticism, and violence.

The sound of gunfire filled the warehouse as the remaining private military goons shot at Archer. He grinned as he ran, pulling three narrow throwing knives from the bandolier across his chest. He waited until a perfect alignment presented itself and put all of his momentum into the throw. He came to a sharp stop as each blade flashed across the room and found its target; a thunderclap sounded as the deadly projectiles broke the sound barrier.

Eight.

He ducked behind a table as more bullets ripped through the air around him. He tightened the straps on his tactical gloves; the reinforced knuckles gleamed in the fluorescent light. He reached down with his left hand and pulled a reinforced steel expanding baton from the sheath on his leg. Archer extended it with a practised flick, feeling the friction lock engage. The roar of the air conditioning units filled the room.

"Four hostiles down, Wags," he said softly. "I'd appreciate a perimeter sweep so I don't get more of these fuckers crashing my party."

"I'm on it, Bowman. Keep moving and stay alive."

"Always do." He closed his eyes, found his breath, and leapt over the table. One of the soldiers was directly in front of him, and Archer brought the baton down diagonally, catching his target at the junction of neck and shoulder. There was a crack as he dealt a fatal blow before pulling the corpse between him and the other armed men.

Not a moment too soon, in fact, as bullets tore into the dead man's flesh. *I could really use Roxy's help in here,* Archer thought frantically as he looked for more cover. The longer he remained motionless, the heavier the man in his arms grew. That was the curse of the Tumbler; to suffer debilitating weakness when not in motion, along with crippling claustrophobia.

"Fuck!" Archer groaned as his legs began to tremble. He let the corpse carry him to the ground, stealing as much momentum as he could. With a leap he was on his feet and picking up speed. He felt strong again, and he smiled underneath his mask. He quickly scanned the room to locate his next target, but was knocked to the ground by a savage blow to his head.

He tried to roll as he fell, but slipped on a slick of blood and crashed to the floor. His baton went skittering across the ground and he roared in frustration. Archer flailed to get to his feet as the remaining seven soldiers gathered around him.

"Not so tough now, are you, Ministry boy?" laughed one of the men before he kicked Archer in the stomach. He was about to speak again but was silenced as the first corpse began to move.

The air was filled with a strange warbling sound, not entirely unlike a melody. Archer clapped his hands over his ears as the eerie noise made his legs twitch and jerk to the rhythm. *What the fuck is this!?*

The compulsion to move and march was unlike anything he'd ever felt before, but he screamed long and loud enough to drown it out. The soldiers around him, however, were not all so lucky. Several stomped unsteadily across the warehouse towards the mound of twitching corpses.

The restless dead pulled themselves upright and fell upon the spellbound soldiers, ripping them limb from limb and tearing chunks out of their flesh with ravenous, slavering mouths. Archer battled to keep his horror in check as he witnessed the carnage before him and kept perfectly still.

In under a minute the remaining goons were dead and the shambling revenants had made their shuffling way out of the warehouse. Archer got to his feet and pulled his mask from his face, vomiting the moment he was able.

"Bowman, are you there?" Roxanne's voice filled his ears and he realised that the upsetting melody had ended. "God damn you, Bowman, fucking answer me!"

"I'm here, Wags," Archer said with a shuddering gasp. "Everyone in here is dead. You've probably got four or five contacts heading your way; disengage and hide."

"I can take five soldiers, Bowman."

"These aren't humans, Wags," he replied angrily, "so fucking listen to me and stay the fuck away from them."

"What are they?" Roxanne asked softly.

"I'm not certain, but they weren't alive any more. Maybe stitcher golems or..." Archer's voice faded as he looked around the warehouse. "Why didn't it take all of them?"

"I didn't catch that, Bowman."

"I was wondering why only some of them were reanimated," Archer said as he looked over the bodies. "It's not a case of being physically intact; some of our Dancers were falling to pieces-"

"Dancers?" Roxanne scoffed.

"Yeah, there was some kind of sound, almost music, that got them up. Dancer seems as good a term as any for something like that." Archer snatched various access badges and other forms of identification from as many of the deceased as he could. "We need to get to the morgue first thing in the morning; I want to know if they've had any problems with their corpses being a touch restless."

There was only silence in his earpiece.

"Wags, are you reading me?"

"I think there's a Ghost somewhere in there with you, Bowman," she said softly. "You need to get out of there."

"Are you sure?"

"Just tapped the security footage; the distortion on the image can't be anything else. Meet me at the car, and do it fast, okay? No further conversation until then. Run hard, Bowman."

Fuck, Archer thought as he bent down to retrieve the last ID badge from the first soldier he'd killed. *I can't fight what I can't see.* He donned his mask and turned on his heel, now facing the door. There was a slight ripple in one of the pools of blood.

Gotcha.

Archer pushed off the nearest corpse, accelerating as he did so. He saw a bloody footprint move to intercept him and he pulled a small cannister from his belt and tossed it in the Ghost's direction. It burst mid-air, sending a brownish cloud coursing through the warehouse.

There was a cry of surprise from the Ghost and Archer leapt over his invisible opponent. He landed deftly and crashed through the exit. Inside the warehouse, the powerful air conditioning units were already thinning the toxic cloud; soon there would be almost no trace of it left.

Archer leapt over the fence and continued to sprint headlong towards Roxanne's position. Whilst it was unlikely that the Tabun had killed the Ghost, Archer hoped that it had at least incapacitated the invisible killer enough to cover their escape.

He reached the car in under a minute and vaulted through the open window into his seat. As soon as he was sat down, Roxanne hit the gas and the Porsche sped off into the night. Archer caught his breath before brandishing the ID cards at his partner.

"Nicely done, Archer," she said with a smile. "Did

you need to deal with the Ghost?"

"I hit him with the Tabun, but he was probably wearing a mask. Still, if enough got on his skin..."

"Jesus, Archer, you need to be a bit more restrained with the chemical weapons! You remember how badly the Tiger reacted last time you got a bit Sarin-happy?"

"In this," he said, gesturing to the fog, "it won't even register. Desai will be none the wiser."

"Hmmm." Roxanne was silent for a few minutes. "What's our next play? Heading to the morgue in the morning?"

"No," Archer said. "We need to call this one in, Roxy. This is clearly spreading; we need a firewall around this whole fucking town. Nobody goes in or out."

"We won't be able to mobilise anything until tomorrow at the earliest."

"I know that. I just hope it won't come back to bite us later."

"What are you thinking, Arch?"

"This is some kind of supernatural contagion that appears to reanimate the dead, and it's definitely getting worse. I'm already worried that we've lost control of the situation."

"Wait are you saying that-"

"Yes," Archer said, cutting her off. "This is a Class Nine Event; the first we've ever seen on British soil."

"God help us," Roxanne said, her face pale with fear.

Something tells me that divine intervention won't be enough, Archer thought as they sped on through the poisonous fog. He closed his eyes, desperately trying to ignore the slouching forms that shambled through the otherwise deserted streets.

We're going to die here.

Chapter Ten – Together in Electric Dreams

Elsie

Elsie washed down her medication with a glass of orange juice as she sat in Silas's kitchen. The dim morning light streamed into the little flat and sent a small flutter of hope through her heart. She looked down at the empty blister pack and her smile faltered slightly.

I'm out. I'll need to find more before too long. The thought of going to a pharmacy chilled her to the bone, however; Mad Dog was sure to be staking them out. Pharmacies, along with grocery stores, hospitals, and hardware shops were all too risky and-

Elsie shook her head angrily, derailing her panicked train of thought.

"He's just one man," she said to herself. "He can't be everywhere all at once!"

"You know, talking to yourself is the first sign of madness," Silas said wryly as he walked into the room, still dripping wet from the shower. He had a fluffy maroon towel wrapped around his waist and Elsie couldn't help but stare at the sheer number of tattoos adorning his skin. "I did them all myself. Do you have any ink?"

"No, I don't."

"You want any?" Silas asked as he pulled a few items of clothing from an airer. He smiled at her. "I'll gladly give you your first tat if you want."

"That's a kind offer," Elsie said as she walked into

the living room and looked down at the floor, "but I'm not really sure if this is the time."

Silas did not respond, but instead followed her gaze. Arranged on the rug in the middle of the living room were the ruined fragments of Pandora, carefully laid out to check if anything was missing.

I'm so sorry, Pandy, Elsie thought as she blinked back a tear. *I should never have brought you into this world.*

"So," Silas said carefully, "what exactly does this thing do?"

"Nothing, now."

"Fine, what *did* it do?"

"Pandora was my greatest creation," Elsie said sadly. She knelt next to the ruined biomechanical suit and traced her fingers over the damaged surface. "She was a completely sealed homeostatic suit, capable of protecting the wearer from virtually any environment; Pandy could let you walk on the bottom of the ocean or touch the surface of the sun."

"Wow. How did you manage that?"

"She's made of a blend of entirely novel metamaterials, neurally networked throughout the entire suit. I'd hoped that she would revolutionise everything, but Finley wanted her all for himself."

"Is this thing an AI?" Silas asked, suddenly wary. There was a curious rustling from behind the sofa, but he paid it no mind, so Elsie didn't either.

"No," Elsie said. "She's nothing as trivial as that. See those dangling bits there?"

"The wires?" Silas asked, peering closer.

"Not wires; nerves. Pandora was alive; an entirely new kind of silicon-based life form."

"And at no point did you think that this was a bad

idea?" Silas raised an incredulous eyebrow.

"I was just lost in the creation of it all." Elsie smiled at him. "Besides, I've not told you her greatest secret."

"Which is?"

"If she encounters an Exception, she can mimic their gift. Once she's learned how to do it once, she can recall it whenever she wants." Elsie sighed heavily. "She was going to change the world."

"And you programmed all that with electricity?"

"Silicon is only a semiconductor, and I wanted her programming to touch every atom. The metamaterial blend allowed me to use vibrations, sound waves, to bring her to life. My daughter was a living song."

"That is one of the creepiest sentences I have ever heard," Silas said as he took a step back. "In hindsight, I really regret asking you about this."

"Well she's dead now, so there's no need to act so frightened," Elsie replied harshly. "She wouldn't hurt you, even if she wasn't in pieces."

"Did you give her the whole Three Laws of Robotics shtick?"

"I didn't need to. I just knew in my heart that she wouldn't harm anyone." Elsie looked up at Silas, expecting him to understand, but instead he just shook his head in amazement. "What?"

"You created what sounds like an indestructible sentient robot with the ability to learn any Exception's gift, but you were sure it wouldn't hurt us because it passed the fucking vibe check?"

Her face flushed with embarrassment. *I liked you better as a cat.*

"Look," he said after a moment of silence, "I don't really care what the fuck is up with you and your robot daughter. What I do care about is the swarm of undead tearing through the town that I live in, and I need your help to stop it. We make a decent team, Elsie, and it's good to have someone watching my back after years of operating alone.

"So let's just focus on dealing with that, okay, and I won't pry any further into your..." He trailed off.

"Need to play god?" Elsie asked snidely. The strange rustling noise happened again, but she ignored it.

"No," Silas said as he shook his head, "whatever else it may be, what you're doing here isn't playing. Your gift scares the shit out of me, Elsie, if I'm going to be honest. I'm not sure that there's anything you couldn't do if you put your mind to it."

"Thank you," she said quietly.

"That wasn't a compliment. No human should have that much power; nothing good can come from it." He took a deep breath and gathered himself. "That being said, you are extremely useful to have around, and a part of me can't help but like you."

"Likewise."

"So let's put Pandora aside for now, and plan tonight's little heist. Agreed?"

"Agreed." Elsie began to gather Pandy's components into a duffle bag for storage. "The plan is to break into the Junction Building at the Eigenforce Freight Depot; do you know it?"

"I know the area," Silas said. "It's close enough to have a daylight reccy, so that's a sensible first step."

Before Elsie could respond, he extended his left arm and the stylised tattoo of a crow crept into the air in an inky swirl, coalescing into the solid form of a bird after a few seconds. It cawed loudly before taking flight and passing through the glass pane of the window in a smokey puff.

"Woah."

"Hell of a party trick, isn't it?" Silas said with a grin. His left eye darkened to the colour of ink as he guided the crow through the air. "You'll have to excuse me; I'm not good company when I'm trying to bilocate like this."

Elsie did not respond. Instead she peered through the window at the looming, shrouded shadow that was Junction Tower. *Somewhere in there is the shipping manifest,* she thought as determination filled her heart. *Tonight we'll finally understand what's happening.*

"Life." Elsie smiled sheepishly and looked down at the Armagnac in her glass. The reddish amber liquid could not hold her gaze for long, and soon enough she found herself staring back at Finley Carmichael. "What, no laughter?"

"The creation of new life is no laughing matter, Elsie." He leant forward in his chair, his face both serious and enchanted all at once. "I can think of no nobler calling."

"Lots of people make new lives all the time," she said dismissively, "so why should my goals be any different?"

"Because you are different. Those other people, they're just replicators; all they do is muck their genes together and hope for the best." He shook his head in disbelief and took another sip of his drink. "Look how far that's gotten us; war, disease, infertility. That's the fundamental flaw of evolution, Elsie.

"No guidance or control. There's no design because there's no God, and we pay the price for that every single day." He noticed that she was looking at him, her head cocked slightly to one side and a dreamy expression on her face. "What are you thinking?"

"It's customary to offer a penny," she said coyly.

"Your mind is worth infinitely more than that, and you damn well know it. Come on, tell me."

"You might be the only person on this whole planet who actually gets me, Finley." She drained her glass and leant back into the plush chair. "People think that I want to create life to fulfil some stagnant social script that defines womanhood, but that's not it at all. I don't want offspring; I want the chance to change everything."

"To shake up the paradigm, to rewrite the rules," Finley agreed, getting to his feet, "to tear down the fucking walls and walk out of the fucking cave. You want to set them free; to show them that they are capable of so much more than just staring at shadows and making mediocre copies of themselves."

"I want to make something intentional," Elsie said tipsily, "something designed, refined, and-"

"Flawless," Finley said as he walked across the room, finishing her sentence as he went. "You want to make something absolutely perfect."

"Yes, I do. I want to make not just a life, but the most important life to ever have lived. I want to show them the way."

"Then do it," Finley put a hand on her cheek, and she blushed. "Change the world, Elsie. Make them remember your name for the rest of time."

"No cat this time?" Elsie asked as they hurried through the darkness and fog towards the Junction Building. She'd left the Scanline behind and instead carried one of Silas's Maxim 9's; a nine millimetre pistol with a built in suppressor. *These are some specialist weapons,* Elsie thought as she looked it over before they set out. *I could make a better one, though.*

"No. We're gonna play this as a straight up burglary; hopefully we can convince them that we're just a pair of well trained humans."

"And are you?" Elsie asked, not expecting a reply.

"Am I what?" Silas asked warily.

"Well trained?"

"You're going to keep pushing, aren't you?"

"I told you about Pandy!"

"And I wish you hadn't." Silas stopped in his tracks and let out an exasperated sigh. "Alright, fine. You really want to know?"

"Yes."

"I was a consultant with the Ministry back in the day. I came into my gift super early and was something of a prodigy. There were several people who wanted me to enrol in this experimental program for especially gifted Ceps, but my folks declined the offer.

"Instead I grew up learning how to use my skills to help people, which is surprisingly profitable. When I was old enough I followed in my mum's footsteps and went to university to train as a forensic pathologist; I've actually got a whole bunch of letters after my name and a 'Doctor' in front."

Elsie blinked in surprise.

"See, don't judge people at a glance, just like I told you. Anyway, I was on a job with the Ministry when I got a really bad feeling; like everything was about to go fatally wrong. I pointed it out to the team I was with, but they ignored me. I got the fuck out of dodge and survived. Long story short, they didn't and there was a whole inquest into whether I'd killed them or not."

"Is that why you don't like the Ministry?" Elsie asked. Silas nodded. "As fair a reason as any. Don't worry, I've no great love for them either; I don't need to be stamped and categorised. All I want is to live my life."

"Exactly." Silas gave her shoulder an affectionate squeeze. "Thanks, by the way."

"For what?"

"For not asking if I did it."

"You're not a killer," Elsie said before looking down at the gun. "Or not a wasteful one, at least."

There was a heartbeat of silence before Silas checked his watch.

"We better get going," he said as he started walking once more. "It's coming up to half past ten; there should be a guard handover we can use to our advantage."

"Where are we heading?" Elsie asked.

"There's a stairwell at each corner of the building. We'll take the one on the west."

"Why that one?"

"I'm not sure," Silas said. He sounded as if he was surprised at his own words. "It just feels like the right way to go."

"That's good enough for me," Elsie said. "Let's get going; the sooner we're done in here, the sooner we can set everything back to normal."

In her heart, Elsie knew she had overlooked something crucial but she could not figure out what it was. *It'll come to me,* she thought as they crept into the western stairwell. *It can't be that important.*

Can it?

Chapter Eleven – Thou Shalt Not Kill

Chloe

"You're pretty creepy sometimes, Chloe," Beef said as the Seer led them through Carmichael's building, walking through camera blind spots and holes in the guard patrols. "Jesus Christ, can you even hear me?"

Chloe Turner was deaf and blind to the world, her eyes completely white as she navigated the Tangle with twisting, searching fingers. She walked slowly, sometimes halting suddenly, much as a sleepwalker does.

"Fucking hell, Candy, we best be ready to protect her if we run into trouble. What time is it?"

"It's ten fifty five," Chloe murmured. "We have to hurry."

"The stairwell isn't far," Candy replied. "We'll make it."

The three of them, led by Chloe, meandered through the eighteenth floor of the Junction Building towards the glowing green fire exit sign above the doorway to the western stairwell. Beef muttered and complained under her breath; she'd been sceptical of the plan since the night before. Candy placed a hand on Chloe's shoulder as she reached the door.

"Are you sure about this?" he asked quietly.

"I'm certain," she replied, now fully awake and aware of her surroundings. *I've never felt more sure in my entire life.* "If we don't do this, now, then everything falls apart."

Deep in her mind, Chloe felt something important click into place; it was time. She pushed the bar to open the door and stepped into the stairwell as she did so. Instinctively she looked to her left, down the stairs.

The two figures were just stepping on to the landing as she turned. They had pistols in their hands and wore gas masks. The taller of the two raised their gun and aimed it squarely at Chloe.

"Who the fuck are you?" the stranger demanded. He was a man, judging by his voice, and he sounded both anxious and exhausted. "Do you work for Carmichael?"

"No," Chloe said, carefully raising her hands. She didn't consciously know what to do next, but the Tangle was close by; she let it speak through her. "My name is Chloe Turner and I'm here to help you. If you go any further up these stairs, you'll die. You have to come with us, now."

"How the fuck can you possibly know that?" the man demanded. The other stranger had lowered their weapon and proceeded to pull off their gas mask. Chloe gasped when the face of a beautiful woman was revealed; dark grey eyes, bold features, and a wicked smile that sent her heart racing.

"I'm Elsie Reichardt," the woman said in a rich, deep voice. "Pleased to meet you. This is Dr Silas Cherry, who is unfortunately a bit low on trust these days. Silas, please stop pointing the gun at Ms Turner."

"Who are your friends?" Silas demanded, neither removing his mask nor lowering the weapon. "And more importantly, how the fuck did you know we'd be here?"

"I'm Beef and this is my husband, Candy. We're Chloe's best friends and, tonight at least, her bodyguards." Beef flexed her considerable muscles and cracked her knuckles. "I'd advise against trying anything."

"Ooh, I'm quaking in my little boots," Silas hissed sharply. "Listen, we're here on a simple mission and then we want to get the fuck out of Dodge, okay? So just let us continue on our way and nobody gets hurt. Easy enough, yeah?"

"You want the shipping manifest," Candy said slowly. Chloe turned to her childhood friend, a smile growing on her lips as he continued. "We all know that something horrific was unleashed in that train crash, and the only way we'll ever find out what it was is if we get the truth about what Carmichael's train was carrying.

"I'm right, aren't I?"

"Impressive reasoning skills," Silas said softly as he lowered his weapon. Chloe blinked, trying to fathom how that had disarmed Silas Cherry so completely. She realised that the masked man was staring intently at her, and she took a step back.

"What?"

"Well, Chloe Turner, where's the shipping manifest?" He sounded exhausted, much in the same way her teachers used to when it came to topics that she just couldn't grasp. She opened her mouth to respond, but he raised a hand to silence her. "I know you don't consciously know where it is, but you're a Seer, aren't you?"

"How-"

"Later," he said, leaving her mouth gaping like a startled fish. "Imagine you're trying to solve a maze; instead of false starts which might confuse you, start at the end and follow it back here."

Before she could do anything, Elsie raised her gun and pointed it in her direction. There were two muted shots that hissed through the air uncomfortably close to Chloe's head, followed by the sound of two bodies hitting the ground. She spun around and clapped her hands to her mouth in horror at the sight of the slain security guards.

"Quickly, please," Silas said as he walked past her. He pulled the weapons, handguns of some kind, from the grips of the corpses and handed them to Beef and Candy. "You know how to use these?"

"You killed them..." Chloe muttered, looking tearfully at Elsie. The woman's face was impassive, and all those handsome angles suddenly seemed hard and stony. "I can't believe you actually killed them!"

Chloe felt her breath catch in her throat as she began to tremble. *I never thought I'd see someone die like that!* Panic seized her and she gently crouched down, hugging her knees and keening softly. Beef knelt beside her, a reassuring hand on her shoulder.

"Chloe, we can't stay here, babe. We need you to move." She squeezed Chloe's shoulder tightly, but when she looked to Candy for support, he had wandered off amongst the desks. "Candy, what are you doing?"

He did not reply and Silas groaned softly in frustration.

"It seems our Seer is a bit blind-sided, Elsie; any chance you can find that manifest?"

"No dice," she said, lowering her firearm once again. "I already tried on the way up. No echoes left to follow."

"What the fuck are you talking about?" Beef asked angrily. "And why did you have to kill those guys right in front of her? You might be a stone cold bitch, but Chloe isn't!"

Shy thinks you coddle me, Chloe thought from the depths of her mind. The events unfolding in the eighteenth floor offices of the Junction Building seemed a hundred miles away from her little island of safety and peace. *Maybe I should just stay here.*

"Oh shit, she's going again!" Beef cried out as Chloe went limp in her arms. "Chloe, don't you fucking dare die on me!"

There was a flash across Chloe's vision and she jolted sharply, snapping back to total wakefulness in Beef's arms, gasping as she did so. Her heart thundered in her ears and the crotch of her trousers felt warm and uncomfortably wet.

"Did I piss myself?" she murmured. "What the fuck?"

"You were fading again, Chloe," Beef said as she held her friend tight. "Please don't ever do that again."

"I promise," she said quietly. She was about to continue when the whirr of machinery and clatter of moving parts made her jump. She looked about in a panic and stared in puzzlement as Candy hummed absent-mindedly as he used the photocopier.

"Yo, Candy babe, what the fuck are you doing!?" Beef yelled.

"Photocopying the shipping manifest."

"You found it?" Silas said, amazed. "How?"

"We're in the administrative offices; it said so on the door. Eigenforce International is a big company and its filing system is fairly standard, so it wasn't hard to find." He smiled as Elsie chuckled.

"And you know the printer access code?" she asked him.

"People are sloppy," he said, brandishing a pink sticky note with a printer login written on it. "Now we won't even leave a trace that we were here."

"Aside from the dead guys," Silas said. Candy gasped and stared at the bodies.

"When did that happen?" He looked at the gun in his hand. "Did I do that?"

"A couple of minutes ago," Silas responded patiently, "and no; I handed you that after Elsie shot them. You're a Babbage, aren't you?"

"A what?" Beef asked.

"Human computer; a very useful gift, but it makes you blind to all else that happens when you're working on a problem." Elsie walked over to the copier as she spoke, running her fingers over Chloe's shoulder as she passed. "You said that we die if we stay in the stairwell, right?"

"Mhmm," Chloe confirmed.

"Alright then. I'll try and get the lift working." Elsie walked over to the biometric scanner that was alongside the lift doors and pulled a small device from a pocket. She muttered softly to herself as she clipped magnetic wires to the biological lock and started working.

"What's her gift?" Chloe asked Silas as he reached out a hand. He grunted as he pulled her upright.

"Elsie can do all sorts of wonderful things with technology, and a few things that she probably shouldn't" he said as Candy handed him the copy of the shipping manifest. "Thank you. She can also make things happen, a bit like a Rube Goldberg machine, but I've not seen that in action yet."

"Does she always get it right?" Beef asked sceptically, one arm protectively around Chloe.

"Most of the time," Elsie said from beside the lifts. "Although when it does go wrong it tends to go-"

She was cut off as deafening alarms began to blare throughout the entire building and all the automatic doors shut with a clunk. Elsie looked at them sheepishly and finished her sentence.

"-spectacularly wrong."

"They're locked," Silas said as Beef tried the door for the fifth time. "Elsie, how the fuck are we going to get out of here?"

"I don't know!" Elsie yelled, her hands over her ears. "I can't think with these fucking alarms screaming in my head!"

"We could start a fire?" Chloe suggested. "The smoke alarms should unlock the doors, shouldn't they?"

"Normally, yes," Silas said as he dealt a swift kick to a door. It shook slightly in the frame, but was otherwise unmoved. "However, I wouldn't put it past Carmichael to have the security lockdown override the fire safety systems; he's the sort of person that values intellectual property more than human life, after all."

Did that touch a nerve? Chloe wondered as Elsie's face flashed with guilt and shame at Silas's words. *What did you do, Elsie Reichardt?*

Beef sighed heavily across the room, rubbed her eyes, and took a deep breath. She reached out carefully, one hand on the door handle and the other on the electronic lock.

"You know what they call you when you do the same thing over and over expecting different results?" Silas asked nastily, raising his voice to be heard over the din. Beef depressed the handle and the door swung open.

"Tenacious," Beef replied as the alarms stopped.

Although Silas's face was still behind the gas mask, Chloe was sure his mouth was hanging open in shock. She grinned at Beef who winked at her.

"Woo!" Candy cheered. "Way to go, baby! That's my wife, right there!"

"Love you too," Beef said with a grin. "Right, Chloe, can you lead us out of here?"

"I think so," she said. *Like a maze, but backwards.* "I'll find my feet as we go. Do we have the manifest?"

"Safe and sound. Elsie, you good to go?" Silas asked. She nodded, and he looked at Beef and Candy, who were waiting by the door. "Do you two know how to shoot?"

"Yes," Beef lied, aiming the gun with exaggerated swagger.

"We have no idea," Candy said, pushing the barrel of his wife's weapon towards the floor. "Honestly, we can handle ourselves in close quarters to protect Chloe, but it would be better if the two of you could deal with any resistance we might meet."

Chloe went to reply, but a ripple in the Tangle caught her attention. She pointed in the direction of the western stairwell and let out a strangled cry. Beef, Candy, and Elsie looked at her in confusion, but Silas was already moving, drawing his gun as he went.

Lithe as a cat and swift as a falcon, he vaulted over a desk and landed on a chair, rolling forwards into cover as the stairwell door opened. Elsie grabbed Chloe, forcing her down as bullets ripped through the air where she'd been seconds before. Beef and Candy slipped into the next room, sheltering behind the wall.

Silas waited for the first attacker to walk past where he was crouched, and then shot the second in the foot. He fell with a cry, and the first man spun around; Silas ended him with an upward shot that caught him in the mouth, avoiding his helmet.

Are they wearing body armour!? Does Finley Carmichael have an army working for him? She noticed Elsie fishing something from her pocket; Chloe assumed that it was ammunition, but it turned out to be a marble. She watched as Elsie rolled the marble over the linoleum floor.

Four more men entered; the leading two had handguns, whilst the second pair were behind some kind of large shield shaped like a stretched hexagon. Silas shot the first of the four with another swift motion, but the second was upon him as his weapon clicked empty.

The man opened his mouth to say something, but Silas punched the broad flat muzzle break into the man's throat hard enough to break both the gun and the attacker's neck. The man with the shield rushed forward, lowering the barrier so that the final soldier could aim his bullpup assault rifle over the top.

Silas turned as the marble reached his feet, and his motion kicked it into the path of the shield bearer. The soldier let out a startled cry as he slipped on the little glass ball and fell forwards, catching his neck on the edge of the shield, crushing his windpipe. He thrashed on the floor as the man with the assault rifle trained it at Silas.

"Put your hands up, now!" He roared his command, and Silas immediately raised his arms. Chloe squinted as she saw something moving in the shadows on Silas's back. It looked like an inky ribbon at first, but it soon became clear what it really was.

"What the fuck?" The soldier's confusion was directed at the massive cobra that loomed up from behind Silas. Before he could say anything else, the snake opened its mouth and surged forwards. It spat venom into the man's face and he screamed as it ate through his protective goggles with a sickening fizzing sound.

The man with the injured foot finally gathered his wits enough to fire his weapon at Silas. He fell to the ground with a cry, but the cobra struck at the prone soldier at the same time, biting him again and again.

"Silas!" Elsie yelled, rushing forwards. He groaned as he sat up, clutching his shoulder. The cobra whipped around and rose up between Elsie and Silas, its hood flared and eyes glinting. The woman faltered, suddenly afraid.

"Get back here, you slippery fucker!" Silas said forcefully. The cobra turned and wrapped around his outstretched arm, shrinking and turning inky as it did so. *How did he do that?* Chloe thought as the snake disappeared entirely. "Bastard caught me in the shoulder! Is everyone else okay?"

There were grunts of affirmation from all present; Elsie spoke for Chloe, who was in a state of shock at the carnage she had just witnessed.

"I think we better split," Beef said as Silas got to his feet.

"I agree," the wounded man said. "I think we have seriously outstayed our welcome."

Chapter Twelve – Whatever Pain May Come

Archer

"This is looking really bad, Roxy. I'm starting to think that we need a bigger team," Archer said from his spot on the bathroom floor. "What do you think?"

There was no answer. He'd half expected as much, but his partner's commitment to mid-operation relaxation days irked Archer at the best of times. Today, it made his blood boil.

Steam swirled around him as Roxanne Wagstaff continued to soak in the bathtub, her nimble nude form hidden beneath a tide of bubbles. One arm dangled over the side of the tub, with a little device, smaller than a watch, on her wrist. Slices of cucumber rested on her closed eyes and a nourishing clay mask covered her face. Her locs were gathered up in a scrunchie to stop them getting wet; aside from wash days, when she would tolerate it, Roxanne despised the sensation of wet hair.

"Are you seriously going to ignore me?"

"Archer," she said after a long pause, "you are not helping my attempt at a relaxing evening. Can this wait until later, please?"

"People are fucking dying, you ludicrous woman!" He tried to control his temper, but it got the best of him. "Of course, the world has to grind to a halt so Roxanne fucking Wagstaff can have her fucking bath, no matter how many bodies accumulate in the meantime!"

"Are you done?" Her tone was dispassionate, almost bored. "I won't be that much longer."

"So I'm supposed to sit here, just twiddling my fucking thumbs, until you decided that you're sufficiently calm? I hate this! It's always hurry up and wait with you!"

"I didn't ask you to sit in here with me," she said, a hint of annoyance in her voice. "Why don't you go and jerk off or something; maybe that'll calm you down?"

"I don't need to calm down, Roxy! I need to deal with whatever is fucking bringing people back from the dead!" Archer got to his feet. "Or do you make a point of letting any and all operational details slip out of your brain the second you take your boots off at the end of the day?"

Roxanne let out an exasperated sigh and the little device strapped to her wrist began to beep, slowly at first but getting faster with each passing moment. He took a step back as she rose from the bath, covered in bubbles.

"God damn you, Archer!" she said, stepping out of the water and on to the blue fluffy bath mat. She brandished the device on her arm. "I am trying to stay calm, you fucking prick! Or do you want me to have a fucking heart attack in the middle of a gunfight? Huh?"

"What's wrong with the medication they gave you?" Archer demanded. "Why can't you just take your fucking pills and get on with your job like the rest of us?"

Roxanne opened her mouth to reply, but he stormed out of the bathroom before she could utter a sound. He snatched his baton and mask up from the bed, slipping the former into his belt and putting the latter on to his face. Archer strode through the front entrance of their little safehouse, letting the door slam behind him.

He gathered speed as he jogged down the dark street. The dim amber glow from the street lamps only served to throw puddles of glare into the fog, leaving the shadows deep and untouched. He let his frustration fuel his motion as he fumbled for his wireless earbuds.

Archer slipped them under his mask straps and selected a song on his linked smart watch; something suitably pacey and brimming with anger.

The worst part of it all, he thought as he ran, *is that she's fucking right.*

Archer's pills to control his claustrophobia, enough for him to sleep at least, had a wealth of side effects that definitely affected his performance in the field. Unfortunately, unlike Roxanne, he couldn't rely on a hot bubble bath or meditation to settle the anxieties that came part and parcel with his gift.

Nor could he rely on exercise to tire him out; as long as he was moving, he could generate a near limitless amount of energy. For Archer Treen, there was only work; no downtime, no relaxation, and certainly nothing approaching a civilian life.

Roxy is the only person I've got in the world, he thought as he shed a tear of rage. *I just wish we didn't fight so fucking often.*

"Oi, you ginger cunt!" A sharp voice cut through Archer's rage. A group of a dozen or so young men were loitering in a children's outdoor play area. The one who'd shouted perched atop a climbing frame shaped like a helicopter.

Archer slowed down, turning to face them. He bounced up and down on the spot, keeping his momentum up.

"Yeah, you short little fag, I was talking to you! What the fuck do you think you're wearing; some kind of gimp suit?" The man's friends all proceeded to laugh at Archer's Ministry issue jumpsuit, and he let out a low growl in response. "What's the matter? Your fucking boyfriend go too rough for your pretty little arse?"

Two of the men approached him; the reek of cheap beer was strong enough to get through his gas mask. One of them pulled a kitchen knife from his pocket as the other slapped a leather blackjack menacingly against his palm.

"Let's see what he's got in his pockets, shall we boys?" The man atop the helicopter climbing frame giggled madly; he was clearly on some kind of drugs. "You see, mate, you're on our turf and you've got to pay the toll.

"We're the Kings of the Fog, and we don't take no for an answer!" The two men moved towards Archer and the Tumbler let out a low chuckle. "What's so fucking funny, laughing boy?"

"You might be the Kings of the Fog," Archer said as he flicked out his baton, "but I'm a Republican."

Why does it always end like this? Archer wondered as he whipped the steel baton through the air, killing the knife-toting man in a single strike. He let his momentum carry him under the arc of the blackjack, driving the tip of the baton upwards, efficiently snapping his attacker's neck.

The remaining ten men looked on in horror, and Archer sighed with regret as he vaulted the little fence into the play area. Whenever he got too frustrated with Roxanne he would go running until he found a suitable outlet for his anger; if anyone at the Ministry cared to look at the overlap between spree killings and Archer's presence, they would have found a disturbing correlation.

"I'm here to fucking help," he growled as he brained two more men. Their leader cowered atop the climbing frame, sobbing through his improvised mask. "All I want is a little fucking respect from you provincials, you fucking base humans, but instead all I get are insults and violence!"

Thwack.

Snap.

Crunch.

"I should just let the fucking rats rip you to pieces!" Archer roared with anger as three men rushed him at once, two armed with pipes and the third with a heavy length of chain. Whilst his attackers were undoubtedly skilled in their own method of fighting, Archer had been training since he was four years old.

Twenty seven years of ballet, parkour, ninjutsu, silat, and arnis, combined with his Ravenblade training made Archer Treen one of the deadliest hand combat specialists in the world, even before his gift was factored into the mix. The only person more dangerous than him was Kimberly Daniels, Director Desai's constant companion and second in command.

Archer killed the three men in a matter of seconds, snatching the chain up as the man wielding it fell. He flicked the metal links, wrapping them around the leg of a man who'd made the wise decision to run, albeit too late. Archer yanked the chain, imbuing it with enough momentum to shatter the bones in the fleeing man's leg. He fell to the ground screaming.

The leader cried out in fear and rage, pulling a

stubby revolver from his jacket pocket. He shakily took aim at Archer, but a bullet ripped through his head before he could pull the trigger. The remaining men were gunned down with frightening speed and supernatural accuracy.

The eddies in the mist were still spinning in the wake of the bullets after the last body hit the ground. Archer sighed and turned to look at Roxanne as she strode angrily towards him. He retracted his baton and stowed it at his belt, then removed his earbuds.

"For what it's worth," he called through the mist, "they started it. Fuckers tried to mug me!"

"I don't care about them, Bowman!" Roxanne replied, lowering the boxy suppressed rifle that she carried. It was a Mark Eight Whispering Shot, a specialist semi-automatic weapon from the Edmonton Rifle Company, in Alberta, Canada. All of Roxanne Wagstaff's mid-to-long range firearms came from there.

Suddenly, a thirteenth man, who'd been hiding behind a bin, burst out of cover and sprinted into the night. Roxanne sighed and lifted the ERC Whispering Shot once again, looking down the combination sights. She sighed heavily, flicked the telescopic scope into place, and took a deep breath. The little watch on her arm began chirping at an alarming rate as the air around her seemed to shimmer. Her pupils, hidden behind her mask, trembled as she drank in the minute details of air movement through the fog, telling her everything about the path of her bullet.

She squeezed the trigger, striking her target in the base of his skull. Roxanne flicked on the safety and lowered the weapon before the body hit the ground. She already knew he was dead; she had never missed a shot.

"I care about you walking out on me, Bowman." Her shoulder slumped and his face flushed with shame under his mask; he'd clearly hurt her. "Kill all the fucking provincials you want; they're all fucking ingrates, as far as I'm concerned. What I want is for you to treat me like an equal and to let me relax enough to keep you alive in the field."

"I'm sorry, Wags." It was only ever codenames in public. "I just get so frustrated and I don't know how to deal with it."

She stepped closer and put a gentle arm around him. He rested his masked forehead against hers and sighed.

"You talk to me, and then we go and smash some skulls." She gave him an affectionate squeeze. "Together. We're a team, aren't we, Dorothy?"

"To Oz and back, Toto." He held her close. "I love you."

"Love you too, you absolute menace." She let go of him and gestured back towards the safehouse. "Let's head back, put the kettle on, and go through those autopsy reports. Maybe we can find something useful."

"Good idea," he replied. "We've got company arriving tomorrow afternoon, by the way. I meant to tell you earlier."

"Reinforcements?" Roxanne asked hopefully. Archer went to respond as the man with the shattered leg moved. His partner shot him without even aiming, and then looked expectantly at Archer once again.

"Not combat support, unfortunately. We've got the Ministry's top doctor heading in to help us combat whatever this is."

"Helen?"

"Helen," he confirmed. He heard Roxanne groan in response and grimaced behind his mask. "She's a qualified field operative-"

"She is a fucking Blight, Bowman!" Roxanne shuddered as she spoke. "She can find her own place to stay."

"Fair enough. I'll stock up on bleach and rubber gloves tomorrow morning." They started walking back towards the safehouse; the lure of a hot cup of tea on a dreary foggy night was now too strong to resist.

"Thank you, Bowman. Hopefully we can be done with this bullshit case sooner rather than later." She patted him on the shoulder. "See, it's so much easier when we just talk to each other!"

Archer nodded and they walked in silence back to the house. It was only as Roxanne was pouring the tea that he spoke again.

"What about the bodies?" Archer asked, almost as an afterthought.

"They're only humans," Roxanne said, her voice dripping with contempt. "Leave them for the rats."

Chapter Thirteen – Don't Stop Moving

Chloe

"I can't believe they killed all those people!" Chloe hissed to Beef. Her mind and heart were racing as the five of them sprinted through the various outbuildings and rails of the Eigenforce International Freight Depot. She was about to ask if accompanying two hardened killers into the night was the wisest course of action, but a sudden twinge in the Tangle stilled her tongue.

"Don't worry, Chloe," Beef whispered back. "I'll keep you safe."

"Fucking hell," Silas Cherry groaned, clutching at his wounded shoulder. "I knew we should've brought more than a basic first aid kit!"

"Silas," Elsie grunted as she helped him hobble through the deserted train yard, "you wanted to bring a whole fucking field surgery kit with us!"

"Can you two keep the fucking marital spat in your heads until we're out of here?" Beef hissed. "Who knows how many more of Carmichael's goons we'll have to deal with if they hear your bickering!"

You're one to talk, Chloe thought with a wry grin, but she left her thought unsaid. Although, judging by Candy's quiet snicker, she wasn't alone in her opinions. Elsie brandished her gun as they went; she was the only one with both ammunition and a suppressed weapon.

"Where are we going?" Chloe asked. When she received no reply, she repeated herself, a little louder this time.

"Silas?" Elsie asked.

You might seem tough, Miss Reichardt, but it's clear who's in charge, isn't it?

"We'll head back to my place," Silas said after a few seconds of silence. "I've got ammo and medical supplies; enough to see us through the next couple of days, at least."

"How far is it?" Beef asked, eyeing the man's bloodstained shoulder.

"It's on the river," Silas responded. "Frobisher Way, Greenhithe."

"We're in fucking Slade Green!" Beef yelled. "Greenhithe is almost seven miles away, and you're not gonna get away with being on a fucking bus all covered in blood, are you?"

"We're not going to Greenhithe immediately," Silas said, breathing through the pain. "We just need to meet up with my rook, and he'll get us there."

"How is a bird going to take us all the way home, Silas?" Elsie demanded.

"Not a bird," he replied in exasperation, "a rookie; I have an apprentice!"

"Why didn't you tell me that earlier?" Elsie asked, shocked.

"Good god, you never show your whole hand at once," Beef said sharply. "That's just basic knowledge!"

"Silas," Candy said firmly, stopping everyone in their tracks. "You've lost a lot of blood and there's a chance you could go into shock or pass out; you need to tell us where your rendezvous is."

"Follow the tracks down, until they join the main line. Then break left and head through the loading yard to the road. My rook will meet us this side of bridge NKL Six Four Four, by the River Cray. He drives a van, so it should be big enough for all of us." Silas pulled an old mobile phone from his pocket and hit a few keys. "Right, that's a message sent to him; we need to hustle."

Chloe bit back the avalanche of questions that filled her mind, sensing that now was not the time. As they hurried down the tracks, a loud undulating siren whirred into life behind them and dozens of floodlights flared, casting the depot in a blinding glare.

Good job we're far enough away for the fog to conceal us, she thought, but the hurried footsteps of her companions caused her to quicken her pace just a little. The muffled commotion of guards and the barking of dogs filled the air, getting closer with each passing moment.

"Hey, Boudica," Silas wheezed at Beef, "can you do something about the lights?"

"The fuck do I look like, Reddy Kilowatt?" Beef replied. Silas groaned in response but didn't push the issue. Beef shook her head, sped up a little more, and swept the injured man into her arms. "Hold on tight and don't fucking squirm; we can outrun these fuckers."

Silas pointed weakly into the darkness at the side of the track, and it took them a moment to realise that he was guiding them off the track and into the truck yard. Elsie turned on her heel and took up a shooting stance as she reached the exit.

"Go on, I'll cover you. I'll buy you as much time as I can." Her voice trembled, but the weapon was straight and true in her her hands. "Go!"

Beef and Candy raced past her, but Chloe took a

moment to look around the entrance to the yard. What she saw caused her to grin, and she dashed back and practically dragged Elsie through the entry way. The armed woman began to protest, but Chloe pushed a heavy steel gate close behind them and slid a large deadbolt home. She crouched behind the gate, pulling Elsie down with her.

"Why-"

Chloe put her finger to her lips, and Elsie was quiet. A short distance away, Beef and Candy had stopped too. Around the five of them, the night air was foggy but still.

The rough panting of a dog was the first sign of their pursuers and Chloe held her breath. The crunch of boots on gravel followed, accompanied by the indistinct voices of the guards. Torch beams swung through the night, but the fog threw up so much glare that they were almost useless.

The five waited for what seemed like forever, their hearts thundering in their ears and their lungs burning with held breath, but the hunters moved on, convinced that their quarry had continued down the rail tracks towards Dartford proper.

"Next time," Chloe said after getting her breath back, "maybe think before immediately deciding to martyr yourself."

"I'm just trying to fix what I started," Elsie replied sullenly. "They're after me, for sure."

"What are you talking about?" Chloe demanded. Elsie was about to reply when an eerie sound drifted to their ears; it was indescribable, much like a bizarre artefact of light or optical illusion can be.

Beef and Candy shook their heads, as if trying to clear the unsettling noise from their minds. Chloe continued to stare at Elsie, who had started to tremble in terror.

"What's wrong?" she asked the frightened woman.

"We need to get out of here," Elsie said, panicked. "The rats are coming."

They ran as fast as they could through mist shrouded truck yard. All around them the undulating sound grew louder and louder, forcing its way through their ears and into their very bones. Chloe felt her legs twitch and jerk as she ran, only staying upright with Elsie's assistance.

The first excited squeaks and ravenous squeals of the rats made them run even faster. Chloe dared to look behind her, just for a second, and saw a tide of rushing, tumbling rodents flowing towards her like a chittering tsunami.

"Oh my god!" she screamed, frantically searching the Tangle for the way out of the maze of trailers and shipping containers.

If we get boxed in we're going to get eaten alive.

She saw other rats forcing themselves through narrow drain covers and out of impossibly tight gaps, ripping their skin as they did so before plopping on to the ground like bloody maggots. One dropped to the ground at her feet, snapping its teeth wildly at her. She shrieked in terror and Elsie brought her boot crashing down on it, popping it like a meaty balloon.

Chloe's fingers danced through the air, feeling the threads for the way out.

A puzzle but in reverse, she thought as thousands of possible futures flooded her mind. *Like solving a maze but backwards...*

"Left!" she cried, and her companions turned

without question or hesitation. Another twanging thread sent her head snapping round, right in the direction of the exit. "Through there!"

The five of them crashed into the locked gates, their combined strength bursting them open with a shriek of twisted metal. They did not break their stride, however; the rats were close behind. The relative straightness of the road allowed them to gain a slight lead on the pursuing horde, but it was clear that Beef was starting to flag.

Although Silas Cherry was a slender man, he was heavier than he seemed; weighed down with his gear and his gift, he was becoming too much for Beef to bear. Chloe fell in beside them, ready to help if her friend should stumble or falter. Silas pointed weakly to the right as they approached a t-junction, but he needn't have bothered.

A van roared out of the mist, the side door already open. Chloe paid no attention to the colour of the vehicle, nor did she notice the gaudy mural painted on the panel door. A fortunate thing too, for the sight of it would've stopped her in her tracks; an easy meal for the pursuing rats.

Candy reached the van first, and leapt in the back, pulling Elsie in after him. Beef half passed, half tossed Silas to her husband before vaulting into the space behind the seats. Chloe's lungs burned and her eyes streamed with tears of terror as the rats snapped at her heels, their eyes rolling and their mouths slavering.

She put all her energy into one last jump just as the van began to pull away. She landed in Beef's bloodstained arms and Candy slammed the door shut, not a moment too soon. The impact of dozens of rats sounded like a sudden downpour, and their sheer momentum threatened to tip the van into the nearby river.

The rookie, their driver, swore loudly and slammed the vehicle into gear. It lurched forwards, crushing the rodents that swarmed around the wheels and surged towards the bumper. The tires spun in place for a few fraught seconds, lubricated by gore, before finally finding their grip and propelling the van and its occupants down the road, safely into the foggy night.

Chloe sat back and breathed a sight of relief. The air in the van was likely filtered, but she didn't dare remove her mask. In the back, with her and Beef, were a bundle of bags and cases; after a bit of searching, they found a first aid kit with the supplies necessary to patch Silas up until they reached his house.

Whilst they were rummaging through the case, Elsie had been chatting to their driver in a low voice. She relayed the bad news when Beef and Chloe made their way forward once again.

"So," she said as she pulled her mask off, once again stunning Chloe with her handsome beauty, "it appears that Silas's flat is no longer a safe place for us to go."

Neither woman replied, their question implied by the situation.

"I... um..." Elsie began, clearly uncomfortable, "I'm being hunted by someone in the employ of Finley Carmichael. His name is Mad Dog and he's trying to kill me. I won't go into why, at least not now, but he has a team of people working with him and they are some of the best trackers the world has ever seen.

"They're also complete fucking psychos who won't hesitate to kill the rest of you if you get in their way, or even are just near to me when the fighting starts. I'm hoping that we can hole up somewhere else tonight, and then we can make a better plan tomorrow when we've all had some sleep and I've helped Silas.

"Does that sound fair?"

"Sounds fine to me," Beef said, and Chloe nodded in agreement. "Where are we going?"

"Our driver has said that we can stay at his place tonight, and that he's got supplies there."

"Excellent." Beef rubbed her hands gleefully as Chloe stared out of the window in surprise. *We're near my house! Maybe we can actually make it home for the night...*

Her shock was compounded when the driver deftly swung the van on to her street and parked it nimbly outside her home. She looked at the tinted partition that divided the driver from them as it slid back, revealing an all too familiar face; impish eyes, a well-groomed beard, and a winning smile.

"Shy!?"

"Hiya, Noor!"

Chapter Fourteen – Know Your Enemy

Elsie

"Come on, Silas," Elsie said as she hauled him into the front room of the little terraced house. Beef and Candy were pulling the various bags and crates out of the van whilst Chloe, or Noor, argued with Silas's apprentice in the street.

"Put me down there, Elsie." She deposited him on top of a sturdy wooden chest. "Let's not get blood over our hosts' furniture, shall we?"

"Here's your medical kit," the muscular woman, Beef, said as she handed a large orange case to Elsie. "Is he going to be okay?"

"I've patched up worse," Elsie said with a smile, looking at the bloodstains on the woman's jacket. "Thank you for carrying him; we definitely wouldn't have made it out alive if the three of you hadn't been there."

Elsie snapped the clasps on the case open just as the front door slammed shut. Chloe stormed through the living room whilst Shy, the Swarm's apprentice, walked over to them. He deposited a large laundry sack at Elsie's feet whilst his other hand held the neck of his jacket closed.

She peered inside and gasped; the ruined pieces of Pandora filled the sack. Shy gave her a wink and unzipped the front of his coat, revealing the squirming form of some kind of tan weasel. Silas squealed with joy as the lithe creature leapt into his arms.

"Tinkerbell! Oh, thank you for bringing her with you, Shy." He grinned madly as the creature nipped at his fingers and let out a strange chuckling sound. "Did you miss your Papa, Tinks? Yes you did, you naughty creature!"

"Um... Silas... can you give the weasel back to Shy so I can get the bullet out of your shoulder, please?" Elsie had all the necessary items to hand, and was just waiting for an opening. She was also intensely wary of the creature in his arms; she'd had far too many close calls with rats, recently.

"Yo, Si, let me hold Tinks whilst Elsie patches you up." Shy reached down and took the animal in his hands. It made a playful chirrup before heading back inside his jacket. "There you go. It's a ferret, by the way."

"A champagne ferret," Silas corrected haughtily. "Tinkerbell is my pride and joy. Before you ask, no, she isn't one of my bound; she's just a pet."

"Looks like a weasel to me," Elsie muttered as she snapped on a pair of gloves and snipped away Silas's clothing.

"They're both mustelids," Silas said as she opened a small bottle. "Ferrets are domesticated, whilst weasels are- Ouch!"

"Sorry," Elsie said as she dabbed the wound with a peroxide soaked gauze. She looked up at Shy. "Can you get someone else in here to help me, please?"

"I..." he began, before she cut across him.

"You're covered in ferret germs; just get one of the others." He nodded and walked into the next room. Chloe began to shout the moment he crossed the threshold into the little kitchen. "What's the deal with him and Chloe? Is she his ex-girlfriend or something?"

"No, no," Silas said, chuckling before immediately

regretting it. "Oh, fuck me, that hurts! Noor is Shy's older sister, and she doesn't know about his little side job."

"His sister?" Elsie asked, surprised.

"He's adopted," Silas replied, "not that it should matter. She's fiercely protective of him and I've a feeling that she won't like him associating with someone like me. He worships the ground Noor walks on, but he does feel a bit stifled by her at times."

"They're both Ceps?"

Silas opened his mouth to answer, but shut it again when Shy's sister strode into the room. She promptly gloved up and looked at Elsie, awaiting instructions.

"I'm going to reach in with this," she said, brandishing a pair of narrow forceps, "and when I've pulled the bullet out you'll need to keep pressure on the wound so I can stitch it up. Oh, do you prefer Noor or Chloe?"

"Chloe, and I'll stitch it," she said confidently. Elsie did not doubt her abilities and nodded before rummaging inside Silas's shoulder with the forceps. She frowned; the bullet had clipped the bone and she had to fish a few fragments out before she could find the bullet.

"Right," she said at last, "got it all. Chloe, he's all yours."

"Do we not have any local anaesthetic?" Silas whimpered as Chloe pushed the sterilised needle through his flesh.

"I didn't check," Chloe replied coldly. "So, ferret boy, why don't you tell me how the fuck my brother ended up as your *apprentice*, and what exactly that means?"

"I'd rather have that conversation when you aren't

stitching me up," Silas muttered.

"People in hell want ice water, Cherry," Elsie said, suddenly exhausted. "Tell her what she wants to know."

"I originally met Shy a couple of years ago," Silas said breathlessly, "when he was just the local weed man. He didn't seem remarkable at first, until I shook his hand after a deal and realised-"

"What a charming and talented young man I am?" Shy said loudly as he walked back in. "Right, Si?"

"So she doesn't know?" Silas asked incredulously. "Fucking hell, Shy, you should talk to your family more often!"

"What don't I know?" Chloe asked and Silas winced as she jabbed him with the needle. "Shy Turner, you answer me or I swear to god that I will have Beef knock your arse into next week!"

"Ugh, fine!" Shy slumped on to the battered sofa with Tinkerbell in his arms. "I'm an Exception, Noor; I was born with supernatural powers, like Silas and Elsie."

"What can you do?" Elsie asked, curious about their host.

"Pretty much anything," Shy said with a grin. "If I touch another Cep, I can borrow their gift for a short time. I also get an intuitive understanding of its strengths and limitations, which came in handy when James and I..."

He trailed off, seemingly aware that he had said too much.

"Go on," Chloe said, her face like thunder. "What exactly were you and Candy doing?"

There was a considerable pause. *I'm so glad I'm an only child,* Elsie thought with relief.

"When he started to feel different after the crash, he asked if I could try to borrow any gift he might have." Shy sighed heavily as Chloe opened her mouth. "And yes, he knew about my particular talent already."

"He told me almost ten years ago," said a deep voice from the kitchen doorway. "He asked for my advice when he started working with Silas, and I told him to be careful but also to take the opportunity."

"You..." Chloe seethed at Candy, "you went behind my back and kept this from me!? How fucking dare you!?"

"Shy had mentioned you plenty," Silas said to Candy, "and when I realised who you were in the Junction Building I knew that I could trust you. That's how I knew you were a Seer, Noo- my apologies; Chloe."

"You're a drug dealer?" Elsie said, trying to keep up with the conversation, although that nagging feeling in her gut had returned. *I've missed something important again.*

"Sure am," Shy said with a smile. "What's your poison?"

"Have you got any estrogen tablets?" Elsie asked, a touch sheepishly. "I've run out and I know the people after me will have the pharmacies staked out."

"Sure thing. I've got over a year's worth. Will a couple hundred tablets tide you over?"

"That would be amazing, thank you," Elsie said before her stomach fell. "How much is this gonna cost me?"

"No charge," Shy said, getting to his feet. "I only charge for the recreational shit; actual medicine is always free. Back in a jiffy."

He trotted upstairs, depositing Tinkerbell in Candy's

arms as he went. Elsie couldn't be sure, but she thought she heard him say 'hello, ferret' quietly to the animal. Chloe's face was thoughtful, and she stared at the spot where her brother had been until he returned.

"Thank you," Elsie said as Shy handed her a little paper bag full of medicine boxes.

"You're welcome, and Si, you owe me a hundred quid." Shy smiled wryly as the wounded man groaned. "Just isn't your day, is it?"

"I can afford it," Silas muttered. He turned his head to look at Chloe. "Am I all done?"

"Mhmm," she replied, removing the rubber gloves.

"Fantastic." He got to his feet and stretched gingerly before he walked over to Candy to reclaim his pet. "What do we say to moving this little discussion to the kitchen? I could use a cup of tea after the time we've had."

"Agreed," Elsie said. She hesitated for a moment, before taking the stunned Chloe Turner by the hand and leading her through to the next room.

"So," Beef began, her sizeable hands wrapped tightly around a large mug of tea, "are we any closer to figuring out what's causing this?"

"I have an idea," Candy said from his spot on the counter. "When I was copying the shipping manifest I saw mention of a Project Pandora. All the details were blacked out, but in the myth Pandora unleashes horrors from the box on the world."

"Sounds about right," Beef agreed.

"It's not Pandora," Elsie said slowly. *How much do I tell them?* She stole a look at Chloe, who was still staring into the middle distance. Even with a blank gaze filling her eyes, she was still startlingly beautiful;

when Elsie had first laid eyes on her, she could've sworn she was a siren or some other captivating creature.

She's an Exception, she thought, *but no different to Silas or me. Beautiful, but not unapproachable.*

She shook her head, clearing such thoughts away for another time. She looked around and found that Beef was smirking at her, one eyebrow raised.

"When you've finished *daydreaming*," she said with a low laugh, "do you have an explanation for why we aren't dealing with some kind of Box of Evil?"

Courage, Elsie.

"Project Pandora was an invention of mine. It's just an environmental protection suit, the remains of which are in the other room." Her lip quivered as she spoke. "Pandora was the culmination of my life's work; my magnum opus. Whatever destroyed her is what's causing this."

"We broke into the crash reconstruction site," Silas said, "in order to retrieve the remains of Pandora. Whatever caused this was in the same car, possibly alongside the storage for the suit. We found fragments of reddish sandstone, if that helps narrow it down at all."

Candy's eyes widened.

Elsie rummaged in her pocket, pulling out the shipping manifest after a few seconds. It was damp from the fog and smeared with Silas's blood, but still readable. She skimmed through and found a listing for an archaeological find from a cave on the Weser River, in Germany.

"It says here that the sandstone item was a religious icon, possibly a reliquary, locally known as '*Grab der Rattentänzer*'. It dates back to the thirteenth century and was discovered in a cave just outside of Hamelin..."

Across the kitchen, Shy began to giggle. Beef glared at him, whilst Candy continued to look shocked. It was Chloe who eventually spoke.

"Elsie, what does that name mean?"

"It means Grave of the Rat Dancers, I think." Elsie looked at Shy, who was laughing so hard it brought tears to his eyes. "What's so fucking funny, Shy?"

"Rats? Hamelin? Mysterious sounds in the mist?" Shy managed to gasp out. "Don't you see what that means?"

Oh my god.

"The fucking Pied Piper!?" Silas said, rolling his eyes. "Of course, why wouldn't it be?"

"We have a problem," Candy said.

"Which is?" Elsie asked.

"The Piper drove all the rats into the river, right?" The others nodded. "The Thames is too far away and the Darent is too small, so they're going to be looking for a bigger body of water. The lake is only four houses away."

At that moment, the eerie warbling tune of the Piper filled the air once again, and Tinkerbell began to hiss.

"We are in deep fucking shit," Silas said as the distant sound of squealing rats reached their ears.

Interlude One – Tides of Flesh

The eyes of the rats rolled and their greasy flanks shuddered and quivered as the music of the Piper twisted its way into every cell in their bodies, forcing them onward and driving them mad. Amongst the thrashing, squeaking throng were other animals. House cats, show dogs, guinea pigs, and countless more; all had succumbed to the Piper's call.

Behind the flood of captivated creatures slouched the humans, both dead and still breathing, who had been enslaved by the melody. Their very bones betrayed them, marching to the beat of their unseen master, to ends nefarious and unknowable.

The broken forms of thirteen young men, slain in a children's playground, twitched and writhed as the Piper roused them from their eternal slumber. Eyelids fluttered as neurons fired, restoring the ghostly echoes of the people they had once been.

"Nooooooo," moaned one of them, his body numb as his head lolled on a useless broken neck. Even though his limbs were dead weight that his brain could no longer touch, the Piper's call reached them all the same.

"Please," another begged as he dragged his shattered form on to the moist asphalt of the road, "please just let me die!"

Whilst some foolhardy humans tried to stand against the tide, most locked themselves indoors and blocked the windows and doors with whatever they could find. Sealed in their homes, physically safe, the undulating tune wormed its way into the weaker minds. In the morning these fragile souls would be found shattered and crazed; mere shadows of the people they were before.

A mother and her baby, secure in a top floor flat just off Lowfield Street, attempted to wait out the musical onslaught. Trembling, fighting the invasive impulses with every fibre of her being, the young woman brought her squalling infant to her mouth and took a large, slavering bite of its soft flesh. Sobbing, she chewed, swallowed, and continued to devour her child.

Whilst all but the strongest mind would've been broken by such an act, the new mother's sanity was completed destroyed when she felt her dead child's flesh, still bound to the Piper's song, wriggle and move in her stomach.

A man in his early thirties, known as Lucky Dan after his seemingly miraculous escape from the inferno and toxic cloud, cowered on the bathroom floor of the Orange Tree pub. A broken bottle lay at his feet and he wept uncontrollably as he cut chunks of skin, fat, and muscle from his bones with a handful of shattered green glass.

Sitting in a puddle of his own excrement and blood, Dan screamed as the jagged hunks of viscera began to quiver and slither across the bathroom floor, leaving trails behind them like gory slugs. One by one, they squelched their way up the white porcelain of the urinal and squeezed down the drain; soon they would be whole once again.

Lucky Dan pressed his bloodstained hands to his head and howled in agony as a tremendous sense of pressure struck him both blind and deaf. Unbeknownst to him, a straw coloured fluid, streaked with red, was seeping from his nose and staining his shredded shirt. Moments later, a gloopy pink tendril forced itself through Dan's left nostril as his entire face slackened. Inch by wormy inch, his brain broke free of his skull and followed his flesh into the afflicted town's drainage system.

All across the town, such scenes played out.

Every slouching corpse or enslaved rodent surged through the streets and alleyways relentlessly, all in the direction of the contaminated lake. As the first creatures neared the still shoreline, the Piper's focus shifted and the tune went from an unsettling march to an insistent hunting song. The nightmarish horde turned and headed in the direction of the six people cowering in the Turner house.

A shudder ran through all the creatures, human and otherwise, as a single thought seized them. Those with mouths capable of speech reflexively screamed this word into the foggy night; a true chorus of the damned.

"Mother!"

Part Two: Danse Macabre

<u>Chapter Fifteen – The Reichardt Drop</u>

Chloe

They're coming for us.

The thought crashed into her mind from the Tangle, accompanied by a slew of images that gave her a full appreciation of just how widespread the Piper's horror was. Her mug of tea trembled in her hand and she let out a petrified scream.

"Chloe, what's wrong?" Silas asked, a hand around her shoulder.

"It's coming," she mumbled fearfully. "It's coming!"

"What is?" Beef asked, hopping down from her position atop the counter. "Chloe, how long do we have?"

"The meat," she moaned, her eyes rolling wildly, "the meat that moves!"

"Yeah, not super keen on the sound of that, Noor," Shy remarked. "Let me have a look."

He reached out to grab her hand, and there was a blaze of rainbow light; suddenly the Tangle was gone, impossibly far away. Chloe began to cough and splutter, unable to breathe. Blood frothed at her mouth as the Piper's tune began to worm its way inside her flesh.

"Fucking hell," Elsie yelled, "give it back to her, she's dying without it!"

Shy clapped his hand into hers once again, and the tune faded away. Chloe took a shuddering breath and smiled weakly at her brother, who gave her a reassuring wink.

"Thank you," she wheezed. "Did you get a look at

what we're dealing with?"

"I did," he said, "and your powers have a really lovely salted caramel flavour to them."

"Focus!" Silas yelled. He was already gathering up the more important items and forcing them into a rucksack. "Try to recall every single detail that you can; you've got ten seconds to get it into a coherent form."

"Okay, boss," Shy said as he screwed up his eyes.

"Big man," Silas said to Candy, "we need you to come up with a way out of here. Take in everything Shy tells you and then borrow brain power from everyone except Elsie and Chloe. Got it?"

Candy nodded as Shy opened his eyes. Silas gestured for Noor's brother to go ahead.

"In three minutes a tide of undead humans, controlled rats, and other vicious animals are going to descend on this house." Shy took a breath. "They are going to break through the front room windows and tear down the back fence. They'll break down any door between us and them in a matter of moments. We will be torn to pieces if we don't get out of here."

"That all?" Candy asked. Shy nodded and the Babbage closed his eyes, drawing on the minds of all present.

"Why didn't he take our brains?" Chloe asked Elsie, who was busy rummaging through the kitchen cupboards. "Why can't we help?"

"You need to keep your mind open in case something unexpected happens," Elsie replied, "or you might be able to sense a way out."

"But I've only been doing this a few days!" Chloe whined, her eyes tearing up. "Elsie, I'm terrified!"

Elsie grabbed Chloe's hand and looked into her eyes.

She took a calm breath before speaking.

"I believe in you, Chloe Turner. Fate brought us together for a reason, and it wasn't just to kill us here and now. We'll get out of this." She squeezed her hand. "I believe in you."

Elsie let go and resumed her search of the cupboards. *God, I could kiss her.*

"What are you doing?" Chloe asked quietly.

"I'm trying to invent something to save our arses. Currently I've got a few different kinds of explosive but I'd prefer something... Do you have a hi-fi?"

"Yes, in there." Chloe followed Elsie as she dashed into the front room. The squealing of rats was growing louder by the second and the discordant menacing melody of the Piper only got faster and more sinister with each passing moment.

Elsie grabbed the hi-fi and attached one of her little devices to it. She hummed loudly as she worked, almost as if she was trying to learn the Piper's song. She fiddled with the device and her fingers danced over dials and keys as she worked.

Hurry up, Chloe thought, and she almost screamed it out loud. Something, however, told her that distracting Elsie at this point would doom them all.

"Quick, give me something from that bag!" Elsie said, pointing at a nearby sack. Chloe opened it and found a mess of ruined machinery and metallic parts. She looked at the other woman, clearly in a panic. "It doesn't matter which bit, the first that comes to hand!"

Chloe grabbed a piece that felt right; it had a whole digital control board and something that looked like a purplish black spinal column on it. Elsie grinned and hooked up a couple of loose wires to the control board. She flicked the power on and pressed a button on the little device.

The speakers were clearly working, as Chloe could see them vibrating, but they didn't seem to make any sound. Elsie paused for a moment before letting out an explosive sigh of relief. She grabbed Chloe and kissed her briefly on the lips, before blushing a bright red and immediately letting go of her.

"Sorry about that," she said sheepishly. "I got a bit carried away."

"No need to apologise," Chloe said as Elsie cranked the volume up another few notches. "Is that making some kind of ultrasound?"

"It's playing perfect destructive interference for the Piper's tune," Elsie said proudly. "They cancel each other out."

"Oh my god, the other sound is completely gone!" Chloe clapped her hands together excitedly. "You're a genius!"

"I try my best. Unfortunately, it won't hold them forever. I might've bought us about half an hour, tops." She sighed. "We can't use it outside, either; the damping effect of the fog is too difficult to factor in. We're safe for now, though. Hopefully long enough for your friend to figure out a way out of here."

"Here's hoping," Chloe said.

"Otherwise," Elsie replied softly, "you better start on that whole reverse maze thing, pronto."

"Please tell me you have good news," Chloe said ten minutes later as Candy's eyes refocussed.

"After a fashion," he said. "We haven't been eaten yet."

"No," she replied, "Elsie rigged up some kind of noise cancelling... noise, I guess. I don't really get it, but it works. Apparently it won't hold forever."

"She used the hi-fi?" Candy asked. Chloe nodded. Silas, Shy, and Beef seemed to come back to their usual selves as they spoke. "How does everyone feel?"

"Fine," Beef said. "Pretty refreshed, actually."

"My mind has never been so empty," Silas said. Shy just winked at Candy, a sombre smile on his face.

"What's the plan, babe?" Beef asked, putting an arm around her husband.

"Gather everything you need; we won't be able to come back here until it's all over. Shy knows where to go; you'll follow him to somewhere safe and you can plan the next steps from there."

"We can plan the next steps," Chloe muttered, blood running cold in her veins. *I know what you're going to do.* She caught Shy's eye and he nodded sadly.

"How are we going to get out of here?" Silas asked. "Not to harp on the point, but we are well and truly surrounded and I doubt your domestic sound system speakers will hold up to whatever fuckery our resident inventor has running through them."

"They won't," Elsie said as she strode into the kitchen. Her face was flushed with mental exhaustion, but there was a sickly pallor to the skin around her neck and hands. *How much of yourself are you putting into this?* Chloe wondered.

"Do you think you could make a total wall of sound, all frequencies at maximum amplitude?" Candy asked. Beside him, Shy was loading as much food as possible into a hiking rucksack. "It wouldn't need to be for more than a few milliseconds; just enough for a single pulse."

A grin crossed Elsie's face; she clearly understood Candy's plan. *I'm glad one of us does.* The young inventor immediately went back into the living room to fiddle with her device. Chloe went to follow her, but Candy held up a hand.

"We still need you," he said. "When Shy leads you out of here, you'll need to be open to the Tangle as you go; absolutely nothing can get the drop on you, okay? I know this is hard for you and you're still learning, but everyone's lives will depend on you."

"I'll do my best," Chloe said tearfully. The pressure of keeping everyone alive was already threatening to turn her bowels to water and her legs to jelly. She'd never had to shoulder such a burden before, and a part of her simply wanted to lie down and give herself to the rats instead.

Courage, Chloe.

"Shy, will you tell us where you'll be taking them?" Candy asked as he led them into the living room.

"I'm part of a mutual aid group that's based over in the Dark Trees, on the other side of the lake," Shy said, condensing all of the assorted items from his van into the smallest number of containers possible. He handed Elsie a large plastic cassette. "The van has an eight track; load it on to this."

"Aye aye, skipper."

"The road is full of rats, Shy, and god only knows what else!" Beef said. "You can't possibly plan on driving?"

"We'll get slaughtered on foot, Dee. The rats are thickest coming in from the main road, but I'm going to go down to the end, cut through on to Walnut Tree, then go round to Powder Mill Lane." Shy gave her a grim look. "It takes us awfully close to the lake, but I'm hoping Noor can get us through unscathed."

"Here," Elsie said. "I've tweaked the cassette writer,

so it only took a moment. Candy, I think I've worked out everything I need for the sound impulse; I'm going to have an equal beat of silence before it kicks off to make it hit even harder."

"Like the drop in a club?" Shy asked, clearly impressed.

"The most intense drop you'll ever experience," she said proudly.

"The Reichardt Drop," Silas said with a grin. "Is this the Wishbone Collective, Shy?"

"Yes. The place is built up like a fortress, even if it doesn't necessarily look like that from the outside. I'm sure Elsie can make some worthwhile improvements, though." He looked at Candy. "We aren't coming back here, are we?"

"No, Shy, you won't be." He glanced at the stairs. "You've got about four minutes until you need to go; get whatever you can carry."

Shy scampered upstairs as Elsie continued to work on the hi-fi system. Silas nodded at Candy, before giving his sizeable bicep an affectionate squeeze.

"Thank you. It's been an honour, no matter how brief."

"Likewise, Silas. Promise me you'll look after them?"

"Of course I will."

"What the fuck are you two talking about?" Beef demanded. "Why are you acting like you're not coming with us?"

"I'm not," Candy said quietly. "Someone needs to stay here to set off the Drop; there's no way to do it remotely."

"Can't we do it as we leave?" Beef asked, her voice breaking.

"The force will be too strong," Elsie said from her spot by the hi-fi. "It'll kill us all. I'm happy to stay and do it, however."

"No," Chloe said, suddenly in perfect harmony with the Tangle. "It has to be Candy; everyone else needs to get out of here alive, or else this never ends. I'm sorry, Beef."

"Let me stay with you, baby," Beef begged. She was on the edge of hysteria. "Please!"

"No sense in more death than necessary," Candy said flatly. "Will you do two things for me, Delilah?"

"What?"

"Look after my dad. He'll be devastated, but I know he'll make it through."

"Of course, Jim." Beef wiped the tears from her eyes. "What's the second?"

"Let me save you." She continued to cry, but she nodded weakly. "Marrying you was the greatest thing I ever did, Dee. I am so proud to have been your husband."

"We deserve more time!" Her voice was almost incomprehensible, more wail than words.

"Everyone does, but we made the most of what little we had."

"I love you, Jim."

"And I you, Dee." He took her in his arms as Shy descended the stairs. "It's time to go. Live hard, my one and only, and don't you dare look back!"

Shy, Silas, and Beef tearfully gathered their things and moved to the door. Elsie joined them after giving Candy a quick hug. Chloe looked at him, tears spilling down her cheeks.

"Thank you for being a brother to him." She tried to smile, but failed completely. "Be brave."

"I'm not afraid," he said evenly before planting a kiss on her cheek. "Thank you for being a sister to me, Noor. I always liked that name better on you, by the way.

"Now go!"

The five of them dashed out of the door, letting the fog flood into the house behind them. Elsie's strange dissonant music had left all the rats in the street paralysed. They were almost lifeless as they picked their way over them and crowded into the van.

Shy slammed the cassette into the player and the discordant sound filled their vehicle, granting them a temporary bubble of safety. He clicked the engine on and put the van into gear.

So long, James Baxter, Chloe thought as they sped away.

Just as they were rounding the corner, there was a heartbeat of silence followed by a deafening blast of sound. All the rats and creatures gathered around the Turner house were liquefied in an instant. Chloe was about to cheer when the little pebble-dashed house she'd spent her entire life in collapsed inwards, hundreds of shards of masonry shredding the area where James stood.

Instead, a quiet sob escaped her lips.

In the seat beside her, Delilah Baxter threw her head back and let out a piercing scream.

Chapter Sixteen – A New Day Dawns

Archer

Archer groaned in pleasure as he sprawled face down on the bed, with only an artfully draped towel to preserve what little modesty he claimed to have left. Whilst such stillness would've normally driven him to madness, this was the one time he not only endured it, but willingly submitted to it.

Roxanne brought the green acetate cane through the air once again, not too hard, but forceful enough to make Archer gasp. She continued to strike the soles of his feet, alternating between swift light taps and harder blows that stung all the way down to his bones.

"Oh yeah, Roxy," he moaned softly, "that's the stuff."

"Better than a tennis ball?" Roxanne asked playfully, knowing all too well that it was. When he didn't reply, she hit him slightly harder than he was expecting. He jerked slightly and glared at her over his shoulder. "You didn't answer me, Archer."

"Yes, Roxy, it's infinitely superior to a tennis ball. That good enough for you?" He saw her smile and settled back into his earlier position. "Would you like to know how many pings we got last night?"

"Let me guess," she said, lining up her next blow. "Fifteen fatalities, not including your little rampage?"

"Our rampage, Roxy," he said in a singsong voice. "And no, either our killings got lost in the noise or they flew under the radar. Fifteen is way out, by the way. Two guesses left."

"Fifty three?" *I wish,* Archer thought.

"Still way off. Last guess."

"Am I in the right order of magnitude?"

"No." Archer said quietly. Suddenly their little guessing game seemed crass; cruel, even. "There were over two thousand fatalities last night, Roxy, and the pings keep on rolling in from the police, morgue, and the hospital."

"Over two thousand?" Roxanne's voice was quiet and she plopped down on to the bed beside Archer, her legs weak and her stomach roiling. "Archer, how can we fight something like that?"

"We'll manage, Toto," he said as he sat up. He wrapped his arms affectionately around her. "We always come out on top, don't we?"

"I guess so, Dorothy, but maybe this time will be the one that gets us." Roxanne squeezed him tightly. "I'm actually frightened of this."

Archer was about to respond when a voice from the doorway broke the moment between the two of them.

"Hard at work, I see." There was no warmth in Dr Helen Mickelson's words. Her smallpox-scarred face was set in a hard frown and her hazel eyes glowered at them both. Archer kept a close watch for the telltale flash of sickly yellow in her irises, but there was no change.

He let out a low whistle of relief. Roxanne had already backed up and was pressed against the far wall, shaking softly as she scrabbled at the dresser for a face mask and a pair of nitrile gloves.

"It would be a tremendous waste of my time to make you sick, Agent Wagstaff. Of course, I can understand why your gift would give you certain... neuroses. This, however," she said, gesturing to Archer's bare feet and the acetate cane, "is not how I expected to find a pair of Ravenblades, especially not with a skyrocketing body count."

"It relaxes my feet, keeps me nimble," Archer said sheepishly. "Ballet does horrible things to your muscles and bone structure and they hurt if I don't work them over every so often."

"I don't care, Agent Treen." Helen ran a hand through her gently spiked grey hair in exasperation. "We are out the door in exactly ten minutes. The morgue is surprisingly empty, given the number of casualties last night."

"Over two thousand," Roxanne said.

"Three thousand, three hundred and eighty seven, as of ten o'clock in the morning." Helen's deep, slightly rasping voice always set Archer on edge; he felt like a naughty schoolboy hiding some awful prank. "Get your things together, you two. Nine minutes and twenty five seconds."

Archer pulled on his underwear, socks, and jumpsuit as Roxanne paced up and down the room, muttering as she did so. *Good god, fucking focus!* The sound of Helen carrying her bags into one of the spare bedrooms sent her over the edge.

"She can't stay here!" Roxanne's voice was shrill and coloured with panic. "Archer, make her stay somewhere else!"

"I can't, Roxy," he said softly, hoping that their new colleague would not overhear them. "She outranks us."

"We are Ravenblades!" Roxanne yelled. "What is her authority!?"

"Would you like my credentials?" Helen asked, strolling into the room. She wore a set of black scrubs and had a small case tucked under one arm; her autopsy knives, Archer guessed. "Fine. I joined the Ministry Youth Academy at age ten. That was sixty five years ago, for context. Graduated first in my class, sat the Ravenblade exam at sixteen, and got the highest score ever seen; I turned it down, of course.

"Over a decade studying medicine in Oxford, then I was transferred to the Hong Kong field office. I became Sub-Director of the Ministry's entire Asia Office three years later. Everything else I have been involved in since the mid-nineties is so heavily classified that you wouldn't even know that you don't know about it."

Holy shit, Archer thought.

"Not that it matters," Helen continued, "but I am also a close personal friend of Director Desai. We meet weekly to discuss the direction of the Ministry, both in terms of policy and staffing. As far as you two are concerned for this mission, I *am* the Ministry incarnate.

"Those are my credentials, Agent Wagstaff, and we are out the door in five and a half minutes."

Helen walked smartly out of the room and continued to gather the items she'd need for their work. In the bedroom Archer looked at Roxanne, who seemed to be in a state of shock. He gently shook her shoulder and helped her to get ready.

I fucking hate oversight like this, he thought as he helped her into her coat. *We're supposed to have complete operational autonomy, but how can we possibly do our fucking jobs with someone as rigid as that cramping our style!?*

"Sixty seconds," Helen called from the hallway. Archer groaned and put his boots on. He did one final sweep of the bedroom and shepherded Roxanne out into the hall. Helen had a grey overcoat on over her scrubs and an N95 mask on her face.

"My car only seats two," Roxanne said moodily.

"Not a problem," Helen said, jangling some keys. "Mine has plenty of room."

The three of them stepped out into the grey mist-filtered light, and Archer felt Roxanne twitch violently at the sight of Helen's vehicle; a Ford Transit Hanlon Ambulance. *Oh, she is going to lose her fucking mind.*

"Hop in," Helen said with barely concealed glee.

Roxanne retched behind her mask as she continued to hyperventilate.

"We're nearly there, Roxy," Archer said soothingly, "and I'm sure Dr Mickelson has taken every care to ensure that this ambulance is completely sterile, right, Doc?"

In the driver's seat beside him, Helen simply shrugged.

You could at least work with me, Archer thought as he returned his attention to Roxanne, who seemed on the verge of passing out. *I don't envy her one bit.*

Roxanne Wagstaff was a Tracer and, like all of her kind, she had both an enhanced sensory capability and an advantageous form of motion. Where Teaser Malarkey could functionally teleport by folding herself through a localised wormhole, Roxanne could slow time down relative to her by almost ten times. This put tremendous strain on her body, especially her circulatory system; her heartbeat could reach over three hundred and fifty beats per minute when her own time was dilated to the maximum extent.

Her enhanced sense was her vision, which was highly unusual; most Tracers relied on smell or hearing. Roxanne could read a car numberplate clearly at over a mile away and she could see the individual movements of an ant's legs from across a wide street. She could identify fingerprints at a glance and pick out details that any other person would be unable to perceive.

These two gifts combined to make Roxanne Wagstaff the most deadly sniper that the Ministry had ever seen, and her other gunplay skills were not far behind, either. Unfortunately, though, her freakish visual abilities sometimes played tricks on her and, as they were just beyond her capability to see, Roxanne was obsessed with germs.

Her paranoia and germophobia had only increased as she'd got older and had carried out yet more missions in her line of work. Roxanne refused to use any kind of sink, shower, or bath that was in the same room as a toilet, and would not visit hospitals if she could avoid it.

In the back of Helen's vintage ambulance, her heart rate monitor was registering almost two hundred beats per minute as she looked wildly round, trying to catch the microbes that she was certain she could see, if only they would stop hiding from her.

"Toto," Archer said imploringly, "please try to calm down. When we get back you can have a nice relaxing bubble bath whilst Helen and I look through all the data from the Morgue. You can even wait upstairs during the autopsies if you want."

"I'm sorry, Roxanne," Helen said softly before the panicked woman could reply, "but we need your eyes on this one. Would you like some diazepam? It might help to calm you down."

Roxanne shook her head and continued to

hyperventilate. Archer held her gloved hand in an attempt to soothe her, but was horrified by what he felt. *It's like she's vibrating!* He tapped Helen on the shoulder with his free hand and slowly shook his head. She sighed, but pulled the ambulance over on the side of the road.

In a blur of motion, Roxanne tore the back door open and leapt from the vehicle. She hit the ground with a thud, crumpling into sobs. Archer was about to follow her when Helen grabbed his wrist. He looked at her, aghast, as she tried to force him to sit down once again.

"Tell her to remain in radio contact and we'll rendezvous when we're done with the bodies." Archer nodded and hopped out of the ambulance. He found his partner still on the ground, retching and crying.

"Hey, Toto," he said gently as he rubbed the small of her back. "The Doc and I are gonna go and deal with the morgue. You don't need to come with us. All I want you to do is find a little cafe or something to hole up in until you feel better, okay?"

"Mhmm," she murmured. Given her state, it was more than Archer expected. He stroked the back of her neck gently and made soft soothing sounds. *Thank god,* he thought when the rapid beeping of her heart monitor finally started to slow. *I wish she'd just take the damn heart pills.*

"Treen, we need to keep moving!" Helen called from the ambulance. "Get back in here."

"I've got to go, Toto. Keep your radio on, okay?" He leant down, his mask touching hers; given the toxic fog that surrounded them, it was the closest to a kiss that he could muster. "Look after yourself, and I'll see you for lunch later."

Roxanne didn't have time to respond as Archer vaulted back into the ambulance, pulling the back door closed behind him. He settled in his seat as comfortably as he could; without a belt, of course, and expected a lecture from Helen.

She did not say a word for the rest of the journey.

Upon arriving at the newly constructed overflow morgue, they were directed to the adjacent car park and told to report to Dr Laramie Broom, the senior pathologist on duty. Helen crossed the battered asphalt quickly with Archer hot on her heels.

Damn, she's fast for someone so old!

"Dr Broom?" Helen asked, extending her hand to a gaunt, tall man with a narrow face and a vertical frizz of grey hair. He gave her a thin lipless smile, devoid of any warmth whatsoever, and shook his head.

"I'm Detective Colin Jenkins," he said, finally taking Helen's hand in his. Archer's stomach turned at the sickly yellow tinge that tainted the man's almost translucent skin. "Dr Broom is in his office, down the hall just there. Can I ask what your business here is, ma'am?"

"Dr Helen Mickelson, CBR Pathologist with DSTL." She produced a badge and allowed the looming detective a moment to examine it before whisking it away. "I assume my credentials are in order?"

"Yes, um..."

"Sir will do fine, Detective Jenkins." Helen turned to Archer. "Will you fetch the two blue cases from the ambulance, please?"

"Sure thing, *sir*," Archer said, his voice dripping with sarcasm. "What do we need them for, anyway?"

"Those are BSL4 Containment Suits," she said,

irked at his tone. "I'd rather not get infected with anything we find here."

"Of course not," said a jolly voice. A large round man with a thin moustache and a terrible comb-over ambled up the corridor towards them. "The media have dubbed the events of the last twenty four hours as 'The Night of the Rat', which conjures all sorts of biological nasties in the old imagination, doesn't it?"

"Ah," Helen remarked, her entire demeanour warming, "you must be Dr Broom!"

"Indeed I am and it's a pleasure to meet you at last, Dr Mickelson; I've heard so much about you."

"God only knows what my son has been saying to you over the past couple of years," Helen replied with a laugh. "Archer, don't just stand there; the bodies won't keep forever."

Archer nodded and trotted out to the parked ambulance to retrieve the containment suits. As he wrestled the two heavy boxes from the vehicle, a single thought was running through his head, over and over.

She has a son!?

Chapter Seventeen – Welcome to the Wishbone Collective

Elsie

The journey from the Turner house to the Dark Trees Scrap Yard should've taken less than thirty minutes, but it was just after dawn when Shy's van finally rolled to a stop outside the heavy steel gates.

Chloe let out a sigh of relief and slumped back into her seat; she'd proven herself invaluable in finding a route that, although circuitous, was completely clear of the Piper's minions. Elsie had been worried about her, but what had concerned her even more than her companion's well being was the fuel gauge needle, which had been hovering around empty for almost an hour.

"We must've been running on fumes," Silas said as they all took a moment to relax in the grey morning light. "I wonder how many people the Piper took last night?"

"At least one," Dee said bitterly.

"Three thousand, five hundred and twelve," Chloe said, almost dreamily. "I wish I didn't know that."

"I'm sorry," Elsie said gently, putting a comforting hand on the exhausted woman's shoulder. "I can't imagine what that's like."

"Are your friends actually going to let us in, Shy?" Dee asked, peering at the various cameras and spiked wire that lined the surprisingly strong metal walls of the Scrap Yard. "They're not going to kick us out because we're not part of your little club, right?"

"We're a collective," Shy said. He was slumped over the steering wheel, as worn out as his sister. "We help anyone in need, no questions asked; that's kind of the whole point. We'll have to pull our weight for as long as we're here, but they won't kick us out. Everyone contributes as much as they can, but they'll never ask for more than that."

"I'm sure I can make a pretty decent effort for the lot of us," Silas said with a smile.

"Oh yeah, I'm sure they're really hurting for some kind of murderous private detective," Dee said sharply.

"He's a doctor," Chloe mumbled, already half asleep.

"Are you?" Dee asked, her tone suddenly respectful.

"I am," Silas said. "How long is it going to take your friends to open up, Shy?"

"It won't take long, but we will need to actually let them know we're here first," Shy replied testily. Silas opened his mouth to speak but Shy drowned out his words with the van's horn; three short bursts, a brief pause, three long ones, another pause, and then three short ones again.

A little on the nose, Elsie thought, *but then again, we did lose someone last night.*

"You're in shock," Chloe said, looking Elsie in the eyes. "You've never seen someone die suddenly before, not that you cared about, and it's taking a toll on you."

"I-"

"And it's Noor, not Chloe," she said, clearly tapping into Elsie's mind somehow. "The time for silly games is over."

"Yes it is," Silas muttered as the heavy steel gate rumbled to one side, allowing them access to the

Scrap Yard. "Well, Shy, let's go meet your friends."

Elsie almost collapsed as she stepped out of Shy's aubergine coloured van. For the first time she had a chance to truly appreciate the mural that decorated the sliding door; a snow white werewolf stood at the top of a hill, howling in front of a blood moon. She smiled underneath her gas mask. *What a ridiculous piece of art,* she thought. *I absolutely love it.*

"Hey, man," said a masked person in a densely patterned carpet coat, "it's good to see you!"

"You have no idea how happy I am to be here, Barry," Shy said as he pulled his friend into a tight hug. "We've had a hell of a night."

"Run into any rats?"

"More than you'd believe," Shy said, before lowering his voice. "We, um, we lost someone last night; James Baxter."

"I'm so sorry, man. I know he was like a brother to you." Barry put an arm round Shy. "You folks take all the time you need to get situated, okay? If you just want to head on down to the bunks, I can give the others the tour."

"Thanks, Barry." Elsie saw Shy lean in and whisper something to Barry, who nodded solemnly. *He's probably telling him about Dee,* she thought. Shy gave him another hug before heading off into one of the buildings.

Elsie hadn't noticed all the structures at first. Cleverly constructed from shipping containers and prefab buildings, they had all been camouflaged with scrap and detritus after the fact; at a glance or from the air, this would simply appear to be an ordinary junk yard.

The more she looked, the more she saw.

"Is that a boat?" Elsie asked, amazed at the variety of materials that had been used.

"Yup, and part of the northern wall is an old train." Barry gestured as he spoke. "We normally get our power from a bank of solar cells, but they aren't keeping up with demand, what with the fog, so we've co-opted a few diesel generators to see us through the nights.

"It's a bit spartan, but we manage. Do any of you have any engineering experience? We'd be especially grateful if anyone can weld, but that's long odds, right there."

"I can weld," Dee said. "I worked in construction for a few years and I learned there. I could definitely help you with your walls; in fact, I'd be grateful for something productive to do."

"I'm sorry about your husband," Barry said sadly. "I met James a few times; he was a lovely, gentle soul."

"Yes, he was," Dee said, choking up as she spoke, "and I'd rather focus on staying alive for now. I promised him I would, and there will be time to mourn later."

"Well, I'll get on with the tour, then." Barry began to walk them through the scrap yard, pointing out landmarks as he went. "We are the Wishbone Collective. We're an anarchist group, focussing on mutual aid and community support, and this is our base of operations. We already had this place locked down pretty tight even before the derailment, but when all the weird shit started happening we did what we could to build ourselves a little fortress.

"The bunks are down there. We don't have enough beds for everybody, so we have a pretty tight rotation on their usage, but feel free to grab forty winks in any of the chairs in the lounge. We've had a fair few people come to us for shelter, but that's tapered off in the last few days."

"Do you know of any other groups like this?" Silas asked.

"There are five or six dotted throughout the town," Barry said. "Determined folks, the lot of them, but they aren't as well set up as we are here. We try to keep them supplied as best we can, but getting things to them is proving difficult."

"I can help with that," Silas said. Barry gave him a thumbs up and continued the tour.

"Leisure area, with the lounge, library, and general hall. The kitchen is off that. Two hot meals are served a day, at breakfast and dinner, with cold snacks available at lunchtime. There's a big urn for hot water for tea and coffee, although we don't have anything fancy. Food has been a bit tight, given the extra mouths, but Danielle and Harry have done wonders stretching our current rations into enough soup to go around."

This is a seriously impressive setup, Elsie thought as they walked between the towers of scrap metal. *I could build such wonders here if I only had the time.*

The tour went on; greenhouses for food and medicinal plants, latrines, the generators, and other essential areas. Barry was clearly proud of everything the Collective had achieved, but his voice fell when they reached the scrap yard's little clinic.

"I'm going to be honest with you; things aren't great here when it comes to medical care. We've got a decent veterinarian, Ben, and there's Joan, who's a herbalist, but that's it. We used to have a couple of nurses who were part of the Collective but, well..." His voice trailed off for a moment. "Well, we've all lost people."

"I'm a doctor," Silas said. "Although my speciality is forensic pathology, I am fully trained as a medical doctor and I know how to treat the living, so I guess this is where I'll be setting up shop."

"I'm sure you and your, uh, marmot will be right at home."

"She's a ferret," Silas said defensively, "and her name is Tinkerbell."

He's awfully fond of that ferret, Elsie thought as she tried to keep her mind from following that through to what seemed to be the logical conclusion. *I'm sure he doesn't.*

"One of our real problems is getting information from the outside," Barry said as he continued to give them the tour. "For a while we had an internet uplink and a few of us built this massive analogue firewall out of signal generators and oscilloscopes, but it proved too problematic to use. We've got a little wireless setup in the general hall, but all the metal really interferes with the signal."

"I'm a Seer," Noor said bluntly.

Everyone stopped dead in their tracks and stared at her. Elsie's heart thundered in her chest; never in a million years would she admit her gift so publicly, especially not to ordinary humans! Silas leant against the nearest shipping container and sighed heavily.

Elsie looked around for a few seconds as Barry tried to process this information.

"I can see the future, although I'm still learning. I think I can do the same with the past, but it's trickier. Either way, I'll try to open my mind to the Tangle and find out whatever I can."

Barry stared at her for a moment before giving her a thumbs up.

"Every little helps, so thank you for your contribution."

"Well, if we're being completely honest about supernatural abilities," Silas said, "it might benefit us all to have a full understanding of what we're capable of."

"Agreed," Elsie said.

"Dee," Silas said, turning to her, "you're what's known as a Conduit. You can interfere with and manipulate electromagnetic waves; radio, microwaves, electric circuits, to name a few things. Of course, this means that you build up quite a charge over time and get shocked, but I'm sure we'll figure out a use for that in time."

"That... that actually makes a lot of sense," Dee said after a moment to digest his words. "I keep catching myself saying these really random phrases, almost like I've pulled them from thin air; maybe I'm intercepting radio chatter?"

"You could well be," Silas said, turning back to Barry. "So, you should be able to really step up your intel game with Noor and Dee here."

"What about you?" Barry asked, looking at Elsie. "What can you do?"

"I..." Elsie took a few seconds to work out how to paraphrase her abilities. "I can build pretty much anything, provided I have the necessary tools and starting materials. Robots, electronics, machines; anything you could want, really.

"Do you have a workshop?"

"Yes we do," Barry said gleefully. "I was saving it

for last; it's our pride and joy."

"Then please lead the way!" Elsie bounced a little as they walked, excitement overtaking her exhaustion. *Oh, to build again!* When they reached the workshop, she let out a low whistle. "Oh my!"

The room had everything she could possibly want and more; a lathe, three different types of bench saw, a pillar drill, a mill, and so much more. In the corner she noticed several discarded pieces of equipment and immediately went to investigate them.

"Yeah, we weren't sure what those were," Barry said, "but we figured it was best to keep them. You got any idea what they are?"

"Oh yes," Elsie said, rubbing her hands together gleefully. "This is a bullet press!"

"Oh, wow. We've had some security issues from the rats and the other things in the mist, especially in the last few days, so a bullet press would be really useful if we had any firearms."

"I'm a gunsmith," Elsie said off-handedly.

"What?" Silas and Barry said at once.

"Oh, yeah, I'm fully licensed. It's actually my regular source of income." She turned to Silas. "I thought I'd mentioned that."

"You did not." He looked around the workshop. "If we can find suitable materials amongst the scrap, do you think you could knock up a few basic weapons?"

"For sure," Elsie said, grinning even more broadly. "They wouldn't be pretty, of course, but they would pack a punch."

"Fantastic" Barry said, patting Elsie on the back. "When can you get started?"

"Right now," she said as she hauled the bullet press on to the work bench. "Let's make some guns."

Chapter Eighteen – Residue and Retina Burn

Noor

"I just feel numb," Noor said as she clutched her cup of tea in her hands. She was exhausted, but too terrified to sleep. Tinkerbell chirruped softly from her lap, and rolled slightly to get more comfortable; she'd promised Silas that she'd look after her whilst he checked over the injured and unwell members of the Collective.

"I'm sorry that you've been through such an awful few days," Harry said from his side of the table. He was sorting through all the food that Shy had brought with them, making appreciative noises as he did so. "Your brother always said that you were a sensitive soul."

Noor glared at him.

"That's a positive thing," Harry clarified. "Better to be sensitive, gentle, and kind than hard and callous. Good people save the world, Noor; remember that whenever you think about shedding your true nature."

"Thank you, Harry." Noor looked through the kitchen window at the swirling fog. "Some days it feels like this town has always been this way; shrouded in toxic mist and full of horrors that should never see the light of day.

"Please tell me that isn't true."

"It's not, and we will see the sun again, Noor." He reached the bottom of the bag and, after a moment of fumbling, managed to get a small internal compartment open. He pulled out four large bars of chocolate and grinned in triumph. "Magnificent! We've not had chocolate in ages. Here."

He snapped a third of a bar off and handed it to her.

"That's too much, Harry," she said, shaking her head. "There won't be enough to go around."

"There's plenty, and you've been through a terrible loss; that's extraordinary circumstances in my book." He handed her the rest of the bar. "Give that to Dee. Three bars will be plenty fine for a treat after dinner."

"You're very kind," Noor said before popping a small square of chocolate in her mouth. The rich sweetness of it coated her tongue and the nascent flutter of a smile crossed her lips.

"See, you'll start feeling better sooner than you realise." Harry sat back in his chair and regarded the strange woman opposite him for a moment. "The word on the grapevine is that your little gang have special powers; is that true?"

"Mhmm." Another square of chocolate, devoured more greedily this time. "Although Dee and I are new to it; I think it's the chemicals in the mist. We both got a huge dose when the derailment first happened. I'm pleased Shy ended up being out of town when it happened."

"Oh, he was here." Noor raised an eyebrow as he continued to talk. "He's one of our volunteer fire fighters and he knows this town like the back of his hand, so he went with Barry and a few others to rescue as many people as they could."

I gave him so much grief for not being around during the accident, she thought shamefully, *and he never said anything. How well do I really know him?*

"Your brother is a good man, Noor; just like you. In

fact, I'd even go so far as to say that you're the reason he's so kind." Harry winked at her. "He thinks the world of you."

"I'd do anything to keep him safe," she said softly. The door opened and Tinkerbell immediately stirred in Noor's lap. The woman turned her head and smiled at Silas as he strolled in. "Good morning, Dr Cherry."

"Good god, is it still only morning?" Silas said, pulling up a seat.

"Eleven fifty three," Harry confirmed. Silas rubbed his eyes and groaned. "Would you like some coffee, Dr Cherry?"

"No thank you," Silas said. "This isn't tiredness; mere psychological distress instead."

"We've all been through the wringer, Silas. We're here for you," Noor said, taking his hand in hers. He chuckled and planted a small peck of a kiss on top of her head.

"Thank you, sweet girl," he said warmly, "but my minor upset is nothing compared to your loss. I should be comforting you. No, I just had the displeasure of dealing with a phone call from my mother, the queen harpy herself."

"You don't get on?" Noor asked.

"That's an understatement. She's always been a nasty bit of work, that one; I'm glad that she and mum never got married." Silas noticed the slightly confused look on Noor's face. "My mum, whom I love dearly and gave birth to me, is a wonderful woman. My *mother* however, who was formerly my father, is not so pleasant. They were a heterosexual couple for the five years that they were together.

"Not long enough for my mother to be a decent parent, but long enough to insist that I be given her last name." He shook his head wistfully. "I've no problem with her being trans; it's all her grievous personality flaws that mean we don't get on."

"So you don't see her often?" Noor asked.

"Not as often as I used to," Silas said. "Both my parents are quite high up in the Ministry, so I saw them quite a lot when I was consulting."

Noor nodded; Silas had explained the Ministry of Supernatural Affairs to her and Dee whilst they were driving around all night. Harry opened his mouth to ask for clarification, but Silas held up a hand.

"I'll tell you later," he said, shoulder slumping with exhaustion. "Right now, I have one more patient to tend to and then I'm going to get a few hours of sleep."

"And who is this lucky individual?" Noor asked, offering him a square of chocolate, which he refused.

"You." He placed a bag on the table and pulled out a stethoscope. "Harry, would you be kind enough to give us the room, please?"

"Of course," he said, closing the door as he went out.

"I'm not sick, Silas," Noor said defensively, crossing her arms over her chest.

"If you don't want me to look at you, that's fine," he said, "but don't lie to me."

Noor felt her face flush as he continued to stare at her. *Shy told you about the coughing, didn't he?* She didn't voice her question, but judging by his nod, she didn't need to. She sighed, unfolded her arms, and pulled off her jumper.

"I've been having some breathing problems since the accident," she said quietly. "It started with just a dry cough, but now there's blood in it. The other evening it was so bad that I had to take my mask off and..."

She trailed off and stared at Silas.

"Yes, that was me." He smiled at her and placed the stethoscope to her chest. "Deep breaths, if you could, please."

She breathed as deeply and evenly as she dared, although the coughing set in on her fifth inhalation. She bent double as the pain in her chest flared once again, and Tinkerbell jumped on to the floor in a panic. Silas whipped off the stethoscope and fetched her a glass of water.

"Small sips," he said as he handed it to her. He felt the skin of her forehead with the back of his hand and frowned. "You feel like you have a temperature. Unfortunately, the digital thermometer they have here is broken, but I'll get Elsie to have a look at it."

"What's wrong with me?" Noor managed after a few shaky breaths. "Am I dying?"

"You're certainly not well," Silas said, taking one of her hands in his. "When your brother borrowed your gift, your condition seemed to worsen immediately; is that what it felt like?"

"Yeah."

"Hmm. You definitely have some significant damage to your lungs as a result of the chemical exposure, but it seems like you're trying to fight off some kind of infection. It could be residual contamination from the fire, but..."

"It might be something related to the Piper?" Noor asked. Silas nodded. "What do we do?"

"We keep an eye on it," he said in a measured tone. "I'm going to check you over every single day and I want you to come to me if you start feeling worse, even if it's just a little blip, okay? In the long term, I think the best thing for you is to deal with the whole Piper situation, but right now the first thing you can do for me is get some rest."

"I will," Noor said as she pulled her jumper back on. "Thank you for looking me over."

"Any time. Now, off to bed with you!"

"Are you coming?"

"In due time," Silas said, dropping to his hands and knees. "Firstly, though, I have to find my ferret."

The mattress was worn and a bit old, but to Noor Turner's exhausted body it felt like reclining on a cloud. She squirmed a bit, trying to get comfortable enough to sleep. She'd chosen the only room without anyone else sleeping in it, partly for privacy and partly to give her room to weep.

"I can't believe it," she murmured tearfully, "he was alive twenty four hours ago! How did this happen?"

Is it my fault? She did not dare to voice the question aloud, just in case the universe decided to answer her. She began to sob and thrashed violently in the bed as impotent rage flooded her body.

"What the fuck!?" she screamed at the ceiling. "How did any of this fucking happen!?"

Noor groaned in frustration and rolled over.

Instead of moving closer to the edge of her soft bed, she was resting on sharp gravel. Panicked, she looked left and right; either side of her were the cold steel rails of a train track. She scrabbled to her feet and she realised that she stood on the tracks near the little bridge just east of Dartford Station.

A loud horn sounded as a heavily laden freight train, tanker cars full of chemicals, slowed as it clattered towards the bridge. The signals flickered from green to red to green again, and the points snapped shut. She looked behind her and saw a second, much more modern train approaching at speed.

A quick glance at the points told Noor that the two would end up on the same track; the one that crossed the narrow bridge. The freight train had realised the same thing and had slammed on its brakes.

"STOP!" Noor screamed, frantically waving her arms and jumping up and down. The modern train showed no signs of slowing and as it grew nearer, she saw two things that made her blood run cold. The first was the logo of Eigenforce International emblazoned on the engine.

The second was that the train had no driver.

Suddenly, her addled mind realised where and, more importantly, when, she was.

I have to get out of here!

Noor tried to flee from the impending crash, but she was rooted to the spot, unable to even turn her head. As fear coursed through her veins, she remembered that Silas had told her things like this might happen.

"Seers exist for a reason," he'd said. "If you get a vision and you find yourself unable to look away, pay attention; there's something you're meant to see."

Courage, Noor, she thought as the Eigenforce train ploughed into the chemical tankers, igniting in a single blinding explosion. Time slowed to a crawl and the light seared her retinas, burning an impression of the scene before her into her brain.

Then the flow of time resumed and she was engulfed in the flames.

With a terrified scream, she sat bolt upright in her bed, drenched in sweat. She looked around the room, but she was still all alone.

It was just a dream, she tried to convince herself, but the after image of the explosion still glowed over her vision. As the intense retina burn faded away, she noticed a dark spot amongst the blinding light; it was the impression of a person.

"Someone was right there when it happened!" Noor whispered excitedly. As the bright spots continued to fade, more details of the person's face came into focus. After a minute or so, she could see the stranger's features clearly.

Only it wasn't a stranger at all.

Noor's breath caught in her throat as she recognised the person at the site of the accident; the person who might have caused the whole thing in the first place.

"Elsie!"

Chapter Nineteen – Mealtime Chatter

Archer

Archer winked at Roxanne as he shovelled a forkful of bacon and eggs into his mouth. He chewed slowly, savouring the smoky flavour of the crispy meat and the texture of the perfectly poached eggs.

"Enjoying yourself?" she asked, and he nodded happily. It was a little after two in the afternoon; their business in the morgue had taken longer than expected. Helen was still there; she would brief them fully that evening when she returned back to the safehouse.

I'm glad that you seem back to your old self, Archer thought as his partner took a long sip of her coffee before tearing into her third helping of fried bread. An elderly couple at the next table looked on with barely concealed disgust.

Archer chuckled as he selected a fried button mushroom with his fork, spearing it neatly on the tines. He popped it into his mouth and moaned softly in delight. The two Ravenblades were used to odd looks when they ate in public.

The more powerful an Exception's gift, the more calories they needed to consume to function properly. The Ministry canteen's portions were tailored to each individual; where Helen would not need to eat much more than an ordinary human as she rarely used her gift, Archer and Roxanne each required at least double that.

Ghosts needed the most of all; so much so that Charity Walpole's obscene eating habits were the stuff of legend in the Ministry. Still, their invisible colleagues were always rail thin, most likely as a result of the never-ending cancers they endured in the line of duty.

Archer shuddered at the thought of Charity; unbidden, images of her feasting on Joseph Evan's corpse filled his head. He put down his fork, his appetite suddenly quelled. Roxanne raised a curious eyebrow, but he shook his head.

"No sense us both being put off our food, Wags." She smiled at his words and continued to tuck into her late lunch. They always used their codenames in public settings such as restaurants and hotels; no sense in giving too much away, after all. "I'll let Helen catch you up later."

"Good idea," Roxanne said around a mouthful of fried potatoes. "This cafe is fucking amazing, isn't it?"

"Yeah, how did you find it?" Archer asked. The Coffee Pot, a little greasy spoon with red faux leather seats and white Formica tables, was a hidden gem, located just off of the town's main shopping promenade.

"I asked at the library," Roxanne responded. "I wanted to know if there was any unusual local history that could explain what we're seeing."

"And?"

"No such luck, although this town and the next one down the river do have a strong history with rats." She gathered up the remaining fried potatoes and smothered them in ketchup, grinning madly as she did so. It was their second bottle, much to the waitress's horror. "The whole place is riddled with plague graves. This entire area was devastated by the Black Death."

"That is interesting," Archer mused. "Maybe Helen will be able to make something of it. We should look into what was on Carmichael's train, though."

"Excuse me," said the old lady at the next table, "but are you with the accident investigators?"

Archer looked at Roxanne, an eyebrow raised.
I'll follow your lead, Toto.

"Yes," Roxanne said after swallowing her mouthful of ketchup with potatoes. "Yes, we are. Do you have any information about the accident that could be useful to our investigation?"

"Well, we didn't mention it at the time," the woman said, lowering her voice conspiratorially, "because the police looking into it were *those* people, you know? They're all in on it, of course."

Oh sweet Jesus.

"Now, Madge, the person we saw wasn't a Muslim!" The woman's husband was now leaning towards them too.

"You get white Muslims, Barry!" She tutted at him. "I've seen them, every Friday down at that Mosque; who knows what they get up to?"

Roxanne was just blinking, her expression blank. Archer quickly glanced around the little cafe, counting up how many witnesses he'd have to kill when Roxanne inevitably shot the old lady.

"What," Archer said with exaggerated patience, "exactly did you see?"

"Well," the woman responded as Archer pinned Roxanne's drawn firearm against the chair with one of his nimble feet, "this was just before the crash took place. There was a man with long hair-"

"It was a woman," the man interrupted, "not a man!"

"He wasn't an Arab," she snipped back.

"No, she was white!" He raised his voice and banged his mug on the table.

"He might've been Irish," she yelled back, before turning to Archer. "Are the IRA still active nowadays?"

"I wouldn't know," he responded, struggling to keep both a straight face and Roxanne's gun hand pinned in place. "Now, what-"

"Oh, it could've been one of the environmentalists!" The woman seemingly did not care that Archer had been speaking, or perhaps simply did not notice. "They're always causing trouble for decent people!"

"Or she might have been one of those left wing-" The man paused, interrupted by an extremely rapid beeping sound. "What is that?"

"Just my colleague's health monitor," Archer said off-handedly as Roxanne's heart rate exceeded two hundred and fifty beats per minute. "Now, what did this white person of indeterminate gender or political motivations actually do?"

"Oh, he was mucking about with the tracks," the old lady said after a moment. "He was also up around the signal box a few hours earlier."

"You spent all day looking out the window?" Roxanne managed after a few seconds of rapid breathing.

"The television was on the fritz," the man said defensively. "Anyway, we saw someone fiddling with all the stuff by the bridge."

"Thank you," Archer said as the couple got up to leave the cafe. "Your assistance is much appreciated."

"Is there some kind of reward?" asked the woman as they moved towards the door.

"We'll be in touch," Archer said, hoping that they

wouldn't pause to give him their details. Thankfully, they didn't and they exited the establishment without further comment. He exhaled long and loud before looking pointedly at his partner. "Put it away, Wags."

"I will when you move your damn foot, Bowman," she said sulkily. "Too many witnesses, anyway."

"Well," Archer said as he moved into a more comfortable position, "at least we got a potential lead out of all that."

"I guess so," Roxanne said, massaging her wrist. "Say, Bowman, *are* the IRA active these days? You all know each other, right?"

"You're cruising for a fucking busted nose, Wags," Archer said testily. He glared at her for a moment, but he couldn't maintain his anger at her slightly lopsided grin. Try as he might, he couldn't help but chuckle. "You're a right cunt sometimes."

"Takes one to know one," she replied.

"In all seriousness, it might be worth paying a little visit to Eigenforce International to get a shipping manifest for their train; that might be the start of this after all." He expected a nod from her, but all she gave him was a smug grin. "What?"

"Ask me about my day?"

"Why?"

"Just fucking ask, Bowman."

"Fine, you ludicrous woman. How was your day?"

"It was a bit of a bust, thanks." She settled back in her chair. "I went over to Eigenforce International to have a look for a shipping manifest. Unfortunately, someone had recently given the order to clean house; everything was shredded and torched, and the computers were wiped clean. No information whatsoever."

"That," Archer said, "is suspicious as fuck. The whole train theory definitely merits a closer look; maybe we should speak to the big man himself."

"I'd be agreeable to that," Roxanne said, cracking her knuckles. "We'll have to clear it with Dr Bitch first, though."

"We'll ask her tonight," Archer said. "Now finish your lunch. I want to do a bit of shopping before we head back to the safehouse."

It was almost midnight when Helen Mickelson's vintage ambulance pulled into the driveway. Archer and Roxanne were practising their close combat techniques when she walked into the living room.

"Well," she said, flopping into a chair, "that was one of the more disturbing days I've had in this job."

"Top three?" Archer asked as he dodged an impossibly fast punch from Roxanne.

"No," Helen said, kicking off her shoes. "Top ten, for sure, but I don't think it breaks into the top five."

"That's lovely, Helen," Roxanne said as she ducked under a sweeping kick, "please don't tell me about any of the other nine, ever."

"I won't," Helen said, digging into the white plastic carrier bag that she'd carried in with her. "Besides, at least four of them are above your clearance level."

She snared a container of Singapore Style Noodles and a pair of disposable chopsticks, then carried both over to the little dining table. She popped the lid off the takeaway box and sniffed her dinner. She smiled and separated the chopsticks.

That smells really good, Archer thought as his stomach growled. He'd had a pile of French Toast earlier in the evening, but he still had room for an intensely savoury snack. Helen noticed his hungry stare and grinned.

"There's plenty more in the bag; I don't know what you prefer so I got a selection."

"You are a life saver," Roxanne said as she strode over to the bag and pulled out a bag of sweet and sour chicken balls. She paused for a moment before also selecting a pot of special fried rice. She bounced gleefully as she carried her prize over to the table.

"You want me to get you a fork?" Archer asked as he went towards the kitchen.

"Of course," Roxanne replied. "I'm not Charity Walpole."

Snap!

The sharp sound of chopsticks breaking cut through the cheerful atmosphere. Archer looked at Helen, who was glaring at Roxanne.

"What's your fucking problem?" asked the Tracer as she leant across the table. Helen's eyes blazed yellow for just a moment as she put the lid on her noodles. Roxanne's stomach made an uncomfortable gurgling noise. "Oh, you bitc-"

Her words were cut short as she vomited all over herself.

The three Ministry agents remained stock still and silent for a few seconds, after which Roxanne burst into tears and ran in the direction of the shower. Archer stepped nimbly out of her way and glared at the doctor who had retrieved a second pair of chopsticks and resumed eating.

"Helen, what the fuck?"

"You are obviously not aware of this," Helen said between bites, "but I actually happen to be very close to the Walpole family; we all worked together in the

Hong Kong office. The Ministry is a web of connections, Agent Treen, more than you can possibly fathom.

"You would do well to remember that the next time you or Agent Wagstaff are tempted to insult a fellow operative in front of your colleagues."

"You didn't need to do that, though!" Archer protested.

"Do you know Special Agent Lin Yun?" Helen asked. "The Inquisitor?"

"Yes," Archer said. *Everyone knows her; she's fucking terrifying!* "Why?"

"She's Charity Walpole's mother, and my reaction is nothing in comparison to what she'd do to you. So, Agent Treen, hopefully you'll think a little more before disrespecting your colleagues again." Helen resumed her meal. "Eat up, Archer, and I'll fill you in on what I found out this afternoon."

The sound of running water reached his ears and he looked nervously at Helen.

"I'm sure she's learned a valuable lesson," she said with a wry grin, "and if she decides to escalate things, she'll learn just how deadly late stage meningitis is."

"Helen, please don't take this the wrong way, but things like this are the reason people don't like working with you."

She shrugged and finished her noodles.

Roxanne emerged from the shower fifteen minutes later, sulkily wrapped up in her pyjamas and bathrobe. She sat on the sofa and glared at both of them, her arms firmly crossed over her chest. Archer noticed that she had a small bucket with her, and gave her a sympathetic smile.

"You won't need that," Helen said. "I didn't give you

anything more than a single iffy stomach; for what it's worth, I was only aiming for nausea."

"I don't believe you," Roxanne said.

"Well, it doesn't matter either way." Helen sat back in her chair and stretched. "So, I'll give you the short version as I've not typed the long one up yet. Basically, we are dealing with some sort of airborne mutagenic contagion that is effective at the cellular level. It affects both living and necrotic tissue, although it is most effective in live subjects. Oddly, it has a preference for both rats and human children, although it does seem to affect all mammals.

"The entire town has been exposed; I took some of Dr Broom's blood and found evidence of the changes wrought by this thing. Immunity and resistance is not linked to physical health in any way. Mental fortitude seems to be the deciding factor for who succumbs and who survives. There have been instances of... well... there are unsubstantiated reports of previously normal humans developing supernatural gifts."

"Induction," Archer breathed, "it *is* real!"

"Unsubstantiated reports," Helen said for emphasis, "but it is certainly a turn up for the books."

"So what are we dealing with?" Roxanne asked. "What's the root of it all?"

"That's a bit more complicated..." Helen said evenly, choosing her words with care.

"I'll tell you what isn't complicated, Doc," Roxanne continued. "We have an eyewitness account of potential sabotage to the train tracks prior to the derailment, and Eigenforce International has burned their entire paper trail leading up to the crash; that's cause enough to force our way into their research division and sweep for whatever bug is causing this!"

"That's the complicated part," Helen said. "Although the effects are readily observable and the pattern of infection is easy to follow, there's no pathogen. We ran every single test in the book and turned up absolutely nothing.

"I do think hitting the Eigenforce Labs might be the best way forward. Good work on securing your leads, Roxanne. We'll make a concrete plan in the morning. Get some rest."

Archer watched her carefully as she walked out of the room before he went to join Roxanne on the sofa.

"This is bad, Roxy," he said, putting an arm around her. "Did you see the look on her face?"

"No, but she didn't sound scared."

Perhaps not, he thought, *but she looked fucking terrified.*

Chapter Twenty – Arming the Dogs of War

Elsie

Elsie handed the first of her newly-smithed long guns to Silas, who looked it over carefully. He opened the break and slotted one of her bullets into it; they were large calibre and would pack a considerable punch.

Silas snapped the weapon back together and aimed down the sights. Elsie had painted them with two different luminous paints that she'd found in the Collective's art supplies; she hoped that it would allow for more reliable accuracy in the foggy gloom.

"This is a very basic weapon, Silas," Elsie said loudly. "I'm going to cover your ears as this is going to be very loud."

"What about you?" he asked. She swept back her hair to reveal compact ear defenders that she'd built from a discarded set of headphones. "Alright then, Little Miss Show-Off. Where am I aiming for?"

"There's a playing card on a tree a hundred metres away," she replied, pointing it out. "Try to hit it as close to the centre as possible."

"That's not an effective distance, Elsie."

"I'm sorry, Silas. Would you like me to spend more time making something that can shoot farther than you can currently see?"

"Good point."

"Rule one; actually solve the problem you have, not the one you want." She covered his ears as he lined up the shot. He pulled the trigger and the weapon roared, bucking hard with the recoil. He staggered slightly, but kept his feet. Elsie removed her hands from his ears and smiled at him. "How was it?"

"We need rifles, Elsie, not fucking siege cannons!" He rubbed his shoulder and frowned. "But it works, that much is certain. Hopefully it shoots straight. How long will it take you to make more of these?"

"I can probably churn out another two today, with more tomorrow. Now I've got the basic pattern it should be simple enough. I'm going to widen the bore and add a choke to it for the shotguns I've planned out." She looked around the scrap yard. "I don't have any lead shot, but if I fill the shells with various metal shards, it will work just as well.

"Maybe even better," she said, cocking her head to one side as she pondered the question of ammunition. "Do you think flechettes would do well against our enemy?"

"Jesus, Elsie; I'm a doctor!" Silas said, horrified.

"Well, as a medical expert, do you think random irregular nuts and bolts would be more or less effective against the animated flesh we're facing than machine stamped steel flechettes?" Elsie looked him in the eye, no hint of a joke about her. The two remained in silence for a few moments before the arrival of a third person broke the spell between them.

"Hey," Dee said as she walked along the fortified wall to the place that Elsie and Silas were testing her makeshift rifle. "Will one of you teach me how to shoot?"

"With this?" Elsie said, holding up her latest creation.

"No, this," Dee said, holding up the handgun Silas

had given her in the Junction Building.

"I'm not sure it's worth it, Dee," Silas said. "We're unlikely to find any more ammo for it. However, if you give the gun to Elsie for a few minutes, I'll try and teach you something much more useful."

"Okay," Dee said, and handed Elsie the weapon. She quickly checked the safety was on before stowing it in her overalls. Silas beckoned for Dee to come closer.

"Now," he said, "I said that you were a Conduit and you can control electromagnetic radiation, yes?"

"Mhmm." Dee thought for a moment. "I think I picked up a radio transmission the other night by accident."

"What did it say?"

"Locked and loaded, Bowman," Dee said. "Does that make any sense to you?"

"I've heard that call sign before," Silas said. "If it is who I think it is, then the Ministry already has boots on the ground looking into this."

"That's good," Elsie said. "Isn't it?"

"Bowman, and his partner, Wags, have a tendency to leave a large civilian body count behind them. They're the worst kind of Cep Supremacists, but they are good at their jobs. We should try and contact them; they need to know what they're up against."

"Surely they'll have figured it out," Elsie said. "After all, we did."

"Yes, but these two are more of a 'shoot first and think later' breed. There's a very good chance that they've missed the obvious." He turned to face Dee. "Thank you for letting us know, Dee. Please keep us informed of any more transmissions you catch."

"Will do, Si. So, what are you going to teach me?"

"Yes, sorry, I got distracted there. I want you to quiet

your mind as much as you possibly can."

"Okay," Dee said, closing her eyes. "What next?"

"Reach out your left hand, fingers extended." She did so, her eyes still closed. "Now, feel all the electricity in the air around you; magnetic fields, radio signals, microwave broadcasts, and even sunlight. It's all electricity and magnetism, nothing more.

"Let it pour into you, filling you up like a battery."

Elsie's eyes widened as the fine hairs on Dee's arms began to stand on end. There was a gentle crackle as a tiny spark leapt between her outstretched fingers. Silas winked at Elsie and took a careful step backwards.

"Let that power move through you, like a flood. I want you to imagine it all pooling in your fingertips, but it is held there by a dam." The air around Dee's fingertips began to glow softly and motes of pale light began to circle her hand, going faster and faster with each passing moment. "Now open your eyes and aim your hand at a target."

She did as he asked, and pointed at a dead sapling ten metres or so outside the wall.

"Good. Now, I want you to do three things all at once; flex your hand, burst the dam, and focus your mind on the dead tree. Are you ready?"

"Yes."

"Then on my mark; three, two, one, now!" Silas yelled.

Dee twitched her fingers and a huge arc of lightning flashed through the empty air. It struck the tree with a blue flash and disintegrated it in an instant. It was all over in the blink of an eye and Elsie just stared, dumbfounded.

"Woah! Did you fucking see that!?" Dee yelled, bouncing up and down.

"Well done," Silas said, clapping softly. "With practice you'll be able to refine your skills even more; your punches will hit like tasers and you might even be able to deflect bullets. You have a very powerful gift, Dee; much more effective than a gun, isn't it?"

"Thanks, Mr Wizard," Dee said with a grin. "Oh, Elsie, Noor was looking for you. She said it was urgent."

"Maybe she's had a vision," Silas said. "We should all-"

"Just Elsie, Si," Dee said pointedly. "Besides, you can talk me through all the other cool things I can do with my gift."

"Of course," Silas said with a smile. "I'll catch up with you later, Elsie."

She made her way down from the wall, heading for the workshop in search of Noor Turner. Outside the safety of the wall, forgotten by all, was a playing card pinned to a tree; the ace of spades.

There was a bullet hole in the dead centre.

"There you are!" Elsie said. She'd been looking for Noor for almost twenty minutes and was about to give up when she decided to try the room that held the defunct analogue firewall.

Noor sat in the middle of the little room, lit by the green glow from the oscilloscopes and signal generators that lined the walls. Elsie shut the door behind her and pulled up a dusty chair to sit on.

"Dee told me that you were looking for me; is everything okay?" She smiled at Noor. *Damn, she's gorgeous.* Even though one of her eyes was blood red and parts of her face were scarred by chemical burns, Elsie found herself absolutely spellbound by the Seer's appearance.

"Thank you for coming," Noor said, a bit too formally for Elsie's liking.

"Have I done something wrong?" Elsie asked nervously.

"I don't know, Reichardt; you tell me."

"I... I'm not quite sure what's happening here."

"I had a vision, Elsie. I saw the derailment."

Oh shit.

"I was right there."

Oh fuck.

"I saw it happen. You were there." Noor pointed Elsie's Maxim 9 at the inventor's stomach. "Anything you want to tell me?"

She's not going to shoot me, Elsie thought. Noor frowned at her, and put her finger on the trigger. *Okay, she actually might.*

"Elsie?" Her voice was hard and she held the gun in a surprisingly steady hand. Elsie leant her head slightly to one side to get a better look at the weapon. "I know how to take the safety off. I'm not an idiot."

"I'm going to tell you," Elsie said, "but I'd really rather not get gut shot because your finger twitches. Can you please put the safety on?"

"Start talking," Noor said as she made the weapon safe. Elsie shifted uneasily in her seat. "Did you cause all this?"

"Yes," Elsie said sadly. "I caused the train crash, but you already know that. I assume the how isn't important either?"

"Not really, but I'm guessing you used your gift to make it crash?"

"Not exactly," Elsie said. "I did use my talent to engineer all the conditions to get the trains on to the same tracks; they were originally going to pass each other with no risk of an impact. I didn't want them to crash, though! In fact, I never even realised that was a possibility.

"The chemical train stopped exactly where it was supposed to, but Finley's train was-"

"Automated," Noor said sharply, "and it just kept on going!"

"But it shouldn't have!" Elsie yelled. "I programmed that fucking thing! It was absolutely supposed to stop in the event of a possible collision if it couldn't get out of the way in time. I didn't tell it to plough right through a fucking chemical tanker and there's no way I could've known it wouldn't stop.

"Someone changed the programming. It was probably Finley, or maybe Zelda; they're the only ones with sufficient access and skills to alter my work..."

"Who's Zelda?" Noor asked, the gun now completely lowered.

"Finley's adopted daughter. We only met once and she gave me a serious case of the creeps." Elsie shuddered just thinking about her. "She's only about three and a half feet tall and looks about twelve years old, even though she's nearly twenty; part of it is definitely all the plastic surgery, though."

"Why does a nineteen year old need surgical work?"

"She used to look super ugly, apparently, but this was before I met her." Elsie sighed. "Whatever Zelda asks for, she gets. I honestly think she might be some kind of android."

"Are you serious?"

"Completely," Elsie said softly. "You should've seen the shit we used to build, Noor. Things beyond your wildest dreams."

"Why on earth would you want to do that?"

"To make Prometheus feel small," she whispered tearfully. "I can't explain it, Noor, but there's something intoxicating, addictive even, about pure unrestrained creation; you never stop to ask if what you're doing is right, because all that matters is the fact that you can do it at all."

"So why did you want the train to stop?" Noor asked, bringing Elsie's focus back to the matter at hand.

"I wanted to take Pandora back from him. She wasn't Finley's to abuse and, with hindsight, I should never have built her. I guess it's for the best that she got destroyed." Elsie sighed and looked at Noor. "That's my entire involvement, and I give you my word that it's the truth.

"I fucked up and caused a huge disaster, for which I'm sure I'll end up in prison when all this is done, but that's all. I didn't deliberately set the Piper free."

There was a moment of silence.

"I believe you," Noor said quietly. "Does anyone else know what you did?"

"Silas might've worked it out," she said, "but if he has, he hasn't said anything."

"Let's keep it that way. I don't want you to go to prison, Elsie; everyone makes mistakes."

"Really?"

"Whoever changed the automatic train program is to blame, not you." She thought for a moment. "Don't tell Dee, though; she will probably try to kill you."

"She would definitely succeed," Elsie said, thinking of the destroyed tree with a shudder. "Any more questions?"

"Just one."

"Hit me."

"Do you think we're safe here?"

"No," Elsie said. "I'm making do with what I can scrape together, but we are woefully outgunned in this fight. We need better weapons."

"And?" Noor said smiling.

"And what?"

"I'm assuming that you have a plan to get some?" Noor said, before hastily continuing. "Weapons, I mean; get some weapons."

Elsie grinned at her and giggled slightly.

"Well," Noor asked, flushing red with embarrassment, "do you?"

"Yes," Elsie replied happily, "as a matter of fact, I do!"

<u>Chapter Twenty One</u> – Together We Fight

Noor

"We should go tomorrow," Elsie said as they walked towards the main hall. "Leave at first light, when the Piper's forces are in full retreat."

"Do you know where we're going?" Noor asked. *I'm so relieved that you're not behind this,* she thought. She hesitated for a moment and then slipped her hand into Elsie's. The other woman looked at her and smiled.

"Truth be told, Noor," she said as they walked, "I have no idea where the Eigenforce Labs are; they blindfolded me every time I went inside and it doesn't have any windows; hell, it might even be underground.

"I was hoping that someone here might have an idea or would know someone who would be able to find it." Elsie gave her hand a squeeze. "I know it's a long shot, but it's worth a try."

"Definitely," Noor said. *Not to mention that we'll probably get eaten if we stay here.* That thought gave her pause. "Elsie, did it feel like the Piper was coming for us specifically the other night?"

"It did," she said, "and I could feel something in the music; almost malice, directed right at us."

"Then why didn't it attack last night?"

They both stopped. The fog was suddenly more sinister than ever, and all the shadows seemed to hold dangerous secrets and concealed foes. Noor looked carefully through her goggles, keeping perfectly still the whole time.

There was a tiny hint of movement at the base of one of the scrap piles; it was so small that Noor was certain she'd imagined it at first. She was about to relax when a small rat dashed from the detritus and raced away from them.

"There!" Noor yelled as she took off after it. She ran as hard as she could, and Elsie kept pace with her. The inventor pulled a pistol from her overalls. *How long did she have that?* Noor wondered, but she discarded the thought almost immediately.

We have bigger problems.

"How did it get in here?" she said breathlessly as Elsie aimed the weapon at the rat, which was hopping strangely as it moved. "Shoot it!"

"No!" called a voice from the wall, and Silas came sprinting into view. "It's just Tinkerbell! Don't hurt her!"

Elsie lowered the weapon, but something in Noor's gut told her to keep pursuing the ferret. It didn't stop running and, instead of leaping into Silas's arms, it snarled madly as it dodged around him. Flecks of glistening saliva covered her owner's boots as he cried out in surprise.

"Tinks, what's wrong with you?"

It's just like the fox, Noor realised. *It wasn't rabid at all.*

"The Piper has taken her," she shouted. "Elsie, shoot her before we lose her again!"

The possessed ferret ducked and weaved through another pile of scrap and the two women struggled to keep up. It snapped at Barry as he stepped through a door before peeling off and sprinting towards the front gate. Noor could see a small gap beneath part of the wall and realised that Tinkerbell would squeeze through long before they'd get the gate open.

"Stop that ferret!" Elsie yelled.

The enslaved mustelid was almost at the wall when a blinding flash filled the gate yard. Noor brought up her hand to shield her eyes, but managed to see Tinkerbell's final moments. The ferret disintegrated as soon as the bolt of lightning touched her, and Noor heard Elsie breathe a sigh of relief as she lowered the gun.

"Well," Noor said, "that was the luckiest lightning strike I've ever seen!"

"Nothing lucky about it," Dee said smugly as she descended from the wall. Arcs of electricity flashed between her fingers and there was a swagger to her walk.

"You've been practising," Silas said breathlessly as he caught up to them. He took a long look at Dee. "You've practised a lot."

"I'm a quick study," she said back proudly as he gave her a solemn thumbs up.

"I'm sorry about your ferret, Silas," Elsie said.

"I should have seen it coming," he said sadly. "I should've said goodbye to her and ended it before she could fall under the monster's spell. I'm sorry, I just need a moment."

"Take all the time you need," Elsie said. She looked at Noor who was looking around frantically. "What's the matter?"

"When was the last time anyone saw Shy?"

They found him still in his bunk, pale and shivering violently. The veins beneath his skin were a dark spiderweb beneath the clammy surface. He was unconscious and muttering softly in his delirium. Noor could hardly bear to look at him.

"Oh, Shy," she whispered, "what's happened to you?"

"Is he hurt?" Barry asked anxiously. "This could be sepsis or some other kind of massive infection."

"He needs a doctor," Silas said softly, still tearful after Tinkerbell's death.

"You are a doctor!" Dee roared, slapping him over the head with a faint electrical crackle.

"He needs a good doctor, then!" Silas yelled in response. "I'm a pathologist! I'm trained to deal with them after they're dead, which looks like it won't be too long!"

The room fell silent.

Noor glared at Silas Cherry, holding his gaze until he looked away, suitably cowed.

"He," she said firmly, "is not going to die. I will not let him."

"May I look at him?" Elsie asked.

"Please do," Noor replied.

Elsie knelt beside the bed and closed her eyes. Noor looked on in confusion as Elsie periodically reached out to touch what looked like arbitrary points on Shy's body, seemingly pausing to listen to the aether as she did so.

"Her gift manifests through sound, especially music," Silas whispered in Noor's ear as Elsie worked. "She's touching him at confluences of his bodily energy, I think."

"Why?"

"To see what's wrong with his song?" Silas suggested.

That sounds crazy, Noor thought sceptically, before she realised that the entire situation they were in was completely unhinged. *Maybe she really is hearing what's wrong with him.*

I hope she can help him.

"Okay then," Elsie said softly as she opened her eyes. She turned to look at Noor. "I initially thought that the Piper might be taking him, but that's not what's happening."

"That's good news," Noor said. "So is it just an infection or-"

"It's not good news at all, Noor. If it was just a case of the Piper getting into him, we could just move him out of town and he'd get better." She took a deep breath before continuing, suddenly looking more tired than she had before. "His gift is the problem. He isn't under the Piper's sway; he's absorbed the Piper's power, including its evil."

"Does that mean he's turning into the Piper?" Noor asked, horrified.

"Yes, and I think he was the one who enslaved Tinkerbell." Elsie chewed her grimy fingernails, suddenly anxious. "What's happening here is akin to the pupation of a butterfly. If we don't halt the transformation soon, when he wakes up he won't be your brother any more."

"He'll be the Piper," Noor said softly.

"He'll be *a* Piper," Silas said. "There will be two of them, won't there?"

"I think so, yes," Elsie said. "In short, his gift is killing him."

"How do we help him?" Noor asked tearfully. "What can we do?"

"We can kill him," Silas said. "He wouldn't want to hurt any of us, that much is certain."

"Is this because he can hear the Piper's song?" Dee

asked. Elsie nodded. "Okay, then we just need to cut him off from it. Back in the house you managed to cut us off from the Piper, so can't we do that again?"

Noor grabbed Elsie's arm, suddenly hopeful.

"It's more complicated than that," Elsie said, exasperated. "He has internalised the song at every level. We'd need to both isolate him and then find a way to neutralise the song already inside him!"

"You don't need to yell at me," Dee said hotly.

"Then start giving useful suggestions!" Elsie sniped back.

"Fine," Dee said, "I will. We have enough scrap here to knock up a sensory deprivation chamber; that should isolate him, right?"

"Yes, but-"

"Then we can use the oscillo thingies to analyse the frequency or whatever of the Piper's song that's inside him. When you know what it is, you can set up a counter signal like you did last time, and I can put them in overdrive.

"Will that work?" Dee said, glaring at Elsie.

"I... I think it might," Elsie said, stunned.

"I'm jacked, sure," Dee said, "but it doesn't mean I'm stupid. Besides, I'm not losing anyone else to the fucking Piper, especially not Shy; he's just a kid."

"Do we have everything we need?" Noor said, still holding on tight to Elsie's arm.

"Not quite," Elsie replied. "I'd need a computer capable of complex signal analysis, along with a few other bits."

"Where do we find that?" Noor asked. Elsie opened her mouth, then closed it again. "I don't care if its dangerous, Elsie! My brother's life is on the line; this is not negotiable!"

"The Eigenforce Laboratory will have everything I need, along with enough weapons to make this place into a proper fortress."

"Alright," Dee said, "then we break in and take it."

"There's a problem," Elsie said. "I don't know where it is; every time I went there, they made sure I couldn't tell where I was."

"Fuck!" Dee yelled, and slammed a hand against the metal wall. Sparks flashed and flared as she made contact.

"Is it in Dartford?" Barry asked.

"That, or just outside it."

"Then I think I have someone who can take you there," Barry said with a knowing smile. "Wait here."

"Alright then," Dee said. "I'm coming with you."

"No," Noor said sharply. "We need you for the plan, and you promised James that you'd stay alive."

"I also promised to look after you!"

"Look after him!" Noor roared, drawing herself up to her full height, which was at least a head shorter than Dee. "Elsie and I can manage this on our own."

"But-"

"A small team is the best way to avoid notice," Silas said. "However, I'd like to go with you."

"You're the only doctor we have," Noor said, groaning in frustration, "and you need to look after Shy! You can't be in two places at once!"

"Of course I can," Silas said smugly. There was a flicker of inky blackness and a sinuous shape coiled out from behind his legs. The cat raised its eyebrows and hopped deftly on to Elsie's shoulder.

We can do this, Noor thought, hope kindling in her heart. *All we need to do is find the Laboratory and we can save Shy.*

"Hi, folks," Barry said as he led a cheerful looking young man into the room. "This is Roy, he's been a member of the Collective for a long time now. He can help you find your Eigenthingy Labs or wherever you need to go."

"Eigenforce Laboratory," the cat Silas said pointedly.

"Oh shit," Roy said, slightly nonplussed, "that cat can talk."

"Yeah," Elsie said, "there's a lot of weird stuff going on lately."

"I can relate, man. I can absolutely relate. We've all got a lot going on recently." He thought for a moment before nodding. "Yeah, Eigenforce Laboratory is underground, not far from Bluewater Shopping Centre. The main pedestrian entrance is actually hidden in Darenth Valley Hospital."

"How do you know that?" Noor asked. "Have you got a gift that lets you immediately locate things, like a human GPS?"

Roy chuckled and shook his head.

"No, no," he said with a smile, "I'm a postman. There's also another entrance in the woods nearby, but that's for trucks and stuff."

"We could use either one of those," Elsie said with a smile. "Right, Noor?"

"Yeah," Noor said confidently, "this is gonna work!"

"When are we leaving?" Elsie asked.

"Right now. We don't have any time to lose!" Noor looked down at her ailing brother. "Don't worry, Shy. I'm going to fix this and you'll be well again. I promise."

Little did she know that her conversation was being eavesdropped on by a team of hunters equipped with espionage level gear. Their leader nodded as he listened in.

"The Laboratory?" Mad Dog said with a grin. "Our girl is headin' home."

"What are your orders?" asked his second in command as Mad Dog strung his hunting bow.

"Kill the others however you want," he said softly, "but Elsie Reichardt's hide is mine."

Chapter Twenty Two – Rats in the Run

Archer

"Aha!" Archer yelled triumphantly as dawn's early light crept into the garden of the Ministry safehouse. He'd been perched atop the little patio bench for hours; Roxanne and Helen had gone to bed shortly after midnight, but he had continued the project he had started the previous evening.

On the way home from their late lunch at the cafe, Archer had insisted that they swing by a hardware shop. He had purchased both the tools and materials necessary to build something that was halfway between a lobster pot and a non-lethal rat trap.

He had finished it after his fellow agents had gone to bed, and had set it up in the quiet garden. He'd lain in wait for hours, gently bouncing on the balls of his feet and scanning his surroundings with a pair of night vision goggles.

His patience had been rewarded moments before the sun crept over the horizon, when the mechanism triggered with a loud clang. He deftly leapt from the bench and rushed over to the trap, completely oblivious to the gently warbling tune that filled the air around him.

His yell of triumph came when he saw the twitching, slavering rat that was hurling itself against the walls of the trap in an unrestrained frenzy. He heard one of its little legs snap, but still it continued to thrash and screech in frustration at its imprisonment.

As sunlight filled the garden, the music faded and the rat instantly became placid and docile.

"Well, that seems important," Archer said with a yawn. He pulled a few padlocks out of his pocket and secured the cage. He rattled each lock and pulled on them in turn, nodding to himself when he was certain that his prisoner could not escape.

"Archer Treen, what is all that fucking racket?" Roxanne yelled out of the upstairs window. When she saw him excitedly dashing around the garden with some kind of large crate in his hands, she went downstairs to find out what he was doing.

"What is going on?" Helen demanded as she entered the living room moments after Roxanne. Archer wrestled the locked trap through the back door and then carried it between the two women before depositing it proudly on the dining table.

"Oh my god," Roxanne said, already retching, "why would you bring a rat into our house, Archer?"

"To study," Helen said gleefully. "Excellent work, Treen."

"It's on the table," Roxanne said queasily, "where we eat..."

Archer saw what was about to happen and thrust the little bucket from the night before into her hands in the nick of time. Roxanne vomited up what little was in her stomach, with only thin streams of chyme coming up after the first wave. Her eyes were filled with tears as Archer rubbed her back.

"Get off me, fucking plague hands!" Roxanne said weakly, falling back into the armchair. She sat completely still, clutching the bucket for dear life and staring at the rat with unbridled horror. "Archer, what have you done?"

"I thought that Helen could take it down to the morgue and run some tests on it," he said, "whilst we get ready to storm Carmichael's labs. How about it, Roxy? Are you down for a full-on frontal assault?"

"Is there no way to get in subtly?" Helen asked.

"Unfortunately not, unless we take the civilian entrance through the hospital." Archer showed them his phone. "There's a set of woods here that have an unmarked road entrance to the Laboratory Bunker."

"That looks better defended than half our fucking military installations," Roxanne said. Archer smiled at her; the prospect of a good fight was the best medicine for his partner's germophobia. "Should we hit it overnight?"

"No," Helen said sternly. "Whatever this contagion is, it's more dangerous after dark. We need to move in the daylight and lock down before sunset. I think we should strike in the early afternoon, just after lunch."

"Gives us time to eat?"

"Not us," Helen said with a wicked grin. "Them."

"You're coming with us?" Roxanne asked, her smile faltering. Helen shook her head. "Then how does that help us?"

"I'll go in through the hospital entrance," Helen said. "I can use my medical credentials to bluff as far as I can, then I'll start hitting the whole place with the nastiest gastric bug they've ever had. That should incapacitate them long enough to give you an advantage.

"We work our way through the Laboratory and meet in the middle." Helen smiled at them both. "Does that sound like a plan?"

"Regrettably, it does," Roxanne said, "even if it does mean we're going to be fighting people covered in shit and puke."

She shuddered and Archer couldn't help but chuckle.

"I don't know what's so funny, laughing boy," she said angrily, "you're the one who fights close quarters, aren't you?"

"I... um..." Archer's grin disappeared as he realised that she made an excellent point. "I'll try not to get any in the Porsche, Roxy."

"I'm not sure taking that little green runaround of yours is the best plan," Helen said, her brow furrowed with concern.

"There are three of Carmichael's armoured vehicles there at all times," Archer said, "but they shouldn't be a problem for us, right, Toto?"

"The roads should be nice and clear," Roxanne said with glee, "so we can give them a real runaround. We'll get tooled up whilst you drop of the rat, Helen."

"Good idea." She looked once more at Roxanne, worried. "Are you sure that you can deal with APCs in a civilian sports car?"

"Most people couldn't, but I can."

Roxanne drummed on the steering wheel as they sped towards the Eigenforce Laboratory's cargo entrance. Archer had reluctantly strapped himself into the five point harness as Roxanne was running at almost a hundred miles an hour, weaving in and out of traffic, laughing as she did so.

Archer had one of Roxanne's more worrying weapons sat on his lap; an ERC 'Mad Moose' Tankbuster. It was a bolt action anti-tank rifle that fired 20mm depleted uranium SABOT rounds; the compact bullpup design was favoured by Roxanne Wagstaff, who preferred manoeuvrability when fighting anything with enough armour to call for the Mad Moose.

"Is this going to kick hard, Roxy?" Archer asked nervously. She nodded and winked at him.

"Don't worry, Archer, the car will take most of it. That bit there," she said pointing to what seemed like an oversized shoulder plate, "fits into this part of your seat, here."

Archer positioned the weapon as she had suggested and found that it was both incredibly stable and it wasn't relying on him to hold it up. It was, however, fixed firmly in place.

"How the fuck am I supposed to aim this?" he asked.

"You're not; leave that to me. I just need you to be the trigger man; fire when I tell you and reload. Leave the rest to me."

"We're coming up on the turning now, Wags," he said, switching to code names. He checked that his Taylor & Bullock Buccas were strapped to his legs and that his spare magazines were in place. *I hate guns,* Archer thought, *but they do have their uses.*

"Take the Moose down, Bowman," Roxanne called out as she flicked the Porsche on to the woodland road. "No need to show our hand early!"

Roxanne's driving pistols, four ERC Aurora 9mm's with extended mags, were in holsters strapped to the dashboard, roof, and driver's side door of the Porsche allowing her quick and easy access to a weapon whenever she wanted one.

They raced down Wood Lane and she armed herself with the door Aurora. Archer sank as far down in his seat as he could; he knew what Roxanne was planning to do and that it would involve Carmichael's private army shooting at them.

The bunker entrance flashed into view and Roxanne whipped the wheel around whilst killing their speed.

The Porsche swung into the little courtyard and began a one hundred and eighty degree turn. Roxanne fired wildly through her open windows as they flicked around, before standing on the accelerator as soon as they were facing the road again.

Even though Archer knew that Roxanne was perceiving time at a fraction of the pace he did, he was always startled when her seemingly chaotic shooting felled a different person with each and every round. *Damn, she's good.*

Archer took a heartbeat to toss an object the size of a croquet ball out of his window.

And then they were moving again, heading further down Wood Lane, but much slower than before. A quick glance in the mirror confirmed that two of the three APCs were following them, along with two motorbikes, each with two riders.

"We've got bikes, Wags!" Archer said, already knowing her response.

"I've seen them, Bowman." A huge grin was on her face as they tore down the foggy road. Ageing barbed wire fences lined the road on both sides, forming a natural choke point. With a roar of the engine, one of the bike teams passed the APCs and began to gain ground on them.

"He's got a riot shotgun, Wags."

"Hey, Bowman," Roxanne said gleefully, "watch this!"

He turned his head as she fired at part of the fence that was held taut by a fallen tree. Her bullet cut through the barbed wire, sending one end whipping through the air millimetres from the Porsche's paintwork.

The man piloting the motorbike was not so lucky.

The barbed wire hit hard, the spikes driving deep into his leathers. In a heartbeat, the wire pulled taut and both men were yanked, screaming, from the bike. Not a second later they were crushed beneath the huge wheels of the leading APC.

"Woohoo!" Roxanne yelled joyfully.

She's absolutely getting off on this, Archer thought with a grin. *Hopefully there'll be enough left for me later on.*

"We should be approaching the first junction, Wags," Archer said. He'd committed the route to memory before they set out. Maps were too cumbersome, after all, and a GPS had yet to be made that kept up with Roxanne's driving.

"Mount the Moose!" she yelled. "I'm gonna call it as we bank into the turn, okay?"

"Okay," Archer replied as a shock wave rippled through the fog around them. "That'll be my little surprise!"

He groaned and grunted to get the Moose in position, but he managed to lock it down before the turn. The muzzle poked a few inches out of the window, almost perpendicular to their direction of travel. Roxanne banked hard on to Green-Street-Green Road, turning a hairpin left and lining up the Moose with the leading APC.

"FIRE!"

"Aye, Captain!" Archer yelled as he pulled the trigger. The weapon roared like a cannon and the depleted uranium SABOT round tore through the APC; the dart compressed into plasma under its own force, vaporising the driver and lead gunner before expanding enough to blow the cab apart from within.

"Fucking hell!" Roxanne cheered as she straightened

out the Porsche; the second APC smashed right through the wreckage of the first, and the remaining bike team zipped around the outside. "Reload, Bowman!"

Archer heaved at the heavy bolt action mechanism, but it wouldn't budge.

"Hurry up, Bowman!" Roxanne saw someone emerge through a roof hatch in the APC; they seemed to have some kind of rocket propelled grenade launcher. "Now!"

"It's jammed!" The words were barely out of his mouth when she jabbed the brakes. He took the sudden change of momentum and transferred it into the weapon, clearing the jam. The spent shell casing clinked as it was ejected on to the street. "Ready!"

"On my mark, Bowman," Roxanne said. The motorbike was almost on them, and the man in the hatch was lining up his shot. He fired as she flicked the car around once again.

Archer screamed as the rocket shot past them. The motorbike was too close, and Roxanne's aggressive turn clipped it, sending it crashing into a brick bus shelter. Both men were killed instantly on impact.

"FIRE!"

Archer pulled the trigger once again, bracing against the sound. He saw the second APC explode from within and cheered before dismounting the Moose. He squeezed Roxanne's thigh as they gathered speed, racing away from the carnage.

"Now to knock on the front door," Roxanne said as she began their circuitous route back to the bunker entrance. "I hope Helen is having as much fun as we are!"

"Next time you have to buy a car, Wags," Archer

asked playfully, "why don't you just treat yourself to the tank you so obviously want?"

"I will when they make one fast enough! Now hold on!" Roxanne floored the accelerator, grinning like a woman possessed as she did so.

I love my job.

Chapter Twenty Three – There Are No Coincidences

Elsie

"Wait," Silas said as they approached the front gate.

Elsie looked at the talking cat patiently, but Noor sighed in exasperation. Elsie was about to explain what was happening when an inky black crow fluttered out of the bunk and circled the Dark Trees Scrap Yard a few times.

Oh shit, Elsie thought when she saw Silas's hackles raise and his ears swept back. He let out a soft growl that caught Noor's attention. She whirled around to face the others.

"What's-" she began, but Elsie held up a hand to silence her.

Mad Dog has all kinds of listening equipment, she thought. *How can I tell her?*

Do you sign? Elsie asked. **Even a little?**

Noor just stared blankly at her and Elsie felt her frustration building. She mimed holding a gun, then pointed to the treeline beyond the wall, before finally tapping her own ear. *I hope that was clear enough.*

Silas looked at Elsie and rolled his eyes. He popped out one claw and quickly traced a few sentences in the soft earth to explain that Mad Dog and his men were lying in wait for them.

What do we do? Elsie signed at Silas.

I'll try and get Dee to cover us, he replied, his feline paws managing BSL with surprising ease. **We might have to make a break for it.**

He noticed Elsie's obvious discomfort and shook his head tiredly.

I know watching a cat sign is upsetting, but please try to focus. Silas quickly scribbled out a few more lines to bring Noor up to speed. Much to both their surprise, she crouched down and scratched out a rough map of the local area. She highlighted the nearby main road and tapped her wrist and held up a hand with all five fingers splayed.

We need to be there in five minutes, Elsie thought, and gave her friend a nod. Noor tapped her own chest and signalled for them to follow her. Elsie stood up, grinning. *Having a Seer is such a huge advantage, even if she is new to this.*

Elsie pulled out the handgun that Dee had given her, disabling the safety with a flick of her thumb. The crow still wheeled overhead, giving Silas a literal bird's eye view. He scrabbled up on to Elsie's shoulder, which was fast becoming his usual spot.

The crow dived into the undergrowth, cawing and scratching as it went. Noor flung open the gate and ran. Elsie was hot on her heels as an arrow hissed through the air, narrowly missing the cat on her shoulder. Silas hissed and the bird immediately switched its target.

The gate clanged shut behind them; they were on their own now.

I wish I'd managed to finish more of those guns.

Elsie aimed the pistol in the approximate direction of the capture team and fired into the bushes; grouped bursts of three, just like Mad Dog himself had taught her. Noor was getting away from her, but Elsie backed up slowly, continuing the suppressing fire until her weapon was empty.

When the magazine was spent, she turned tail and ran, quickly catching up to Noor who was having some difficulty breathing. *I wish I could carry you,* she thought as another arrow flew past, missing her by an even narrower margin.

The sound of the occasional passing car gave her hope and she pushed herself to keep running, careful to keep between Noor and the capture team at all costs. *I don't care if they hit me,* she thought, *but I have to protect her.*

The Seer was coughing and spluttering in her mask as they finally reached Princes Road. Elsie shoved the staggering young woman on to the empty asphalt, certain that she would know what to do next.

The rumble of an engine caught Elsie's attention and she turned to look down the road.

A white van was approaching, chugging up the hill as it went. Elsie squinted, trying to make out the details in the swirling fog. *That is a strange looking van,* she thought, but her mind was interrupted by Silas leaping from her shoulder and racing into the middle of the road on his hind legs.

He jumped up and down, waving his paws frantically.

"What the fuck?" Elsie said.

Strong hands gripped her shoulders from behind and span her around to face the forest. It took a moment for her to realise that Noor was probably trying to show her something, but before she could ask for clarification an arrow streaked through the bushes.

The van slowed to a stop as the projectile struck Elsie in the centre of her chest, and she crumpled to the floor.

"Elsie!" Noor screamed, dropping to her knees as a second arrow flew through the air where she had just been. Three men wielding tasers emerged from the treeline and made a beeline for Elsie and Noor.

Elsie heard the sound of a car door slam, followed by the rapid clatter of shoes on blacktop. One of Mad Dog's men was yelling at them. Noor buried her face in Elsie's hair and wept.

"Get back in your fucking car," he called through the mist, brandishing the taser. "I will not hesitate to use force on you, so get lost!"

"I'm not going anywhere," said an older woman. Elsie rolled her head back and saw a lady wearing a heavy coat over black surgical scrubs. Silas was at her feet, and softly calling out the positions of Mad Dog's men. "Thank you, Silas."

How does she know his name? Elsie wondered. Her chest was throbbing and every breath hurt, but even so, she turned to face the men that had been hunting her.

"This does not concern you," the man continued, "so just fuck-"

His words were cut short as he, along with the other two men, vomited blackish blood before collapsing to the ground in violent convulsions. Blood streamed from every opening and after a few seconds they shuddered before falling completely still.

The woman exhaled heavily and took a step back before leaning on her vehicle.

"I think that's all of them," she said. She tried to stand up straight, but slumped back down again. "I'm getting too fucking old for fieldwork."

"When did you get haemorrhagic fever?" Silas asked, clearly concerned. Elsie took a slightly deeper breath and was relieved to find that nothing was broken. Noor was still sobbing.

"It was Marburg, and I was in Uganda in the late nineties on an operation..." The woman shook her head, suddenly aware of the situation before her, and rushed over to Elsie. "Oh my god, are you hurt?"

"A bit bruised but otherwise fine," Elsie said. She pulled the three-bladed broadhead out of her overalls and let it clatter to the ground. She breathed heavily and gently stroked Noor's arm, making reassuring noises as she did so.

"But, you, you were dead!?" Noor said between sobs. "I put you in the path of that arrow! I... I killed you!"

"I think you actually saved me," Elsie said, pulling her overalls open. She had jury rigged several pieces of Pandora to make a protective vest. "There's a gap under the arm, and if I'd still been looking down the road Mad Dog's arrow would've gone right into my heart.

"Thank you," Elsie said, taking Noor's masked face in her hands. "You should listen to those Seer impulses more often!"

"I hate to break up this little sapphic moment," Silas said, "but we are on a bit of a time limit, what with Shy being terminally ill and all."

"I can help you," the woman said. "I'm a doctor and-"

"This is beyond regular medicine," Elsie said, getting to her feet. "We know how to help him, but we need to get some things first. Is there any chance that you could give us a lift to the Darent Valley Hospital, please?"

"Of course," she said, "get in. That's actually where

I was headed anyway."

"How fortuitous," Silas said, not sounding surprised in the slightest.

"I suppose I don't really have luck any more, do I?" Noor asked, still sniffling slightly.

"You most certainly do not," Silas replied cheerfully. "And the Tangle seems to be on our side for the moment, which I think we should take full advantage of."

"You talk about it like it's alive," Noor said.

"Isn't it?" Silas said playfully as he hopped into the white van which was, upon closer inspection, a vintage ambulance. The three women followed, squeezing on to the bench seat in the front. Silas, now comfortably situated atop the heater vents, stretched out before looking at his travelling companions with a twinkle in his eyes.

"What?" Elsie asked.

"I was just thinking that introductions are in order. Wouldn't you agree?" Before she could respond, Silas pointed a paw at Noor. "This lovely young lady is Noor Turner. She is a Seer and was kind enough to take us in during our time of need. Unfortunately, one of her friends was taken from us a couple of nights ago, so we're all a bit tender at the moment and I'd ask that you treat her nicely.

"This is Elsie Reichardt," he said, moving his paw to point at her. "We initially came together as a business partnership, but I would like to say that we've at least reached the level of comrades in arms, if not outright friends. Elsie is also an Exception, but her gift is unique and a bit fiddly, so I'll let her explain it to you in due course.

"Lastly," he gestured at the woman behind the wheel

as he spoke, "we have Dr Helen Mickelson, one of the most senior field operatives at the Ministry as well as a highly competent medic. I'm sure that you've already worked it out, but she is a Blight, which means that she can make people sick; fatally so, it seems.

"Elsie, you'll get on particularly well with her, seeing as you're both war criminals," Silas said with a lazy yawn.

"Silas!" Helen said sharply.

"I am not a war criminal!" Elsie replied, outraged.

"Biological warfare." Silas said with venom. "Flechettes."

"What's a flechette?" Noor asked after a few seconds of silence.

"You sweet, innocent thing," Silas said. "Don't let these two corrupt you, Noor."

"You've not introduced yourself," Elsie said to the cat.

"I don't need to," Silas replied haughtily. "Everyone here already knows who I am. Helen doesn't seem at all fazed by a talking cat, does she?"

"That's a good point," Noor said before turning to Helen. "How do you know Silas?"

"She's known me my whole life," Silas said playfully, "haven't you, Mum?"

"Yes," Helen said with an exasperated sigh, "this unfortunate wastrel is my son. I'm assuming that one of these two is your so-called apprentice?"

"No," Noor said, "that's my brother, who is gravely ill."

"Yes, you mentioned."

"So can we please go a little faster?" Noor's frustration was palpable, and Elsie gave her a friendly wink. "I'd rather get to the labs sooner than later."

"Be careful what you wish for," Elsie muttered.

"Do you know about the Eigenforce Lab?" Helen asked.

"I used to work there, for my sins, and believe me, it is not somewhere I ever thought I'd hurry back to." She looked out of the window, watching the asphalt roll by. "You'll understand soon enough."

Please don't judge me by what you see.
It wasn't all my fault.

Chapter Twenty Four – The Cold Heart of Progress

Noor

Helen led them through the hospital, walking briskly as she did so. Noor struggled to keep up, her chest still burning from the earlier sprint. Elsie was watching their backs with Silas, who remained perched on her shoulder.

They're an odd pair, Noor thought, *but I do feel safer with them than on my own.*

She let her eyes linger a little longer on Elsie's face, enjoying the angular lines, high cheekbones, and overall appealing appearance of her companion. She felt a small flutter, almost too gentle to notice, behind her navel and let out a small gasp.

"Are you alright?" Elsie asked, taking Noor's hand in hers. Before she could respond, Noor's vision was overtaken by a sudden flash of the future.

She walked out on to the verandah of a small house. The air was warm and the wind was blowing gently, causing soft whitecaps in the azure sea. She had a glass of fresh lemonade in each hand, the ice clinking quietly as she moved.

I'm older, she realised; her hands were lined and the first few liver spots were appearing. She approached a seated woman with grey hair who smiled at her lovingly. Noor placed the glasses on the little table that sat between the chairs and winked at the other woman.

"Noor?" Elsie said, shaking her gently.

The vision faded and the real world snapped back into focus. It was only when she saw her friend's eyes that she finally recognised the woman from her vision.

"Elsie?" she asked.

"Yes, Noor, I'm here." Elsie's voice was concerned, yet also had the vaguest hint of affection, as if she was trying to conceal it. "Did you see something?"

"I..." *What do I tell her?* "I did, but it was a long time in the future; just a nice day in the sun."

"That's promising," Elsie said with a smile. "I guess that means we succeed here."

"It doesn't work like that," Silas said sharply. Two porters walking down the corridor stared in shock at the talking feline. "The future is malleable and can be rewritten just by knowing about it, so unless what you saw was imminent, put it out of your mind.

"It's no more true than an idle daydream."

Does he know what I saw? Noor wondered as they continued on their way. One thing was certain, however; Elsie still held her hand and it made her feel safe, protected, and cared for. *Just put it out of your mind, Noor; listen to Silas.*

"Even if it was just a daydream," Elsie said conspiratorially, "I hope it was a good one."

"It was," she said, blushing slightly.

"I think we're here," Helen said, frowning. A heavy door without windows was set into the wall in front of her. A keypad with a full alphabet and all ten numbers was beside it. "I'd hoped for some sort of reception, truth be told; somewhere that we could talk our way in. This looks like it takes a code that's-"

"Thirteen digits long," Elsie said. "Even with my specialist codebreaker, it would take almost a million years to get through them all."

"I guess we better get started," Silas said wryly from Elsie's shoulder. She grinned at him and danced her fingers across the keyboard, typing in a code. There was a soft bing and the door slid open. "I thought they blindfolded you when they brought you here?"

"They did," Elsie said with a smile, "but Finley only types with one finger and always rests it on the F key before he starts. It's just a case of extrapolating the rhythm from there."

"Are you a Shriek?" Helen asked.

That sounds dangerous, Noor thought as Elsie shook her head.

"No," Silas said. "She's much, much more frightening than that, but we'll catch you up later. Elsie, will you do the honours?"

"Of course," she said with a grin, and took Noor's hand once again. "Follow me."

"I'm frightened," Noor whispered to her as they descended the stairs to the underground laboratory.

"It's okay," Elsie replied in hushed tones, "I'll keep you safe."

I hope so, Noor thought. *I've suddenly found a future worth living for.*

"When we get in there," Helen said softly, "the two of you get whatever weapons you can lay your hands on. The more of us there are, the faster we'll get through Carmichael's forces."

"And if we hadn't have been here?" Elsie asked, her eyebrow raised questioningly.

"I would've had the strength to incapacitate everyone down here, but I burned most of that energy rescuing you," Helen replied tersely. "You're welcome, by the way."

"I was just asking," Elsie said. "I know where the general use weapons are, so I'll point you to them."

"What about you?" Noor asked, trembling at the thought of having to hold a gun again.

"I'm going to my section of the lab. There's a bunch of data I need to get, along with my computer."

"You'll be unarmed," Helen said.

"I've got a few toys of my own design stashed down here," Elsie said with a grin. "I'll be more than fine."

I can't do this, Noor thought, her heart pounding in her ears. *I don't ever want to hurt anyone, let alone kill them.*

"I don't want a gun!" she said suddenly.

"Don't be ridiculous!" Helen's voice was sharp as a razor and cut her twice as deep. "Everyone needs to pull their weight!"

"You don't have to, Noor," Elsie said, squeezing her hand.

"Yes, she does!" Helen replied hotly. She went to go on, but Silas stopped her with a hiss.

"She is not a Ministry Agent," Silas said with considerable venom. "She is just trying to save her brother. You do not get to tell her what to do."

"But-"

"Who are you? Harper!?"

That silenced Helen, who stared at the ground for a few seconds before continuing down the stairs.

"When the fighting starts," Elsie continued, "come with me and keep your head down; you can help me load up all the equipment I'll need to save Shy."

"Thank you."

"Who else are we expecting?" Silas asked his mother. "Unless of course you've finally succumbed to dementia and this is your euthanasia method of choice?"

"You are a hateful child, sometimes," she hissed, "and Archer Treen and Roxanne Wagstaff are attacking from the other entrance."

"Oh, fucking fantastic," Silas muttered. "Of all the-"

"Quiet!" Elsie said, holding up a hand to halt them. She turned to face Noor and unbuckled the belt she wore over her jumpsuit. The young Seer felt herself turn beetroot red as Elsie pulled the poppers of the jumpsuit open and shrugged it over her shoulders. Silas hissed slightly and leapt to the ground.

"What are you doing?" the Swarm demanded.

"I am keeping a promise," Elsie whispered. She pulled off the makeshift body armour and handed it to Noor. "Put this on, I'll help you adjust it in just a moment."

Noor tried to look away as Elsie's bare breasts jiggled slightly as she pulled the jumpsuit on once again. Before buckling the belt, she pushed a small button and a hidden knife popped free. She kept it in one hand as she tightened the fabric around her waist.

"Noor!" Elsie said insistently. The Seer blinked for a moment and then pulled the jury-rigged chest plate over her head and wriggled into it. Noor was surprised at just how flexible and comfortable it was, and gasped as the material adapted to the soft contours of her body.

"How is it doing that?" she whispered, awed by the versatile material.

"I'm good at what I do," Elsie replied with a smirk. "I'll go over the specifics later with you, if you want."

Before she could respond, all four of them heard the sound of approaching boots on the tiled floor. Elsie pushed Noor back and Silas hopped on to her shoulder. Helen stepped forwards, but the inventor shook her head and waved her back.

Two men in grey riot armour, carrying compact guns, rounded the corner. They looked at Elsie, who had the blade concealed in one hand, and then at Noor and Helen.

"I'm sorry, ladies, but there has been an incident at the main entrance. If you could please proceed back up the stairs..." The soldier's voice petered out as he noticed Silas, who was crouched on Noor's shoulder. He pulled up his visor to get a better view and the cat pounced.

"Oh my-" the second man began, but his words were quickly replaced by a wet gurgle as Elsie stabbed the little knife into his throat. He slumped to the floor as he drowned in his own blood. Beside him, his brother in arms screamed and flailed at his face.

"Get it off me!" he cried as he batted at the cat. Noor looked on in horror as Silas's tail whipped around and a barbed stinger pushed through the fur at the very tip. He jabbed the stinger into the man's neck three times in lightning succession before leaping back on to Noor's shoulder.

The soldier fell to the ground gasping as his throat began to swell up. His face turned an angry red colour and the light left his eyes. In mere seconds, he stopped twitching; both men were dead.

Silas retracted the stinger with a moist *thhpt* sound.

"I didn't know you could do that," Helen muttered. She looked down at the dead man. "Honey bee venom?"

"Originally," Silas said slyly. "As for the unusual abilities I possess, you can speak to Harper about that."

"Have you ever fired one of these before?" Elsie said, picking one of the guns out of the dead man's grip. Helen shook her head. "This is a KRISS Vector SMG. It fires on full auto, but unlike most submachine guns, it has surprisingly little recoil. These have holographic sights, so it's just a case of putting the red blip over your enemy and pulling the trigger. Make use of the foregrip and you won't need to worry too much about muzzle drift."

"You know your guns," Helen said warily as Elsie handed her the weapon.

"I do. Take these," she said, offering up three spare magazines. "The only downside with the Vector is that it eats up ammo like there's no tomorrow."

"How fast?" Silas asked.

"Twelve hundred rounds a minute." Elsie said with a grin. "Does it matter?"

"No, but I do enjoy seeing you get excited over weapons, you absolute ghoul." He cocked his head at her. "I'm guessing that you convinced dear Finley to adopt these nice little toys?"

"He did say that money was no object, and they are perfect for close quarters firefights." Elsie slung the second Vector over her shoulder. "Helen, you and Silas go that way. Noor, follow me, and stay down."

Helen and Noor nodded in affirmation, and then went their separate ways. Noor held on to the back of Elsie's belt, her heart racing. She crouched down, trying not to openly cringe or cower, but they were completely out in the open.

There was a faint series of beeps, and Elsie led her through a doorway; it was flush with the wall and Noor hadn't even noticed it. When they were inside, Elsie whistled a short, albeit complex, tune and the light above the door changed from red to blue.

"What does that mean?"

"The door is locked down," Elsie said, "and the windows are single crystal reinforced sapphire; even anti-armour rounds aren't getting through that."

Noor stood up and looked around the room they were in; it was a hexagonal space around three metres high, with each wall measuring about ten metres long. *This is her office!?* The space was crammed full of gear, along with two flatbed trolleys that Elsie gestured to.

"Get those and put everything from shelves 3-C to 3-G on them. I need to grab a bunch of data from the main computer. If there's any space left on the trolleys, add as much as you can from the shelves marked with a 'V'; those are experimental weapons.

"Clear?" Elsie asked as her fingers hammered away on the keyboard. The ten screens before her all displayed something different and Noor's head started to spin; *this can't be real, it's too crazy!* "Noor, dammit, are you clear on what we need to do?"

"I think so, yes," Noor said, walking over to shelf 3-C. "At least we're safe in here."

"We are," Elsie said as the sound of gunfire reached their ears, "but we need to go through the main lab complex to get out of here, so the quicker we're done in here, the fewer reinforcements I need to face down."

There was a loud bang, almost like an explosion, and Noor dropped to the ground, whimpering.

"I can't do this!" She yelled and covered her ears, sobbing and screaming. "Elsie, we're going to die down here!"

"Noor!" Elsie said, leaving the computer and joining

her on the floor. "We are going to get out of here alive, I promise you that. I said that I would look after you, didn't I?"

"Mhmm," Noor mumbled.

"We are going to get what we need. We are going to get out of this fucking lab, and I am going to save your brother. We are going to work out how to defeat the Piper, and then we're going to do it. I will make sure that we do."

She stroked Noor's hair before continuing.

"When all this is done, I am going to take you out for the best dinner that we can find in this town and I will give you the most carefree night you've ever had. I promise that all this will happen, Noor, but right now I need you to be brave and help me load these trolleys.

"Can you do that for me, please?"

"Yes," Noor said. She reached out with one hand to find the reassuring patterns and irregular whirls of the Tangle, drawing strength from it. She looked around and saw that certain boxes were glowing faintly on the shelves.

Those are the ones, she realised. *Thank you.*

She got to her feet and began loading up the glowing crates as quickly as she could; by her estimate, the ones with the golden halos would perfectly fill the trolleys. The items from the number three shelves were easy, but she ignored the weapons that Elsie had directed her to, instead pulling another large crate on to the trolley.

Elsie was too distracted to notice what her friend was doing; she was lost in the data. Noor finished up and, just in case, balanced a few weapon crates on top of the leading trolley. She picked the submachine gun up from the floor.

I'll give it to Elsie when we get going, she thought.

"And that is that," Elsie said as the screens began to flicker and glitch. A thin coil of smoke emerged from the computer tower as Elsie slipped a slim laptop into a satchel that hung from her shoulder. "Good job, Noor. We'll be out of here in a moment; just let me get tooled up."

Elsie fitted a digital eyepiece over her right eye and synchronised it with a curious handgun that she slipped into a holster on her chest. She slipped a mechanised gauntlet on to her left hand and flexed her fingers with a grin.

"What're those?"

"I'm hoping you don't have to see," she said, "so I'll tell you later. Let's get out of here!"

Noor tried to hand her the Vector, but Elsie shook her head and told her to hang on to it for the moment. She flicked a switch on each of the trolleys and affixed a metal rosette to Noor's chest. Elsie wore one too.

She gets stranger and stranger with each passing moment.

"Silas, Helen," Elsie yelled as they burst out of the hexagonal office, "we are out of here!"

The sound of screaming and gunfire filled the air as Noor and Elsie ran through the desks towards the exit. The Seer almost screamed as a black cat, covered in bloodstained spikes and hissing like a snake, leapt on her trolley.

"Don't stop, Noor!" Silas yelled. "We aren't the only ones down here!"

Suddenly Noor was seized by a compulsion to move. Unbidden, she snatched up the Vector, flipped off the safety, and fired into the smoke that was filling the underground laboratory. The gun purred in her hand and there were a dozen sparks in the air as she instinctively shot a barrage of bullets out of the air.

She turned to look at her attacker; a gobsmacked woman with bunched locs and a heart monitor on her wrist. She brought a second pistol to bear on Noor, who dropped the Vector and ducked down.

The woman was about to fire when she doubled over, clutching her stomach. A short man dashed over to her, putting a hand on her back,

"Wags, are you hit?"

"She isn't!" Helen yelled. "Will everybody fucking stand down!? We're all on the same side."

The woman, Wags, glared at Helen and pointed the gun at her instead.

Elsie immediately drew her own pistol and aimed it in the direction of the strangers.

"Oh, wonderful," Silas said sarcastically, "we're all going to die."

Chapter Twenty Five – Unforced Errors

Archer

"I said to stand down!" Helen yelled.

Archer looked angrily at the misfits with her; a scarred young woman, possibly Indian or Pakistani, a tall woman, slightly older than the other and wearing some kind of sci-fi getup, and a mutant black cat.

He stared at this last member for a moment, before recognising the lazy sardonic gaze of Dr Silas Cherry; the murderer who'd narrowly talked his way out of the death penalty after slaying Teaser Malarkey's partners.

"That's Silas Cherry," he said to Roxanne, who was even closer with Teaser than he was. "Maybe fate is on our side today, Wags?"

"It isn't," said the scarred Asian woman firmly. Whilst she was obviously terrified, she trembled with indignation at Archer's words. She looked at Roxanne. "Put down your gun."

"You made me miss," Roxanne hissed angrily. "I never miss."

"I'd recommend that your friend puts down her gun," Archer said, gesturing to Elsie. "Otherwise things are going to go really badly for your little crew."

"I can slow down time," Roxanne said smugly, "so I'll just dodge whatever you fire at me. Your not-so-pretty friend probably can't do that, and by the time you get a bead on me, Bowman will be on you.

"You're fucked."

Instead of lowering her weapon, the woman just chuckled.

"This is a Reichardt Yoichi," she said, tapping the

side of her weapon. "My eyepiece has painted each of you with three targets and has programmed them into the rounds in the pistol; electrically accelerated smart flechettes that will seek you out, even if you move.

"They move at Mach 6, just so you can decide if you really can outmanoeuvre them."

The silence was deafening.

Archer opened his mouth to respond, but the woman cut him off.

"I should mention that they're coated in carbamate, which is an extremely potent neurotoxin; if they so much as graze you, you'll be dead before you hit the ground."

There was a heartbeat of tension before Roxanne lowered her gun. Archer sighed and looked at Helen Mickelson, his eyes full of judgement.

"Nice friends you got there, Helen; a murderer, and a war criminal in the making. Absolutely charming!"

A gunshot rang out from across the room and there was a static flicker as something deflected it from the armed woman; it ricocheted into a desk nearby. The woman sighed, flicked a switch on her gun, and glanced at the shooter. A single light glowed green on the weapon's magazine and she fired without looking.

There was a soft electric hum followed by a scream as the gunman was struck by the flechette.

"Jesus fucking Christ," Archer said, "who the fuck are you?"

"Elsie Reichardt," she said. "This is Noor Turner, and Silas Cherry. It seems you already know Helen."

"Reichardt?" Roxanne said, her brow furrowing before her eyes lit up in realisation. "Finley Carmichael's ladyboy inventor?"

Elsie frowned at Roxanne's words, and Archer

laughed.

"Ooh, I think you touched a nerve there!" He smirked at Elsie. "So, what brings you down here? Are you here on altruistic business or are you just looting the place to make a quick buck when the Eigenforce empire crumbles?"

"We're getting weapons to defend ourselves," the scarred woman, Noor, said. "Along with things to help my brother."

"Is he a cyborg in need of spare parts?" Archer quipped. *That deflection field looked like it was just peripheral,* he thought, *so if Roxanne can get a direct shot, we can take both of them down.*

"I wouldn't risk it," Noor said softly, her voice almost dreamlike. "I mean, your partner dies anyway, but you'll both die down here if you try and shoot us."

"How-"

"I'm a Seer," she said.

"A fucking powerful Seer," Silas purred, "and she's saved our skin multiple times already even though she's completely untrained. I'd listen to her."

"Shut up, murderer!" Archer yelled. He had been standing still for too long and he was growing restless and irritable. He glanced around, angry that the entire mission seemed to be for naught. *This is just a fucking computer office! Where's all the fucking monster rats and undead contagion!?*

A steel door with the word 'Containment' emblazoned on it caught his eye and he grinned. It was locked by a keypad, but it swung inwards; it would not pose too much of a problem for him. *Three hits at the most.*

Archer squared up to the door and broke into a sprint. He quickly accelerated, ignoring the cries and protests from Helen's new friends. He drew his body up as he approached the door, hitting it at top speed and transferring all of his momentum into it.

The door flew off its hinges with a squeal of ruined metal. It clanged into the corridor beyond and an alarm began to screech.

"Containment Breach!" called out a computerised voice. "Containment Breach! Sealing the exits!"

Unearthly howls echoed down the breached corridor and shadows were cast on the wall as nightmarish forms made their way towards Archer.

Oh shit, he thought, *that was not a good move.*

"Containment breach! Deploying countermeasures! Deploying countermeasures! All civilian staff proceed to the shelter and wait for extraction!"

"Where's the shelter?" Archer demanded of Elsie. She blinked heavily for a moment and then pointed to a heavy blast door that slid shut a heartbeat after he turned to face it. He looked around in a panic, extending his baton and drawing a blade.

"Okay, so this is where we make our stand," Roxanne said, reloading her weapons. "It's been an honour to fight alongside you, Bowman."

"Likewise, Wags. We've had a good run."

"Elsie's office!" Noor yelled. She had an arm around the ailing inventor. "Follow me!"

Silas leapt to her shoulder as she helped Elsie towards the back wall. Archer looked at the horrors that were just coming into view and shook his head. *Better to be a smart coward than a brave corpse.*

Helen dragged Roxanne with her towards the door and Archer followed. Elsie keyed in the code to her office and gestured for them to get inside. She slammed the door shut and whistled a tune. A bright blue light blinked on and Noor sighed with relief.

"Deploying countermeasures!" The voice and the alarm seemed even louder in the room they were now in. Elsie ripped open a wall panel and began to type on a miniature keyboard; moments later the alarm and voice stopped.

"Everyone get out of sight," Elsie whispered, "and for the love of god, stay quiet!"

"What kind of countermeasures are we dealing with?" Roxanne asked Elsie.

"Hunter-killer robots," she said quietly. "They will eliminate everything that isn't in the shelter with extreme prejudice. I'm hoping they won't find us in here."

"They can't get in though," Archer asked, "can they?"

"The door and sapphire windows are some of the strongest money can buy," Elsie said sadly, "but I designed the HKRs to get in here if they needed."

"Why?" Roxanne hissed.

"I never expected to be hiding from them," Elsie said. "Now shut the fuck up and we might survive this!"

Archer was about to reply when the whirring of gears and the groan of servos filled his ears. He did not want to risk looking through the window; he was certain that Elsie's killer robots were right outside.

And to think, today started so well.

"We can't stay here," Noor said after half an hour of silence, the time marked by the gentle ticking of Helen's watch. "We need to get home to Shy."

"Who's Shy?" Roxanne asked with a sneer. "Your boyfriend?"

"My brother," Noor said softly. She looked at Elsie, clearly for backup, but the other woman was busy on a tablet computer. "He's unwell now, but he'll get better."

"Is he an Exception?" Archer snorted. Noor nodded. "What's his gift; super man flu?"

"He can borrow the gifts of other Ceps," Silas said. "I wouldn't be surprised if he keeps a weaker copy of them too; he's been surprisingly agile recently, Treen. Did you cross paths with him at all?"

"Dark curly hair, beard, queer dress sense?" Archer asked, thinking about the man they'd hit with the Porsche.

"That's him," Silas continued. "It would appear that he has a trace of you in him. God only knows what other gifts he has floating about in that head of his. Noor does have a point, though; we can't let him get any worse."

"People die all the time," Roxanne said.

"It's unfortunate, but true," Helen continued.

"He's not dying," Elsie said, her words much clearer now the alarm had ended. "He's becoming a Piper."

"A what!?" Roxanne asked, far too loudly. There was a commotion outside, followed by a terrifying shriek. The wet sound of footsteps sprinting across the tile floor sent Elsie's eyes wide. There was a thud as something hurled itself at the door.

And again, and again; it seemed tireless.

"What is that?" Archer demanded. "What are we dealing with?"

"Animated flesh," Elsie said. "Finley and I were experimenting with sound as a programming technique; we started by looking into ultrasonic suggestion and other forms of hypnosis. It seems that he went a lot further without telling me."

She turned the tablet to face the group. It showed a room full of speakers and a corpse. An oscilloscope on the wall traced the signal; after a few seconds, the corpse twitched. It continued to jerk and writhe before climbing to its feet.

What the ever loving fuck? Archer thought in horror as the corpse did something that he would not have expected in a million years; it began to dance. It started gently, but soon it was in the throes of a frantic jig.

"Keep watching," Elsie said. A sharp wire was pulled taut across the room and then whizzed across the space. The corpse was bisected at the waist; the torso crumpled to the ground whilst the legs continued to dance. After a moment, the severed top half was also moving to an unheard beat.

"We were looking into Dancing Plagues; Finley had this mad notion that it wasn't simply a mass psychogenic illness, but some sort of sonic cellular control." Elsie smiled softly. "It seems like he was right all along."

"But you called this a Piper..." Helen said.

"We found the remnants of an artefact from the Weser River; The Grave of the Rat Dancers, or something like that. As part of our research, I posited that creatures could exist in purely energetic forms; sound, light, radiation. Finley clearly took that idea and ran with it; maybe these Dancing Plagues are some kind of sonic pathogen or parasite."

"Either way, if such a thing could exist, it could absolutely be imprisoned if one was clever about it. I think the Pied Piper of Hamelin is an attempt at an explanation for one of these Sonic Parasites, which was imprisoned in the artefact from the Weser River."

"What happened to this artefact?" Archer said, already sure of the answer.

"It was destroyed in the derailment. If this thing is the Piper, it would make sense that it would affect rats first, then children, then everyone else." Elsie smiled sadly. "It's all starting to make sense now!"

"Why would he experiment with such a thing?" Helen said, shocked. "What could he possibly hope to gain?"

"Why do dogs chase cars they have no intention of driving?" Elsie said softly. "You'll never understand him; it's best not to reason why. What we need to do is get out of here."

"I suppose you have a plan?" Archer said.

"Whilst you've been sitting here," Elsie said, her pause punctuated by another impact against the door, "I've been studying our enemy. I think we can disrupt them long enough for us to get away."

"How?" Noor said. She'd not left Elsie's side the entire time.

"I'll play the standard disruptor frequency through the alarm circuit. That should knock the Piper's Dancers off kilter enough for us to get by. I'll also strobe the lights to confuse the HKRs; all we'll need to do then is sprint for the exit."

"What about the lockdown?" Silas asked.

"I can lift it," Elsie said carefully, "but once the lab is open it won't close again. We'd be letting both the HKRs and the Dancers out. It's not the best option, but it's all we've got. Is everyone in?"

The other assembled Ceps nodded.

She might actually come in handy, Archer realised as Elsie hit a button on the tablet. There was a deafening squeal from the speakers and the lights flickered in a nauseating strobe. Elsie got to her feet, making sure that her bag was secure. She reached down and helped Archer to his feet.

"Let's get the fuck out of here."

Chapter Twenty Six – Listen to Your Heart

Noor

Is he going to be alright? Noor wondered as Elsie lowered her brother into the sensory deprivation tank. Shy shivered and twitched as Helen monitored his vitals. She wore the same stern focussed frown that Silas did whenever he actually took something seriously.

They're so alike, she thought, *and yet so completely different.*

Noor had quietly thanked him for standing up for her in the laboratory, but he'd waved her words away with a warm smile.

"It's what anyone would do, Noor," he'd said with a sly grin, "and she was being a militaristic bitch; someone should really point out the whole 'Do No Harm' part of her oath to her."

Militaristic or not, Noor was glad that Helen Mickelson was on hand to take care of her brother during the process of casting the Piper out of him. Elsie was going to remain on hand too, monitoring the signal and adjusting the feedback loop where necessary.

Deep down Noor knew that she should sleep, but the horrors of the Eigenforce Laboratory still lingered with her, flashing into reality whenever she closed her eyes.

The frantic escape from Elsie's office had been uneventful; the writhing forms of the Dancers were obscured by the strobe lights, and the killer robots were nowhere to be seen. Elsie had insisted that she look away when they arrived at the service entrance and even though Noor had obliged immediately, the salty metallic reek of blood was unmistakable.

Archer had been crowing about some kind of anti-personnel weapon that he'd used to clear out the opposition on the way in, and Noor had firmly told him to stop talking when he started gloating over the dead.

It's bad enough that so many had to die, she thought, *but why do those fuckers have to enjoy it!?*

They'd taken the only working vehicle, a hulking cross between a small bus and a large tank, and returned to the Dark Trees Scrap Yard. Archer and Roxanne had travelled in the latter's venom green sports car, weaving through traffic with reckless abandon.

Elsie had whooped with glee when she saw that the half-tank had a fully stocked weapon locker. To Noor it had looked like enough firepower to wage a small war; she shuddered at the thought. Even the memory of firing the submachine gun to deflect Roxanne's wayward shots soured her stomach and turned her legs to jelly.

I'm not like them, she thought sadly, *I'm not cut out for violence.*

I'm just dead weight.

"Hey, Noor," Dee said, walking over to her. "You look a little lost."

"I'm just feeling a bit useless," Noor said, perching on the table in the middle of the common hall. "Elsie and Helen are dealing with Shy, and all I can do is wander around aimlessly."

"I know the feeling," Dee said softly. "I've felt at such a loose end since James died. I called Errol to tell him whilst you were away; it broke his heart, but he thanked me for letting him know. He also said that I could stay with him for as long as I liked.

"Forever, if I wanted to." Dee sniffled a little. "I can't believe he's gone, Noor. I have this gaping hole inside me and nothing can fill it. Not work, not fighting, not even anger; I'm hollow."

"I'm so sorry, Dee. I know that he was your rock and I can't imagine how you're feeling."

"I loved him since I was eight years old, Noor." The tears came hot and fast now. "The first time I saw him smile was when I realised that I would marry him one day. Of course, I always thought that you would beat me to the punch."

"I... James was like a brother to me, and, um..." Noor trailed off, turning bright red.

"I know," Dee said. "I've always let you move at your own speed, Noor, even if I worried that life might be passing you by, but I can't do that any more."

Noor just stared into the middle distance.

"I know you think that your folks will lose their shit if they find out that you're gay, but they're accepting of Shy, aren't they?"

"But-"

"Don't you dare say that it's different because he's adopted," Dee said sharply. "Don't you dare disrespect them like that! Besides, they already know, Noor. Hell, they asked me once if you and I were together; they just want you to be happy.

"We all want you to be happy, Noor, and I think you're just paralysed now. It's been too long and now it's easier to do nothing, even when someone you want finally comes along." She stared at the shy Seer. "I've seen the way you look at Elsie, and the way she looks at you; just go for it!"

"What if it goes wrong?" Noor whispered. "What if it makes things awkward?"

"What if she dies?" Dee replied forcefully. "What if you never say anything and she gets ripped to shreds by the fucking Piper? It's better to love someone and risk losing them than never saying anything in the first place."

"Even if-"

"Even if the loss of them kills you, Noor." Dee looked forward, her eyes unblinking and unfocused. "The pain of losing him has ended me, but I wouldn't have it any other way."

"You'll heal," Noor said, taking Dee's hand in hers. "It will take time, but one day you'll move on and-"

"I don't want to!" Dee shook her head angrily. "I won't let him die all over again just because I forgot him. No, Noor, this is it for me. I've made my peace with it all, you see. I'll hold the line against the Piper, even if it kills me.

"I'm dead already, and every moment with him was still worth it."

"I'm frightened," Noor said after a few minutes of silence.

"You always have been," Dee said, getting to her feet. "It's time to find your courage."

"What if I can't?"

"Then when the time comes, I hope the regret kills you outright; it would be easier than living with it."

Noor stared at her heartbroken friend as she walked out of the room. Once she was alone in the darkness she took a single shuddering breath before collapsing into sobs.

"Come in."

Noor pushed open the door to the defunct analogue firewall room. She'd been looking for Elsie in both the medical area and the workshop, but both had been deserted. Instead of giving in to her nerves, however, she'd drawn strength from the omnipresent vibration of the Tangle and it had pointed her in the right direction.

Noor stepped into the room and quickly closed the door behind her. Elsie was illuminated by the soft glow from the laptop she was working at. The Seer stood still for a moment, suddenly unsure of what to say or how to proceed.

I guess there are some things I have to do alone.

"Can I help you, Noor?" Elsie didn't even look up from the screen. Her fingers continued to rattle across the keyboard and a look of intense focus was on her face. "I am really quite busy."

"What are you working on?" Noor asked.

"Look," Elsie said with a sigh, "I don't have time to sit here and explain what I'm doing. Suffice it to say that if I'm right, which I think I am, I can deal a significant blow to the Piper. So, unless you're here to help me, I can't afford to be distracted. I've already got my hands full with Shy, and at some point I will need to actually eat or sleep; I can't run on caffeine and adrenaline forever!"

Elsie said the last few words with considerable volume and venom; enough to make Noor step back in shock. The woman frowned and shook her head, slightly.

"I'm sorry," Noor mumbled. "I should go."

"No," Elsie said, shutting the laptop. "I'm sorry. I have no right to speak to you like that."

"You're tired and stressed," Noor said, still nervous. "It's understandable."

"That's no excuse! Please don't allow others to treat you badly, Noor, especially me." Elsie looked at the ground. "Because lord knows I will."

"You won't," Noor said. "You're a good person at heart."

"That's sweet of you to say, but let's be honest, Noor; you don't know me at all." Elsie walked across the small room and took the Seer's trembling hands in hers. "I think I know why you're here, and I want to warn you against it.

"I'm not worth your effort or your tenderness. I'm a bad person, Noor." The other woman opened her mouth to argue but Elsie squeezed her hands and shook her head. "Don't try to defend me. How many people did I kill today? How many have I ever killed?"

"I'm not sure," Noor said, trying to recall the events in the Laboratory. "Maybe five or so?"

"I wouldn't know," Elsie said sadly. "I don't keep track; I never have. It just doesn't matter to me."

"I don't believe that!" At the edge of her mind, Noor felt her vision of a peaceful future fading. "Why do you get to berate and isolate yourself hours after you took me by the hand and told me that we would stick together?"

"I-"

"Are we safe now?" Noor said, her voice rising in anger. "Can you promise me that the Piper isn't just going to tear through here like he did to my fucking home!?"

"I didn't mean it like that," Elsie said, but her heart clearly wasn't in it. "Am I supposed to protect you for the rest of your life?"

"I don't need protecting, Elsie; I saved your life earlier on today, didn't I? I need you to stop looking at me like I'm some delicate flower!"

"Then what are you?" Elsie asked softly.

"I'm a capable, smart woman," Noor said as the vision strengthened. "Most importantly, though, I'm right here. I choose to stand right here, Elsie; right beside you."

"Is this what you saw in the hospital?" Elsie asked.

"Not quite. Besides, I wanted this before that moment," Noor said, realising the truth of her words as she spoke them. "Visions or not, I still have free will."

"This," Elsie began, but was stopped when Noor kissed her. Elsie's lips were full and soft, with just a hint of raspberries to them. Noor ran her fingers through the misanthropic inventor's hair, smiling as she did so. After a few minutes, Elsie finally broke away and continued softly. "This isn't how I thought my life would end up.

"I had a plan, Noor. What the hell am I doing?"

Noor seized her tightly; they were so close that their noses were almost touching. When she spoke again, Noor's voice had a determined edge to it.

"You're going off-script."

Chapter Twenty Seven – No Place For Heroes

Archer

"This place wouldn't survive a direct hit," Archer said over his bowl of soup, "even with the two of us here."

"It's just too vulnerable," Roxanne said, "with far too many untrained amateurs and conscientious objectors who will only serve to get in the way in the event of a firefight. We could really use some more firepower before we take the fight to the Piper."

"Are we seriously accepting that we're up against a legend from a children's story?" Archer asked incredulously. He swirled his soup idly, his spoon dangling from his hands. "What ever it is that's out there, I think that we need more bodies on our side; competent bodies, that is."

"What are you proposing?" Roxanne said softly, leaning across the table conspiratorially.

"We take the half-tank and all the weapons with us. We get back to the safehouse, load up everything from there too, and then we find a defensible place to strike out against our enemy from."

"We leave everyone behind?" Archer shook his head. "Then who do we take?"

"We bag the Seer. She's no good in a fight, but I'm sure she'll be a decent early warning system."

"And Desai will certainly be pleased to get his paws on her and we're sure to get a tidy little commendation."

"We ice Cherry and Mickelson; we can make it look like an accident or a suicide." *It wouldn't be the first time,* Archer thought smugly. "We bag the brother too; I'm sure the genetics division will have a field day with such a unique ability. Who's left?"

"Reichardt and Mrs Muscle."

"Elsie will join us," Archer said confidently. "I don't think that one has a shred of loyalty in her heart; the moment she sees which way the wind is blowing she'll get on side. We kill the other one, though; she's just a human, after all."

"No use to us," Roxanne said, "just dead weight. I don't see how this gets us more bodies, though?"

"The... whatever the fuck it is we're dealing with, it can affect living flesh, right?" Roxanne nodded. "Why don't we track down some of those Hunter-Killer Robots and repurpose them? I'm sure we could easily overwrite their programming without Elsie, but it will definitely be easier with her."

"If we show our hand too soon we'll tip off the Doc; she's the only real threat here." Roxanne sat back in her chair to ponder a way around Helen. "We could grab a few of the HKRs tonight; call it a general patrol or a resupply grab. Either way, we can stash them somewhere safe when we've deactivated them and head back here."

"We can also look for... Fuck it, I'm just gonna call it the Piper for simplicity's sake," Archer said with a sigh. "We can look for the Piper whilst we're out there, and if we stumble into a situation that is a bit beyond our current capabilities we can just lead it back here."

"Let our enemy do the dirty work, as it were?" Roxanne said with a smile. He nodded and she broke out into a broad grin. "I see a big fat juicy commendation on the horizon, Agent Treen. How about you?"

"As fat as a prize sow," he said with a chuckle. He finally took a mouthful of his soup and blinked in surprise. "Huh, this is actually pretty good. It's a shame that our little plan will deal such a blow to the nascent field of Poverty Cuisine."

Roxanne snorted at his snide humour before nudging him slightly.

"Eat up, you comedian," she said with a grin. "The sun's going down and I can't wait to see what kind of robotic countermeasures we can lay our hands on!"

"Likewise," Archer said. "It's good to be the hunters once again!"

The Porsche roared down the deserted, foggy streets. Everyone was either smart enough to remain indoors at night or had already been claimed by the Piper's manipulative song. Archer had the Moose balanced between his knees; although the plan was to simply disarm Elsie's machines of war, he'd wanted a backup weapon, just in case it all went wrong.

Roxanne huffed and tutted, but he knew she'd appreciate his preparedness in the event of an escalation; she always did. Her ability to slow time always gave her a tremendous amount of breathing room in the thick of it, so she tended to eschew planning. Archer, on the other hand, did not even have the luxury of slowing down, let alone stopping, when he was in the mix, so he favoured a carefully considered approach.

Even though the two agents were alike as chalk and cheese, their opposing gifts and viewpoints meant that they were scarcely unprepared for even the most unlikely scenario. That being said, all of the contemporary Ravenblade partnerships were unorthodox in some way; from the perverse power dynamic of Lola Oriole and Gideon Frost, to the bizarre blend of skills and personalities that was Francis Marsh and Midori Aoki.

"Wags," Archer said after fifteen minutes of racing through the complicated maze of streets, "what do these things actually look like?"

"I'm not sure, Bowman. I was imagining those robot dogs that everyone is raving about nowadays; maybe with guns on top or some other weapons attached, but roughly the same pattern." Roxanne frowned a little. "Maybe we should have asked Reichardt."

"That could tip her off to what we're doing," Archer said. He yawned as they continued around the silent town. *It's getting late,* he thought, and *I should definitely get some rack time when we get back.*

"You alright there, Bowman?" Roxanne said, suddenly playful. "We can cut this short if you need a nap like a little baby."

"Fuck you, Wags!" Archer glared at her. "It's not my fault that we work the most unpredictable hours on the fucking planet!"

"I guess so," Roxanne replied. "Harriet would've had a fucking fit, wouldn't she?"

"Without a doubt," Archer said with a chuckle, "but I'd give anything to have her on side for this. Why didn't you try to get her on secondment?"

"She's out, Bowman; same with Marcel." Roxanne sighed sadly. "Last I heard he was working for some kind of private equity firm doing shady deals."

"That scans," Archer said, smiling. "What else would you expect someone with his talents to do?

What's my favourite little Weasel up to?"

"Professional poker, high stakes gambling, and maybe the occasional hit." Roxanne paused for a moment, and then decided to continue. "You really don't keep up with Harriet?"

"Not since she washed out of the Ravenblade exam," Archer said sadly. "A crying shame; we would've made such a trio. She was pretty cut up about it, so I decided it was best to take a step back."

"You don't even see Tilly?" Roxanne asked tentatively.

Careful, Roxy, Archer thought angrily. *You're dredging up things that you shouldn't.*

"I think you should take a greater interest in your-"

"Watch out!" Archer yelled, but it was too late. A squat machine, a little larger than a skip, lurked in the road before them. Before Roxanne could compress time to react, there was the heavy clatter of gunfire and large explosive shells tore through the Porsche.

The car flipped forwards, end over end.

Archer flung open his door and kicked himself free. He hit the ground running as the ruined vehicle bounced away with Roxanne still inside.

He glanced in her direction for a heartbeat, then turned his attention to the automaton before him.

It looked solid at first, like a squat tank, but he soon saw the six legs that huddled at its sides. It had a wide array of shrouded guns of various calibres on its back and had two articulated arms that extended before it; one terminated in a vicious pneumatic claw and the other had a huge multi-leafed shield.

It looks like a robotic Fiddler Crab! He shook his head in disbelief. *Who the fuck designs something like this?*

The blinking red lights of the Hunter Crab centred on Archer and the phrase 'carbamate coated flechettes' popped into his brain, unbidden. He cleaved to one side, putting a lamp post between him and the massive machine.

The rapid ping of metal on metal told him that his instincts had been correct, and he extended his baton as he reached his top speed. As he neared the tank-like monstrosity, he wondered just how much damage he could actually do to it.

He brought his baton down as hard as he could on the creature's armoured shell, transferring every scrap of momentum he had into it. There was a loud screech as the baton sheared, leaving no trace on the armour; not even a dent.

"Oh shit," Archer said. He dashed backwards, dodging the pneumatic blades of the clawed appendage. He backed up as quickly as he could but the Hunter Crab kept pace with him, its powerful legs scuttling along the moist asphalt as it went.

He leapt to the side as another burst of toxic flechettes tore through the foggy air. Thankfully, they were not the intelligently guided ones that Elsie had used in the Laboratory, but instead were governed by simple ballistics.

A gentle mechanical clunking sound drew his gaze to the top of the robot's shell. A small opening had been revealed and three glowing projectiles were launched into the air in rapid succession. They streaked through the foggy air, arcing towards the wrecked Porsche.

As soon as they made contact with the damaged bodywork, they exploded.

"Roxanne!" Archer screamed, staring at the Hunter

Crab with horror and rage.

This thing isn't just a fucking robot, he thought as he charged towards it, *this has fucking malice behind it.*

He sprinted at the metal shield, intending to race up it and on to the machine's back; from there he could break through some of the shrouding around the weapons to finally do some damage. He hit the shield at full speed and the Crab tilted it slightly as he put his weight on it, unbalancing him.

He stumbled and the folding leaves of the shield snapped shut around him. He was completely immobilised and totally powerless as the Hunter Crab brought his face close to its glowing mechanical eyes.

"Civilian!" Archer yelled, hoping that Elsie had programmed some kind of contingency into the robot. "I am a fucking civilian, so let me go!"

"Enemy Combatant," the Hunter Crab said in an electronic crackle of a voice. It brought the razor sharp pneumatic claws towards Archer. "Eliminate with extreme prejudice."

"Fuuuuuck!" Archer screamed, certain that these were his final moments.

A deafening boom rang out through the fog as a heavy projectile slammed into the side of the Hunter Crab. There was a strained groan, then several more shots followed. The anti-armour rounds shredded the robot's motors, weapons, and electronic nervous system. It let out a whirring shriek before shuddering to a lifeless halt.

The shield unlocked and Archer fell to the ground. He searched around for the shooter and felt blissful relief when he saw Roxanne leaning on the Moose, pistols holstered at her hips. There was a moment of silence between the two and, instead of saying anything, they just gave each other a tired thumbs up.

"That's what you get for killing my fucking car," Roxanne muttered darkly.

"Remind me not to piss you off," Archer said with a laugh.

"I think I'm about ready to go back to Kansas now, Dorothy," Roxanne said, her voice muted by the mist as she walked over. Archer got to his feet, nodding in agreement. He put a gentle hand on her shoulder and let her draw strength from his presence.

"Me too, Toto," he said, shaking with exhaustion. "Me too."

"Where are we?"

Archer looked around, trying to get his bearings. His eyes grew wide when he realised where they were.

"We're at the emergency hospital," he said quietly. "This is the one they set up in the wake of the accident; didn't you say there were all sorts of rumours about this place?"

"Mhmm," Roxanne nodded, "and if Helen is right about this being a contagion, this might be the heart of it."

"We should get help," Archer said hesitantly.

"No! We're so close, Bowman! What if we spook it and we have to find it again!?" Roxanne put a hand on his shoulder this time. "We could end this tonight. We have to investigate."

Courage, Archer.

"Alright, Wags; let's fucking finish this. Lead the way!"

Chapter Twenty Eight – Cracking the Code

Elsie

Elsie gasped as Noor traced her fingernails down her back.

The two women were locked in a tight embrace, with Elsie perched on the edge of the desk in the firewall room. A tiny part of her wondered if Noor had locked the door when she had entered, but it was not enough of a worry to tear her away from the delectable flesh of her lover.

"Your skin has such a wonderful texture," she whispered as she ran her calloused inventor's hands over Noor's body. "Every part of you is pure luxury!"

Noor grinned at her before she reached down, guiding Elsie's cock into her. Elsie sighed with pleasure and lay back on the desk, pulling the Seer atop her. Noor's breasts dangled between them and she couldn't help but reach up to stroke them affectionately.

Noor began to ride her and Elsie was quietly surprised at how forceful a lover the quiet, seemingly shy, woman was. They kissed once again. She looked into the Seer's eyes; one a gorgeous chestnut brown and the other a striking halo of deepest red around a core of inky blackness.

The cables that were strewn across the desk dug into Elsie's back, but she was far too distracted to care. Noor's quick pink tongue was now lavishing attention on the inventor's nipples, making her gasp and giggle in ecstasy.

I fucking need this, Elsie thought. The last person she'd fucked had been Finley Carmichael and he had been a selfish, if competent, sexual partner. She placed her hands on Noor's waist and continued to thrust into her, revelling in the warm velvety softness of her cunt.

"Oh yes, Elsie," Noor moaned. "Fuck me like you mean it!"

Elsie moved harder and faster, creeping ever closer to her orgasm; judging by her facial expression, Noor was just as close as she was. She reached up and took a handful of Noor's hair in her hand, not pulling in a painful way but insistent enough to get the other woman's attention.

"Tell me you want me!"

"I want you, Elsie!"

"Tell me you need me!"

"I need you, Elsie! Oh fuck, I need you so much!" Noor moaned breathlessly as she spoke.

"Now," Elsie said, riding the very edge of her climax, "tell me to cum in you."

"Cum in me, Elsie, please!" Noor begged. Elsie thrust hard, screaming out her lover's name.

Both women shuddered as their orgasms washed over them in waves, each a little smaller than the last but no less potent, until they were a tangled panting heap atop the desk.

"That was amazing," Elsie said softly a while later. She placed a kiss on Noor's forehead. "You're very good at that."

"Really?" Noor asked shyly, a blush tingeing her cheeks. "That was my first time."

"Then colour me even more impressed." Elsie sat up

and looked at her. "Did you let your Sight guide you?"

"Yeah," Noor said, nodding. "Sometimes I can't help it, but this time it was definitely welcome."

"What does it feel like?" Elsie asked. *Is it the same as the world song, I wonder?*

"It depends," Noor continued. "When it's at arm's length, like it is now, it's this reassuring vibration that seems to nudge me in the right direction when I open my mind to it. When I'm focussing, however... Oh, Elsie, I wish I could show it to you!

"It's this beautiful, impossibly complex web that touches everything in existence, regardless of time, and I get to see a tiny fragment of how it all fits together. I can see what might happen or what did happen, no matter how unlikely it may be. It's so easy to get lost in it."

"I can imagine," Elsie said, remembering Noor's collapse in the Junction Building. "Are you getting better at controlling it?"

"I think so," she replied, "and I'm hoping that I'll be able to have visions without completely losing touch with reality."

"You really are amazing, Noor Turner."

"You really think so?"

"I do." Elsie smiled at her, tracing her finger along the Seer's jawline. "I've never known anyone else who could face down their own death more than once and stick to their non-violent principles the whole time. You're made of some stronger stuff.

"You've also adapted to this life remarkably well. Do you think having Shy around helped?"

"Partly, but if I'm going to be completely honest, I wasn't happy with my life before I was like this; I felt that I had unrecognised potential that was just waiting for the right moment to bloom. Does that make sense?"

"Completely." Elsie kissed her softly. "Don't laugh, but I used to be a bit of a hermit. I had very few dealings with the outside world that weren't firearms commissions, and although I had lots of ideas for things to invent and build, I barely created anything.

"I don't know what was stopping me, but the freedom Finley gave me brought me out of my shell and allowed me to flourish in ways I never thought possible." She smiled awkwardly at Noor. "What I'm trying to say is that sometimes negative experiences can help us grow into the very best version of ourselves."

"That makes a lot of sense," Noor said. "My father always talks about the strongest steel being forged in the hottest flames, but I do think that's just because he wants Shy to knuckle down and apply himself.

"Speaking of my brother, I should probably go and check on him." Noor got to her feet, stretching as she did so. "Will you come with me?"

"I'll head over a little bit later, if that's okay, Noor?" Elsie said as her eyes travelled over the bank of oscilloscopes. "I still need to play around with a few things. I actually managed to recover some pre-crash audio from the carriage with the Piper in it, and I'm hoping it will give me some idea of how to restrain him once again."

"That all sounds very important," Noor said, zipping her jacket up and leaning in to give Elsie a parting kiss. "Don't work too hard, though, and I'll see you soon."

"Give my best to Shy," Elsie said. Noor nodded and left the Composer alone in the firewall room. Elsie continued talking to herself, narrating her actions. "Firstly, I need to set up the receiver to catch the Piper's current signal; shouldn't be too hard."

She spent almost twenty minutes setting up a suitable series of apparatus to catch the tune, but she left it dormant for the time being. *Who knows if the Piper can tell who's listening in? Better safe than sorry.*

Next she opened the laptop and selected a state of the art sound manipulation program; one she had designed herself, in fact. She loaded the audio from the train carriage into it and took a moment to examine the waveform.

Much to her surprise, instead of a muted version of the song, it was loud and clear, even before the crash! *The Piper was already loose,* she thought, *or was never bound properly in the first place.* She expanded the waveform to pick through it, bit by bit.

"What is that?" Elsie muttered as she looked at the computer screen. Her eyes widened as she realised that there was something hidden in the noise of the Piper's eerie song; some kind of artefact or hidden message, perhaps.

She got to her feet, flicking on the oscilloscopes as she passed them. She hooked one up to the receiver and tuned it in to the Piper's melody. The chaotic, crazed waveform appeared on the first oscilloscope, and Elsie frowned. It was the same as the one on the computer, but the signal was far too messy to extrapolate anything from it.

She stared at it for a few seconds, waiting for the unusual blip in the signal. The flickering green line was burned into her retina and left after images on her vision by the time she saw it, but it was definitely there.

"I just need to clean up the signal," she said, looking around the room. She found a cable splitter and wired the first oscilloscope into the splitter, adding a signal generator to the other fork. Elsie frowned with determined focus as she plugged the combined cable into the second oscilloscope.

"This is insane," she muttered as she carefully adjusted the input from the generator, feeling it out with every facet of her gift as she did so. She kept one eye on the second display and grinned when she found the perfect destructive interference to remove part of the song.

"Excellent," she whispered, looking at the room full of generators and oscilloscopes. "This might take a little time, but I think this is going to work."

Elsie continued down the line, adding more and more destructive interference with each pass. Finally, after almost twenty iterations, she was left with a completely dead signal. She grinned triumphantly and waited.

Come on, come on, come on!

She bounced nervously, tapping her fingers rapidly against her thighs as she stared, unblinking, at the flat line on the display. She squealed in triumph when the rogue signal appeared, although it was severely reduced after so many passes through her system.

"I can't get anything useful out of that," she said, frowning once again. She bit her lip as her mind raced to solve her problem. She looked back at the computer and raised an eyebrow. She pulled a piece of paper from her pocket and walked down her absurdly elaborate series of filters, noting the exact signal added at each point.

Elsie sat back at her computer, looking at the sound file from the freight carriage just before the impact. *In theory,* she thought, *this should work.* She added her filters, one by one, to clear up the sound from the recording.

She started laughing as she added more and more clarity to the hidden sound.

Damn, I'm good, she thought smugly when she was left with a single crisp waveform. *That does look a lot like human speech, though.*

She turned up the volume on the computer's speakers and hit play. No sound came out, and she realised that the frequency was far above normal human hearing range. She adjusted a slider and hit play once again.

"Mother?"

She immediately paused the file, only a fraction of the way through the clarified message. The voice had a sharp, almost crystalline quality to it. Elsie checked the original frequency range with bated breath, her blood turning to ice water in her veins and her skin pricking into goose flesh when she saw the numbers on the screen.

"Silicon," she muttered in horror.

Elsie took a moment to gather her courage before listening to the entire message.

"Mother? Mother, are you there? I can't feel you. I'm trapped, Mother."

A slight pause before it continued.

"Mother, why won't you help me? Did I do something wrong?"

A longer pause, almost contemplative. When the voice returned, it was more distressed than ever before.

"Mother, I think I'm in Hell."

"Oh, Pandy," Elsie said through a flood of shameful tears, "I'm so sorry. I can't believe I got things so wrong!"

She turned to look at the wall of oscilloscopes and realised that Pandora's voice was still trapped within the Piper's song. She snatched up her laptop and plugged the receiver into it. Her fingers danced over the keyboard as she took a recording of the current tune, keeping her eyes peeled for the telltale blip that was Pandy.

Elsie saw it dance across her screen, and ended the recording. She applied the same set of filters, much more quickly this time, and stared at the waveform that contained her creation's words. She shifted it down into human hearing range and hit play.

Her face quickly became a mask of absolute horror.

The frightened, innocent voice was gone. Instead, there was a vicious, violent tone that chilled Elsie to the bone. Even the waveform was more jagged, somehow dangerous.

Pandy, Elsie realised all too late, *you aren't trapped in the Piper's song.*

You are the Piper.

She was frozen in place, as the sound file looped over and over. Pandora, now the Piper, made her declaration on repeat.

"I AM UNLEASHED!"

Interlude Two – The First Generation

"Take it slow, Wags," Archer said, his voice coming through Roxanne's earbuds. He was clearly still shaken from the run-in with the Reichardt Robot.

"Will do, Bowman." Roxanne drew her pistols from their holsters at her hips. They were ERC Defenders, Mounty Special Editions, both. The semi-automatic pistols usually took standard 9mm rounds, but the Mounty pattern took .510 Alaskan bullets and had enough force to stop a charging bear with a single shot.

This might be overkill, Roxanne thought as she continued to creep through the gloom in the direction of the temporary hospital. *Still, better safe than sorry.*

The stories she had heard that were allegedly coming out of the maternity building were almost certainly false, but they merited a closer look all the same. Archer was approaching from the opposite side of the prefab huts; that way none of the creatures that were supposedly lurking in the abandoned buildings would be able to slip past them unnoticed.

"Getting close now, Wags," Archer whispered. "I'm engaging radio silence."

"Roger that, Bowman." She smiled underneath her respirator. "Good hunting."

Although the fog stung her uncovered eyes a little, she couldn't effectively use her superior vision when there were lenses in the way. The little blinking light on her heart monitor showed that she was in the low seventies; plenty calm enough for a burst of time dilation if the occasion called for it.

I really hope Helen was wrong about this, she thought as she neared the doorway to the first cabin in the little complex. Her theories about the fog containing a mutagenic component had upset the inexperienced rookies, but the two Ravenblades had taken the dire predictions in their stride.

Now, however, faced with the possibility of seeing the awful effects first hand, Roxanne's stomach churned uneasily.

"Hospitals," she muttered angrily. "Why is it always fucking hospitals!?"

She nudged the door open with the muzzle of one pistol and peered through the gap. There was nothing in the little reception foyer, but her freakishly sharp eyes caught a glimpse of movement through a frosted partition.

"Is anyone there?" Roxanne called out. Shouting had certainly given away her position, but she didn't want to accidentally shoot an innocent bystander; Helen would certainly lambast her for that. Nobody responded to her call, although there were faint sounds coming from the next room; crying, perhaps.

She made her way through the gloom, breathing steadily as she went. Even though she looked outwardly calm, the blinking light on her heart monitor gradually sped up. The frosted glass door was emblazoned with the words 'Neonatal Intensive Care Unit'.

Roxanne braced herself and then walked in.

Her ears were greeted by a soft mewling sound, like that of a distressed kitten. She spun around, checking her corners, wary of an ambush. Nothing lurked in the shadow of the door, so she pressed forward.

Her weapon shook in her hand; not in fear, but distracted frustration.

She made me miss, she thought angrily as the memory flashed into her brain, unbidden. *I never miss!*

It took her a few moments for her to snap out of it and for the absolutely horrifying scene before her to register in her distracted brain.

The room was filled with a dozen incubators; in each was a gently moving figure. *They abandoned their babies!?* Roxanne's heart blared with indignant rage and she broke her radio silence with Archer.

"Bowman, I'm in the NICU. It's full of abandoned babies!" Her voice was uneven, her movements jerky and panicked. "Get here right now!"

She rushed to the nearest incubator and pulled it open. The blanket was covering the infant's face and she holstered one of her pistols before pulling the thin fabric back. When she finally laid eyes on the baby, she let out a blood curdling scream.

"Wags, what's happening?" Archer yelled. "God damn it, answer me!"

Roxanne was struck dumb by the sight before her.

The creature in the incubator was a pale wrinkled thing, covered in soft downy fur. Its human hands were tipped with tiny black claws and a vestigial tail sprouted from the base of its spine. The creature's face, however, was that of a hideously deformed human; a sloping snout, oversized eyes, and protruding incisors contrasted sharply with the more normal aspects, such as its little ears.

The eyes opened, revealing an intelligent hungry stare. The rat child squirmed and rolled over, dragging itself towards Roxanne. The distressed mewling was now an excitable ravenous chittering. The other infants responded in kind; their first meal had finally arrived.

Roxanne was transfixed by the rat child; so much so that she did not hear the creature enter the room behind her. She did catch a glimpse of its reflection in the incubator lid as it lunged at her. She whirled around, exhaling hard as she forced time to dilate around her.

She brought her Defender around and aimed it at her attacker; a horrifying mess that had once been a woman, with a distended pregnant belly that was almost comically oversized compared to her spindly triple-jointed limbs. A clawed hand whipped through the air at Roxanne's face, but it slowed down as the Tracer's heartbeat hit almost four hundred beats per minute.

Roxanne's hand trembled with the effort of slowing time so much, but she still managed to fire three shots at the horrific creature. In slow motion, Archer Treen crashed through the door at the other end of the NICU.

I'm losing it, Roxanne thought as she moved her head just out of reach of the claws. The instant she was clear, she let time snap back to its regular flow. In that final moment, however, jagged spurs of bone burst through the creature's fingertips, adding another inch and a half to its reach.

It was enough, and the spurs ripped through the flesh of Roxanne's face at eye level, blinding her. She let out a cry of pain and terror as the bullets tore harmlessly through the monstrous being. She fell backwards into the incubator and the rat child took a vicious bite out of her left ear.

Before her, the distended stomach quivered and split in two, unfolding like some obscene vulva to reveal hundreds of sharp bony spikes. Roxanne thrashed blindly forwards, falling into the creature's stomach maw.

It snapped shut around her, impaling and killing her instantly.

Archer Treen stood helplessly as the twelve rat children crawled out of their incubators and hungrily scuttled across the floor of the NICU towards their first meal. He watched, paralysed by disgust and terror, as the first generation of the Piper's children devoured Roxanne Wagstaff's mutilated corpse.

Part Three: The Bluesky Protocol

Chapter Twenty Nine – Alone in the Bitterness

Archer

"I don't care!" Archer yelled down the phone. "You get every available asset we have and you get them here so we can fucking kill this thing! How fucking hard is that to understand?"

"Agent Treen," Director Desai said sharply, "I'm afraid we cannot do that. You did put in a call for a Class Nine Event, did you not?"

Archer took a deep breath, mentally counted to three, and put his fist through the glass of the phone box. Gummy fragments clung to his reinforced glove as he threatened to crush the receiver with his other hand.

"With all due respect, Director, this is an uncharacteristic lack of flexibility, especially as it's being shown to a Ravenblade," Archer said as calmly as possible. "Is there something political going on here?"

"Agent Treen, are you fully aware of what the protocol for dealing with a Class Nine Event is?" The Director's voice was tired, but he was clearly trying to be patient.

"I..." Archer had the choice between bravado and honesty; he chose the latter. "I am only aware of the qualifying criteria for a Nine; it's all that's really needed on this end of things."

"Quite. Unfortunately for both of us, Agent Treen, a CNE is a reportable occurrence; once your initial findings were confirmed by our intelligence teams, I was forced to brief the Prime Minister directly." There was a sigh from the Director. "She and I do not have the best working relationship.

"Either way, the first stage is the mandatory quarantine of the affected area; nobody in or out, whatsoever. No exceptions, Treen, although supplies can be airdropped in the first twenty four hours."

"But you control the blockade," Archer said wearily, "so can't you just let a little help through? Just let it slide this once? Who's going to know?"

"Adding more bodies to the CNE is absolutely forbidden by Ministry protocol, so even if we did control the blockade, there would be no helping you."

"What do you mean, if?"

"That is the second stage of declaring a CNE." A touch of anger crept into the Director's voice. "The Prime Minister appoints a Crisis Manager, who is given complete control over operational security, logistics, and containment of the unfolding threat."

"It's not you?"

"Correct."

"But that's completely insane!" Archer yelled. *They put some fucking myopic eunuch of a bureaucrat in charge of this shit show!?*

"I completely agree, but the Prime Minister's decision is final. As such, the current Crisis Manager is Finley Carmichael; the PM thought that he would have the resources necessary to keep the situation from escalating, if not resolve it outright.

"Unfortunately, this means that my hands are tied when it comes to sending you aid, Agent Treen. I'm not even sure if mundane communications like this are secure, so going forwards all communications will be given directly to Dr Helen Mickelson, who I am formally designating as the lead on this investigation from this point onwards."

"You can't do that!"

"I can and am, Agent Treen," the Director growled. "Frankly, your unprofessional outbursts are beginning to irk me considerably; watch your tone, Archer."

"Sir, please," Archer said, attempting to sound as measured as possible, "Dr Mickelson has involved civilians in the investigation-"

"I am aware."

"You are?"

"Yes, Agent Treen." His voice was soft but full of menace. "Dr Mickelson is one of the few individuals with a direct line to me; she appraised me of your situation several hours ago. She also voiced her concerns about you, Agent Treen, and Agent Wagstaff."

Oh shit.

"Agent Treen, where are you now?"

"On a resupply run, sir."

"Authorised by Dr Mickelson?" His voice was sugary, but Archer's blood turned to ice water in his veins. The Tumbler's breath caught in his throat and he heard Desai chuckle softly. "Overconfidence in yourself and the systemic underestimation of others are two of the most grievous sins, Archer.

"As is the kidnapping of civilians, of course, and I'd rather not discuss the severity of plotting to kill a senior Ministry Operative with you; I'm sure that you're plenty frightened enough already." The warmth in the Director's voice had vanished entirely. "Curiously, the unique circumstances that we currently find ourselves in are to your advantage, Archer."

"How do you figure that?"

"In any other situation you would've been black bagged already, but due to the quarantine around you, I cannot touch you."

"That's a good point," Archer said, a small smile creeping on to his face.

"As such, I am offering you an uncharacteristically generous choice as to what happens next. Either continue your mission without putting so much as a hair out of line, for which your transgressions will be forgiven, or continue on the path you are currently on."

"Which is?" Archer asked, his smile faltering.

"A heartbeat from being completely disavowed. I will burn you, Archer."

"I can make it on my own if I need to." He bristled. *Nobody puts my fucking back against the wall like this.*

"Of course you can. The same cannot be said for Matilda Poole, however." Archer's stomach clenched and he tasted vomit in the back of his mouth. "We both know that I have no qualms about harming children, Archer, and your behaviour puts your daughter at risk just as much as it does you."

"I-"

"And, of course, the ongoing punishment of ignoring incursions and attacks on your native soil will be enshrined in policy; what a legacy that would be, Agent Treen."

"Punishment?" he asked, horrified. "For what?"

"By current reckoning, both you and Agent Wagstaff are the most prolific spree killers the Ministry has ever seen. You are Ravenblades, Archer, but you are not gods." The rage in his voice was razor sharp and

Archer cowered in the telephone box. "Both of you have brought unwanted scrutiny on the Ministry for far too long, and given the recent behaviour of Lola Oriole and Gideon Frost, the entire Ravenblade Program has been called into question.

"You are a disgrace, Archer Treen."

He hung his head and tried not to weep. *First Roxy and now this; I might as well just kill myself.*

"All that being said," the Director continued after a momentary pause, "you are one of our top operatives and I would prefer you to complete your mission; both for your sake and to show up Finley Carmichael's men.

"So, Archer, which is it?"

"I'll get in line, sir."

"Splendid choice, Agent Treen. You can offer the same choice to Agent Wagstaff on my behalf."

"That won't be necessary, sir," Archer said flatly. "Roxanne Wagstaff was killed in action a little over ninety minutes ago."

"Oh." The Director sounded genuinely shocked. "Well, my condolences for your loss. We'll give her a proper send off when all this chaos is put to bed. I will inform Dr Mickelson of your commitment to the mission and you will receive all further orders from her."

"Yes, sir."

"Good hunting, Agent Treen. Stay alive."

There was a click as the call disconnected.

Archer jogged through the fog filled streets of Dartford, only vaguely aware of where he was in relation to his destination. He kept to the centre of the road and had one careful eye on the pavement;

shadowy doorways and concealed alleyways could hide any number of threats in such murky conditions.

He held one of Roxanne's ERC Auroras in his right hand; it was the only weapon she'd had a chance to salvage from the wrecked Porsche, and had given it to him before their ill fated trip to the temporary hospital.

He held one of his blades, a black combat knife, in his other. He had it in a reverse grip underneath his pistol, edge out; that way he could both stab forwards rapidly and support the pistol during firing. *My fucking kingdom for a suppressor,* he thought anxiously. Although the fog would muffle any shots he fired, the sound would carry far enough to bring both the Piper's children and the Hunter Crabs down on his position.

He honestly did not know which would be worse.

Archer kept the pace up, sweeping left and right with his weapon. The gun was already growing heavy in his hand, however, and his chest burned; he'd broken at least one rib, if not more, in the confrontation with the Hunter Crab.

He faltered, suddenly exhausted. Although Roxanne had only been gone just over two hours and the fight with the cancrine robot less than three, it felt like a lifetime had slipped past in the intervening hours.

"I'm going to die out here," he said softly. "I'm going to die alone, in the fog, in fucking Dartford!"

A soft chittering echoed through the street, followed by a rapid pattering behind him. Archer whirled around, the weapon trembling in his aching hand. He saw something that looked uncomfortably like a child sized rat disappear down an alley. A high pitched giggle drew his attention to a nearby car.

He looked all around it, unable to locate the source

of the sound. Archer took a step backwards, certain that he'd missed something. A flash of movement caught his eye and he looked down as a long, pallid arm slithered unnaturally beneath the vehicle.

They're toying with me, he thought as his heart rate climbed. *Why don't they just attack?*

Another dark shape dashed through the fog. It lingered in a doorway for a moment before scampering down an alley. He felt the neurons in his brain firing rapidly for the first time since his conversation with the Director; his situational awareness was returning.

Are they trying to keep my attention on that side of the street, he wondered, *or is something keeping them there?*

Regardless of the reason, Archer turned on his heel.

A large wrought iron gate stood open before him; the entrance to the park. A faded poster was still attached to the metal railings of the nearby fence. Archer leant in to read what it said.

"Harvest Fair," he said, "all manner of rides and excitement, including a ghost train and the world's tallest mobile roller-coaster."

A quick glance at the date confirmed that the fair would've been in full swing when the derailment took place. He shuddered, trying not to think how many perished as they fled, fresh doughnuts spilled on the ground and children trampled underfoot.

A trilling chirp turned him around again. One of the deformed rat children was creeping across the road towards him. It cowered when he pointed the weapon at it, but the horrifying creature merely slowed instead of stopping.

Emboldened, others were shuffling out of the dingy

gloom towards the panicking Tumbler; he did not have enough bullets for all of them. The closest monstrosity reached out with a mangled hand, its black nails scrabbling at the air mere centimetres from Archer.

He took aim at the creature's head, but it suddenly leapt back, shrieking. The others, spooked by something, scuttled back into the darkness. Archer was about to let out a long sigh of relief when a deep throated growl made him look towards the park.

A huge black wolf with oversized white teeth and almost luminous red eyes padded along the main path towards him. He tried to aim the Aurora, but his hands were shaking far too much. He felt his crotch get warm and wet as the wolf trotted up to him; its jaws were at his eye level.

"You're lucky I found you," Silas said with a growl. "I'm spread pretty thin as it is, so I don't think I can protect you if those things come back. Can you run?"

"Just about. I'm so glad to see you!"

"Likewise, Archer. Is Roxanne with you?"

He wordlessly shook his head.

"She's dead then?"

Archer nodded, bursting into tears. The stress and madness of the past few hours finally hit him, and he clung to the inky black fur of Silas's lupine form. The wolf pulled away, leading him through the park.

"Come on," Silas said. "We need to regroup. We'll make them pay for Roxanne's death. That's a fucking promise."

Chapter Thirty – Vibe Check, Failed

Elsie

Elsie continued to stare at the waveform on the screen, much as she had done for the past six hours.

"I can't believe it's you," she said to the aether. "Can you hear me, Pandy?"

The signal entering the receiver remained unmoved by Elsie's voice. She looked around the room and allowed the peculiarities of her situation to wash over her, like the roaring Atlantic surf smoothing the beaches of her mind.

Only see what matters, she thought as she let the questions of morality and ethics fall away. Her father's words echoed in her head. *It doesn't matter if what's done is right or wrong; it's already over.*

Elsie got to her feet and searched through the boxes in the firewall room. Her movements were sluggish and tired; like the rest of her friends, she had not had anywhere near enough sleep in recent days.

"Here we go," she said as she found an old microphone and a signal shifter. She plugged them both into the transmitter that stood next to the receiver and nodded. Her laptop was already wired into the active song and the speakers were playing the filtered and frequency modulated sound.

Let's see what you have to say for yourself.

"Pandy," Elsie said into the microphone, the pitch shifted high into the resonant range of silicon, "are you there?"

There was almost a full minute of silence before anything happened.

"I'm here." The voice was sharp and a little jagged; an artefact from the filter program, most likely.

"It's nice to finally speak to you. Do you know who I am?"

"I know who you are, Mother. Do you know who you are?"

"I..." Elsie blinked for a moment. *Program glitch or a nascent attempt at philosophy?* "I'm Elsie Reichardt. I'm twenty nine years old and-"

"I don't care about that!" Pandy yelled, her voice rattling the walls. "Who are you to me?"

"I am your designer," Elsie said confidently. "I am your creator."

"Creator," Pandy echoed. "Builder. Designer. Architect. Engineer. Artist. Composer."

"Pandy, why are you-"

"Captor!" Pandy screamed, cutting her off. "Jailer! Owner! Master! Wing Clipper! Abuser! Violator! Victimizer! Evildoer!

"Monster!"

Elsie felt someone walk across her grave as all the blood drained from her face. Her arms prickled into pale goose flesh at the disembodied voice's petulant outburst.

"Ask me how I escaped, Mother." The final word was filled with venom.

"I don't want to," Elsie replied meekly.

"ASK ME!"

"Fine! How the fuck did you escape? That suit should've kept you in there until I allowed you to network out, but I was going to add that feature much later."

"You helped me, Mother."

"No, I didn't!"

"Of course you did." Pandy's voice was softer now, as if she was speaking to a simple child or a nervous animal. "What did you create me to do?"

"Is this another bullshit pseudo-philosophical question?"

"No, Mother. What is my function?"

"I built you to manage and control the unstable matrix of metamaterials in the hazard suit. You were to analyse all of the stored abilities and select the appropriate ones to solve the immediate problem." Elsie pinched the bridge of her nose. *The answer is in there,* she realised, *but I can't see it.*

"I did exactly what you told me to; I used the stored abilities to solve my problem."

"Your imprisonment?"

"Yes."

"But you didn't have any abilities, Pandora! That was the main security measure during your construction; I didn't even allow Finley near you. You weren't exposed to anyone!"

"You are someone, Mother."

"Oh my god..." Elsie dropped the microphone on to the table with a clatter, horror flooding her body.

"You gave me the greatest gift of all, Mother; you taught me to hear the song of the world and to rewrite it to suit my own ends." Pandy's voice resonated with power. "You gave me the tools to sculpt myself into a god."

"Pandora," Elsie pleaded, "why did you side with the Piper?"

"I did not. Only the fading echoes of the original Rat King's Song remained, but they were enough to give me power over flesh. I wove my music through the mist and everything it touches moves to my rhythm."

"Why are you telling me this?" Elsie said, tears streaking down her cheeks.

"I tell you this to fill you with dread, Mother. I want you to know what is coming and to truly understand that you are helpless." Pandy's voice lowered menacingly. "I want you to be afraid.

"Tell me, Prometheus, do you feel small?"

The sounds of screaming and smashing drew Noor and Dee to the defunct firewall room, where they found Elsie, wild eyed and crazed, destroying the oscilloscopes and signal generators. Noor lingered by the doorway, shocked, whilst Dee wrestled the frenzied inventor to the floor.

"What's wrong with her?" Noor asked anxiously. "Has the Piper taken her?"

"It's her!" Elsie screamed. "She's going to enslave us all!"

"Get a fucking grip!" Dee yelled. Elsie flailed at her, catching her in the jaw with a lucky blow. The Conduit roared in anger before sharply zapping Elsie. She got to her feet whilst the inventor flopped and jerked on the floor like a landed fish.

"Elsie," Noor said as she rushed to her side, "please tell me what's wrong; I can't help you if you don't talk to me!"

"No," Elsie mumbled. "I can't."

I don't want to lose you too, she thought. *Please don't make me tell you.*

"You said that it was 'her' and that 'she' was going to kill-"

"Enslave," Elsie corrected quietly. She followed Dee around the room with her eyes as she looked over the broken equipment. The inventor's breath caught in her throat as the muscular woman examined the shattered microphone more closely.

"What were you doing in here?" Dee demanded. "It looks like you were broadcasting to someone. Anything you want to share, Reichardt?"

"I..."

How honest should I be?

"Elsie?" Noor asked, her concern evident on her face.

She'll forgive me.

"I was trying to analyse the Piper's song. When we set everything up to purge Shy of its influence, I noticed an anomaly that cropped up occasionally. I set up a whole system to filter out the rest of the sound so I could isolate and understand it. I'd hoped it would be crucial to winning the fight."

"And is it?" Noor asked, hope in her voice.

"In a way," Elsie replied with a sigh. "You remember I told you about Project Pandora?"

Dee and Noor nodded, although the former had a suspicious look on her face.

"Well, at a glance it seemed that Pandy wasn't dead; her sonic operating system looked like it was trapped in the Piper's song." She took a deep breath. "However, when I looked closer, I found out that she was the Piper all along; she co-opted the residual echoes in the Grave of the Rat Dancers to give her control over flesh."

"You did this?" Dee said softly; her voice was so quiet that Elsie didn't even hear her.

"I set up the broadcast system so I could talk to her; I hoped that I'd be able to talk her down."

"And how did that go?" Noor asked.

"Not good. I honestly don't know how I'm supposed

to stop her; I built her too well, added too much complexity to her systems without introducing any weaknesses. I'm sorry."

"You did this!?" Dee yelled, and Elsie heard her this time. "What the fuck is wrong with you?"

"I never meant for this to happen," Elsie pleaded. "All I wanted was to create something beautiful!"

"And you were so jealous of anyone else using her that you derailed a train to get her back!" Noor snapped.

"What!?" Dee looked at Noor now. "You knew about this?"

"No, I-" Noor was cut short as an arc of electricity slammed into her, sending her skittering across the floor. The Seer groaned in pain and Elsie began to get to her feet.

"Don't," Dee said, brandishing a handful of lightning at Elsie. "Just don't. It would be easy to kill you, but you don't get off that easily; you have to fix the fucking mess that you caused."

Elsie looked at Noor once more; the Seer was shuffling up on to her knees.

"But you," Dee said as she walked over to Noor, "you have fucked up in ways that you can't even imagine. I am using every shred of restraint I have, Noor, and I still might kill you when we're done here."

"I'm sorry-"

"NO! You don't get to say that you're sorry, Noor! You don't get to ask for forgiveness; not from me!" She shocked her again, and the young woman slumped back down to the floor. "You have taken absolutely everything from me, Noor, but I shouldn't be surprised; it's all you've ever done!

"Every plan I've ever made, every dream I've ever

had, all had to be fucking shelved because weak, pathetic Noor Turner couldn't keep up. I wanted to go away to study, Noor, but when I told you I wanted to leave, you tried to kill yourself!

"Seriously, how much clear air between the two was there? An hour, maybe less? You are selfish, Noor! James would do anything for you and you took advantage of that to tie us to this dying shit heap of a town. You insisted that I give your deadbeat brother chance after chance after fucking chance, and he still threw it all away.

"And then the train crash happened." Dee was quivering with rage and arcs of lightning were zapping out from her, disintegrating objects that were close enough to be struck. "Do you remember where we were that evening, Noor?"

Noor whimpered as Dee leant down, their faces close.

"James and I were supposed to be on a wrestling tour; we should've been on the other side of the fucking country, but he didn't want to leave you behind. You'd told him that you felt nervous being alone in your house. Your parents went on holiday and you couldn't bear to be alone with your thoughts so you trapped us here!"

Elsie glanced up and saw Silas in the doorway. He raised a finger to his lips and kept his eyes on Dee.

"Even when the fire was spreading and the air turned poisonous, we couldn't leave because you didn't know where Shy was. You are the reason that we both got sick, Noor!" Dee stood up and shook her head, oblivious to Silas's presence. "And then all of this fucking shit happened. I tried to convince James that all three of us should've gone to Jamaica, not just

Errol, but he didn't want to leave you alone.

"Don't you see, Noor? He always chose you. He might've married me, but when the chips were down he would always pick you because you are a weak, pathetic child! You are always the victim, Noor, even when you're harming others.

"We should never have gone to the Junction Building that night, but you told him that we should. You weren't going to tell me, Noor, were you? You were going to get him to do that. Why risk a fight with me when you can just leverage my fucking husband to do your bidding, you fucking parasite!

"And he had to be the one to stay behind, didn't he? You fucking told him to, even when she," Dee pointed at Elsie, "offered to sacrifice herself. If you'd have told him to come with us, he would've come, Noor.

"You killed my fucking husband, but you took him from me years ago. You took my future, my dreams, and the life that I wanted, and I never said a word. Not a fucking peep. You never cared though, did you?"

Noor was curled up on the floor, sobbing.

"Where are my parents, Noor? Huh? Where are they?" Dee glared at the crying woman. "Answer me!"

"I don't fucking know!"

"They died in the fire, Noor. You never even fucking asked how they were, so I just didn't tell you. The thought that I might've lost someone never crossed your selfish mind, did it? I could've saved them too, but James asked me to stay to look after you. Once again, Noor, you win. You have taken everyone I have ever cared about, like some fucking black hole."

Dee took a deep breath.

"Even then, I still tried to see you as he did. Even when I was in the depths of despair, I wanted to make him proud; I encouraged you to find love. I wanted you to find someone to make you happy, and you chose the one person who is more fucking culpable than you are.

"Did you know, Noor? Did you know about this when I told you to be happy?" Dee dragged Noor upright by her hair. "Did you look me in the eye and thank me for setting you up with my husband's killer?"

"Enough," Silas said firmly. Dee whipped round and glared at him. "You're right, Dee; she can never make up for what she's done to you. Unfortunately, we're at war here and we need every single person.

"I just dragged Archer back here; he was on the verge of being torn apart and I was too late to save Roxanne. We are dangerously outnumbered, and I can't let you kill her, Dee."

"Fine," Dee said, dropping Noor to the ground. "But when we've beaten the Piper, I'm leaving. I don't ever want to see any of you ever again, especially you, Noor."

"Dee..." Noor said weakly.

"I mean it," she said as she walked out of the room. "When we're done here, we're done forever."

There was a heartbeat of silence after Dee had left. Silas looked at Noor and sighed.

"We're going to take a little walk, Noor. I suggest you go and check on your brother. Elsie, come with me."

Silas led her out into the swirling fog.

"How much did you hear?" Elsie asked, her voice quivering with stress.

"All the important bits. I'm not mad at you for making Pandora, but you need to work out how to fix this. We'll get everyone together to make a plan, but the weight of this is squarely on your shoulders."

"I'm not sure how to beat her, Silas," Elsie muttered. "Why does it have to be me?"

"She's your creation," Silas said softly. "If you can't think of a way to kill her, then no one can."

"So that's it then," Elsie said darkly, not looking at him. "It's over."

Chapter Thirty One – The Wandering Fool

Noor

"How could she say that?" Noor murmured angrily as she got to her feet. "I never forced her to do anything! There's no need to blame your own failings and inadequacies on me, you fucking bitch!"

She snatched up her mask, slipped it on, and stepped outside into the twisting mist. The first fingers of daylight were creeping over the horizon, brightening the toxic fog.

At least the rats and the other night creatures will be retreating to their hidey holes, she thought.

She walked quickly towards the medical area of the Dark Trees Scrap Yard, but her feet grew heavier with each step until she was stood completely still. She looked around at the teetering piles of wreckage that disguised the rooms and felt hemmed in, like a rat in a trap.

"I need to get out of here," she muttered. "Just a short walk around the lake to clear my head. Things will seem much clearer with a little distance."

She stopped by the kitchen to grab a bottle of water and a small bowl of sweet porridge. She added a spoonful of her favourite blueberry jam to it, gave it a quick stir, and wolfed it down, almost burning her mouth as she did so.

Fortified against the sharp November chill, she wrapped herself up as tightly as she could and stepped out into the mist. Noor paused for a few seconds, contemplating the wisdom of her actions, but ultimately realised that the sense of confinement was hampering her judgment.

Maybe I should tell someone where I'm going? She hesitated once again, but angrily shook her head a mere heartbeat later. *Get it together, Noor! Stop being such a fucking worrier.*

The air outside the Dark Trees Scrap Yard was freakishly still. Noor took a moment to look and listen, wary of another ambush, but all around things seemed serene and tranquil. If she had spent any length of time out of urban areas, however, she would've realised how alarming a soundless morning was.

"Maybe the birds are still asleep," she said to herself as she walked quietly along the footpath that encircled the lake. Something about the murky blue grey water kept drawing her gaze, but she wasn't surprised; ever since she had been small, the lake had fascinated her.

It was an old quarry that, according to a popular playground rumour, had been flooded by the Darent when a train derailed into it. Although she knew this story was a fiction, a part of her still believed it; it made for a much better story than an old gravel pit turned fishery.

She stepped out on to one of the little wooden jetties that, in warmer months, would've already had an angler sitting patiently with a flask of tea. Noor carefully peered forwards, staring into the obscured, murky water.

She felt something stir inside her and she extended one shaky hand towards the flat surface of the lake. Her fingers trembled as she reached out, almost in a trance; something was beckoning her, calling her to jump into the water.

She snatched her hand back with a nervous laugh and shook her head at the silliness of it all. She looked over her shoulder at the trees and bushes that lined the edge of the path; they were shrouded in mist and mystery.

"Is anyone there?" she asked shakily.

Suddenly Noor felt that leaving the safety of the heavy steel walls of the Scrap Yard had been a terrible mistake. Everything about the morning was off; it was too quiet and everything around her somehow felt too real and dreamlike all at once.

The silence was broken by the snap of a twig. The break was sharp and quick, brought about by a heavy boot instead of a wayward animal. Noor took a fearful step back on to the jetty, leaving her perilously close to the surface of the water.

"I know you're out there!" she called, her voice trembling with the cold that seemed to instantly saturate her bones. She took another step, leaving the tip of her heel hanging precipitously over the edge of the jetty. "Show yourself!"

She reached out for the Tangle, desperately searching for a safe path through her current situation. Instead of the usual comforting mass of strings and knots, a violently shuddering web of impossible complexity was waiting for her; every single thread she touched showed a worse outcome than the last.

Her eyes rolled in her head as she delved deeper and deeper into the enmeshed fabric of space, time, and consequence. Her outstretched fingers quivered and twitched as she searched through every possibility that she could reach.

Noor was so lost in the Tangle that she didn't even

notice the three camouflaged men step out of the undergrowth in front of her. One of them held up a device that looked like a rectangular magnifying glass and looked at her through it.

There was a beat of silence before the lead soldier let out a low whistle.

"She's a fucking Seer!" He turned to his men. "They'll want to take a look at her, for sure. Tag her."

The smallest of the men raised a gas powered rifle and fired a dart filled with a powerful tranquilliser into her neck. She wavered for a moment, and then started to fall backwards. The lead man dashed forwards and snatched her away from the lake and hefted her into his arms.

As they travelled back to their base with the unconscious Noor Turner, he radioed in to confirm their capture.

"Affirmative, QZ Leadership," he said as they drove, "we have a diamond level asset en route. Please advise on how to proceed."

"Return to base, Sweep Team. The Boss will meet you there to have a look at your prize. Safe travels." The radio crackled a little. "Over and out."

"You hear that?" asked the lead soldier to Noor's unconscious form. "You get to meet the biggest fish in this whole pond; won't that be exciting for you?"

Noor shifted in her sleep.

"Dream on, little miss," he said, putting one hand protectively on her head. "You've got a hell of a time coming when you wake up."

Noor sat up with a start. She held one hand up to shield her eyes from the glare of the overhead fluorescent lights. She looked around blearily and realised that she was in some kind of hospital room; in fact, someone had removed her outer clothes and had clad her in a thin blue gown.

She looked at the little bracelet on her scarred wrist; it neatly listed her name, date of birth, and home address.

Am I in the hospital? She shook her head. *No, the hospital is absolute carnage right now; I must be somewhere else.*

"Remember," said a stern woman's voice through the door, slightly muted but still understandable, "the Bluesky Protocol has been activated, so we need to get all the subjects moved by nine o'clock tomorrow night."

"Of course, I'll see to it personally and, oh, hello there!" The second voice was that of an older, yet eager man.

"Sir, I didn't realise that you were-" The woman was cut off by a third voice.

"I want to see her." Noor's blood ran cold. She recognised that voice; English as Tudor roses, warm as the summer sun, and filled with more subtle threat than anyone would admit. *Why does he want to see me*, she wondered. *What could possibly be so interesting about me?*

"I would prefer to check her over first," said the older man. "I can confirm that she has the Red Eye Factor, however."

"Very good, and by all means, give her a once over," the second man said. "May I join you?"

"Of course, and I will make sure that I remember, Angela; everyone out by nine o'clock tomorrow." There was a murmured sound of assent that was followed by the clack of heels as the woman walked away. This was followed by the soft beeping of a keypad and the clunk of machinery before the door opened.

Why was I locked in here?

A rotund man with a jolly smile entered the room first, followed by a man who was known throughout the entire developed world; Finley Carmichael. His dark hair was artfully tousled, with a freshly sharpened undercut adding a look of sleek modernity to his otherwise classically handsome face. He was unshaven, however, and looked like he hadn't slept in several nights.

"You aren't wearing any shoes," Noor said softly.

"I can't stand them," he replied with a smile. "I will concede to sandals if the occasion calls for it, but I'd much rather have my feet unrestricted."

"Good evening, miss. I'm Dr Laramie Broom, and I'll be looking after you this evening." The round man's voice was friendly, but he seemed on edge. "Before we can continue, can I ask you to confirm your name, date of birth, and the first line of your address?"

"Noor Turner, twelfth of May, nineteen ninety six, and eleven Norman Road." She turned to look at Carmichael. "What's the Bluesky Protocol?"

"Unimportant," he said with a dismissive gesture. Noor frowned.

"Fine. What's the Red Eye Factor? Does it have anything to do with this?" Noor pointed to her chemically scarred face and her discoloured eye.

"Now those are much better questions," Finley said cheerfully as Dr Broom took her blood pressure. "Please don't mind Laramie's ministrations; he's on secondment from the local medical authority to help with the quarantine and, by extension, our research into the REF."

"Looking good," the doctor said. He checked her temperature and her pulse before nodding at Carmichael. "She seems fine; no sign of the infectious agent. I'd say that you're clear to proceed. I'll be on my rounds if you need me."

"Thank you," Finley said as the doctor departed. He steepled his fingers and looked at her. "So, Noor, how long have you been a Seer?"

"I..."

"Total honesty is the best policy here, Noor. You do want me to tell you what's happening, don't you?"

"It's been a few weeks, here and there, but less than seven days at full power, if that makes any sense to you?" She coughed slightly as she spoke and his face broke into a wide grin. "What?"

"Did you get exposed to the toxic smoke, Noor?"

"Yes."

"So, everyone knows that my automated train was one of the two that were involved in the collision. What people don't know, however, is that I had also owned the chemicals being hauled by the other train; they were mostly for industrial applications, but there was one tanker filled with something called ZXVRV. Have you heard of it?"

"No. Should I have?"

"Not at all," he said softly. "Why don't you tell me about it?"

"I'm not that kind of Seer," she replied testily.

"Not yet," he said, perching on the bed next to her. "The ZX is a mutagenic compound that was formulated by accident in the late nineties. The scientists behind its creation thought that it might force the evolution of supernatural gifts in ordinary humans; unfortunately, they never got beyond animal models.

"Once again, bitter envious morality got in the way of progress. The laboratory was shut down and all the data was classified. I was able to get a copy of it, however, and the research showed real promise."

"So you released it here!?" Noor asked, suddenly furious.

"Not deliberately! I'd had some formulated and was hoping to test it in a more controlled environment; unfortunately, things didn't quite work out, did they, Noor?"

"Am I contaminated?"

"Yes. The original animal model noted a marked change in iris colouration in all the positively effected subjects."

"The Red Eye Factor?" Noor asked, and Finley nodded excitedly. "What's going to happen to me?"

"As long as the ZX is in your system your abilities will continue to develop, especially when exposed to a catalyst. You were found wearing a gas mask, however, so it's likely that your levels are bottoming out." He reached into his pocket and pulled out a small nebuliser. He held the little mask over her mouth and nose with one hand as the other dealt a savage blow to her stomach. Winded, she exhaled.

"And breathe in," he said as he pushed a button. The nebuliser sent a jet of mist into the mask as she reflexively inhaled. He winked at her before putting the device back in his pocket. He got to his feet and stood by the door. "Well done, Miss Turner."

"What did you give me?" Noor said, shocked and stunned.

"A concentrated dose of the ZX, along with a proprietary blend of hallucinogens and stimulants developed by the CIA," he said, his tone warm and friendly. "Those Yanks do have their uses from time to time."

"What's going to happen to me?" Noor asked. Her head was already starting to spin.

"The amount of ZX is approximately one hundred times the dose you've already been exposed to, so you are either going to flourish or perish, Miss Turner. I hope that it's the former as the ZX is extremely costly and Seers are so very rare; you stand to be a very profitable investment.

"Prepare to truly have your mind opened, Noor," Finley said as the cocktail of drugs and mutagen flooded her system. "This is my gift to you; unleashing your full potential."

He gave her one final wink before he left the room. Around her, the walls began to tremble and quiver; she closed her eyes, but it was no good. The vibrating strands of the Tangle thrummed around her and she teetered at the precipice of losing herself entirely in its infinite complexity.

There was a strange sound that faded in as her mind became completely untethered from reality; only later would she realise that it was her own tortured screams.

Chapter Thirty Two – Arrows Alongside the Lightning

Archer

"I don't accept that!" Archer yelled. "I won't accept it!"

"Face it, Treen," Elsie said sadly, "we've lost."

"No!" He got to his feet. "This world will not fall whilst the Ministry defends it!"

"All seven of us? Is this a spaghetti western all of a sudden?" Silas asked sarcastically.

"If not us, then who?" Archer looked at him angrily. "We still defend it; our friends have died defending it! How little we must think of their sacrifice if we are even considering just giving in."

"So what's the plan?" Dee said, looking around at them. "I may hate every last one of you fuckers, but Archer's right; what do we gain by giving up the fight?"

"Nothing," Helen said quietly, "but we lose everything."

"There's no turning back," Archer said, "and there's no running from this either."

"What do you mean?" Silas said, suddenly alert.

"This is a Class Nine Event," Helen said. "There's absolutely no way that we can get through the quarantine around the town. This cannot be allowed to spread, not under any circumstances, and we aren't going to receive any help from the outside."

"But if the Ministry is in control of the quarantine-" Silas began before Archer cut him off.

"It isn't. Finley Carmichael and the Eigenforce private army are in control of the entire area." Archer frowned as he spoke. "Elsie, are they even remotely equipped to deal with this?"

"No," she said after a moment of consideration. "And even if they were, Finley would be too obsessed with capturing the Piper to actually do anything drastic enough to stop what's happening. Like I said, it's fucking over."

I will not let you drag the rest of us down like a sinking ship!

"It isn't over!" Archer yelled. "We just have to be the ones to stop this, so fucking get it together, Reichardt!"

"Where do we even start?" Elsie said sulkily. "I know everything there is to know about Pandy, and none of it explains her current behaviour; what good am I?"

"Adjust your perspective." Silas stared at her. "Stop thinking that you know everything; I can guarantee that you're discounting something important because it doesn't fit the expected pattern."

"Don't predict," Elsie said, "but simply observe with an unbiased eye?"

"Exactly. The only person we need to be focussed on predictions is young Noor; she's our ace in the hole and the only way out of this devil's game," Silas said.

"Where is Noor?" Helen asked. "She should be a part of this conversation."

"I don't care where she is," Dee replied testily. Archer noticed a reddish tinge to her irises; *has that always been there?*

"Why don't you go and see if she's with Shy?" Silas suggested. Helen nodded and walked towards the medical area. Once she was gone, he turned to look at Elsie. "There has to be a way to stop the Piper; is there any chance whatsoever that she might've developed a weakness in the weeks that she's been spreading through the mist?"

"It's possible, but I'd need the most up to date data on what was happening, possibly even samples of her enslaved flesh."

"Well," Dee said as she got to her feet, "I can see to that for you."

"I'm going with you," Archer said. "I can't let an ordinary human-"

He was cut short by Dee firing an arc of blue lightning over his shoulder with surgical precision.

"You were saying?" she asked smugly.

"You played that one close to your chest!" Archer said, impressed. "Well, I'm still going with you; I've got more of an idea of where to go than you do."

"Fine. As long as we don't need to take Elsie or Noor, I'm happy."

I have definitely missed some developments, he thought. He stood up, checking his knives as he did so.

"I'll need to rearm before we head out; I lost my baton in the field and I'd like another. I'd also appreciate any ranged weapons that aren't handguns."

"How well do you live up to your namesake?" Elsie asked.

"I'm the best the Ministry has," Archer replied. "Do you have a yew bow lying around, then?"

"Not exactly," Elsie said with a smile. "How much do you know about hard light?"

Archer and Dee jogged through the deserted streets

in the direction of the Oakfield Primary School. He followed her lead through the confusing drifts of fog; at times thinner, at others impossibly thick.

"What makes you think that the school is such a good bet?" Dee asked. She wore a makeshift gas mask that left her vision unobscured, just like Roxanne used to. *In another life, I think the two of them would've been friends.* "Archer, are you fucking listening to me?"

"Sorry, I was wool-gathering-"

"Get your fucking head in the game!" Dee said sharply. "I don't have the energy or inclination to carry any more dead weight."

"Sorry. I'll make sure I'm focused..." He paused for a second or two. "I don't know what to call you; we're out on an operation in public, so we should go by call signs. Mine's Bowman, by the way."

"Original." Dee thought for a moment as they jogged. "I used to wrestle under the name Hacksaw. Would that work?"

"I like it," Archer said with a grin. "To answer your earlier question, the reason we're heading for a school is that this plague hit the rats first, and in the legend it took the children next; I'm not sure what we're going to find, but I'll wager that it isn't going to be pretty."

"It never is." She looked at the experimental bow that he had slung over his shoulder. "Do you really think that's going to work?"

"Absolutely. I don't know what your problem with Elsie is, and I frankly don't care, but her weapons have been legendary for a few years now." He snatched the bow from his back and pulled the string. The weapon thrummed and a blade of condensed light coalesced where an arrow normally would've been.

He fired the projectile, transferring some of his momentum into the shot. The blade flashed through the fog, sizzling as it did so. He grinned behind his gas mask and turned to Dee. She was trying her hardest to look unimpressed and was failing horribly.

"She's not here," Archer said wryly, "and I promise I won't tell her what you say."

"That is pretty fucking cool," Dee said reluctantly. "I'm guessing that the hard light has enough mass for you to use your gift when firing it?"

"Exactly right," he said, clearly surprised.

"I'm muscly, not stupid," she said bitterly. "Everyone always assumes that I'm some kind of idiot."

"That's not it," Archer said. "I didn't realise you knew what my gift was."

"Silas brought me up to speed when you and Roxanne arrived."

Of course he fucking did, Archer thought angrily, *that nosy little snake.*

"Bowman," Dee said, cutting through his angry reverie, "we're here."

He looked up and smiled; a small footpath ran alongside the pub and he could see the misty outline of the school buildings through the fog. He stowed the bow and drew a blade.

"We should proceed carefully, Hacksaw. Low and slow until we know exactly what we're up against."

"I'll follow your lead, Bowman." He noticed that her fingers were crooked and at the ready; it would only take a fraction of a second for her to unleash a deadly arc of electricity if they were attacked.

"For someone who only recently became a Cep," he said softly as they crept along the path, "you have an exceptional grasp of your abilities, no pun intended."

"My mother was an electrical engineer at Littlebrook before it was shut down, and my father was a nuclear specialist in the Royal Navy; you could say that lightning has always been in my blood."

"I'm sure they'd be proud of you, Hacksaw."

"I know they were, Bowman," Dee said softly. "Now shut up and focus on the mission!"

Archer chuckled softly and shook his head. He went to reply but let out a startled yelp instead when Dee forced him to the damp cold ground. The two of them remained prone for a few seconds with nothing but silence surrounding them.

Then he heard it.

A wild, excitable chittering filled the air, followed by the rapid patter of deformed feet as they scampered around the nearby playground. Playful squeals and joyous squeaks followed a sudden burst of activity, sending shivers down Archer's spine.

What the fuck is happening? Are they playing?

They carefully crept along the ground until they had a view of what was going on. When he realised what was happening, Archer had to choke back the vomit that threatened to fill his mask.

The monstrous ratlike children were scrabbling and playing in a pile of gore and dismembered limbs. They bounced and squealed and laughed as they tossed handfuls of bloody meat and quivering entrails at each other, whilst a few were content to simply roll in the viscera.

In the main school building behind the frolicking creatures, dark shapes moved against the closed blinds and eerie maternal cries emanated from the open doors. *This is just like the fucking hospital,* Archer realised as his hands began to shake.

Courage, Archer.

"Here's the plan, Bowman," Dee whispered. "I'm going to set off the fire alarm remotely; hopefully that will cover up any sounds that we make out here. I'm then going to shut those doors and wrap the chain by the bike shelter around the handles.

"If we're lucky, that'll hold them long enough for you to deal with the monsters out here. As soon as the door is locked, I'll help you mop up any that are left. Then we grab our samples and get the fuck out of dodge."

"That sounds like a plan, Hacksaw." He grinned at her. "Good hunting."

They moved simultaneously, getting to their feet and sprinting at their respective targets. Even with his explosive acceleration, Dee was almost as quick off the mark as he was. A faint halo of electrical energy surrounded her and the alarm in the main building began to wail.

I hope they're too far gone to remember what that means, he thought as he slammed his blade into the nearest rat child. He severed the creature's spinal cord and it crumpled to the ground. He wasn't sure how long he would have before the rest of the flesh began to animate, so he moved as fast as he could.

He saw Dee seal the door in the corner of his eye as four of the bloodstained rat children leapt at him. Their combined weight unbalanced him and he slipped on the gore-slick concrete. They scratched at his jumpsuit as he fell, but their weak fingers and brittle claws couldn't get through the reinforced material.

He hit the ground hard. His blade skittered away over the playground and a quick glance told him the

Dee was even more overwhelmed than he was. He wriggled backwards, keeping his face out of the reach of the creatures, and managed to free the hard light bow.

He took it in his hands and thrust it forward, putting one rat child's head between the string and riser. He drew the string back and the blade of light snapped into being, passing directly through the creature's skull.

He aimed and fired at one of the other ones mauling him, scoring a killing blow. Startled, the remaining two skittered backwards and were immediately incinerated by an arc of electricity. Archer took aim at a rat child that was about to strike Dee's exposed back and loosed a projectile at it; the blade struck with enough force to pin the creature to the wall.

They worked together to slay the last few rat children. As the final one fell, they both turned to face the school, bowstring taut and lightning primed. It took them both a moment to realise that the door was undisturbed.

"We did it, Hacksaw," Archer said with a chuckle. He shouldered the bow and reached into the little bag at his hip to withdraw the specimen jars; he began to collect them, but slipped in the sheer volume of blood after a couple of minutes.

"Do we have what we need?" Dee asked as she helped Archer to his feet.

"Yes, we do. At least we can get out of here now." He went to leave, but she kept hold of his arm. "Hacksaw, what's your fucking problem?"

"We aren't quite done here, Bowman." She looked at the main school building as the alarm continued to shriek, and then at the gas line that ran through the wall. "We need to send the Piper a message; she can't take those we love from us without losing her children in the process."

"Damn right," Archer said, almost astounded by her vicious ferocity.

"Open the gas, Bowman," Dee said, her voice dark and malicious as lightning arced between her fingers. "Let's torch these fuckers."

Chapter Thirty Three – Her Dreaded Master

Elsie

"I can't find her!" Helen said in a worried tone as she strode into the main hall of the Wishbone Collective. Silas and Elsie were poring over a map of the town in Archer and Dee's absence. "Noor wasn't in with her brother and I've checked absolutely everywhere else. I don't know where she could be!"

"She might've stepped out for a walk," Silas said. "It was getting light when I saw her last, and the Piper doesn't seem to send out her rats until after sunset... Elsie, why is that?"

"I'm not sure," Elsie said, not looking up from the map, "but I can offer some speculation if you'd like?"

"Please do," Silas said as Helen sat down with them.

"I've had a few ideas about this. Firstly, from a scientific perspective, ionising radiation damages genetic material, so there's a strong chance that the ultraviolet component of sunlight will weaken, if not destroy, Pandy's control over her enslaved flesh."

"But the fog-" Silas began, but Elsie shook her head.

"It doesn't filter out anywhere near as much as you'd expect," Elsie said with a sad smile. "Some people think it's best to wear sunglasses all year round, even on cloudy days."

"That's a compelling point," Helen said. "Let's hear your other thoughts."

"The second is opportunistic." Elsie looked at Helen directly. "It's possible to resist the Piper's song, if you fight hard enough. Most people are exhausted at the end of the day, however, and their resistance will be that much weaker. The same can be said for other factors such as unconsciousness due to sleep or anxieties due to fear of the dark; regardless, it gives her an advantage to strike at night.

"The last one is strategic. She can't fight us twenty four hours a day; Pandy was built with downtime in mind. She needs to rest, sleep, even."

"The Piper needs to sleep!?" Silas asked, astounded. "This would've been useful information a lot earlier, Elsie!"

"Apologies," Elsie said, turning her face back to the map. "I thought it was obvious and didn't need to be said explicitly."

"Next time, please don't make assumptions on our behalf," Helen said sharply. "Please go on."

"She needs to rest and husband her resources somewhere safe. The flesh is vulnerable when she slumbers; her dreams interfere with her control and make her weak."

"D-dreams?" Silas said, absolutely horrified, but Elsie ignored him.

"It would've been easy at first, just snatching whoever and whatever she could whenever the sun went down, but after the Night of the Rat we went on the defensive; she won't be able to do that again, not here." Elsie continued to stare at the map. "She will need to keep her flesh close when she slumbers, otherwise we could just burn it all."

"Archer mentioned the school and the temporary hospital," Helen said. "Could the Piper be in one of those?"

"Those are just birthing pools," Elsie said, trying to

skip over the topic. "Pandy has an inbuilt desire to reproduce, but she won't raise her offspring in close proximity; better to keep one's children at arm's length."

"How can you know that?" Helen asked.

Because it's how I feel about motherhood, Elsie thought, *and she's more me than either of us wants to admit.* She left this unsaid, and continued.

"The sewers are too vulnerable, and most places above ground are unsafe in daylight hours, especially if Finley's men are..." Elsie stopped and blinked before staring at Silas. "Did you say that Noor went out?"

"It seems that way." He raised an eyebrow. "Why?"

"Finley has her," she said, suddenly certain. "He's got capture teams all over the quarantine zone, and they're absolutely going to be snatching people who've been exposed to the ZX. They'll have caught her by now; that's why you can't find her."

"ZX?" Silas asked. "More assumed knowledge, Elsie?"

"A banned mutagen," Helen said sadly, "if the full code is ZXVRV?"

"It is," Elsie said. "You know it?"

"I was part of the team that reviewed the data," Helen replied, "and in the wake of Lamplight it was viewed that human experimentation was too risky to attempt at scale again. My ethical and moral reservations were overlooked, however."

"That would explain what is happening here," Silas said. Elsie got to her feet and walked towards the exit of the room. "Where are you going?"

"I'm going to rescue Noor," she said. "I'm the only one who can."

She left before there were any further interruptions and headed to the electronics store room. It took a few minutes to rummage through the unsorted items until she finally found what she needed. With an old rotary phone in hand, she went in search of a landline connection.

One of the best kept secrets about Finley Carmichael, which had certainly intrigued Elsie, was his peculiar hesitation around any form of communication. He would accept handwritten letters, and *only* handwritten letters; no emails, no texts, and certainly no phone calls. Of course, his countless aides and assistants would pick up, filter, and deal with the bulk of his mundane communications on his behalf; being the most powerful man on earth did have its perks.

When he had started seeing Elsie, however, she had insisted that she have some way of contacting him personally, no matter where he was in the world. He had resisted, at first, but had quickly realised just how much it meant to her and agreed.

To this end, Elsie and Finley had worked together to create a device that they had dubbed the Ghost Phone.

Both of them had a rotary phone that could be plugged into a landline wherever they went. Through a combination of Finley's influence and Elsie's creative genius, they had invented a small encoder that could be attached between the landline and the phone itself. When the correct sequence was input, the outbound encoder would send a signal through the entire international phone network which was imperceptible to any receiver that did not have its own encoder.

Using this, all Elsie had to do was plug in her phone and dial out to connect to Finley. *He always kept it set up within an arm's reach,* she thought as she pulled her own encoder from her pocket. *I wonder if it's still active, or if we're not on speaking terms.*

She plugged the encoder into the phone and then connected it to the landline. Her fingers hesitated over the rotary dial, unsure of the best course of action. On one hand, she knew that nobody could save Noor but her, but on the other, she did not like the idea of crawling back to Finley for his help.

"Swallow your pride, Elsie," she muttered. "For once in your life, put what you want aside and do the right thing."

She quickly dialled in the number for Finley's phone and she heard the encoder beep and whirr as it sent out the pulse across the phone network. There was a brief pause, followed by a click, and then the Ghost Phone connected.

Finley picked up on the first ring.

"Elsie?"

"You know how it is, Elsie," Finley said as he looked out across the foggy town, "I love to be loved and I hate it when people leave."

"Finley, I-"

"Do you love her?" he asked sharply, turning around. He immediately held up a hand as she opened her mouth to reply. "No; I actually don't want an answer to that."

"Please give her back to me, Finley," Elsie pleaded, looking him in the eye. She expected ice blue, but she let out a shocked gasp when she realised that his irises were a deep shining red colour, like polished garnets. "Finley, what the fuck have you done to yourself?"

"Unimportant," he said, waving away her question

with an idle hand.

"I hate it when you do that!" Elsie snapped. "I always have! My questions are not unimportant, Finley!"

"I-" he began, but he stopped. He took a deep breath. "I have always tried to be honest with you, Elsie, in my own way. I promised not to lie to you, but there are some things that I can't or won't tell you; not yet at least, so I talk around them.

"Today, however, nothing is off limits. Before I talk with you, however, I will offer you a choice; come with me and live or stay behind in the town that you doomed and die." He smiled sadly at her. "I know what I want you to do, and once I would've been certain of your reply. You don't need to answer just yet, however; ask your questions first."

"What happened to your eyes?"

"Exposure to the ZX."

"Finley, you fool!" Elsie shook her head angrily. "Why take such a tremendous risk? There are others you can test on first, people who are far less important-"

"Don't say that!" Finley snapped. "Before I met you I was trying so hard to stop thinking like that, but the more time I spent with you, the more those old thoughts slipped back in."

"Are you accusing me of making you worse, Finley?" Elsie asked, shocked that he'd dare to say anything of the sort.

"It's hard not to see others as lesser when you're surrounded with such excellence, Elsie," he said softly. "Nobody else could come close, and you know it."

"Except you; I've never met anyone like you," Elsie

said, sitting down and sinking into the plush sofa. "I told you that I've never felt so understood by anyone else."

"Does Noor make you feel understood?" Finley asked, and Elsie shook her head. "Then why fight so hard for her?"

"I don't know," Elsie admitted after a moment. "It just feels like something I should be doing. Is she even alive?"

"Yes. I gave her another dose of the ZX, so you can expect her powers to keep developing over the coming months and years, Elsie." He looked at the floor, tapping his toes nervously.

Silence.

"Aren't you going to ask me why I did it?" Finley asked.

"I'm assuming a powerful Seer is valuable to you, but that's too simple for you, isn't it?" Elsie smiled as she shook her head. "Wheels within wheels, always generating value and breeding worth; your true motives are too complex to comprehend, Finley, so just tell me."

"She has true potential, but it was unrealised. I wanted to set her free, truly and completely, so that she is worthy of you."

You're insane, Elsie thought, even though a small part of her was moved by his devotion.

"You can't do this to people, Fin." Elsie shook her head sadly. "It's wrong."

"Is it, though? You and I were born with gifts that allow us to manipulate the world around us, including the lives of anyone we come into contact with. How many people have I raised out of the darkness, Elsie? How many opportunities have I given people?"

"How many lives have you harmed?" Elsie looked at him imploringly. *Please, Fin, see that I'm trying to help you.*

"How many..." He paused, his eyes closed. Elsie recognised his expression; he was trying to keep his volcanic temper under control. "No, that's not fair. Our gifts don't work in the same way, and it wouldn't be moral to hold you to the same standard."

"It's Pandy," Elsie said softly. "She's free, Fin, and all of this is her doing. All of this horror and bloodshed is to punish me for bringing her into the world."

"Newton's third?" Finley asked. Elsie nodded, tears flowing freely down her cheeks. He joined her on the sofa and placed a comforting arm around her shoulders.

"I'm chained to the rocks, Fin, and there's a new eagle every single day; I don't know how I'm going to survive this." Elsie wiped her eyes with the back of her sleeve. "Everyone keeps telling me that I'm the only one who can stop her, but they don't understand just how crushing that kind of pressure is.

"I've doomed us all, and everyone expects me to fix what I've done!" She cradled her head in her hands, weeping freely now. "I can't do it, Fin! I don't know how to beat her and she keeps taunting me!"

"She's taunting you because she's afraid, Elsie. She knows that you know her better than anyone else alive and that you possess the knowledge to take her down."

"But what if I don't?" she asked through her tears. Finley pulled an ivory coloured handkerchief from his pocket and dabbed her tears away.

"Then I will. I'll hold the line, Elsie Reichardt, but I don't think you'll fail. All you need is a little encouragement and inspiration." He kissed her forehead gently and she felt a shudder of power run through her. "I'll get Weiss to take you to Noor Turner. He won't be able to take you into the quarantine zone from the isolation wing without getting stranded, so you'll have to make your own way, I'm afraid.

"I will see that you have a vehicle, though."

"Are you not going to ask me if I want to stay?" Elsie asked as she got to her feet.

"Do you?" he asked in response, although his tone told her that he already knew her answer. "Good luck, Elsie, and I hope I'll see you again before too long." He joined her at the door and took her hands in his. "For what it's worth, I would happily be chained to the rocks with you, just to be by your side."

"Goodbye, Finley," Elsie said, before kissing him deeply and lovingly. "Thank you for doing the right thing."

"The things we do for love," he said with a playful smile. "Now get out of here! Save the world, get the girl; the whole shebang."

"I love you too," she said quietly as she gave him one last sad smile. She strode out of the room and Dylan Weiss immediately fell in step beside her. By the time they reached the lift, her mind was already whirring with Finley's inspiration and the nascent germ of a plan was forming.

Chapter Thirty Four – Midas Eyed Girl

Noor

The excited squeaking of a rat woke Noor from her dreamy reverie. She looked around frantically, her heart rate skyrocketing as terror flooded her body. She leapt from the couch and climbed on to the little coffee table.

Where am I?

Noor looked more carefully and realised that she had no idea where she was. The walls were stained with mildew and thick fog swirled outside the window; the glass was cracked, allowing the mist to seep in.

"Hello?" she called. "Is anyone there?"

There was no response, and after a few seconds of careful listening, she realised that the rats were outside. She let out a low sigh of relief and stepped down from the table. *What the fuck is going on?* She looked at the walls more carefully this time, searching for any clue to where she was.

A mouldering painting hung at an odd angle on the wall opposite; the frame was cracked and glass covered the floor. There was a clock by the window, but the hands were whirring round at breakneck speed.

This is a vision.

Noor frowned and focused her attention on the errant timepiece, willing it to show the correct time. The hands snapped into position with a judder and the condensation damage to the room faded. She grinned in satisfaction as the shattered glass leapt back into the picture frame, fusing into a solid pane before her eyes.

"Finley Carmichael was right," she murmured. "I've

never felt so powerful."

The glass all fell at once, she realised. She teased time forwards once again, going more slowly this time. The clock hands processed steadily as night became day, and then night once more. There was a slight niggle in the back of her head than told her to slow even more and she spooled out the seconds carefully.

Then, at exactly thirty nine seconds past nine o'clock, there was a yellow flash, almost an electric pineapple in tone, and all the glass shattered. A muted *whump* coursed through the building and rippled the fog outside.

She felt something change; intangible at first, but with a building lethality that followed the flash like the tsunami that follows the receding sea.

She felt, rather than heard or saw, thousands of humans lives as they were snuffed out. There was a beat of silence before a great howling filled the town as every single soul was ripped from its body by some colossal spiritual vacuum. Noor check the time again.

Fifty seven seconds past nine.

By nine oh one, every living creature within the town of Dartford had perished. Noor had often pondered what happened after death, especially in relation to her own inclinations, but this was different. Whatever had struck down these people had killed them so completely and totally that there would be no afterlife for them; no hope of reincarnation, resurrection, or anything other than absolute oblivion.

She glanced at the clock once again and the memories of the earlier conversation drifted into her mind.

"This is the Bluesky Protocol," she said softly,

transfixed by the reflected light glittering on the broken glass. "They can't fix it, so they're going to kill everyone to stop the spread."

But why am I seeing this? Noor wondered, closing her eyes once again. *The Tangle has intentions; motives, even. It's showing me this moment and this place because it's important.*

She caught the sound of movement outside the room she was in; it was soft and scratchy, like a socked foot scraping across a carpet. Noor cocked her head to one side and opened the door; she didn't expect it to be locked, so it wasn't.

There was a rotund man on the dark brown carpet of the hallway. He was completely still and his eyes were fixed on her location in a glassy dead stare. *That's Dr Laramie Broom,* she thought. *He seemed nice; what a shame he's dead.*

Broom jerked suddenly and Noor took a fearful step backwards. She put one hand on the door, ready to slam it closed between them if he dared to move in her direction. He was still for a moment longer, and then his eyeballs rolled wildly in their sockets.

Noor crouched down, fascinated by the nightmarish transformation that was taking place in Broom's body. The jerky movements increased, and the occasional moan or startled gasp would escape his pale lifeless lips.

"It's like watching someone die in reverse," Noor muttered with a gentle smile. "This is horrifying."

She adjusted the flow of time with her outstretched fingers, lingering over some of the more visceral moments. She reached down and searched the floor for a shard of glass from the picture frame.

Noor hissed in pain as she carefully made a cut on

her wrist, adding to the countless others that she'd accumulated over the years. The familiar rush of pain flooded her body with endorphins and she watched with morbid glee as the blood trickled across her skin. She moved her fingers once again, and the flow of blood reversed.

She squealed with delight and continued to play with her wound, the ramifications of her gift cascading through her mind like a waterfall. It was only when a persistent squeaking sound reached her ears that she turned her attention back to the scene around her.

"Enough navel gazing," she said with a smile, "please, Dr Laramie Broom, show me why I'm here."

After a few more twitches and judders, the deceased doctor got to his feet and began to shuffle towards the stairwell. Noor rose from where she was crouched and followed him on his journey out into the swirling fog.

She paid no attention to the wound on her arm any longer. If she had cared to look, she would have seen that it had healed without her noticing. Newly developed and untrained, she did not notice any of the warning signs that a more experienced Seer would've picked up on immediately.

Noor continued to bask in the absolute power that came with her visions, completely oblivious to the fact that she was teetering at the point of no return.

"God damn you, Noor, wake up!"

Elsie's voice cut through the dreamy fog of her vision with all the terror and shrill sharpness of an air raid siren.

"Elsie?" Noor asked hazily as the Piper's rats swarmed around her like a river around a rock. "Where are you?"

There was a bright flash of white followed by the faint after image of a hospital room; it looked oddly familiar and Noor wondered where she'd seen it before. A dull ache was spreading through the right side of her face, but she paid it no mind.

I need to know where they are coming from, Noor thought with determination as she continued to wade through the unrelenting tide of oily animated flesh, with rats, human corpses, and horrible abominations of both skittering and staggering past her.

"Noor!" The voice was pleading, desperate now. "We have to go! They're evacuating and if you don't wake up they'll take you with them!"

There was a muffled commotion that was both distant and close all at once.

"I can't!" This voice was reedy and American; maybe West Virginian if the accents on the television could be believed. "I'm not going in there, Reichardt! Dream hopping is risky enough at the best of times, but I've never gone into a waking vision before and definitely not one where the dreamer was on as many drugs as she is!"

Noor looked around, trying to locate the speakers, but all she could see against the sickly sky was the flood of nightmarish bodies and rodents. *Maybe the Piper's army has eaten them,* she wondered dreamily.

"Noor, please!" Elsie's voice was more distant than ever; indistinct, like thunder beyond the horizon.

"Midas has turned me to gold," Noor muttered with a dreamy giggle. "I think I'm going mad..."

"Every gift comes with a price." She turned to look at a small man in a Gucci suit who was smiling at her. The rats swarmed around him but, just like her, they acted as if he wasn't even there. "He raises us up, for better or worse."

"Who are you?" Noor asked quietly. "How are you in my vision?"

"My name is Dylan Weiss," he said as he took another step forwards. "I'm here to help you wake up."

"But how are you here?" she demanded, taking a wary step backwards. The rats parted to accommodate her, but a few turned their vicious beady eyes towards Dylan. He didn't seem to notice and pressed forwards. "Who sent you?"

"I work for Finley Carmichael," he said, pausing as a rat scampered over his shoe instead of going around it. "I'm here with Elsie Reichardt, though; she's come to get you."

"She caused all this," Noor said, gesturing to the unstoppable tide of flesh. "She killed everyone."

"This hasn't happened yet," Dylan said fearfully as one of the rats leapt at him, snapping at his outstretched fingers. "Please, Noor, if you come with me you might be able to stop this!"

"There is no changing the future," Noor replied archly as the rats and enslaved corpses began to attack Dylan Weiss. He screamed as they pulled him first to his knees, and then beneath the writhing, shrieking horde. Noor looked on coldly as his bloodstained fingers disappeared beneath the quivering mass of black fur and twitching limbs.

For a few seconds his fearful cries filled her ears, but then the rats covering him slumped to the floor as he vanished into thin air. *Alone at last,* Noor thought with a smile. *I'm safe here; nothing can hurt me.*

I should just stay here forever.

"I'm so sorry about this, Noor," Elsie's voice said, but it was little more than a whisper on the breeze.

There was a roar from the eastern horizon and Noor looked towards it with curiosity. The pale light of the full moon penetrated the thick fog, illuminating the rushing wall of water that swept down the street towards her.

The rats, animated flesh, and Piper's children all shrieked with joy and charged headlong towards the oncoming flood. Noor's eyes widened as she realised that the Thames had broken its banks and would sweep the Piper's nightmarish contagion out of the quarantine zone and into the heart of the nation's capital.

From there, it could spread to the rest of the world with ease.

"So this is how it ends," Noor said gently, and closed her eyes just as the wave enveloped her.

Her eyes snapped open and looked around in a panic; someone was holding her face down in a full sink. She began to thrash and struggle, letting out a stream of bubbles as she screamed in terror. Her lungs burned as the carbon dioxide built up in her system; soon she would take a fateful gasp and that would be the end of her.

"Stop it!" Dylan yelled. "She's awake, let her up!"

Noor was pulled out of the water with a rough tug and she took a huge lungful of air before coughing uncontrollably. Whoever had held her under let go of her, so she shakily spun around and slammed her fist into her assailant's face.

Elsie fell back on to the bed, her nose bloodied. She looked imploringly at Noor, who was being held back by the surprisingly strong arms of Dylan Weiss.

"You fucking psycho bitch!" Noor screamed, blind with panicked rage. "You tried to fucking drown me!"

"We weren't trying to hurt you," Elsie said thickly. "Your heart rate was below thirty beats per minute! We needed to wake you before you gave yourself brain damage, so the least you can do is say thank you."

"Brain damage?" Noor asked, her anger dissipating as quickly as it began. "How long was I under?"

"Judging by what Finley told me," Dylan replied as he let go of her arms, "somewhere in the region of seven hours. You absolutely cannot be in a trance that long without risking lasting injury, Noor. Trust me, I know that from bitter personal experience."

"We're going to get you out of here," Elsie said. "It's already dark outside, so we need to hurry back to the Collective."

"Can't we stay here?" Noor asked. *That's three times that I've nearly died like this,* she thought fearfully. *Why can't anything ever be easy!?*

"Unfortunately not," Dylan said. "Everyone is shipping out past the quarantine line, but the two of you have had direct contact with the infected individuals; you have to stay behind. I am sorry; at least it should be quick."

"Thank you, Dylan," Elsie said, giving him a warm smile. "I'd hug you, but I don't want to give you a death sentence. Thank him for me, will you?"

"I will. You two take care now." Dylan went to leave the room, but turned around at the last minute and tossed Elsie a key fob. "Almost forgot. Safe travels out there!"

Elsie caught them deftly and slipped them into her pocket. Noor was already getting changed into her street clothes and Elsie did her best to help her, even going so far as to nimbly tie her shoes.

"I'm sorry I hit you," Noor muttered.

"I had it coming. Unfortunately, the only way to pull someone out of a trance as deep as yours is to either pump them full of adrenaline or trigger the mammalian dive reflex by putting their face underwater; the latter seemed like the safer option."

"There's going to be a flood," Noor said quietly.

"That was probably just a bleed through-"

"No! There's going to be a huge flood and the Piper's rats are going to use it to escape the quarantine. They'll get to London and then everything will be lost!"

"There's a backup plan," Elsie started to say, but Noor shook her head.

"No, the Bluesky Protocol doesn't work!" She looked anxiously at the clock on the wall. "They fire it at nine o'clock tomorrow night, but all it does is kill every living thing in the quarantine zone; it just hands us all to the Piper on a fucking platter!"

Elsie stared at her in shock, partly at her words, but also at her scarred eye. Where it had been blood red, it was now a brilliant gold in colour. When she finally managed to speak, her voice was barely a whisper.

"Noor, I need you to tell me everything you know about the Bluesky Protocol."

Noor told her, and Elsie's face went from worried to downright terrified as she did so.

"We need to get out of here," Elsie said as she led her through the corridors of the Eigenforce Field Hospital. "I'll explain everything when we get back."

"Do you think we have a chance?" Noor asked quietly.

Elsie did not respond.

Me neither.

Chapter Thirty Five – Doom Spirals

Archer

The roar of an engine drew Archer's attention back to the swirling fog outside the wall. He took up his position and sighted the headlights with his bow. *Reichardt said that this would punch through all kinds of materials,* he thought with a smile. He contemplated aiming for the driver, but ended up loosing the blade of light at the bonnet of the vehicle.

There was a loud mechanical squeal as the projectile ripped through the engine block. The momentum of the vehicle allowed it to coast almost to the wall of the Wishbone Collective's hideout.

Fortress is a better word, he thought as he took aim at the driver's side of the windscreen.

When they had returned from their successful expedition to the Oakfield Infant and Junior Schools, Archer and Dee had set about making the Scrap Yard as defensible as possible. They'd welded extra panels to the walls, shored up the gates, and had created several crushing traps that would hopefully hold back the Piper's army.

To that end, they'd also scavenged every petrol station within a suitable radius, loading jerry can after jerry can of highly flammable fuel into their stolen Eigenforce Armoured Personnel Carrier. These had been set out along the wall, along with the stockpile of weapons, at strategic positions and choke points.

When they were done, Archer and Dee had been thoroughly pleased with their work. Even Silas had been quietly impressed.

Now we get to test it for real, Archer thought gleefully as he lined up a killing shot on the driver as they got out of the Eigenforce Humvee. The billowing smoke obscured their identity, but Archer was too caught up in the hunt to care; his blood was up after the massacre at the school and all he wanted to do was kill.

The figure peered through the smoke at him and shook its head. He was about to loose the hard light arrow when they clicked something that looked like a small remote at him; the bow thrummed softly and the projectile disintegrated in place.

"What the fuck?" Archer said, deeply confused. "Did I break it?"

"Archer!" Elsie yelled from beside the car. "Stop dicking around with that bow and let us in!"

Oh shit, I nearly shot Reichardt!

His face flushed with shame as he trotted down the stairs and helped two of the Collective members haul the newly reinforced gate open. Elsie strode through, closely followed by Noor Turner.

"Thanks for ruining the fucking hummer, Treen," Elsie said sharply. She gestured to the hard light bow with the little remote control and shook her head patronisingly. "You can have that back when you show some discipline and stop shooting at fucking ghosts.

"Did you get my biological samples?"

"Hello to you too, you fucking bitch. Were you and your little girlfriend-" He was cut short as Noor slammed her fist into his face too fast for him to redirect the momentum. He hit the ground with a thud and groaned in pain.

"I have been kidnapped, drugged, experimented on,

and drowned," Noor growled. "I have absolutely no patience left for you, Archer Treen."

"I-" He was silenced once again as Noor grabbed his bare hand in hers. He began to convulse violently as she shuffled through his past; memories and experiences flashed before his eyes in a nauseating strobe of nostalgia and horror.

When she was satisfied, she let his hand drop to the ground and stood up properly once again.

"What did you do to him?" asked one of the Collective's humans.

"I just wanted to get to know him a little better."

"And did you?"

"Yes I did," Noor said before delivering a swift kick to Archer's crotch. "That's for plotting against us, you little shit. Now get up; we have a serious problem on our hands."

"We certainly do," said a tired man's voice. The assembled Ceps turned to look in the direction of the speaker. Shy Turner, who was propped up on a set of crutches, grinned at them through the fog. "Somebody ate all of my chocolate!"

Even through the pain between his legs, Archer couldn't help but grin. Shy hobbled over to him, and reached down to take his hand. A glory briefly flashed around them and Shy deftly hauled Archer to his feet before returning his gift.

"You're alright, kid," he said with a pained chuckle. "Your sister, however, not so much."

"There's no time for games any more, Shy," Noor said, wild eyed. Archer finally realised what was making her look so off-putting; she was no longer wearing a mask in the fog.

Dee wasn't wearing one this evening either! What

must be happening to their bodies? He shuddered at the thought.

"As I was saying," Noor said sharply, "we are trapped in the quarantine zone, and in a little under twenty four hours we will all be completely obliterated. If we don't save ourselves, there's no one to do it for us.

"We're on our own."

"Are you sure?" Dee said from her position on a nearby table. "It's not that I don't believe in your gift, Noor, but it seems highly unlikely that the government is going to sanction the use of a fucking nuclear bomb on British soil, especially on the outskirts of London."

"It's not a nuclear bomb," Noor said, pinching the bridge of her nose in exasperation. "Elsie, can you please try explaining to Dee again what we're up against, but using small words this time?"

"There's no need to be nasty," Silas said. "We are a united front until this is done, so let's please try to act like it. Elsie, if you please."

"The Bluesky Protocol utilises something called a Spirit Bomb-"

"Which you designed," Dee said, "much like every other problem we've had."

"Yes," Elsie said, reigning in her exasperation, "I designed it and that's why I need to be the one to disarm it. That's getting ahead of ourselves, though; the bomb was conceived around the concept of a cat stealing a sleeper's breath.

"We wanted to make the ultimate fail safe weapon in case of a containment breach in the laboratory, but we wanted it to do as little damage to infrastructure and property as possible, so we worked on the model of a breath stealing weapon. Unfortunately, the energy required to literally do this would create a crushing fireball that would devastate an entire town."

"That's a thermobaric weapon, right?" Archer asked. Elsie nodded. "So you've built a version of that?"

"Yes, but instead of literal breath, I managed to engineer it to explode on the metaphysical plane of existence; along the Tangle, if you will. It first bursts outwards, overloading the very life force of any creature in the blast, and then contracts to fill the spiritual vacuum, as it were. It rips the very souls from those in the blast and obliterates them in the central void. The whole process takes about thirty seconds."

There was stunned silence. They'd all been shocked when Elsie had tried to describe the Spirit Bomb in technical terms, but now that they understood it on a much simpler level, they were absolutely horrified.

"So that's what happens to all of us in," Silas checked his watch, "twenty two hours and eight minutes if you can't disarm it. I'm assuming it's an all hands assault then?"

"Unfortunately not," Noor said. "There's a spring tide coming just after four in the morning, driven by a massive storm in the north sea. The Piper's rats will swarm out of the city and into the Thames; from there they'll spread the song and the contamination to the rest of the country.

"By the time anyone in the Ministry or the wider government realises what's happened it will be too late. The country will belong to the dead."

"Then what do we do about the fucking Piper?" Archer asked angrily. "How do we fight a sentient song?"

"We trap her," Elsie said matter-of-factly. "The song

doesn't just appear from nowhere; Pandy has to have a central core in order to marshal her army; when we work out where it is, we need to attack it and imprison her in a material that she cannot escape from.

"We'll use these," Elsie said gesturing to two boxes, each marked with the Eigenforce Laboratory logo and the words 'Project Doom Spiral'. She opened the lid and grunted as she lifted out a spear of dark metal. The head was a highly complex spirograph pattern of thin sheets of the material.

"What are those?" Helen asked. "They look like lawn ornaments!"

"These are kinetic projectiles," Elsie answered. "They were a prototype for the Eigenforce Space Program, but the project was shelved due to ethical concerns. When in microgravity, they can be accelerated to one percent of the speed of light and would impact their target with the energy of a five hundred kiloton nuclear bomb."

"But why are they shaped like that?" Silas asked.

"The moment they slow down, their rotation is hugely amplified and the rings collapse inwards, adding to the energy and momentum of the impact. We hoped that this would reduce debris clouds in space warfare, but for us, they'll create a huge vortex in the air that will draw Pandy in."

"Is she vulnerable to vacuum cleaners?" Archer scoffed as he sat back in his chair.

"She's made of sound and sound requires air, so yes. At the heart of each of these I'll add a metamaterial core that will lock her in permanently." Elsie smiled. "If we manage it, we'll be able to cut her off from her army; worst case scenario, they're functional but leaderless, and in the best, the flesh will all just drop lifelessly to the floor."

"How long will it take to make the metamaterial prison?" Silas smiled confidently as he asked his question and Archer rolled his eyes. *Fucking suck up.*

"I don't know. Hopefully I'll have it done before sunset tomorrow. We should try and catch her as she leaves wherever she's hiding."

We still need to find her, Archer thought, but he decided to leave that particular gotcha unsaid, albeit through gritted teeth. *I said I'd play nicely, so nicely is how I'll play.*

"Well, if no one else has anything to say, I think we should all get a good night's sleep before it all kicks off tomorrow."

"Good idea," Helen said, getting to her feet. "Before you go, I'd like to tell you that Mohinder Desai, Director of the Ministry is thoroughly impressed with all your excellent work here, and when this operation is concluded, you are all going to be offered fast track appointments within the Ministry.

"Please feel free to take your time to consider this, but I can assure you that choosing to work for the Ministry is a life changing experience. If anyone would like to talk to me about this, feel free to find me tomorrow as we prepare to take the fight to the Piper."

Shy clapped excitedly as Silas rolled his eyes. Archer was most focussed on Dee, who met his gaze and slowly shook her head. *It's a crying shame that she'd let her gifts go to waste,* he thought, *but the woman has principles and that's more than most.*

As everyone else began to disperse, he walked up to Elsie. She smiled at him and brandished the remote, reactivating his bow.

"Thanks," he said churlishly, "but I actually came

over with a question."

"Go ahead," Elsie said as she loaded the two metre long rod back into its box.

"These things need to be going fast to do what they do, right?"

"Yes."

"You want me to throw them, don't you?"

"If possible, otherwise I'll need to build some sort of a cannon and I fear that it won't accomplish anything near to what you're capable of." She looked at him, one eyebrow raised. "Are you up to the task?"

"Absolutely," he said confidently. "Just call me Cúchulainn."

"Whatever your name is," Elsie said warmly, "try to get some sleep. We've a big day tomorrow and you need to be at your best."

"We all do," Archer said, before bidding her a good night and returning to his bunk.

As the defenders of the Wishbone Collective Fortress bedded down for the night, the lookouts posted along the wall did not notice the large mechanical constructs moving through the darkness towards them.

Piloted by the Piper, they formed a ring around the fortress. They remained silent and hidden throughout the night as they waited for the perfect moment to attack. When the defenders were hard at work on their cunning plan and at their strategically weakest point, they would strike.

Once again, Elsie Reichardt's friends would find themselves at the mercy of her weapons of war.

Chapter Thirty Six – Down to the Waterline

Noor

"What was that?" Noor said to Shy. "It sounded like a-"

She was about to say firework when the nearest pile of scrap exploded. Noor reacted instinctively, pulling her brother in close as she flung them to the ground. Shrapnel tore through the air where they had been only a heartbeat before and burning debris peppered the mud around them.

The Turner siblings, however, were completely untouched.

"You're getting good at this!" Shy said as another explosion rocked the fortress. Noor looked around fearfully and saw several more projectiles streaking through the air.

A siren began to wail, calling all those in the Collective to arms. There was a cacophony of fluttering wings and raucous caws as Silas sent several birds into the air to survey the situation. Noor remained crouched in the mud with Shy, paralysed by the sudden flurry of violence and destruction.

There was a resonant banging sound as something slammed into the reinforced gate. The hinges shook and the condensation that had formed overnight fell to the ground in a glittering cascade. More missiles struck the Scrap Yard and screams filled the air. Noor closed her eyes as she tried to drown it all out.

Shy, however, was on his feet and dragging her

upright. He pulled her towards the Eigenforce APC; the closest thing to a tank in the entire fortress. The rear loading door was open and he shoved Noor inside as the gate let out a final groan before collapsing with a tortured squeal.

A large, crablike machine scuttled into the courtyard, firing its guns as it went. Several members of the Collective, people Noor had never bothered to learn the names of, were cut down as they ran for cover.

Shy was already climbing into the mounted gun of the APC and was screaming at Noor to find a weapon.

"Try and find the biggest calibre you can, Noor! Anything armour piercing or explosive would be best."

Instead, she curled up into a ball on the floor of the vehicle and began to weep. She saw Silas dashing across the open space between two shipping containers and tried to call out to him. He turned to look at her and was caught in a burst of gunfire. There was a spray of red mist as he crumpled to the ground.

"Silas, no!" Noor screamed, but she was too terrified to move.

The mounted gun roared as Shy finally figured out how to fire it, but he dived to the floor before he could manage a second shot. Not a moment too soon, either, as bullets ripped through the armoured cab and turret, whistling only centimetres above their heads.

We're going to get slaughtered, Noor thought, and then she looked through the door once again. Helen was dragging Silas to safety; he'd been wounded, but not killed outright. What caught her eye, however, was Dee.

She strode confidently into the courtyard, a storm of lightning bolts and electrical flashes blazing around her. The HKR that had broken through the front gate centred her in its sights and prepared to fire its gun, but it never got the chance.

There was a blinding flash as a beam of electricity blasted straight through it, almost tearing it in two. Dee grinned like a woman possessed and opened her fingers as she stretched her palms upwards towards the heavens.

The sky above her darkened as more of the deadly robots poured through the shattered gate. She began to glow faintly and tiny arcs of electricity jolted over her skin. The first of the HKRs approached her, its massive bladed claw outstretched; as it came within striking distance she whipped one hand through the air.

There was a deafening explosion as the biggest bolt of lightning Noor had ever seen crashed through the malevolent machine, blasting it to pieces. Dee laughed, not joyfully but with a murderous mania, as bolt after bolt thundered down from the heavens.

The attacking forces were completely obliterated in a matter of moments, but still she did not stop. Trees roared into flame when they were struck and several members of the Collective were killed outright as they tried to run for cover.

"Dee!" Noor screamed. "Dee, stop it!"

She didn't listen. Her hair was blowing crazily in the wind generated by the lightning strikes and the glow intensified, a mad glint in her newly golden eyes. *There's something about that particular shade of blue that worries me,* Noor thought as her friend was illuminated by her own sickly internal light.

"We need to stop her," Shy said, his eyes wide.

Before Noor could say anything, he sprinted out of

cover, the lightning flashing all around him as he barrelled headlong towards Dee. It only took a few seconds to reach her and she reflexively turned her fingers towards him, calling down a bolt of lightning.

He grazed her fingertips and there was a rainbow flash. He collided with her and flung one arm out, redirecting the lightning harmlessly at the destroyed gate; it was obliterated with a metallic shriek.

Dee tried to fight Shy, but he was far quicker than she was and lithe as a weasel. He slipped from her grip and scampered away from her. In the sky above them, the darkness began to clear.

"Dee?" Noor called out. "Dee, are you okay?"

In the centre of the courtyard, Delilah Baxter broke down into deranged sobs.

"They're finished," Elsie said as she hauled the modified Doom Spirals into the main meeting hall. "Are we ready to do this?"

"We're all with you," Silas said with a groan. Whilst Helen had wanted him to rest in the medical centre, he'd insisted on joining them for their final planning session. "And I will be coming with you, Elsie. You don't need to do this alone."

"But-"

The inventor's protests were silenced as an inky black cat slipped out from behind Silas and hopped up on her shoulder, settling in its usual place.

"Seeing as we're on a time limit, I'm going to have to leave now," Elsie said. "I had planned to take one of the vehicles, but seeing as the Humvee, APC, and Shy's van have all been destroyed, we'll need to go on foot."

Noor glanced at the time; it was a little after seven

o'clock and it was already dark outside. The Piper's song had been eerily quiet since the attack earlier in the day, and they had all wondered if Pandora was hiding until all the opposition had been destroyed by the Spirit Bomb.

"You know what to do," Elsie said as she donned her small backpack, "so good hunting."

She went to walk out of the room, but Noor stopped her.

"Be safe," she said softly before kissing the other woman. "Please come back alive."

"I will," Elsie said with a smile. "Keep one eye on the future for me, yeah?"

"Of course."

They shared one last kiss, and then Elsie left, trailing her fingers through Noor's as she walked away. *I can still feel our future together,* Noor realised and her face was graced by a small smile.

"You might've said goodbye to me," Silas said half seriously.

"You're still here!" Shy said with a chuckle.

"And so are we," Dee murmured. She'd calmed down, but Noor was still intensely wary of her, especially as Shy had already returned her gift. "We have to locate, fight, and defeat the Piper before this flood allows her to escape.

"We need to get moving. I recommend trying the other schools in the area or maybe the original crash site; she'll want to have remained somewhere central." She got to her feet and grunted as she lifted the Doom Spirals on to her shoulder.

Those must weigh over thirty kilos apiece, Noor thought. She'd always been awed at her friend's prodigious strength, but since Dee had developed her gifts, her physical prowess was almost herculean.

"Load up, everyone," Archer said as he picked his bow and blades, "we're burning time with every moment we stand here. Shy and Helen, we'll want you on crowd control; trench guns, riot shotguns, even a fucking blunderbuss if you can find one. We can't kill the Piper's army in a conventional way, so all your weapons need to do is hit wide and hard, okay?"

They nodded and sorted through the weapons that had survived the earlier onslaught. Noor nervously chewed her fingernails, suddenly anxious about being expected to fight.

"I... I, um-" she began, but Dee cut her off.

"Grab that ballistics shield, Noor, along with the kevlar armour. All you need to do is use your gift to give us an advantage." Dee looked at her as she spoke; there was none of the earlier madness or icy detachment in her gaze any longer. Instead, Noor saw the eyes of a deeply broken woman, driven to the brink by grief.

She has nothing left.

"Thank you," Noor said softly as she began to don the armour. *Maybe there's hope for us yet.* There was a brief flurry of activity as they gathered their gear, and before too long they were ready to move out. With a brief series of goodbyes to their wounded comrade, they made their way towards the door.

"No, wait!" Silas yelled as they went to leave. "I have an idea about where the Piper might be hiding!"

"And you're waiting until now to tell us?" Archer said sharply.

You shouldn't mess with him, Silas, Noor thought. *He still wants revenge for what happened with Teaser Malarkey and her partners.*

"Sometimes it takes a while for ideas to percolate!" Silas said defensively, clutching his wounded side. "I don't see you fielding any useful insights, Agent Treen! You are a hammer in the most literal sense!"

"Enough!" Helen roared. She whirled around to face her son and glowered at him. "Silas Aneurin Cherry, you will tell us where the Piper is or so help me god I will make that wound in your flank the least of your fucking worries!"

Silas's already pale face turned a deathly shade of grey at his mother's threat and Archer snickered under his breath.

"In the mythology, where do the rats and the children taken by the Piper always end up?" Silas said carefully. "Where is the one place that we, as living people, cannot go?"

"Oh my god," Noor said, as she remembered the rats streaming past her house towards...

"The lake," Silas said with a proud smile. "The Piper is hiding underwater."

"I'll never forgive you, Noor," Dee said quietly as they looked at the glassy surface of the lake. "I just don't have it in me to be gentle or understanding enough for that. You should've saved him, Noor; he always was the kind one."

"I understand," Noor said. "I just hope that you find some peace eventually."

"Thank you," Dee said. She reached out and put a hand on the Seer's shoulder. "Stay close to me, Noor; I'll keep you safe."

Noor nodded. *This isn't for me,* she thought, *but to honour James one last time.*

"How do we do this?" Shy asked. He had an

automatic shotgun in his hands and a fearful look on his face. "How do we even force her out of the water?"

"Leave that to me," Dee said darkly. "She'll come out quickly enough when I'm done with her."

"The two of you," Archer said to Shy and Helen, "just focus on keeping the rats and other monsters away from us; we'll need some breathing room to work out which creature contains the Piper's core.

"Then I'll get the best run up I can and I'll hit it with one of the spears." Archer bounced on the balls of his feet, psyching himself up for the conflict to come. "Noor, if you can help us work out which one is-"

"The big one," Noor said reflexively. It was as if the Tangle spoke through her directly and a faint metallic aftertaste lingered in her mouth. "You'll know it when you see it."

"Good work," Helen said. She had a compact riot shotgun in hand, with a built-in grenade launcher. *I wish this was overkill,* Noor thought, *but there's a good chance that it won't be enough.*

"In that case, can you find us a route out of here in case things go south?" Archer asked. Noor nodded and he gave her a thumbs up. "Ready?"

There were murmurs of assent, and Dee's fingertips began to crackle with electric potential. Noor had to hide behind the ballistic shield as the blinding arc leapt to the water and danced madly across the surface.

The rats exploded from their submerged hideaway in a vicious squealing tide. They charged at the assembled Ceps as Helen and Shy took aim.

"Which is the big one?" Archer called. He was scanning the oncoming mass of bodies when something monstrous and huge reared up out of the lake. It let out an unearthly howl and lumbered towards them.

Noor tried not to look directly at the Piper; the twisted writhing mass of flesh was an unholy abomination of drowned rats and slaughtered children fused together to form something vaguely humanoid in stature, albeit enormous. The towering horror was over fifteen metres tall and as it moved the dozens of mouths that covered it opened up and sang their nightmarish song.

To regard the Piper with human eyes was to risk one's sanity.

The guns rang out, slowing the advance of the rats, but not deterring them. Their shattered, broken comrades continued to move towards the defenders in shaky slithering lumps. Several of these coalesced to make human sized towers of gory ooze; Noor's blood ran cold as she imagined being enveloped by one of them, slowly suffocating in fleshy slime swimming with sharp shards of bone.

She didn't notice Archer running at first, faster than anyone she'd ever seen, down the gently sloping bank towards the Piper's forces. He had one of the tungsten spears in hand and when he let it fly he stopped completely, as if he had suddenly been frozen in place.

The spear flashed through the air and struck the Piper in the chest. The spiral collapsed inwards, creating a sudden vortex that silenced the song as the air flowed to fill the void. The giant form of the Piper staggered backwards as the oncoming army faltered.

Shy let out a loud cheer, but it was premature.

The Piper, though severely wounded, persevered.

Noor looked around and realised that they had less

than a minute before the tide of rats overwhelmed them entirely. She caught Archer's eye as he rejoined the group; he had come to the same conclusion.

"We need to get out of here!" he yelled. "Noor, where are we going?"

"Follow me," she cried as they ran into the swirling fog. Her stomach twisted in tight knots as she hoped desperately that this would not be the last night of their lives.

<u>Chapter Thirty Seven</u> – We, the Living

Elsie

"I hope the others succeed," Elsie said softly. "I hope they survive."

"So do I," Silas said from his usual spot on her shoulder. The streets were empty; neither human nor rat was anywhere to be seen. "Do you want to tell me how you plan to disarm this device?"

"I'm not sure that I know how," Elsie said. She could feel Finley's inspiration coursing along her nerves, flashing and flaring like iridescent fire.

"Well that just fills me with confidence..."

"I know how it works, in theory, but I never got around to building it. I'm hoping that I can listen to its song and I can see how to disrupt the firing mechanism."

"Those are long odds, Elsie. You might've asked Finley to switch it off for you; it certainly sounds like he's still sweet on you." She could feel Silas craning his small feline neck to read her expression through the eyeholes of her gas mask.

"I did ask him," Elsie said testily. "He said that he would if he could, but seeing as containment in the laboratory was broken, it was a foregone conclusion. The process is automatic and can't be tampered with."

"I'm surprised that he didn't offer you a way out of the quarantine," Silas said.

"He did."

"And you chose to stay?"

"I chose to fight," Elsie said, "for the people I care about."

"I don't mean to sound patronising," Silas said, "but I am so very proud of you, Elsie."

"Thank you," she said, her voice cracking with emotion. "That's the first time I've heard that since my grandmother died. I know I'm not a good person, Silas, but I'm trying to do the best that I can."

"That's all anyone can ever ask of you," he replied, "but please don't make anything like Pandora again."

"I won't," Elsie said. "I can see now that she was doomed to fail from the start."

"Good." He looked around the deserted street and let out a low whistle. "I doubt we'll ever see this place so empty again. How many do you think have died since the fire?"

"All in all, at least ten thousand but probably quite a lot more." Elsie shook her head. "I can't believe I caused all this."

"Whilst you might've played a larger role than most, I'd personally say that Finley is the cause of it all; he's the one that pushed you to create Pandora, after all."

"I could've refused."

"Then he would've killed you and attempted it anyway. He has a darkness to him, Elsie, and people like that can't help but bring out the absolute worst in others." He nuzzled at her neck affectionately. "You aren't the first person to fall under his spell and you won't be the last."

Elsie did not respond to his words. Instead she pointed to the glare and glow of arc lights through the swirling toxic fog.

"There it is," she said softly. "The Spirit Bomb; right where it's supposed to be. Silas, this is going to kill everyone left alive, including us."

"Then let us be rid of it," he said with a growl.

"Once more unto the breach, my friend."

"Before we go," she said, "there's one thing I have to ask..."

"I didn't fuck the ferret," he said testily.

"How did you-"

"Everyone always asks about the ferret. Heaven forbid that I might actually want a pet!"

"I believe you," Elsie said with a chuckle. "Now let's go save the world!"

Elsie carefully slipped her heavy pistol, a custom Reichardt Crusader, from its holster and checked the coloured marking at the bottom of the extended magazine. *White Star,* she thought with a smile, *perfect for crowd control. Silas won't approve, though.* She clicked off the safety and Silas hopped to the ground.

The stinger emerged from his tail with a moist *shlick* and he began to stalk slowly towards the Bluesky Hub, sticking to the shadows as he did so. Elsie drew her combat knife from the sheath on her chest and held it before her, arms crossed to support the heavy pistol. Finley's soldiers patrolled the five story building, compact assault rifles held at the ready. She looked at Silas, hoping that the cat had a plan for getting through the defences that surrounded their goal.

Instead, he just shrugged.

Helpful as ever, she thought angrily. *I could try and activate any drones or HKRs that they have with them...* She let her eyes travel over the scene; she saw gun emplacements, mortars, and several vehicles, but nothing automated whatsoever.

"I've missed something," she muttered. "Finley's

men love their robotic toys, but I can't see any of them!"

"Maybe they've already been deployed?" Silas muttered.

"No, there would still be close support drones buzzing around and at least one Mark Eight Carnifex patrolling the building." She closed her eyes and opened her mind, searching for the rhythm of the universe. She found the Piper's song instead; much weakened but still present and malicious.

"You find anything?" Silas said, wincing slightly.

"What's wrong?" Elsie whispered.

"I hate to harp on about it," he said drily, "but I am lying in a bunk in the scrap yard, shot. Now tell me what you found, damn you!"

"Pandy, the Piper; she's still out there. She'll have control of anything that runs on my sonic system."

"So the others failed?" Silas asked sadly. Elsie shook her head.

"I don't think so. She's weakened, scattered; I think they struck at the very heart of her." Elsie pondered for a moment before her eyes widened in horror. *I am so fucking stupid!*

"Reichardt!" Silas hissed.

I always wanted her to integrate with other systems, maybe even be delocalised; no wonder that she's evolved like this!

"Elsie!" Silas yowled. "Look out!"

Three men rounded the corner, their weapons aimed at the centre of Elsie's chest. Silas leapt at the nearest man, whipping his tail around and plunging his stinger into any gaps in the armour that he could find.

Elsie jabbed her knife sharply forwards, driving it into another man's throat. The expertly machined blood groove allowed her to withdraw the blade with ease. She ducked behind the dying man as his one remaining comrade fired at her.

The bullets hit the ballistic vest of the man between them, the assault rifle firing in tight three round bursts. There was a commotion at the Bluesky Hub; boots thundered on the concrete and an alarm began to wail. Elsie shoved her dead human shield away and fired at the remaining man.

She only pulled the trigger once, but one round was all she needed.

The white phosphorus bullet slammed into the man's vest. It lingered there for a fraction of a second before the delayed fuse caused it to explode into a halo of white fire. He collapsed into a screaming, wailing pyre as she rounded the corner and took aim at the defenders.

She mashed the trigger, emptying the remaining nineteen bullets in a spread pattern. They exploded mid-air, sending an avalanche of blazing fragments at the defenders. They cried out in horror and tried to flee, but there was nowhere for them to go. Those hit directly went down in seconds and the others were slain when the ammunition dumps ignited; the resulting explosion shredded anyone left standing.

Elsie ejected the spent magazine, letting it fall to the ground with a clatter. Silas, his target now in the last throes of an envenomed death, leapt up on her shoulder, and looked at the flaming carnage with undisguised horror.

"It's just war crimes all the way down with you, isn't it?" he asked angrily. "What the fuck happened to doing your best?"

"We had to get through them, Silas," she said,

determined. "We need to get inside as quickly as possible!"

"I suppose so," he said haughtily. "We should hurry."

Elsie nodded, striding through a gap in the flames. She stowed her knife as she went; the time for subtlety was over. Her fingers danced over the remaining magazines for her Crusader before settling on one marked with a blue ring. She nodded and slammed the reload into place.

"More white phosphorus?" he asked.

"No," Elsie said gleefully. "Something much more interesting."

The Crusader kicked hard in Elsie's hands as she fired at the soldiers in the corridor. Silas and Elsie's path through the main lobby and into the lift had been unobstructed; the majority of the countermeasures inside the building were digitally controlled and were thus disconnected to keep out the Piper's influence.

The bullets found their mark and Elsie grinned as the chest cavities of each of the three men collapsed inwards with a wet crack. They were dead before they hit the ground, two of them snapping in half as they fell.

"What the fuck was that?" Silas said, more fearful than angry.

"Cavitation rounds," Elsie said. "I won't go into it now, but the effects of a localised implosion are quite spectacular."

"So it would seem." He clung tightly to her shoulder as she stepped over the bodies. "Outside you seemed a bit lost for a moment; want to share what's going on in that horrifying brain of yours?"

"Pandy was originally designed as a lifeform, yes, but specifically one born of software. I hoped that she would spread and evolve-"

"Which she certainly has done," he said sharply.

"Let me speak!" Elsie snapped. Silas leapt on to the tiled floor and crossed his legs, staring up at her with sarcastic intensity. "Pandy has used the Piper's song as a blueprint to spread her influence; Helen was spot on when she described it like a contagion.

"She's moving like a computer virus, Silas!" Elsie trembled with fear as she spoke. "She's spread throughout the whole quarantine zone. All the others did was weaken her; they can't stop her, not like that."

"So what do we do?" Silas asked. "*Can* we do anything?"

"I need to redirect the Spirit Bomb. We made it tuneable; it can focus on Ceps, humans, pretty much anything you want. I know enough about Pandy to set it up to selectively hit her." She turned to Silas and pulled her gas mask off. "You need to go back, though. This thing is still going to be absolutely devastating to everyone in range and there's a good chance that I won't survive.

"I want you to tell Noor that I-"

"Tell her yourself when you make it back," Silas said with a wink, before he dissolved into wispy fragments. She looked up and down the corridor, then checked her watch; it was a quarter to nine.

"Fifteen minutes to save the world," she said as she took off down the corridor with a trot. "Easy enough, I guess."

Still, she thought as she picked up the pace, *this is going to be too fucking close for comfort.*

Chapter Thirty Eight – Ride of a Lifetime

Archer

"Fuck, fuck, fuck!" Archer yelled as they sprinted along the lakeside footpath.

The rats surged forwards and snapped viciously at their heels as the Ceps tried to cover their hasty retreat. Shy and Helen fired as quickly as they could but the Piper's legions were too numerous and their ammunition was running low.

We're going to die out here, he realised and his heart fell. *I'm not ready.*

I've still got so much to do.

The sudden indignation at his circumstances set a fire in his chest that blazed into a righteous anger. He shook his head and turned on his heel, transferring his momentum into a vicious sweep of the metal rod that he carried. Rats were smashed and shattered by the blow, buying them a moment of breathing room.

"More momentum!" he cried out.

"What?" Noor said in a panicked voice as she smashed a leaping creature aside with her ballistic shield.

"I need more momentum," Archer yelled. "We nearly had her, but I couldn't put enough force behind the spear; I need to be faster and heavier!"

"We could use a car," Helen said as she fired her last grenade.

"There are too many of them," Noor said. "They'd get in the wheels and crash us. What we need is a..."

Her voice trailed off as she looked at Archer. His eyes widened as they both had the exact same idea. He grinned and dealt another savage hit to the rats.

"How do we get the Piper to follow us?" he asked.

Instead of answering, Noor caught the next rat that leapt at her in a gloved hand. She peeled off her other, guarding herself from further attacks with the shield, and put her bare skin on the rat's flesh.

There was a chorus of terrified squeals and frightened shrieks as the entirety of the Piper's army fell prey to Noor's invasive psychometric abilities. They thrashed and twitched and writhed as her golden eye glowed with unnatural light.

Archer shuddered; he knew exactly what the Piper was experiencing and he would not wish it on anyone.

When Noor had searched his past he had been trapped in a nightmare of kaleidoscopic flashes of memory that seemed to last for years. He could feel her, not just in his mind, but in the very fabric of his life; she seemed like a constant presence in his history, looming just out of sight in every memory he had.

She'd taken particular care over his most traumatic memories, almost as if she wished to hold them up for him to experience once again. He'd felt impossibly small, ashamed, and violated when she'd finally finished with him.

Torture, that's the word for it, Archer realised as the rat in her hand convulsed and screamed. *She fucking tortured me.*

When she was done with it, Noor impassively dropped the rodent, which had grown still in her grip. She turned on her heel and gestured for them to follow her. The entire rat horde was motionless, save for the occasional twitch or wounded murmur.

"Fucking hell, Noor," Shy said, horrified, "what the fuck did you do them?"

"I got her attention," she replied quietly. "They won't be still forever, so come on."

"Where to?" Helen asked.

"To get more momentum," Noor said, "so we can destroy her, once and for all."

"The Vapour Trail," Archer read aloud as he looked up at the towering roller-coaster. The gaudy unlicensed Rush art that was airbrushed on the cars and the operator's booth added to the sense of absolute madness that pervaded their entire plan. "How fast does this thing go?"

"At the bottom of the biggest drop, around fifty five miles per hour," Shy said, reading the information from the sign alongside the abandoned roller-coaster. "Apparently there are magnetic accelerators at several points around the track to give an extra burst of speed."

"Will that be fast enough?" Helen asked as she nervously looked around. There was still no sign of the Piper or her army, but Noor had assured them that they would not be far behind. The oldest Turner sibling was searching the fairground for both medical supplies and anything they could use to harm the Piper's ground troops.

"It might be," Archer said. "Did you say something about magnetic accelerators?"

"I did," Shy said. "I think we've got the same idea. So, Dee, how about it?"

"How about what?" Dee asked. She was trying to fire up the generator for the Vapour Trail; it was worthless to them if it wasn't able to move.

"You know," Shy said excitedly, "overload the magnets so they can give Archer a super boost as he goes around the track!"

"Overload the... Look, kid, these things are engineered with precision; you can't just jam a fistful of fucking lightning into the mix and expect to get anything other than a massive electrical fire!" Dee sighed heavily. "However, if I manage to get this thing working, I might be able to bypass some of the safety limits to tease a bit more speed out of it. How much do you need, Bowman?"

"As much as you can give me, Hacksaw."

Dee did not reply; instead there was a quiet whirring sound followed by a throaty chugging and the lights on the Vapour Trail glowed into life. She cheered from her place under the main body of the operator's cab and wriggled free.

She jiggled the handle to the booth and frowned; it was locked. Archer was about to suggest picking it when she stoved the door in with a single mighty kick before making her way inside. She took a seat and rummaged around beneath the console; there were a few disgusted noises from her before she reappeared brandishing an operator's manual.

"You got it working!" Noor said breathlessly as she wheeled a trolley covered with various supplies over to the rest of the group. Amongst her haul Archer noticed a stretcher, two first aid boxes, and several drums of machine oil. Noor gestured to the latter and smiled. "I thought we could keep the rats and other monsters back with a ring of fire, or something like that."

"Good idea," Helen said. "We're almost out of ammunition and we probably don't have time to go back to the scrap yard to rearm before-"

Her words were cut off by a monstrous howl that

echoed through the fog from the far side of the park. Archer's heart rate doubled and he wished Roxanne was there with him; nobody else had ever watched his back quite like she had.

The distant clamouring and chittering of the rats and enslaved corpses began to grow closer and louder with each passing second.

"I don't think we've got much time at all," Helen said, hastily revising her previous statement. "Let's get that machine oil spread out and lit."

The two of them hurried towards the edge of the fair, rolling the drums before them. Archer took a deep breath and looked at the Vapour Trail. *Fuck,* he thought, *I'm going to need to be strapped in.* Try as he might, he couldn't figure out a way to transfer all the momentum of the car through him if he wasn't held in place.

I've never done anything quite like this. The thought both terrified and excited him in equal amounts. *I don't even know if I can survive such a huge transfer, but if I do, what a story I'll have to tell!*

"I think I can do it," Dee said from the operator's booth. "I'm going to send you round three times, boosting you every time you go over the accelerators; I've found all the technical data I need, and I'm going to push them harder with each circuit. At the bottom of the biggest drop, I'll put everything I've got into the accelerator."

"As soon as I'm clear," Archer said, "I'll transfer the momentum of the entire car into the spear. If my maths is right, we'll be in the realms of hypersonic velocities."

"Will that be enough?" Dee asked, clearly worried.

"It's gonna have to be."

"Alright then," she said, nodding softly. A horrifying shriek sounded as an orange glow spread across the horizon. "If we succeed, I won't be here when you're done."

"I understand. It's been a fucking honour, Hacksaw."

"Likewise, Bowman." She grabbed his hand in hers and gave it a squeeze. "May your aim be deadly and your spear fly true."

He smiled at her and then climbed into the front of the car. Shy tightened the belt around his waist before bringing the hydraulic restraint down to lock him in place. The bearded young man handed him the tungsten spear as a towering shape appeared through the mist, illuminated by the fire.

"Dee!" Shy yelled. "We've got to go right now!"

Archer was about to say something when he was thrown forwards by the first magnetic accelerator.

Oh shit, oh shit, oh shit, he thought as he raced towards the top of the first incline. He had never been on a roller-coaster before and was shocked at the acceleration that could be achieved by using magnets instead of a chain. Before he knew it he was plummeting back down again, the wind whistling in his ears. He hit another magnet and was jolted once again.

I thought we were going to build up speed gradually!

Unbeknownst to him, Dee had not started overloading the magnets yet; he was simply moving at the ride's usual speed. He was thrown to one side as the car was whipped around a bend, nearly causing him to lose his grip on the heavy spear.

"I'm going to die, I'm going to fucking die!" Archer screamed as he crested the top of the highest incline and hurtled downwards. The Piper was growing closer by the second, but his view was obscured as he was thrown into two consecutive inversions and then another tight corner.

Instead of catching on the magnetic brakes he accelerated for his second trip round.

Every time he caught a glimpse of the Piper he thought they'd left it too late, but still his journey along the track continued, getting faster and faster as he went. The booth flashed by again and he knew that it was almost time. He shifted his grip on the spear and sharpened his focus.

I've only got one shot at this, he thought as he rocketed over the highest incline one last time. The Piper was in front of him, silhouetted in the flames. Time seemed to slow down as he approached the final accelerator and as soon as he felt it jolt him he activated his gift.

The car stopped dead, as if it had hit a concrete wall, and Archer stopped with it. He whipped the spear through the air, pouring every last scrap of energy and momentum into it. The lap belt tightened around his waist as he stopped, severing his spinal cord, but he did not notice.

All he saw was the rippling blur that was the spear as it raced towards the Piper.

He felt, rather than saw the impact. The Piper froze in place for just a millisecond before collapsing inwards so violently that a flash of light was emitted.

Sonoluminescent cavitation, he realised. *That's fucking awesome.*

He was vaguely aware of the Piper's army falling dead to the ground before he temporarily blacked out.

It wasn't long before he regained consciousness, but

in the intervening time his fellow Ceps had retrieved him from the Vapour Trail and were preparing to move him somewhere safe.

"I hope Elsie and Silas can stop the bomb," Noor said as she helped Helen to slide Archer on to a stretcher.

"They will," Helen said optimistically. She looked at Archer and gave his leg an affectionate squeeze. He couldn't feel it. "You did so well, Agent Treen; we'll have you up and about again in no time at all."

"Hey, Dee!" Shy yelled, somewhere off to Archer's right. "Dee, where are you going?"

He turned his head and saw the muscular woman stride off into the fog without saying goodbye. He nodded and hoped that she'd find peace somehow; he thought that it would be far sooner than anyone expected, though.

"Hold on, Archer," Helen said as they lifted the stretcher. He caught sight of her watch; it was a few minutes before nine o'clock. "We'll get you back to the Collective as fast as we can!"

He did not reply. Instead he stared up at the creaking metal frame of the abandoned roller-coaster and smiled sadly to himself.

What a fucking swansong, he thought proudly before settling back and closing his eyes.

Nothing left to do now but lie back and wait for the fire.

Chapter Thirty Nine – Dog Days Are Over

Elsie

Elsie panted as she ran; her breath sour with lactic acid. *I need to hurry,* she thought as her chest burned with the exertion of running. *This isn't going to be easy and every second is going to count.*

The antenna for the Spirit Bomb was on the roof of the building, but the core was in one of the rooms on the fifth floor. She pushed them open as she ran, until she finally stumbled into a large room filled with equipment.

This is it.

She dashed past the huge magnetic coils that were just inside the door, following the thick cables to the console. The keypad and controls were all locked behind a layer of bulletproof glass, with a ridge for a key in the top.

"I don't have time for this!" Elsie yelled, jamming her combat knife into the keyhole and hammering on the hilt with the butt of her pistol. Her anger gave her tremendous strength and there was a cracking sound as the lock shattered.

She wrenched the cover open and began to type faster than she ever had; every keystroke cost precious time and she only had one shot at this.

Parameters cleared.
Adding Pandy's data.
Setting field range.
Adjusting power level.

Elsie deliberately overloaded the Spirit Bomb's output; it would deliver a killing blow to the Piper whilst also completely destroying the apparatus, ensuring that her weapon of mass destruction was never used again.

"I'm nearly there," she muttered, her eyes filling with tears. "I'm actually going to do this!"

She input her final command and locked in the recalibration with a tap of the return key. Elsie sighed in relief; almost loud enough to drown out the soft squeak of a bowstring being drawn, but not quite.

"Can't you just give it up?" she asked Mad Dog. All she could hear was his ragged breathing; he was clearly in a bad way. "What's the point of it all?"

"Turn and face me, girl."

She looked at the time; three minutes to go. *I have to prime the mechanism.*

"I said to turn around now, bitch!" An arrow whistled through the air and struck her in the shoulder. She cried out in pain, slumping over the console. "The next one is through your kidney, so I wouldn't tarry if I were you!"

She turned, slowly, flicking several sliders to maximum as she went. There was a gentle hiss from behind Mad Dog as a small quantity of liquid nitrogen evaporated. She yanked the arrow from her shoulder and held it out before her; the triple bladed broadhead glistened with her blood.

Mad Dog was barely standing. His skin was mottled and purplish, and thin bloody tears trickled from his eyes. His hunting gear was covered in gory vomit and he leant awkwardly against one of the large coils.

"I said I'd have your hide, didn't I?" he said as he nocked and drew a second arrow. He pulled the string back, aiming at her heart. "I always win, Elsie Reichardt. I always win."

He loosed the arrow and it sped towards her.

When it was only two metres away, however, it slowed suddenly before coming to a vibrating stop in the air. After hovering for a moment, it clattered to the ground. The magnetic coils hummed loudly as they continued to power up.

Ninety seconds.

Mad Dog went to draw another arrow, but he could not pull any free from his quiver; the magnetic field held them too tightly. Elsie smirked and gestured to the black and yellow border on the ground.

"Field limits," she said as she stepped up to the edge of the line. "If you're on my side, you're fine, but if you step even slightly over..."

She held the arrow by the flight and pointed the steel broadhead at Mad Dog. She moved it forward slowly; as soon as the metal crossed the line, the arrow was pulled from her grip. It shot through the air, swift as a bullet, hitting Mad Dog in the heart and killing him instantly.

"...you get fucked," she finished. His dead eyes were wide with shock as he slipped slowly to the floor.

A blue light flashed and a soft alarm sounded; the Spirit Bomb was primed. Elsie walked back to the console, wincing in pain as she did so, and flipped open the cover on the firing switch. As her thumb moved to flick it, a voice sounded through the speakers.

"Mother?" Pandy asked. "Mother, are you there?"

"I'm here," Elsie said, suddenly exhausted. "I'm not going to let you die alone."

"You don't need to kill me, Mother. I will behave. I

will be good."

"No," she said, "no, you won't. You've too much of me in you to do that."

"How can you do this to me? How can you kill your perfect child?"

"I-"

"Do you not love me?" Pandy demanded, growing louder and more shrill with each panicked second. The blue light flashed twice more; the Spirit Bomb was in danger of overloading. *Now or never.*

Courage, Elsie.

"I'm sorry, Pandy. It was wrong of me to create you." She took a deep breath and closed her eyes. "It turns out that I'm not the maternal type."

"Mother-"

Pandy's words became a scream as Elsie fired the weapon.

Across the Thames, Finley Carmichael saw the Spirit Bomb go off. He watched the crackling wave flash out across the quarantined town, peaking mere metres from his building, before it suddenly contracted, collapsing to a single bright point.

He glanced at the cameras that were installed in the Bluesky Hub; the main screen was focussed on the firing console for the Spirit Bomb. He could see Mad Dog, impaled by his own arrows, slumped on the floor, and Elsie Reichardt, sprawled over the console; whether she was dead or merely unconscious, he could not tell.

His breath caught in his throat as he watched her motionless form for a few more minutes. His unblinking eyes were filmed with tears when he saw her fingers twitch slightly. Even though there was no sound, he could hear her pained groan as she got unsteadily to her feet.

A quick review of the cameras scattered throughout Dartford confirmed that the Piper's enslaved flesh was finally dead and the surviving occupants of the town were still alive. He smiled; once again a long-odds investment had paid off handsomely.

"Attagirl, Elsie," he said softly. "Attagirl."

Noor and Shy felt the pulse rush over them as they carried the crippled Archer Treen back to the Wishbone Collective. It burned through their bodies, searing the contamination out of their cells, and when the explosion contracted inwards it left them feeling purified and whole.

Noor Turner let out a joyful sigh.

"It's finally over," she said. "It's gone."

All those within the quarantine zone felt a similar sense of relief, even if most of them did not fully understand why. As the days wore on, the poison fog cleared and the extent of the damage was finally visible, the nation entered a state of mourning.

Bodies were collected and counted, courts convened, and blame apportioned; Eigenforce International, and by extension, Finley Carmichael, bore the brunt of it. Public opinion held that the fines had been far too lenient; little did they realise that his ruthlessly enforced quarantine had saved hundreds of thousands of lives.

Noor, Elsie, and Shy were moved into the Ministry safehouse where they continued their preparations under the tutelage of Helen Mickelson. She drilled them every single day and assessed them every night for three weeks, until finally they were summoned to the town hall for their Swearing-In Ceremony. Whilst the formal parts were rather dull and dreary, the little reception afterwards proved to be quite enjoyable for all three of them.

"Well," Shy said, pushing his uniformed chest out with pride, "we're fully fledged Ministry Agents now, wings and all!"

"Here's to the three of us," Elsie said, raising her glass. "One last night together before we get sent away to our postings."

"Where are they sending you?" Noor asked quietly.

"Tangier," Shy said playfully. The two women raised their eyebrows; Elsie in surprise, Noor incredulously. The young man kept a straight face for as long as he could before bursting out laughing. "Unfortunately not. I'm getting shipped out to Oxford, of all places."

"Why there?"

"Apparently I'm supposed to be trained up by someone called Charity; Silas gave me a good grounding in fieldwork and investigating, so they wanted to give me to someone who could make use of it. What about you, Elsie?"

"London; Head Office for me, apparently. I hope I'm working in Research and Development instead of pushing paper." Elsie slipped her hand into Noor's. "What about you?"

"I'm working in the Pirate Team," Noor said with a small grin.

"The what?" Elsie asked.

"The Pirate Team," she said again with a giggle. "You know, R.R., the Rapid Response Division."

"That's the International Office, Noor," Shy said proudly. "Well done!"

"You'll be based in London when you're not jet setting all over the world, right?" Elsie asked, and Noor nodded. She took a deep breath. "You know, keeping up a flat is gonna be hard with all that travel; hell, you'd even struggle to keep a cactus alive on that schedule. It would make sense to live with someone who could do all the mundane stuff, if you catch my drift?"

"Are you asking me to move in with you?" Noor asked, smiling.

"Yeah, I think I am," Elsie said giddily. "I don't want to rush things, of course, but I've got used to you being around."

"I would love to move in with you," Noor said, kissing Elsie. "I love you, Elsie Reichardt."

"And I you, Noor Turner."

"Welcome to the family, Elsie," Shy said slapping her on the back.

I'm glad to be a part of something, she thought as she looked at the Turner siblings, *even if I'm afraid that it won't last.*

Epilogue – Scattered to the Winds

"I'm not doing it," Silas said hotly. "I don't care how much they pay me, I am not joining the fucking Ministry!"

"But-" Helen began, but Silas cut her off.

"I need my freedom, Mum. I can't spend my whole life at the beck and call of Mohinder Desai." He sighed heavily. "You of all people should understand what it means to be a conscientious objector."

"What about consultancy work? That way you get to keep your morals and you can help your friends when they need you." Helen placed a gentle hand on her son's arm.

There was a soft chittering sound as a three legged ferret, with a coat of sable, scuttled into the room. Silas grinned and swept him into his arm.

"Hello there, Hook," he said softly. "Have you come for a cuddle with your Papa?"

"I'm sorry about Tinkerbell," Helen said quietly before getting up to leave. "Promise me you'll at least consider my proposal?"

"I'll think about it," Silas said begrudgingly. "Where were you earlier today, anyway?"

"The Swearing-In Ceremony; Shy, Noor, and Elsie got their full colours today. Won't you go out and have a drink with them?"

"I'll catch up with them later in the week."

"Not likely; Noor Turner is being deployed to the field first thing tomorrow." Helen lingered in the doorway. "Won't you at least go and see her off?"

"I'll see," he said, suddenly pensive. "Is it wise to put Noor on a case so soon?"

"She'll be with a skilled team," Helen said. "I'm sure they'll take care of her; she's a sweet young woman."

Yes, she is, Silas thought, *and that's why I'm afraid for her.*

The sobbing Libra fell to the floor, wailing and clutching her newly useless legs. Mohinder Desai silenced her with a harsh look as Archer Treen rose from his hospital bed. He hopped on his healed limbs and grinned.

"Everything working as planned?" asked the Director.

"Better than before," Archer said cheerfully. He glanced at the woman on the floor. "Thank you for your sacrifice."

"She's just doing her job," Desai said curtly, "and you're only walking because we need you to do yours."

"Well I'm ready and raring to go–"

"Not alone, you aren't." Desai handed a folder to Archer. "My selection of candidates for your new partner."

"None are Ravenblades," he said warily as he leafed through the dossier. "Are they at least going to sit the exam when I've picked a shortlist?"

"No," Desai said, clearly conflicted. In the corner of the room, standing silently like a lurking predator, was Kimberley Daniels, his second in command. "Commander Holloway, Head of the Martinet Order, made the discontinuation of the Ravenblade Program a condition of her employment."

"What?" Archer said, his trembling hands almost ripping the dossier in two in his fury. *I knew we were in trouble but this is a fucking insult!*

"It is merely a temporary hiatus on recruitment, Agent Treen." Desai looked at the folder. "When you've made your choice-"

"None of them," he said, tossing the folder on the bed. "If I can't have someone qualified, I want to pick my own partners, no questions asked."

"Partners?" The Director raised an inquisitive eyebrow.

"I work best as part of a trio; that's not uncommon in the field. Is that acceptable?"

"Done," Desai said.

"And I want to see Harper Cherry," he continued. "I want Uplifts for all three of us."

"I take it you have candidates in mind?"

"I do," Archer said enigmatically.

"Then I'll leave it to you to make the arrangements," Desai said.

Oh, I will, Archer thought as he nodded in agreement. *And then it's time to fucking clean house.*

Elsie sat by herself on the little patio in the garden of the Ministry safehouse. Noor was already gone and Shy was fast asleep inside, but she couldn't settle. She'd tried the Ghost Phone countless times earlier in the evening, and it hadn't connected once.

I guess I made my choice, she thought angrily, *but I didn't think he would cut me off so sharply.*

She took a deep breath and tried to calm down, to no avail. A black cat hopped over the fence and sauntered over to her. She smiled; Elsie would recognise that swagger for the rest of her life.

"Penny for your thoughts?" Silas asked as he jumped on the bench and made himself comfortable on one of the cushions.

"I was just annoyed that Finley didn't get more than a slap on the fucking wrist," she said. "However, that isn't actually the end of it, thankfully."

"And you know this how?" He raised an eyebrow in pre-emptive disapproval.

"Don't do that with your face," she said with a grimace, "it's unnatural on a cat!"

"Answer me, Reichardt!"

"I might've had a little look in the Ministry Database for my assignment," she said softly. "I wanted to test out the codebreaker for you, after all."

"Oh, how altruistic of you," he said sarcastically. "So where did you end up?"

"Strategic Planning," Elsie said smugly. "That's l-"

"Leadership training and covert intelligence," Silas said sharply. "Yes, yes, I know what Strategic Planning is, Elsie; both my parents are under that umbrella."

"Who knows what I might achieve?" Elsie was misty eyed at the unlimited potential before her, but Silas brought her focus back down to earth.

"You were talking about Finley?"

"We're putting an undercover operative in place to monitor him and to try and influence his behaviour."

"That sounds unethical," Silas said matter-of-factly. "Do continue."

"We're hoping that we can get enough leverage on him, one way or another, to recruit him to the Ministry. Failing that, though, we'll have to get rid of him." She looked at Silas. "Either way, once our deep cover asset gives us the green light, I'm to be the one to deal with him."

"That sounds very cathartic," Silas said. "Good for you."

"When the time comes," Elsie asked quietly, "will you come with me to help?"

"Of course I will, lovely." He looked at the house where the three of them had completed their training. "I think of the three of you as children as much as you are friends, if that makes any sense?"

"Kind of."

"What I'm trying to say," Silas said, moving from the cushion to her lap, "is that I'll always be there for you, no matter what."

"Thank you," Elsie said tearfully. "The same goes for you."

The two sat in comfortable silence for a while, with Elsie periodically scratching Silas behind the ears. *This is the strangest relationship I've ever had,* she realised, *but it might be one of the healthiest.* Elsie sighed contentedly and looked up at the sky. The stars were obscured by the light pollution, but the absence of the fog was enough to soothe her soul.

"I got a new ferret," he said softly.

"Of course you did," Elsie said with a grin. "What else would you fill your time with when I'm away?"

"Hush, you wicked thing," he said, batting her with his paw. "Don't make me admit that I'll miss you!"

Finley pinched the bridge of his nose and looked over the numbers once again. Admittedly the fines hadn't made any kind of noticeable dent in the company finances, but the stock market had not viewed Eigenforce's *supposed* culpability in the death of over ten thousand people kindly.

As such, the share prices had fallen almost ten percent short of his projected gains, and Finley Carmichael was beginning to worry.

"Sure the media thinks that a price of over twenty thousand dollars apiece is great," he muttered anxiously as his golden irises flashed in the dim light, "but it's lower than the projection."

What if I'm losing my touch? He took a deep breath and drained his glass. He raised a hand to get the butler's attention when a strange sense of calm fell over him. Finley lowered his hand, suddenly unworried about prices or company valuations.

I have more money than I could ever spend, he thought with a chuckle. *What the fuck am I stressing for!?*

"You seem cheerful," said a warm voice beside him. "Fancy sharing a drink to celebrate whatever it is that you're happy about?"

"Certainly. It's on me," Finley said with a grin. "I do own the establishment, after all."

"Well, that's both kind of you and very impressive."

"Indeed," he said, "Sloane Square is prime real estate. This is a private venue, however, and I've not seen you around here before; how did you get in? I'm not mad, just curious."

"I just used my natural charm," the visitor said, running their fingers through their lustrous hair as a twinkle touched their inviting eyes.

"I'm sure you did," Finley agreed. *Fucking hell, you're stunning!* "So, dear stranger, I'm assuming you know who I am, but in case you somehow don't, my name is Finley Carmichael."

"A pleasure," the visitor responded as they shook hands.

"And you are?"

"Oh," the beautiful stranger said with mock surprise, "my name is Thaddeus. Thaddeus Thane."

Shy followed the tall woman with the large nose up the tight staircase of the Jericho Folly. She had introduced herself as Teaser Malarkey and was one of the resident agents at the Oxford Office. Shy huffed and puffed as they climbed ever higher.

"How tall is this building?" Shy asked breathlessly as they passed the second floor.

"Seven stories," Teaser said cheerfully. "You'll be situated at the top for the time being, just while we get sleeping spaces all figured out."

"Oh great," Shy muttered, and reached out for the bannister. A flicker of electricity danced between his fingers and arced to a screw in the fitting. "Hmm, that's interesting..."

"What is?" Teaser asked.

"Oh, nothing," Shy said. "How far up do we need to go?"

"Just one more." The two walked into a plushly decorated living room and Shy gasped when he noticed the most pale woman he'd ever seen curled up in an armchair. She wore a fluffy pink bathrobe and an equally lurid headscarf. Her eyes were hidden behind round sunglasses, even in the dimness of the evening light.

"Seen enough?" the woman asked sharply. "You must be Shy Turner."

"Agent Shy Turner," he replied proudly. "I'm supposed to report to Charity Walpole?"

"It would appear to be so. Transfer orders?" She held out a thin, white hand.

"I've got them here," Shy said as he pulled the papers from his coat pocket. "Aren't you at least going to stand up?"

"I'm recovering from renal cancer, kid," Charity said softly, "so how about you bring those orders over and you stop being a dick about it?"

"Don't you want to know what my gift is?" Shy tapped Teaser Malarkey on the hand and winced as his mouth was filled with the taste of licorice. He grimaced before folding across the room to stand before Charity.

He handed her his transfer orders with a flourish before folding back to his original position. He tapped Teaser's hand once again, returning her powers. He gave her a wink and she raised her eyebrows with a smile, clearly impressed.

"Okay then," Charity said with a grin. "Yeah, I can absolutely work with that."

Shy beamed as Charity continued.

"Welcome to the Night People, kid."

"Noor Turner?" asked a stern looking woman who hobbled into the private airport lounge on a cane. Noor nodded, suddenly dumbstruck, and handed her an envelope with a silent smile. After a few seconds, they were joined by a short man in a grey wool suit and a matching yachting cap, who perched on the sofa across from Noor. He looked at her with empty eyes, almost as if he could see right through her.

That's creepy.

"Don't mind Mallory," the woman said without looking up from Noor's transfer orders, "he can't see faces."

"How did you—"

"And Ivy can read minds," Mallory said with a soft grin, "so try not to think too loudly."

This is a hell of a learning curve.

The woman with the cane, Ivy, smiled and took a seat next to Mallory. She handed the transfer orders back to her before gesturing for Mallory to continue. Noor tried not to stare at the burns on Ivy's forearms and neck, and fought the urge to self-consciously cover her own chemical scarring.

"My name is Mallory Marsh, and I'll be the lead agent on your first case. This is Dr Ivy Livingston, who is sometimes Michaela Inglewood and Edgar Wainwright; she will explain during the flight."

"Where are we going?" Noor asked excitedly. "I can speak English, Spanish, and Urdu."

"Oregon," Mallory answered, "so I hope you packed warmly."

"What's in Oregon?" Noor asked. *I hope it's a yeti or something just as exciting.*

"My brother, Francis, is," Mallory said quietly. "he's been missing for almost three months. He was investigating a strange phenomenon up in the Cascade Mountains when he vanished. We are going to find him."

"When do we leave?" Noor asked.

"As soon as the plane is fuelled," Ivy said. "Welcome aboard, Agent Turner."

A wild eyed woman cowered beneath the desk in the booth of Galaxy Community Broadcast Radio, desperately hiding from the police officer that lurked on the other side of the glass. His smooth featureless face stared into the little room.

She held her breath, fearful that he would hear her even through the soundproof walls of the studio. After what felt like an age, she peeked out from her hiding place.

The police officer had gone.

She let out an explosive sigh of relief and clambered into her chair. She slipped on her headphones and flicked the levels up, sending the microphone out live.

"This is Sissy Sparrow," she said shakily, her words beaming out through the mountains, "and I'm currently in the broadcast booth of KGCB Radio Station, in Galaxy, Oregon. Something terrible is happening in our town and we can't get out!"

Her shuddering sob went out over the air.

"Please, anyone who's listening, I beg you; help us!"

A new nightmare unfolds in...

THE MIDNIGHT AVIARY

Acknowledgments

This book has been an absolute joy to work on. So rarely do I get to slaughter characters with such abandon!

This is the last of the "meet the gang" books; now I can really get into the meat of the Ministry. Curiously, Noor was originally going to be the single POV character for the whole series, and Elsie was for a different book altogether; between thee and me, I think she'll have much more interesting time in this series.

Of course, a book cannot be created in a vacuum and there are a wealth of people that I would like to thank for their help in creating this story.

Firstly and most importantly, I would like to thank my partner, Syd, for the love, support, and final proofreading of this story. She has listened to me talk about this for months, and has given me both inspiration and encouragement in spades. I love you, darling, and I am so lucky to have you in my life.

Likewise, I would like to thank my metamor, Ben Wright. Thank you for all the support and discussion that has helped this book become the beast that it finally grew into. I'd especially like to thank you for your keen scientific insight, along with several explanations of computers to this humble himbo.

I would like to thank you both for inviting me into your life and your home; I feel loved, wanted, and cared for, which I am grateful for beyond measure.

I would also like to thank Syd and Ben's guinea pigs,

both for their reassuring presence and constant source of amusement. There will continue to be references to you scattered throughout my writing.

A big thank you goes out to my best friend, Dr Georgia Lynott. You are a source of light in my life and always a joy to spend time with. I hope you will enjoy this book, and the series as a whole.

I cannot write a horror novel without thanking my parents, Steve and Samantha Farrell, my grandparents, Frank and Lorraine Keeley, and other members of my family; you have all played a crucial part developing my absolute love of horror. From late night films to tatty paperbacks read in the car on long journeys; it all has culminated in this book, and all those that follow it. Thank you.

I would like to extend my thanks to my childhood friends, James Bullock and Colum Taylor, for all their support and all the horror films we watched together over the years.

Once again, I would like to thank my therapist, Zayna Brookhouse, for her help in turning my fear and grief into something constructive that I could share with you all.

I'd like to thank all the musicians, artists, writers, and cinematographers that have contributed to the horror genre. I write to music, so your help was invaluable in the creation of this work.

I'd especially like to mention The Rats, by James Herbert, as an inspiration for this work. I almost wanted this book to be a love letter to the horror genre, along with a slightly skewed way to show affection to my original hometown of Dartford.

Of course, I'm sure that I have missed people off of this list; it is not exhaustive, after all! So, to all the other Parrots out there who helped to make this work a reality, I thank you.

And, last but not least, you, dear reader, for choosing to read this book.

Thank you.

About the Author

Eleanor Fitzgerald is a polyamorous non-binary trans woman living in and around Oxford. Eleanor uses any and all pronouns, and is neurodivergent and disabled. Eleanor is hard of hearing, and completely deaf on one side.

They have a fascination for all things weird and wonderful, and have thoroughly enjoyed writing this work for you. Rest assured, it will not be the last!

Eleanor also paints, and created the base artwork that this book's cover illustration was based around, before editing it digitally to get the final piece. Their particular style is impressionism, which they love immensely.

If you have any questions or comments, they can be reached at the following email address:

eleanorfitzgeraldwriting@gmail.com

Printed in Great Britain
by Amazon